Also by Julia London

JULIA LONDON

The SEDUCTION of LADY X

Pocket Star Books

New York   London   Toronto   Sydney   New Delhi

Pocket Star Books
A Division of Simon & Schuster, Inc.
1230 Avenue of the Americas
New York, NY 10020

This book is a work of fiction. Names, characters, places, and incidents either are products of the author's imagination or are used fictitiously. Any resemblance to actual events or locales or persons, living or dead, is entirely coincidental.

First Pocket Star Books paperback edition April 2012

POCKET STAR BOOKS and colophon are registered trademarks of Simon & Schuster, Inc.

For information about special discounts for bulk purchases, please contact Simon & Schuster Special Sales at 1-866-506-1949 or business@simonandschuster.com.

The Simon & Schuster Speakers Bureau can bring authors to your live event. For more information or to book an event, contact the Simon & Schuster Speakers Bureau at 1-866-248-3049 or visit our website at www.simonspeakers.com.

Manufactured in the United States of America

10 9 8 7 6 5 4 3 2 1

ISBN 978-1-4391-7547-7
ISBN 978-1-4391-7551-4 (ebook)

To Julie Kenner, Kathleen O'Reilly, Dee Davis,
Jacquie D'Allesandro, and Sherri Browning Erwin,
my partners in crime, for their devotion to
our friendship all these years.

PROLOGUE

England, 1809

Twenty-eight souls served the Carey family at Everdon Court, and every one of them, from the young girl who peeled potatoes in the kitchen to Mr. Brock, the head butler, knew to cut a wide berth around Lord Carey if they wanted to keep their position. His lordship had a cold and calculating temper, and with a tot or two of whiskey in him, he could be provoked by the most innocuous thing. With a few tots in him, he could easily be moved to dismiss a groundsman who had served for twenty steadfast years but had failed to trim the shrubbery to the marquis's exacting standards on the day he commanded it done. Or to send a young stable boy to pack his things and leave at once when Lady Carey laughed at something he said as she mounted her horse.

The servants avoided the marquis when they could, and when they did not have the luxury of doing so, they kept their eyes down and their lips sealed. Lady

Carey, however, could not avoid her husband. How she managed to abide her marriage to such a cold man was a source of endless fascination for two old friends in the family's employ: Miss Foster, the cook, and Mrs. Perry, the housekeeper. Miss Foster believed that Lord Carey's prowess in the marital bed was the one thing that must have kept the marchioness loyal to him in the six years they'd been married. "A lady might put up with quite a lot if she's properly handled between the linens, aye?" she'd cheerfully hypothesized.

Mrs. Perry, who had been married quite a while longer than six years, argued, "You are mad if you believe a romp is all that is required. I'd wager what brings her to heel is more likely the threat of being handled in a manner she *doesn't* find the least bit pleasing."

"Nonsense," Miss Foster said. "We'd hear of it from Nancy if that were true," she said, referring to Lady Carey's personal maid. "And besides, she'd not be willing to leave any of this behind her, would she, now?"

Miss Foster was referring, of course, to the monstrosity that was Everdon Court. It had been a keep at one time, but through the centuries the Careys—the surname as well as the title deriving from the borderlands once known as Careyridge—had added wings to the central tower and taken down battlements. Now the house boasted eighteen bedrooms, two courtyards, and a banquet hall appended to the ballroom that could seat one hundred guests. It was filled with the finest French furnishings obtained during the dismantling of the French aristocracy over the last twenty years.

"Aye, but what good is all this when she's married to a man like him?" Mrs. Perry had countered. There was little that would entice her to stay if Mr. Perry were to treat her as unkindly as the marquis treated the marchioness. "These are only things. Lady Carey deserves a man's esteem."

"Perhaps it is a child she wants," Miss Foster suggested. "An heir to all of this would serve her well."

Mrs. Perry gave Miss Foster a withering look. "If there was to be a child born to that union, it would have been born long before now." Every one of the twenty-eight staff knew of the trouble on that front. They waited every month with anxious anticipation— was she, or wasn't she?

"What, you think her ladyship is barren, then?" Miss Foster asked.

"No," Mrs. Perry said pertly. "I rather think it is him, what with all the whiskey."

"Perhaps you are right," Miss Foster said. "And then again, perhaps he's unable." The two ladies looked at each other and snickered.

What they could not know was that the marriage of the Marquis and Marchioness of Carey existed perfunctorily between the linens, and beyond that, scarcely at all. On most occasions, Lord Carey was neither a demanding nor an exciting lover; he performed his marital duties as was necessary to gain the heir and saved his personal preferences for a young woman in town who had been happy to receive him for some four years now.

Four years ago, Lady Carey had thought herself pregnant. As any woman would have done, she'd shared the joyous news with her husband, who was overcome with relief and gratitude. Alas, when two months passed, Lady Carey realized that she was no longer, or had never been, pregnant and the marquis's disappointment was so great that he'd never fully recovered from it.

Lady Olivia Carey, who had enjoyed a highly public and fashionable wedding among England's *haut ton*, had long since abandoned any hope of having a marriage of mutual respect and admiration. There was nothing she loathed more than her husband's twice weekly visits to her room—except for his tendency to drink to excess—and she was ever thankful that it was over within a matter of minutes.

Sometimes, while Olivia lay there as Edward attempted to impregnate her, she wondered what it must be like to have an exciting lover. Or a caring one. She would settle for a lover who did not rut about like an animal answering some primordial need to procreate.

Sometimes she lay there and counted the tiles on the ceiling, guessing what number she might reach before he finished.

And still other times, when he reeked of whiskey and clumsily groped her, Olivia passed the time by imagining the ways she could murder her husband and avoid being found out. Shooting him was too risky, as Olivia wasn't entirely certain how to fire a gun. She imagined fumbling with the thing and losing the element of surprise.

Pushing him from the top of Everdon Court seemed a better alternative, but she might draw attention if she invited him to a meeting on the roof. And then, of course, she would need him to stand at the edge, preferably where she could take a bit of a run at him to have enough force to topple him over.

Poison seemed the most sensible, but Miss Foster would never allow Olivia near his lordship's food. The woman was entirely too conscientious and prided herself on the meals she served. It would take some convincing that Olivia was suddenly interested in preparing a dish for her husband to consume. And really, how much poison was necessary to kill a man? What if she did not use enough? Or so much that the taste of the food was ruined?

Lately, the murderous thoughts had lost their luster for Olivia. For one thing, Edward had not been able to perform "his duty," as he called it, for more than a month due to his fondness for drink. It certainly didn't stop him from trying, but he gave up quickly and Olivia rolled over and stared at the gold silk ties that held the heavy canopy curtains back from her bed. Inevitably, she would feel a well of envy bubbling up for her younger sister Alexa.

She did *not* envy Alexa's disastrous situation. What she envied was the fact that Alexa had fallen so deeply in love with a man that she walked about with a look of yearning in her eyes. Alexa refused to reveal to Olivia who had earned this devotion from her; the only thing Olivia knew was that he was a gentleman Alexa had met in Spain while on tour with Lady Tuttle. Alexa could scarcely speak of anything else but the fine brown shade of his eyes, or the timbre of his laugh, or the intelligence of his speech.

Oh, but Olivia envied the quiet, desperate pining that Alexa seemed to wrap about her like a heavy winter shawl. Olivia wanted to know what that was like, how it felt. She wanted to *feel*.

For the first fortnight of her return from Spain, Alexa had not revealed that she was carrying the man's child. Olivia had guessed it by the way Alexa would unthinkingly place her hand on her abdomen when she spoke of love. And while Olivia admired Alexa's fierce determination to protect her lover from condemnation and scandal, she wanted to strangle the foolish young woman for bringing her insurmountable problem to Everdon Court.

When Olivia confronted her, Alexa had tried to deny it—so typical! She'd been indulged as child and allowed to barter and skate her way out of trouble, and had never learned the art of owning up to her mistakes. She preferred to deny and shift blame where she could . . . and Olivia always picked up the pieces.

Especially since their mother had died.

Alexa was eight years younger than Olivia and her only sibling, the daughter of her mother and her mother's second husband. She was fair-haired, like Olivia and like their mother had been, but her eyes were brown, not blue like Olivia's, and she was smaller in stature than Olivia.

Their mother had always doted on Alexa. Everyone had. Alexa had been a darling child with curly hair and a dimply smile that matched her bubbling *joie de vivre*.

"The devil kissed that girl when she was born," her mother used to say, and it was true that, as a girl, Alexa could be counted on to create mischief. As a young woman, she was free-spirited and disdainful of the societal rules that governed their lives. She'd never really thought of the consequences of her actions, whereas Olivia had always been circumspect. And quiet. And responsible.

Even so, Alexa was generally not as reckless as this.

When Alexa at last did admit to the truth, she collapsed to her hands and knees while great choking sobs wracked her body. "What shall I do, Livi?" she begged. "I don't know what to do!"

It was heartbreaking for Olivia to see her sister so distraught, particularly as Alexa really didn't know what to do. Olivia could guess that the consequences of her actions had scarcely been a thought in the girl's head until now.

Unfortunately, there was nothing they could do but

tell Edward, and that, Olivia knew, would not go well. Edward could not abide Alexa's spirit. "She always seeks to tie her garters in public, then turn up sweet," he'd complained once when Alexa had attended a ball in London and danced with the same young gentleman four times. When Olivia had explained to her sister that this was simply not done unless there was an understanding with the young man, Alexa had been sweetly contrite. "I beg your pardon," she'd said. "I did not know."

Edward had not been placated. "She has no appreciation for the Carey name, and I am second cousin to the king!" he'd railed at Olivia, as if dancing was somehow on a par with treason.

"What shall we do, Livi?" Alexa had asked her sister, artfully twisting her pregnancy into a dilemma for them both.

"We have no choice but to explain it to Edward," Olivia had said wearily.

Alexa had gasped loudly and thrown herself at Olivia's knees, begging for any other fate than that.

"Oh, Alexa," Olivia said sadly, bending over her sister. "What did you expect? Will it not be obvious to us all in a matter of weeks?"

"Yes, but I thought you'd help me without telling *him*."

"I must tell him! How could I ever keep it from him?" There was so much Alexa did not understand— particularly how powerless a woman was in this male-dominated world. Once a woman took her wedding vows, she was doomed to whatever fate her husband would mete out. She could not escape.

"Must we tell him now?" Alexa asked tearfully. "There is the supper party for the Duke of Rutland, and you know how the marquis can be."

Olivia knew better than anyone. Edward would not abide even a breath of scandal when the Duke of Rutland came to dine.

"After the supper party," she said to Alexa. "But not later than that."

She wasn't sure who was more relieved, her or Alexa.

CHAPTER ONE

Harrison Tolly, the steward of the Carey family holdings, was known around the village of Everdon for his affable demeanor and his willingness to help friends in need. Which was why his friend Marcus Dembly, the proprietor of Dembly's Goods, believed Harrison would help him with the problem of having one too many horses for his stable.

He'd brought the horse down to Everdon Court to show Harrison and was working very hard to convince him he ought to give the mount a go.

"I do not intend to buy your horse, Dembly," Harrison said as he openly admired the roan gelding. "You realize that, do you not?"

"I cannot see why not," Dembly said. "Why rely on the Everdon Court stables when you could have your own horse? There is a perfectly good stable here at the dowager house. I should think you would want your own, so that you might call on your Lady X whenever it pleases you." He grinned and cuffed Harrison on the shoulder.

Lady X was how Harrison's friends referred to the woman he adored from afar. Or rather, they did not know he adored her from afar—they'd drawn their own conclusions because Harrison had refused to name her.

He never would have mentioned her at all had there not been a movement afoot for the last few years to provide him with a wife. It sometimes seemed to him that half of Everdon was desperate to see him wed, and the other half just as desperate he not marry into their family, given the circumstances of his birth, which was completely lacking in paternity.

"Your powers of persuasion are quite good," Harrison said congenially. "But I will not purchase horseflesh I do not need and cannot feed. Which, I suspect, is the reason you are so eager to sell."

"Bloody hell, Harry, just try the horse, will you?" Dembly begged, clearly annoyed now. "I've come all this way. You might at least humor me."

"Very well," Harrison said with a shrug. "Give the horse over for the day and I shall humor you properly. By what name do you call this gelding?"

"Lightning," Dembly said.

"How terribly original," Harrison drawled. "Go on, then," he said, shooing his friend away. "I'll not have you breathing down my neck, hoping for a miracle."

He put his foot in the horse's stirrup—Dembly had

put a premium saddle on him, Harrison noted—and swung up. The horse felt good beneath him, strong and sturdy. And big. So big that Harrison could only guess that the beast would require an entire pasture and a bushel of carrots each week.

He spurred the horse on to appease his friend and rode out through the gates to the park behind Everdon Court, en route to Mr. Fortaine's cottage, the tenant he had intended to call on today. He took the forest path that led to the river road, and as he emerged from the forest, he came upon Lady Carey in the grassy clearing beside the river.

She was standing before an easel. She wore a wide-brimmed hat and held a palette in one hand. She was dressed in a white muslin gown and a rose-colored spencer. A footman was sitting on a rock on the river's edge, a fishing pole in his hand.

Harrison trotted up to her. Lady Carey turned her head; when she saw it was him, she smiled beatifically.

That smile drifted through Harrison like stardust. "Mr. Tolly!" she said, her voice full of delight. "What a pleasant surprise! You are just the person to give me an honest opinion of my painting. Will you have a look?"

"I wasn't aware that you were an artist," he said as he hopped down from the gelding.

"No?" she asked, smiling coyly.

He walked over to have a look at her handiwork. He had to cock his head to one side and squint a little, but after careful consideration, he determined that the painting was of a goat eating daisies in a field. And the goat had a man's face. A vaguely familiar face at that. It rather looked like the marquis.

"What do you think?" she asked brightly. "Do you like it?"

"Well . . . it is very colorful," he said.

"Colorful! How kind."

He gave her a sidelong look; she had a playful smile on her lips as she casually studied her work. "My skill at interpreting works of art is lacking," he said, "but if I am not mistaken, you have painted a goat with a familiar face."

Her smile brightened. "I have, indeed! Are you impressed with my skill?"

"Ah . . ." He looked at the painting again. "I am impressed. But not with your skill."

Lady Carey burst out laughing—a deep laugh that made her eyes shine. "I share your opinion," she said laughingly, and touched her brush to the goat's tail. "However, my husband believes ladies of leisure should paint. And therefore, I paint," she said, and dabbed at the palette. "I have an affinity for wildlife," she continued, and began to touch up the daisies that were sticking out of the goat's mouth. "You know, horses and birds. Goats. Even donkeys." She winked.

Harrison couldn't help his chuckle. "You are perhaps the finest painter of goats I have ever seen."

Lady Carey laughed warmly.

"Is your sister about?" he asked, looking around

them as Lady Carey added a few more daisies to her field.

"Unfortunately, no. Alexa is a bit under the weather."

Harrison thought that Miss Hastings was a bit of a problem. Certainly the marquis did not care for her. "She's a light-skirt, that one," he'd said one day for no apparent reason. "A disgusting lack of decorum." Harrison had no idea why the marquis felt that way—he'd never heard any such thing about Miss Hastings. He rather thought the marquis simply did not care for her.

"I am distressed to hear it," he said to Lady Carey.

Lady Carey smiled prettily at him, but her eye caught something behind him. "Is that a new horse, Mr. Tolly?" she asked, leaning to her right to see around him.

"In a manner of speaking," Harrison said. "My friend Mr. Dembly would like me to purchase him. He does not care that I have no need for a horse."

"Haven't you? For this one looks as if he would be a good runner."

Harrison looked at the horse, then at her. "Would you care to ride him?"

She gasped with delight. "May I?" she asked, already putting her palette aside.

"Of course you may. However, the horse is not saddled properly for a lady—"

"Oh, that's quite all right," she said with a casual flick of her wrist. "I shall make do."

She moved around to the side of the gelding, and

Harrison cupped his hands for her, as the stirrup was too high for her to reach. She slipped her foot into his fingers and leapt up as he lifted her. She landed squarely in the saddle and hooked her knee around the pommel. Her other leg was exposed from the calf down, and though she wore white stockings, Harrison could see the line of her shapely leg.

"Oh, he is indeed a fine horse!" she said, and leaned forward to stroke its neck. "And quite strong."

Her breasts strained against her spencer jacket as she reached for the horse, and Harrison unwisely imagined those breasts pressed against him.

"Perhaps you might give him a bit of encouragement?" she asked.

Harrison obliged her by slapping the horse's rump. The horse started off in a slow canter. Lady Carey rode him expertly, leading him to trot around the clearing, making a big circle around her easel and Harrison, who stood with his legs braced apart, his hands on his hips. Her bonnet toppled off her head, but her footman was quick to retrieve it.

"Do you recall the race between Mr. Williams and Mr. Janus a few years ago?" she called out to Harrison as she trotted by.

As if Harrison could forget any moment he'd spent in her company. On that particular day she'd convinced him, with her winsome smile and charming laugh, to make a few wagers on her behalf. "My husband will not allow any wagering, you know," she'd whispered.

"He thinks it quite unladylike. What do *you* think, Mr. Tolly?"

"I think you are mad to wager on Mr. Janus," he'd said low. "He is a stone heavier than Mr. Williams and cannot possibly outrun him on that steed."

"I have faith in Mr. Janus," she'd insisted pertly, and had pressed some coins into his palm. "Would *you* care to wager with me?"

Harrison would do anything to prolong his time in her company. "What do you have mind, madam?"

"If Mr. Janus wins by a length, you shall give me ten pounds."

"Ten pounds?" he'd said, cocking one brow high with amusement.

"I beg your pardon, is that too rich for you?" she'd teased him.

"I think it is too confident for you."

"So you say," she'd said coyly. "If Mr. Janus wins by less than a length, I shall give *you* ten pounds."

"And what if," he'd said, his gaze locked on her sparkling blue eyes, "he doesn't win at all?"

She'd shrugged. "Then I shall give you twenty pounds."

He'd laughed. But he'd taken her bet.

Mr. Janus had won handily that afternoon, putting fourteen pounds in Lady Carey's pocket. But he'd won only by a nose, which meant that she'd lost to Harrison. That didn't dampen her triumphant spirit.

Nothing did until the marquis discovered that the

only person to wager on Janus and win was his wife. He'd been quite angry about her "impudence" and had forced her to give him her earnings.

"You are silent, Mr. Tolly," Lady Carey said as she trotted past him now. "Surely you've not forgotten?"

"You know very well that I recall it," he said. "Particularly how pleased you were with yourself."

She laughed. "Naturally! I proved that I was the only one amongst us who could read a horse." She kicked the gelding in the flank and sent it into a gallop.

Harrison watched as her pale blonde hair was jostled from its pins and began to fly out behind her. When she rounded the end of the clearing and galloped back, the tresses had come wholly undone and drifted down around her shoulders.

"I owe you ten pounds," she said.

"I scarcely remember it."

"I do not believe you. I think you are a dear friend and are gamely trying to conceal the fact that I have failed to honor my wager."

A dear friend. Harrison's chest tingled a little with that admission. "It was a friendly wager," he said. "May I help you down?"

"Please." She reached out to him; he caught her about the waist as she braced her hands against his shoulders and lifted her down. Her skirts and legs brushed against his; her hair drifted between them. God, how Harrison longed to touch that hair, to feel it between his fingers. He set her on the ground and she looked up at him with affection in her eyes.

It *was* affection, was it not? His mind was not playing tricks? Whatever he saw there, it made his blood rush.

Lady Carey's hands slid from his shoulders and she patted his chest with a smile on her face. "I should finish my painting so that I may show my husband I have done as a lady ought." She stepped away from him, and it felt to Harrison as if a draft of cold spring air filled her place.

"You will help me with the seating for the supper party, will you not, Mr. Tolly?" she called over her shoulder as she returned to her easel.

"That depends," he said, and grinned when she turned back to him. "Will Mr. Wallaby be in attendance?"

"Even worse," she said, as Harrison watched her gracefully re-pin her hair. "Lady Ames will be joining us."

"Good God," he said, and clapped a playful hand over his heart. "I shall don my heaviest armor."

Lady Carey's laughter filled the air. "You always make me laugh so," she said as she accepted her hat from the footman. "Good afternoon, Mr. Tolly."

"Good afternoon," Harrison said.

She turned back to her painting, her face once again obscured. He swung up on the horse and turned it about, trotting off in the direction of Mr. Fortaine's cottage, his body a mass of jumbled nerves and conflicting emotions.

Alexa was still in her bed, a cold cloth across her brow, her pillow damp from the tears that never seemed to stop falling. She refused to rise, refused to join the supper party honoring the Duke and Duchess of Rutland.

In all honesty, that was just fine with Olivia. She had enough to fret over without worrying whether Alexa would offend Edward with something as simple as breathing. That was not out of the realm of possibility.

The supper guests were expected at seven o'clock, and at six o'clock, Edward had still not returned from his ride to God only knew where. But Brock had informed Olivia that Bishop Ogden, who was notorious for appearing early, had arrived.

"I shall be down to see him in a moment," she assured the butler, and took one last look at herself in the blue silk gown with the embroidery along the scalloped hem she'd commissioned. She owed Mr. Tolly her thanks—it was he who had brought her the fabric sample from London, then had ordered a bolt of it with other household goods.

She heard Edward before she saw him; there was no mistaking his drunken lurching down the hall. Olivia fit a pearl-drop tiara onto her head as Edward came through the door of her suite.

He paused there, his shoulder against the jamb, staring at her, clearly foxed. He pushed away from the door and sauntered in. "My darling wife."

"Welcome home, my lord," she said.

His gaze raked over her, but she knew no compliment as to her appearance would be forthcoming. Edward put his arm around her shoulders. He reeked of whiskey and perfume, and when he tried to kiss her, she turned her head; his lips landed on her cheek. He tried to kiss her again, but Olivia turned her head even further, leaning away from him.

"Are you refusing me?" he hissed.

"I would prefer," she said, breaking out of his embrace, "that you at least wash the other woman's perfume from your body."

Edward's face mottled. "Do you think *you* are so desirable?" he asked. "You disgust me."

He started for her again, but Olivia put her hand up. "We have guests for supper this evening. The bishop has already arrived and the duke will not be far behind."

Edward glared at her, his jaw clenched shut. But he did not reach for her again.

"If you will excuse me, I shall go keep the bishop's company until you can join us." She walked past him without looking at him, expecting him to call her back.

But he did not. A duke was coming, and Edward was undoubtedly more concerned with how he would be perceived by him than by Olivia.

The duke and duchess had arrived by the time Edward appeared, having bathed and changed into formal clothing. It was remarkable to Olivia that he could manage to gather himself at all, but he'd done it time and again. One wouldn't suspect that just three quarters of an hour ago, he had lurched into her suite reeking of whiskey and perfume.

He was in the company of Mr. Tolly, and Olivia was happy about that. Mr. Tolly was an equable influence on Edward. He had an equable influence on everyone, really. Olivia presumed he was only slightly younger than her husband, but he was much fitter, her husband having grown soft in the last few years. Mr. Tolly was a bit taller than Edward, and where Edward was golden-haired, Mr. Tolly had brown hair the color of mahogany, his eyes the color of a mourning dove.

Edward's eyes were so brown they almost looked black. Two black, bottomless holes.

Together, the two men greeted the duke and duchess, then moved around the room to greet the few other guests, eventually making their way to Olivia's side. She was standing with the bishop, who had taken a liking to her long ago and rarely left her side when in her company. She was showing the bishop her painting.

The easel and the painting seemed to confuse Edward after he'd greeted the bishop. "What is that?" he asked. "Why is it in the salon?"

"It is the painting you asked me to make," Olivia

said. "I asked the footman to put it here. Do you like it?"

He looked at her strangely, then at the painting. "What is it? A goat?"

"A goat!" she laughed. "It is a horse, my love." Standing just behind Edward, Mr. Tolly arched one brow and a faint smile appeared on his lips. Olivia had to bite the inside of her lip to keep from smiling as Edward leaned in, squinting.

"A fine horse it is, Lady Carey," the bishop said. "A bit short, I think, but a fine horse." The bishop was squinting, too, and gripping his second sherry as if he feared it might be ripped from his hand by a gale-force wind.

"A horse," Edward repeated.

"Yes. A horse."

Mr. Tolly looked down. Olivia could see the muscles in his jaw working to keep from smiling.

Edward turned away from her painting. "It is a childish rendition, then. Put it in the nursery where it belongs."

"Ah yes, that would spruce up the nursery quite nicely," the bishop said.

"I agree," Olivia said cheerfully. "I might even add more to the painting." Such as a noose around the goat's head. Or a fiery explosion. But Edward didn't hear her—he'd already walked on.

"That horse has seen a remarkable transformation in the last few hours," Mr. Tolly said.

"Hasn't it?" she asked with a kittenish smile.

"Mr. Tolly, is that you?" Lady Ames bellowed from across the room. "I've a question of considerable importance, sir!"

Mr. Tolly gave Olivia a slight wince before stepping away to speak to Lady Ames.

Supper was served at precisely eight o'clock. Olivia, seated at the far end of the table, was beside the bishop. That was not the seating arrangement she and Mr. Tolly had devised, and she rather suspected the bishop had asked for a change. Edward was at the other end in the company of the duke and duchess. He was relaxed and laughing.

The bishop began to chat as the wine began to flow. Olivia tried very hard to be a good listener, she truly did . . . but the bishop had a tendency to speak in great concentric paths before reaching anything that even remotely resembled a point. Twice, as she labored to keep up, Olivia happened to glance in Mr. Tolly's direction and caught his eye. He was smiling at her with amusement, knowing very well what agony she was being made to suffer. Once, Olivia gave a subtle incline of her head toward the bishop, silently suggesting that Mr. Tolly might want to engage him.

Mr. Tolly just as subtly refused her offer.

The tedious conversation aside, she thought the evening progressed rather well. She did not feel a sense of foreboding, which she often felt when only she and Edward dined. Her husband seemed in good spirits, the guests enjoying their meal and the company. And then the bishop asked Olivia about Alexa.

"Unfortunately, my sister is ill," Olivia said when the bishop asked why she had not joined them.

"Ah, that is a pity. I do so enjoy her company—very lively, that one. Her health is not in peril, I pray?"

Olivia smiled and shook her head. "She is fatigued after such a long journey from Spain."

"Ah, yes. And what is next for our Miss Hastings?" the bishop asked, settling back in his chair.

"Well . . ." Olivia hadn't thought of what she might say about Alexa just yet. "London, I suppose," she said. That seemed safe; everyone would naturally assume she'd be off for the Season to begin the search for a marital match.

The bishop obviously assumed so, for he said rather loudly, "Yes, of *course* she'll be to London now. A young woman as pretty and spirited as Miss Hastings will make a fine match indeed, particularly with the Carey name to sponsor her!"

"Are we speaking of my sister-in-law?" Edward suddenly asked from the other end of the table, startling Olivia. Conversation ceased, and everyone looked to Olivia; she felt the warmth begin to creep into her cheeks.

"We were indeed, my lord," the bishop said, and shifted around in his seat so that he might have a better look at Edward. "I was remarking how fortuitous it is that Miss Hastings might have the Marquis of Carey to sponsor her in the Season."

"Me?" Edward chuckled as if he'd never considered it. "Do you not have an uncle in London who might see after her, darling?"

Olivia tensed. Her father's brother was in debtor's prison, which Edward knew very well. "No," she said, and smiled as she shook her head.

"But I think you do," he insisted. "What is his name, again? Ah yes. Barstow." He looked around at the faces of his curious guests. "Mr. Barstow is the brother of my wife's late father. Her stepfather, Lord Hastings, adopted her. Perhaps because her nearest blood relative was something of a wastrel." He chuckled again, but it was met with an uncomfortable silence.

"I was very young when my father died," Olivia said. "I always considered Lord Hastings to be my father."

"Rather advantageous for you to do so, I should think," Edward said jovially. "And where is our Uncle Barstow, my love? Still in debtor's prison?"

Lady Ames gasped. The bishop frowned into his wineglass. Mr. Wallaby looked rather surprised and turned to Olivia, clearly interested in her answer.

There was a time when Olivia would have tried to make a jest of Edward's jabs, but she no longer had the patience for it. There was no point in denying it. "Yes," she said. "King's Bench Prison, as I last understood."

"Gambling debts, was it not?" Edward asked casually. "Incapable or unwilling to pay his wagers?"

"I suspect he is trying to gamble his way out even as we speak," Olivia said, and smiled at her husband.

"If I may offer a toast, then," Mr. Tolly said. "To your uncle Barstow, my lady. May his luck improve."

Olivia smiled gratefully and lifted her glass. "Hear, hear, Mr. Tolly."

"Hear, hear," the Duke of Rutland said, and laughed as he lifted his glass. A round of laughter went up around the table, and the guests lifted their glasses, calling out a hearty *hear, hear* to Mr. Tolly's toast.

Olivia was aware that Edward's gaze was on her as he lifted his glass. She could feel it burning a hole in her skin.

At half past two in the morning, when the duke and duchess took their leave, most of the other guests followed them, leaving only the bishop and Mr. Wallaby behind. Mr. Wallaby was determined to show Edward an African spear he'd discovered in a London market. The three men disappeared into the study with their ports. Olivia heard Edward instruct a footman to bring a bottle of whiskey.

That bottle and the spear would keep her husband occupied. Olivia retired for the night. She was quite tired and quickly fell asleep, dreaming of paintings of galloping horses.

She was rudely awakened by a heavy weight pressing down on her and found Edward on top of her, clothed only in a shirt. He smelled of drink, and he was pushing her legs apart, jabbing at her.

"Edward—"

He clamped a hand over her mouth and twisted

her head to one side as he tried to enter her. But the whiskey had made him flaccid again. He growled and did his best to bring himself back to life, but could not manage it. "Do something!" he snarled at her.

"What might I possibly do?" Olivia asked, unwilling to touch him and hoping that he did not force her to do so.

Edward tried again, grunting with the effort, and finally rolled off her. He fell onto his side beside her and his arm lay heavy across her abdomen. The drink had finally put him out.

Olivia lay looking up in the darkness with his arm on her, imagining how she could use Mr. Wallaby's spear to pin Edward to a wall. She would need some help, as the spear looked heavy, and there would be the matter of keeping Edward still so that she might spear him. She had in mind to pin him below the waist.

She'd best do it by the morrow, for she could no longer avoid telling him about Alexa. She wouldn't be the least surprised if he speared her first.

CHAPTER TWO

The hallway at Everdon Court that led to the Marquis of Carey's private study was as long and as daunting as the choir aisle at Westminster Abbey, and with every step, Alexa sniffed a little louder and tried a little harder to suppress her sobs.

It felt as if Olivia was slowly leading her toward the gallows, one leaden step at a time. "Buck up, Alexa," she muttered as they passed a pair of footmen, and pulled her younger sister closer into her side. "There is nothing to be done for it. You must face up to the truth."

"Yes, I know I must," Alexa said weakly. "But I do not understand why you cannot tell him for me."

Olivia sighed; Alexa knew very well why. Olivia had waited as long as she might before Alexa's thickening waistline would draw attention, but she could wait no longer. Olivia could guess what sort of suffering Edward would inflict on them, and on that rain-soaked afternoon, Olivia thought it entirely possible that she dreaded telling him even more than Alexa did.

After what seemed an interminable walk, they reached the polished oak doors of the study. As Olivia lifted her hand to rap, Alexa sagged against her. "I am so weary," she uttered. "I do not feel well."

"Stand up," Olivia said, and jostled Alexa, forcing her to stand, then rapped on the door.

One of the twin-paneled doors swung open immediately, and behind it, a footman bowed. "Is my husband within, Charles?" Olivia asked.

Before Charles could respond, she heard her husband's voice. "Come."

Olivia looked at Alexa and entered, half pulling, half leading her sister with her. But as she crossed the threshold, she discovered her husband was not alone; Mr. Tolly was present as well.

Mr. Tolly smiled warmly as they entered, inclining his head in greeting. "Lady Carey. Miss Hastings. How do you do?"

"Ah . . ." Olivia tried to think of an appropriate response, given that they did not fare well at all.

"Yes? What is it?" her husband asked curtly without lifting his head from the papers on his desk.

Olivia shifted her gaze to Edward. "Alexa . . . and I . . . have something we must tell you," she said. "May we have a moment?"

"Go on," Edward said impatiently, "and be quick about it. As you can see, we are presently engaged."

Olivia's gaze flew to Mr. Tolly, whose smile made his gray eyes seem to dance. He bowed as he started to make his leave.

"Where are you off to, Tolly?" his lordship said. "You may stay."

"Edward . . . it is personal," Olivia said quickly. For Alexa's sake, she did not want Mr. Tolly to be present.

"Mr. Tolly has heard more personal and private details about this family than even I. He will stay." Edward lifted his head and looked at Olivia. "What is it?"

Mr. Tolly slowly stepped back, his expression suddenly stoic.

Olivia was thankful Edward had commanded him to remain, for Mr. Tolly was the one person who could reason with him. Where others were quickly dismissed, Edward valued Mr. Tolly's opinion. And once, on a particularly awful day, when Edward had lifted his hand to strike Olivia for some perceived slight, Mr. Tolly had been there to catch his arm and prevent him from striking her.

Shocked, Edward had bellowed, "You think to lay a hand on me? I will have your position!"

Mr. Tolly had calmly returned Edward's gaze, as if the effort of stopping him required no strength at all. "Then have it. If you believe that my position here is more important to me than my code of conduct, you are mistaken. I will not stand by and allow any man to strike a woman."

Olivia had expected his instant dismissal, even a

brawl. But amazingly, Edward had gathered himself. And he'd never tried to lay a hand on Olivia again.

No, he preferred to strike her with words.

He'd not always been so cruel to her. Indifferent, perhaps, but not particularly cruel in the beginning. Yet as the years had slipped by and Olivia had not conceived a child, Edward's regard for her had dwindled to nothing. The cruelty had begun four years ago, when Olivia had believed herself, at long last, to be pregnant. Edward had been so very happy. He'd pampered her, showered her with gifts . . . but after two months, her courses began to flow again, and Edward's cruelty flowed right along with them.

"Why do you keep me waiting, Olivia?" Edward asked curtly, bringing her back to the mission at hand. "I told you I had work to do."

Alexa shuddered; Olivia put her arm around her sister's shoulders and began the little speech she'd privately rehearsed: Alexa had gone to Spain. Alexa had behaved poorly, for which she was terribly sorry. Alexa was with child. From the corner of her eye, she saw Mr. Tolly flinch, and wondered if it was revulsion at what Alexa had done, or recognition that this would not go well for anyone.

Olivia's speech was followed by pure silence. There was not a breath, not a creak, as Edward turned his cold gaze to Alexa, who stood shaking before him.

Edward's gaze flicked to her abdomen, then to her face. "Is this true?"

"Yes, my lord," Alexa admitted, her voice scarcely more than a whisper.

"Who has done this?" he asked, his voice so soft and dangerously low that a shiver shot down Olivia's spine. When Alexa did not answer straightaway, Edward smiled a little and said, "You may trust me, Alexa."

No, Alexa, you cannot trust him! Never trust him!

Alexa lowered her gaze to the floor and shook her head. "I will not say."

Olivia glanced at Mr. Tolly. He held her gaze a slender moment and she thought—or perhaps hoped—that she saw a flicker of reassurance in his eyes. He was always so calm, so hopeful! Olivia wanted to lean on him now, to put her head on his broad shoulder, to feel his arms around her, strong and protective, keeping her safe from Edward.

"You will not say?" Edward asked, rising from his seat.

"I will not," Alexa repeated.

Edward made a sound of surprise. "But my dear, you must surely realize that if you refuse to tell me who has put this by-blow in you, I can only surmise that he is unsuitable in every imaginable way. Or . . . that you are a whore."

Alexa choked back a sob.

"Edward, please," Olivia pleaded.

Her husband shifted his hard gaze to her. "Please what?" he asked, the venom dripping from his cold smile.

"Please leave her be," Olivia implored him. "She

knows her mistake, and the good Lord knows she will pay for it in many ways for the rest if her life. You need not punish her further."

"I see," Edward said casually as he came around to the front of his desk. "You suddenly believe yourself in a position to tell me what I need not do. Shall I tell you what I find interesting?" he asked as he sat on the edge of the desk.

"No," Olivia said quickly.

"I find it interesting that while you are as barren as a Scottish moor, your sister is a whore who apparently will conceive a by-blow with any man who lifts her skirts."

Olivia's face flamed. The conflict between her and her husband was no secret, but it was humiliating nonetheless.

"There is only one," Alexa foolishly tried, but Edward quickly turned on her.

"Only one, eh?" He chuckled as if that was somehow amusing, and gestured to Alexa's belly. "The only difference between the two of you is that one of you is only half a woman. One of you led me to believe she could give me heirs and yet cannot. Or will not."

He shifted that hard gaze to Olivia, and Alexa burst into tears. Behind Edward, Mr. Tolly turned to look out the window, his hands on his hips. Olivia could see the tension in his jaw, as if he were fighting to keep from speaking.

"The question we have before us is what to do with

this one," Edward mused, his gaze raking over Alexa. "With your mother buried, there is no one who will stand up for you, is there?" he asked her. "Certainly not your scofflaw uncle Barstow. You are entirely at my mercy as your benefactor and provider. And yet, I am the second cousin to the king. The Carey name means quite a lot in this country. Do you mean to defile my good name? A name from which you derive social benefit by mere association?"

"No, my lord," Alexa said softly.

"Then why would you allow some man to defile *you?* Did you think of your sister, who bears my name? Did you think of anything but your own base desires?"

She bowed her head and wisely did not answer.

"What shall I do, Alexa?" he continued coolly. "I dare say your sister connived her way into this marriage and there is precious little I may do about that. But I can keep the blight of your judgment from bringing scandal to my family's name, and therefore, the king's name, is that not so? I still hold at least some degree of influence over this family, do I not? Is there not someone else to whom you may turn for assistance in this . . . unpleasant matter?"

Alexa paled. "No," she said, her voice almost a whisper. "I am at your mercy, my lord." She regarded Edward uneasily as she dabbed at her tears with her handkerchief.

Olivia's scalp tingled with foreboding. "Perhaps if we take a moment—"

Edward's gaze turned even harder. "Thank you, madam, but I do not need your assistance in determining what is to be done with the whore. If there is no one to marry her, than I shall send her to St. Brendan's convent in Ireland with a generous endowment. The sisters may determine what is to be done with the child."

"What?" Olivia felt the blood drain from her face.

Mr. Tolly turned from the window, his brow furrowed with a deep frown.

"What do you mean, what is to be done with it?" Alexa asked, stricken.

Edward shrugged. "It is a bastard child. It will be better off raised by an Irish crofter than seeking acceptance in our society. If you think that I intend to put you up and allow you to raise some by-blow at Everdon Court for all to see, and at the end of my purse strings—"

"You will not take my child from me!" Alexa exclaimed.

"And you will not presume to tell me what I will or will not do," Edward said tightly.

The tone of his voice was bitterly cold, and Olivia knew from experience it would go from bad to worse. She stepped in front of Alexa to save her, to keep her from saying anything. "My lord, perhaps you might consider an alternative?"

"By all means," he said grandly, flourishing his hand at her. "Amuse me with your suitable alternative, for the Lord knows I am in need of it after this news."

"Olivia, I cannot give my baby to anyone!" Alexa said tearfully behind her. "I won't!"

Olivia willed Alexa to be silent. "My lord, my father's cousin lives in a small manor in Wales and has four young children. It is quite remote and there is very little society. Perhaps Alexa might go there, and when the child is born, my cousin will take her in."

She heard Alexa gulp down another sob.

Edward's brows lifted. "That is your idea? Send her to this agrarian cousin?"

He was the cat now, toying with the mouse. Olivia never won these rounds, but she never stopped trying. "To remove her from your sight, husband," she said. "My cousin is my father's blood—I know she will not speak of this to anyone," she added desperately, but Edward chuckled as if Olivia was speaking nonsense.

He stood up from his perch on his desk and put his fingers under Olivia's chin, forcing her to tilt her head back so that she was looking into his cold dark eyes. "Dearest Olivia," he said, sighing a bit. "Do you honestly believe I would trust anyone in your family? Was it not your family who deceived me into believing that you were the best match for me?" He lowered his head and touched his lips to hers, sending a shudder of revulsion through her. "We both know that you were the worst choice for me."

She wanted to claw the smirk from his face. But she was aware of Mr. Tolly in the room, of Alexa whimpering behind her. "I am aware of how much you despise

me, Edward," she said softly. "But please do not punish
Alexa for it. She's done nothing to you."

"She will go to St. Brendan's Convent on the morrow, and there she will remain. Or she may go to hell."

"No!" Alexa sobbed, and collapsed to the floor. Olivia
whirled around and knelt beside her sister, trying to
help her to her feet, but Alexa was inconsolable. "Stand
up, stand *up*," she urged her. "Do not let him defeat you,"
she whispered.

"I shall marry her," Mr. Tolly said clearly.

Olivia's heart lurched in her chest and her gaze
flew up. Mr. Tolly had appeared at Alexa's side, and
he exchanged a look with Olivia as he leaned down
and took Alexa by the arm. He hauled her to her feet,
forcing her to stand. Olivia stumbled to hers, gaping at
him. He was mad—*mad!*—to offer such a thing, but
Mr. Tolly had firm grip of Alexa and was looking at
Edward, his eyes slightly narrowed, the muscles in his
jaw clenched.

Edward laughed. "*You* will marry her, Tolly? Come
now, I thought better of you! You cannot demean
yourself to marry her—she is ruined," he said, as if
explaining why Mr. Tolly should prefer whiskey to gin.
"I understand that perhaps you have some sentiment
for the child, as you yourself are a bastard. But you've
pulled yourself up to the top of the trees, Tolly. This
one will merely drag you down to the bottom again."

"*No*, Mr. Tolly," Olivia said quickly, her heart
pounding. "It is a truly noble offer, but—"

"Noble," Edward snorted. "It is half-witted."

"I won't marry him!" Alexa wailed. "I will not! You cannot force me to it!"

"Miss Hastings!" Mr. Tolly said, and put his hand under Alexa's chin and forced her to look up at him. "Please listen to me," he said, his voice softer. "For now, we shall say we are to be married, and we will seek to devise a plan that protects you and the Carey family from scandal." Alexa started to shake her head, but he dipped down a little and looked her in the eye. "Be strong now, lass," he said kindly. "Now is the time you must think of the child you carry and be *strong*."

Alexa's hand fluttered to her abdomen. She seemed to consider what he said as she sniffed back her tears. She conceded by sagging helplessly against him, looking as if the slightest touch would cause her to collapse into pieces.

"Tolly, you astound me," Edward said, almost cheerfully. "I do believe there is little you won't do to protect the good Carey name. One might think you were one of us. But in this case, I think you are a fool. Alexa Hastings will do as well in an Irish convent as she will do as a wife to you."

Mr. Tolly looked as grave as Olivia had ever seen him. "If you will permit me, my lord, I shall address this unfortunate complication so that you may turn your attention to more pressing issues."

Edward eyed Mr. Tolly skeptically for a long moment, but Mr. Tolly steadily held his gaze, not the least intimidated. Edward finally shrugged and turned away. "Do as you wish. But keep her out of my sight. I don't care to be reminded that I have a slut wandering about Everdon Court. Take her down to the dowager house until you find a place to put her."

As if she were a piece of broken furniture.

Mr. Tolly wheeled Alexa about, moving her briskly to the door.

Olivia tried to follow, but Edward stopped her with a hand to her arm. "Lady Carey," he said sternly. Olivia closed her eyes for a moment before she turned back to him. "I did not give you leave." He settled back against the desk, his arms casually folded over his middle. "Go on with you now, Tolly," he said dismissively. "Take her from my sight."

Olivia glanced over her shoulder at Alexa, but it was Mr. Tolly's gaze that met hers, and she thought that she saw a flash of anger in his eyes.

The door shut behind Mr. Tolly and Alexa, leaving her alone with Edward.

Edward gazed at Olivia for a long moment, his eyes wandering over the peach-colored gown she wore, lingering on her décolletage in a manner that made her skin crawl. "How is it," he said at last, "that your sister may spread her legs to God knows whom in Spain and conceive, and yet you cannot?"

The question did not surprise Olivia, but it nonetheless snatched her breath as it always did. He spoke to her as if there were some defect in her, yet he never considered that *he* could be the reason they had yet to produce a child.

"I asked you a question, madam."

"I cannot say."

"It seems to me if one sister is fertile, the next would be as well."

Olivia swallowed. "I do not think it necessarily follows. We are all individuals, no two alike."

"Perhaps," he said. "And then again, perhaps it is because you take some elixir to abort my seed. Brock said some old crone called on you recently."

Confused, Olivia thought back to her recent callers and remembered Mrs. Gates, who had come on behalf of the charity they had begun for the poor. She was elderly, with a shock of gray hair that seemed as unruly as her wards. "If you are referring to Mrs. Gates, she is a patron of the parish workhouse," Olivia said.

"She is a crone."

Olivia struggled to keep her voice even. "She did not bring me an elixir. I want a child every bit as much as you do. You must know that I would never indulge in such tactics. I cannot bear to even hear you speak of it."

Edward laughed and shoved away from the desk, coming toward her. "Do you indeed want a child, Olivia? For I do not see any evidence that you do. One might ask if you desire a child, then why on earth have you not borne one? Either you are incapable, in which case your mother lied to me, or you deceive me every day," he said as he casually studied her face. "I tend to think the latter. I tend to think you want to vex me in any way you might."

Anger began to bubble in her. "That is not true," she said. "I never wanted anything other than to be a wife and mother."

"Liar," he said. "You are surrounded by riches and staff, yet you never bring me joy, Olivia. You burden me with the troubles of your orphaned sister and expect me to somehow make them go away, as if by magic. You tricked me into marrying you, and the one thing I have asked of you, the *one* thing I have required for all the generosity I have bestowed upon you, is to give me an heir. That is all I ask—an heir. And yet, you do not conceive. And when you do, you abort them."

Olivia gasped; her knees quaked with the force of that remark. "How dare you say such a vile thing," she said roughly. "Dr. Egan said that I have done no harm to my body. I am an obedient wife—"

"*Obedient?*" Edward said, surprised. He grinned. "Is that what you would call your performance in our marital bed? Obedient?"

"I cannot call it anything else," she said, her eyes narrowing.

Edward's nostrils flared. He clenched his jaw and walked to the sideboard, where he poured whiskey for himself.

Olivia's belly churned with nerves, and she tried to focus on a painting above the mantel. It was of an ancestor sitting on a rock, staring at the artist while his dog gazed up at him. Olivia felt like that dog. She had to be ever vigilant, to watch everything Edward did.

"I don't find you the least bit obedient." Edward tossed back the whiskey. "I think you plot to remove my seed from your body." He poured more.

The trepidation was making Olivia nauseous, but she was determined to hold her ground with him. "How can that be? You make me lie there for a half hour and watch me so that I don't move. How could I possibly remove it?"

"Women have a bevy of tricks at their disposal," he said, and turned back to her. His gaze began to wander her body as he moved closer. "Perhaps I have gone about this the wrong way," he added thoughtfully. "Perhaps I am not seeking my marital rights as determinedly as I ought." His gaze lingered on her bosom, and Olivia resisted the urge to cover her breasts with her arms. "Perhaps I have not been as forceful as is required."

Alarm shot through her. "What do you mean?"

"I mean, *wife*," he snarled, "that perhaps I have been too gentle in my desires. Perhaps you would make a more *obedient* wife if I were a more insistent husband."

Alarm quickly turned to fear and Olivia looked to the door, gauging her chance at escape.

Edward startled her with a caress of her cheek, and then a hand to her shoulder and neck. "If your sister can get a child in her, there must be some way to put one in you." He pressed his thumb lightly into the hollow of her throat. "If it is your desire that I do not turn your sister out, as I have every right to do, then you will find a way to give me an heir, Olivia. Do not think to defy me. Who will take you and your sister once I am done with you? *Who?* Your cousin in Wales with four mouths to feed? Your mother's brother, who languishes at King's Bench? The entire country will turn against you. No one will touch you and risk the wrath of Carey. Think on that when you take you elixirs and herbs," he said quietly, then released her with a shove backward. "Now go. I have work to do."

Olivia caught herself on the arm of a chair. She watched Edward walk to the sideboard and pour more whiskey, then quickly left the room.

CHAPTER THREE

Alexa Hastings would not stop sobbing. She was bent over the settee, her cries rattling the house, her shoulders shaking with the force of them. Harrison Tolly hadn't the slightest idea what to do for her. He'd tried cajoling her, then bribing her, then simply demanding that she stop. Nothing worked. She would calm for a minute, apologize for the trouble, and then start up again.

He was studying her now as she wept, thinking that perhaps a wee bit of laudanum might do the trick, when Rue, the ginger-haired, round little chambermaid who served him at the dowager house where he lived, appeared at his elbow. She was another one he'd saved from the marquis. Rue was dull-witted; basic math was beyond her, as were most chores. Harrison had taken pity on her when Brock had dismissed her from the main house for her ineptitude. He'd looked into her young round face and realized she'd be quickly devoured by the world at large if there wasn't someone to look after her. So he'd brought her here to the dowager house to be his chambermaid, and had quickly discovered that she might possibly be the worst chambermaid in all of England.

Mrs. Lampley, his cook and housekeeper, had also been saved from Everdon Court. She'd been married for many years to the gatekeeper, who'd died suddenly one night after supper. Carey had no use for Mrs. Lampley after that. He'd instructed Brock to find another gatekeeper and seemed to think nothing of turning out Mrs. Lampley and her young son. Harrison had brought them to the dowager house to cook and clean.

Privately, Harrison suspected he knew what had killed Mr. Lampley, as Mrs. Lampley's cooking was passable at best.

Harrison couldn't really say why he took in these misfits, but he supposed it had to do with his own humble beginnings. Twenty-nine years ago, he'd been born the bastard son of a professional paramour. He'd not even known who his father was until he was sixteen years old. He'd been an outcast from all of decent society most of his life until he'd made something of himself, and even then, it seemed as if every association was tainted by the circumstances of his birth. Harrison supposed that it gave him an affinity for those with no place in this world.

His friends warned that he'd end up with a kennel full of stray dogs if he weren't careful.

"Caller," Rue said, peering curiously at Miss Hastings.

"Caller? What caller?" Harrison asked.

"Dunno," Rue said. "But he said to say it is urgent."

Harrison suppressed a groan. He was up to his knees in problems and didn't need another added to the mix. "Mind Miss Hastings, Rue. Make sure she doesn't drown herself in her tears," he said as he strode out of the room.

In the foyer, he saw no one about and wondered what Rue had done with him. But then he looked to the door and saw that it was ajar. Rain poured from the skies, but Rue had left the diminutive drowned rat of a caller to stand on the porch. Harrison brought the gentleman in, his wool coat and soggy beaver hat dripping on the entry floor.

"Yes?" Harrison asked impatiently.

"Mr. Tolly?"

Obviously, for who but he resided at the Carey dowager house? "Yes, who is calling, please?"

"Mr. Harrison Tolly?"

For heaven's sake. "*Yes*," he said, frowning. "Now that we have established who I am, perhaps you will be so good to tell me who *you* are and what this is about."

"I am Mr. Theodore Fish," the man said, bowing slightly. "I believe I may have some rather stunning news for you."

Of course he did. What had happened to the mundane? What had happened to the simple problems of managing four Carey family properties, like rents not matching expenditures, or flour deliveries arriving late, or beef prices at an all-time low? What happened to the sort of problems that Harrison excelled at solving?

He sighed and wearily leaned a shoulder against the wall. "And what would your news be, Mr. Fish?"

The man seemed slightly perturbed. He undoubtedly wanted a better response for his announcement of stunning news—a gasp of surprise, a cry of alarm.

"Are you familiar with the name Ashwood?" Mr. Fish asked.

Well now, that *was* a bit stunning. Of course Harrison was familiar with that name, but he'd not heard it in years. He straightened up and eyed the man suspiciously.

"I take it that the name is familiar to you," Mr. Fish said, a bit smugly.

Harrison's eyes narrowed. "Who *are* you?" he demanded. "And what the devil is this about?"

"If I may, sir?" Mr. Fish said, with a not-so-subtle glance at the door. "The news is quite convoluted and requires more than a cursory explanation."

Of all the months and the weeks and the days in the year, Mr. Fish had to deliver his stunning news today. Harrison glanced over his shoulder to the sitting room, where the sound of Miss Hastings's sobs sounded like a performance of a three-act tragedy. He shifted his gaze to the Fish fellow again, taking him in from head to toe. "Yes, all right," he said, reluctantly.

"Rue!" he called as Mr. Fish stepped deeper into the foyer and removed his coat. Rue scurried out of the sitting room in the dress that was too small for her. He really must find her suitable clothing. "Find a towel for Mr. Fish and then bring tea to the study."

"To the study, sir? Not the sitting room?"

Harrison gave the young maid a pointed look. She had a soft heart, and as the sounds of Miss Hastings's tears could be heard in the foyer, the girl wanted him to mend things. That's what they all wanted from him—mend this, repair that.

"No, Rue, not to the sitting room. To the study," he said evenly. "And you may tell Miss Hastings that she will feel better in her room with a cold cloth across her forehead." He arched his brow at the girl. He did not exactly rule with an iron fist at the dowager house, and at times such as this, he rather regretted it.

The arch of his brow had the desired effect; Rue quickly looked down. "Yes, my lord," she said softly and hurried off.

"Sir," he corrected her. "And have Mrs. Lampley bring tea!" he called after her. To Mr. Fish, he said, "This way," and gestured in the opposite direction.

Mr. Fish draped his cloak across the back of a chair and put his hat beside it, and glanced in the direction of the sound of Miss Hastings's sobbing.

Harrison showed Mr. Fish into the study, his private retreat and favorite room. The dark wood trim made the green walls look vibrant to his eye.

The shelves were lined with the books he'd been collecting since he was a child; works of fiction, poetry, studies of places he'd never been and people he'd never met.

Among his earliest memories, vague as they were, he could remember one of his mother's so-called friends, a smiling gentleman in a wig and with long lacy cuffs giving him sweetmeats before ascending up the stairs to his mother's boudoir. That same gentleman had taken a liking to him and had seen to it that Harrison had a tutor. Harrison's tutor, Mr. Ridley, had been a lover of books, and had passed that love to Harrison. Harrison considered his books his companions while his mother was otherwise engaged and he was left to rear himself.

He directed Mr. Fish to a leather winged-back chair at the hearth, where a fire glowed. Water from Mr. Fish's muddied boots and trousers pooled on the fine Aubusson rug Harrison had inherited from his mother's house.

Mr. Fish noticed it, too. "I do beg your pardon," he said. "It is quite a deluge, and Everdon Court is rather far removed from the main roads."

It was indeed. A grand estate sitting on a thousand acres of deep woods and tilled fields took a bit of effort to reach. "Think nothing of it," Harrison said, and sat across from Mr. Fish, crossing one leg casually over the other. Rue bustled in with a towel, which she handed to Mr. Fish with a curtsy.

"Pardon, what else was I to do, sir?" she asked Harrison.

"Fetch Mrs. Lampley."

"Ah," she said, as if the sun had just shone through the window, and hurried out again.

"Much obliged," Mr. Fish said, and proceeded to wipe the rain from his face and shoulders and hands. "Can't recall a rain quite like this."

"What's this about Ashwood?" Harrison asked impatiently.

Mr. Fish folded the towel neatly in his lap. "It is rather extraordinary," he said. "My advice is that you should brace yourself, Mr. Tolly, for there is reason to believe that the late Earl of Ashwood may have been some relation to you."

Harrison couldn't help but smile at the careful description. "If that is your way of stating that I may have been his by-blow, I shall spare you any theatrics and confirm that it is true, Mr. Fish."

Mr. Fish's eyes nearly leapt out of his head with surprise.

Harrison never spoke of it, and he did not like to be reminded of it. "If you have come all this way to tell me something that is quite well known to me, you have wasted your time. I was not personally acquainted with the man who sired me, but I am well aware of who he was."

"Splendid," Mr. Fish said, undeterred. "We discovered your lineage in the parish records in a London church. However, that is not the reason for my call, Mr. Tolly."

"There cannot possibly be more." Harrison knew all there was to know of his father, of his long-standing relationship with his mother. Much to his chagrin, there had been few secrets between him and his mother.

"It would seem," Mr. Fish said, as he stretched his hands toward the fire, "that you may be his only true heir."

Still, Harrison shrugged. "I am still his bastard son. I fail to see the significance of your call."

"In this highly unusual case, being his one true heir would make you the heir to Ashwood."

Harrison laughed at that.

Mr. Fish glanced up at him. "I would not have come all this way if I did not believe it were true, Mr. Tolly."

Harrison would have told him he'd come all this way for nothing, but Mrs. Lampley's young son appeared with the tea service. Harrison met him at the door and took it from him, then returned to the hearth and placed the fine silver service—also his mother's—on a small table. "Did you come from London, Mr. Fish?" he asked congenially as he poured them tea.

"I have come directly from Ashwood at the behest of the countess. Except that she is not the countess any longer. The late earl and his wife adopted Miss Lily Boudine, and until very recently, it was believed that she was the sole surviving and rightful heir. However, now that we have discovered your existence, she can no longer assume the title."

"Neither can I," Harrison said calmly. "The laws of primogeniture are quite restrictive and very explicit in the requirement for legitimacy. Honey?"

Mr. Fish shook his head to the honey. "They are restrictive, indeed . . . unless one has been given a title and an estate by a royal edict, as well as the terms for inheritance."

Harrison snorted. "I rather doubt even a royal edict would make an illegitimate offspring worthy of an estate as grand as Ashwood. So let us avoid a lot of discourse, Mr. Fish. Is there some paper I must sign for this countess to have her place? Give it over, and I will sign it." He sipped his tea and glanced at the mantel clock.

Mr. Fish did not move.

"Shocked?" Harrison asked.

Mr. Fish put his teacup down. "After the year I have spent, sir, I am rarely shocked by anything. Nevertheless, I fear you do not understand me. King Henry VIII bestowed the title and estate on the first earl of Ashwood, and specifically entailed it to the blood offspring of that earl, and the earl's issue, et cetera and so forth, without regard to legitimacy. The *blood* offspring. That means, as the only surviving blood male offspring of the last earl, you have inherited the estate. Furthermore, our solicitor in London believes you have legal claim to the title, as well."

The meeting suddenly gained Harrison's full attention. He stared at the man, trying to guess his game. "Forgive me, Mr. Fish, but do you expect me to believe that you have come here to hand me an estate and a title?" He laughed. "I will not believe I have any claim that cannot quickly and easily be dismantled by some enterprising solicitor. I am the bastard son of the late earl, a man I remember meeting once or twice in my life. My blood relation, as you put it, is illegitimate."

Mr. Fish nodded. "Lady Ashwood—Lady *Eberlin*," he corrected himself, "rather thought you might view things that way." He reached into his coat pocket and withdrew a letter and handed it to Harrison.

The damp vellum had a wax seal that was the crest of the Duke of Darlington—a revered named in England. The brief letter introduced Mr. Fish as a bona fide and true agent of Ashwood, and declared that the Duke of Darlington vouched for what he was telling Harrison today. The duke ended his endorsement with the word *Congratulations* scrawled presumably in his own hand across the bottom.

Harrison supposed he should have been happy to hear this startling news, but he was not. He tossed the vellum back to Mr. Fish as myriad thoughts clouded his brain. There was the problem of Alexa, first and foremost. And there was the personal and private problem of Lady X. "I do not want it," he said flatly.

Mr. Fish almost sputtered his tea. "Pardon?"

"I do not want this," Harrison said again, directing his gaze at Mr. Fish. "Tell your countess to send me whatever papers are necessary to deliver the estate to her, and I will sign them."

Mr. Fish looked stunned. He came to his feet. "Do you realize what you are saying?"

"Yes, I do," Harrison said firmly. He pushed his fingers through his hair, trying to absorb this impossible, ill-timed news. His father had never acknowledged him in any way, and now he would have his estate? Harrison was entirely suspicious, certain there was a catch. And Harrison wanted nothing to do with Ashwood and whatever catch that might be for so many reasons that his head began to spin with them.

"You can't possibly!" Mr. Fish argued. "No man in his right mind would dismiss this so easily—"

"Do you think this is easy?" Harrison snapped.

Mr. Fish caught himself. "I would not presume to know. But I do know that it is a royal edict. And much like any child born to inherit, you may not want the riches that have just fallen into your lap, but they are yours regardless."

"Mr. Tolly?"

Both Harrison and Mr. Fish started at the sound of Miss Hastings's voice. She was standing at the threshold, her face pale, her eyes swollen, and her hands clasped tightly before her. She looked at Mr. Fish, then at Harrison. "What has happened?" she asked. "Has something happened?"

"Nothing has happened," he assured her, walking briskly to the door. "Please go back to your room."

But her gaze was fixed on Mr. Fish. "You have inherited," she said, and turned brown eyes to Harrison. "What have you inherited? What does it mean? Does it mean that—"

"It means nothing," he said quickly, and took her by the elbow, turning her around and ushering her out the door. "Please do return to your room, Miss Hastings. I will be with you shortly."

She glanced reluctantly over her shoulder at Mr. Fish before turning away.

Harrison shut the door of the study and chafed at Mr. Fish's sympathetic smile.

"I see at least one reason you may be reluctant to welcome this news," he said slyly.

Harrison frowned. There was nothing he could say about Miss Hastings until he deciphered what had possessed him to take such a drastic step in offering to marry her. And what the bloody hell was he to do about it now? "*Bollocks,*" he muttered, and stalked to the windows, wondering how in the blazes he would extract himself from a quagmire that seemed to get deeper and thicker as the day wore on.

CHAPTER FOUR

Edward made good on his promise to attempt to force Olivia to his will, but as was his trouble of late, he could not force himself. "You do this to me," he'd said bitterly. "You remove all desire from a man."

On Sunday morning, Edward was subdued. He lingered over breakfast, reading aloud to Olivia from the Bible, having decided, what with the rain, that while the servants would make the quarter mile trek to church, the weather was too foul for him and his wife to venture out.

Olivia sat quietly, pretending to listen to his lesson as he droned on. She was anxious for Alexa. She had not come back to the house last night, and Olivia wondered where Mr. Tolly had taken her. At least she could rest knowing that Alexa was in good hands.

Olivia thought of Mr. Tolly, too, standing so proud and capable in Edward's study, prepared to shoulder Alexa's problem as his own to save her from the fate

Edward would have handed her. Olivia tried to imagine how it would feel to have someone make a heroic gesture for her, to have someone gallop into Everdon Court and take her from the hellish marriage she'd suffered for six long years . . .

She shook her head and absently folded her napkin. No one was going to save her. Save her from what? She was a marchioness, living in the lap of luxury, with all the trappings of wealth and privilege that entailed. She was not the first woman to have suffered a grim marriage.

Unfortunately, Olivia had sealed her own fate when she'd agreed with her mother that Edward would make a fine husband.

It was the night her family had dined at Everdon Court for the first time. What a young, inexperienced, silly fool she'd been! Olivia had been so taken by the great house, the furnishings, the artwork, and certainly Edward himself. He'd been charming, touching his finger to her cheek, remarking on her beauty. She'd thought him unremarkable in looks, but pleasant. He'd seemed so confident and assured, and Olivia had been enthralled by the idea of marriage and children.

So had her mother. "Isn't he lovely!" she'd exclaimed in the coach on the way home.

"He seems very nice," Olivia had agreed.

"Nice! He has twenty thousand a year, Livi. You must think of that. It is so important that you marry well. I'll not always be here to care for Alexa, so you must. We can scarcely rely on this one to make a suitable match, can we?" she'd asked, and had laughed as she patted Alexa's knee.

Alexa, who was twelve at the time, had taken great offense to that. "I shall never marry!" she'd declared. "I'll not have a gentleman tell me what to do!"

"I suspect you will marry," Lord Hastings had said. "But rest assured you will scare off anyone with twenty thousand a year."

"Livi, my love, I know that the marquis will offer for you," her mother had said excitedly. "He seems taken with you and he has just come into his title. He needs to be about the business of producing an heir. Now then, you must always present yourself as demure and obedient," her mother had counseled. "Mind that you do not argue. Make him feel pleased."

Olivia blinked back a burn of tears at the memory. God knew how hard she had tried to please her husband, but it was impossible. Even in the days before he'd grown to despise her, he'd had no use for her. He had never given her the same sort of warm smile that she received from Mr. Tolly each day. Frankly, Edward had never really seemed to see her at all.

But Mr. Tolly . . . God help her, Olivia wouldn't have cared if he'd had only five hundred pounds a year, she would still desire him above all others. She'd been seduced by his warmth and kindness, his ready smile. She'd been captivated by his bright light in her otherwise abysmal life.

She thought back to a few weeks ago, when the icy grip of winter would not let go of Everdon Court. She'd gone to the hothouse to collect some flowers to brighten her sitting room and give her a hint of spring. She was examining the potted flowers when Mr. Tolly had come in search of Mr. Gortman, the grounds-keeper.

"Madam," he'd said, tipping his hat and flashing a smile that charmed her to the tips of her toes.

She had been unconscionably thrilled to see him. "You must help me, Mr. Tolly," she'd said instantly. That was her way of keeping his company as long as she might—she asked for his help. She held up two flowerpots. "Yellow? Or white?"

He had looked at the flowerpots. "Red."

"Red?" She'd laughed and looked around her. "But there is no red."

"Ah, but there is," he'd said with a sly wink. "You are not acquainted with Mr. Gortman as I am. Come." He'd taken the pots from her and put them aside, then took her hand and laid it on his arm, escorting her outside to a small shed just beside the hothouse. It was warm inside the shed; off to one side, the coals in a small brazier glowed. But it wasn't the brazier that had made Olivia gasp with delight; it was the red flowers. There were pots and pots of them: geraniums, cocks-comb, dahlias, and miniature roses.

"Mr. Gortman plans to replant the small reflecting garden," Mr. Tolly explained.

"It's beautiful!" Olivia had said appreciatively. It was a small room full of the promise of spring. "Do you not think so, Mr. Tolly?"

"Yes." He'd said it instantly, softly, and Olivia had turned around to him. But he was not looking at the flowers—he was looking at her in a way that had sent a shiver deep through her veins.

But the moment quickly passed as he moved to the door and held it open for her. "I shall inquire of Mr. Gortman for you. I am certain he would be delighted to make an arrangement for you."

She'd wondered if perhaps she'd wanted so badly to see something in Mr. Tolly's expression that she'd imagined it. "Thank you, but I could not possibly impose. He has taken great care to grow them for a particular reason."

Nevertheless, the following morning, Olivia had awakened to a vase of red flowers on her vanity. "Where did these come from?" she'd asked her maid.

"Mr. Gortman sent them up, mu'um," Nancy replied.

Olivia had been as pleased as if he'd sent her diamonds, and thinking of it now, she couldn't help smiling to herself.

"What are you thinking, Lady Carey?" Edward asked, startling Olivia from her thoughts. She reluctantly turned her attention to her husband. He was seated at the head of the table, holding the Bible in one hand, drumming the fingers of his other on the table.

"Pardon?" she asked.

"I cannot imagine that Scripture puts such a lovely smile on your face. You have never struck me as the sort of woman moved to happiness by the good word."

Olivia didn't speak; she hadn't heard a word he'd said.

"I should like to know what you think of the passage."

He knew very well she'd not paid him any heed. Olivia sighed. "I beg your pardon, but I was not listening."

Edward cocked a brow in amusement. "Quite obviously. And why not, Olivia? Do you find me tedious? Am I so uninteresting to you?"

"Not at all," she said, and thought quickly how to smooth over his ruffled feathers. "I'm afraid my thoughts have been occupied with concern for my sister these last few days."

"I see," Edward said, nodding thoughtfully. "Your *sister* holds a place of greater significance than your husband in your thoughts."

"On this particular occasion, yes," Olivia brazenly agreed.

Edward arched a brow, peering curiously at her, as if surprised that she would admit it. "I am sorry if she causes you distress. But it would seem that your distress is even more reason to banish her from our lives."

"She is my sister," Olivia said. "I want her here with

me, as any sister would. She is in an awful predicament, Edward. She will be shunned and ridiculed and disparaging things will be said of her. All she has is her family."

Edward sat back, studying her. "That is precisely the reason we cannot have her here, and well you know it. The association with her would taint *this* family's reputation."

"I understand," Olivia said carefully. "But I thought perhaps no one would need to know." It was a slim hope that he might agree, but a hope nonetheless.

But Edward rolled his eyes and said, "You are either naïve or simple. Frankly, I cannot believe you would even ask this of me. If you were a loving wife, you would seek to remove this blight from our lives by any means possible. If you truly loved me, you would have sent her away instead of bringing her to me. It's as if you forget who I am."

"Of course I haven't, Edward. I brought her to you because I thought you would be very unhappy to hear of it otherwise."

He shook his head. "You have a mountain of excuses at hand. If you won't send her from us, I shall do it for you. I will make sure that she does not disgrace us ever again."

"But Mr. Tolly has offered to give her his name."

Edward snorted and turned a page of his Bible. "She is comely, your whore of a sister. I am certain he looks forward to the pleasure he will find in his marital bed." He glanced up at her. "Pleasure I have been denied in mine."

Olivia's face flamed. She couldn't look at him.

"Tolly knows what he is about," Edward said laughingly.

"Did I hear my name?" Mr. Tolly asked, striding into the room at the moment with his easy smile.

Olivia could feel the tension instantly leave her.

"Ah, Mr. Tolly!" Edward said, his smile brightening. "Thank you for coming. Sit, and allow Lady Carey to do something useful and pour you tea. Olivia?"

Olivia bit her tongue and obediently rose to pour tea for Mr. Tolly.

"I was just asking my wife's opinion on some Scripture," Edward said as she moved to the sideboard.

"I did not mean to interrupt," Mr. Tolly said.

"You did not interrupt," Edward assured him.

Olivia poured the tea and turned around; Edward's eyes were locked on her. He chuckled. "In fact, my dear wife confessed that she had paid little heed to my reading. What do you make of a wife who blatantly ignores her husband's Scripture reading?"

Olivia set the tea before Mr. Tolly. "Thank you," he said, and glanced up at her with a ghost of a smile.

"It is my pleasure." She took a seat directly across from him; his gray eyes remained intent on her.

"I was reading from Ephesians, Tolly. Are you familiar with the disciple Paul's letters to the Ephesians?" Edward asked.

Mr. Tolly grinned. "Not as familiar as I ought to be, I'm afraid."

If he were married to Edward, he would have been exceedingly familiar with the chapter. Edward often selected his readings from the gospel of Paul.

"If you will indulge a man and his wife a bit of spiritual readings, I shall continue," Edward said, as if he were the Archbishop. He lifted the Bible and read, "'Wives, submit yourselves unto your own husbands, as unto the Lord. For the husband is the head of the wife.'" He lowered the Bible and smiled coldly at Olivia.

Mr. Tolly glanced uncomfortably at his teacup and lifted it to his lips.

But Olivia smiled brightly at her husband. She despised him, but she despised being ridiculed in front of Mr. Tolly even worse. "A fine reading, my lord. You should consider the pulpit."

Edward scowled. "Now that you have given me heed, my dear, perhaps you will be so kind as to tell me your interpretation?"

Olivia knew very well what she risked by challenging him, but she was past the point of caring. Let him banish her, too—it would be a blessing of sorts. Let him hit her—it could be no more painful than his company. "My interpretation?" she asked, as if pondering it. "Oh, I hardly know, my love. But I think you are very eager to tell me what my interpretation should be."

Mr. Tolly choked on his tea.

Edward's eyes darkened. He leaned back, studying her. "I think you need to be reminded that the gospel cautions that a wife should revere her husband."

"Does it?" Olivia asked with a doe-eyed look, then shrugged lightly. "I recall very little of the verses, really . . . Except," she said, lifting one finger, "I do recall the verse that says a husband should render the wife due benevolence."

Mr. Tolly's coughing suddenly worsened. "I beg your pardon," he said hoarsely and stood up, walking to the sideboard.

Edward, predictably, was not the least bit amused. "I think you mean to provoke me."

"Not at all!" Olivia said sweetly. "I *never* mean to provoke you."

Edward's lips disappeared into a thin line.

"If I may, my lord," Mr. Tolly said as he returned to the table, "there is much we have to accomplish before your departure."

"Departure?" Olivia asked.

"Yes," Edward said tightly. "Departure."

Olivia resisted the urge to leap for joy. "Where are you going?"

Edward suddenly stood. Mr. Tolly stood, too. "I am to London. And before you inquire, I shall tell you straightaway that you are not allowed to come."

If she hadn't despised him, Olivia might have kissed him. "I would not dream of burdening you with my presence," she said sweetly.

Edward tossed down his linen. "Mr. Tolly, please endure the company of my wife for a few moments. I find I am in the need of a bit of air before we begin," he said and, looking pointedly at Olivia, he strode out.

Mr. Tolly remained standing until he'd gone, then turned about and looked at Olivia, a soft smile on his face. "Ephesians," he said as he resumed his seat.

"We are very select in our readings here. But never mind that—Mr. Tolly, I have been desperate to speak to you."

"Of course."

She leaned forward and stretched her hand across the table. "You *cannot* mean to marry Alexa! I cannot allow it."

"Of course I—"

"No, no," she said, shaking her head. "It was very chivalrous of you to offer, and God knows I cannot thank you enough for it." She spoke quickly, certain that Edward would appear at any moment. "But I will not allow you to saddle yourself with an unwanted marriage and wife for the rest of your life."

"It is—"

"Are you *mad*?" she whispered, glancing nervously at the door. "There is *no* life, no happiness in marriage to someone you cannot love. Your heart was pure, and you meant a kindness, but you and Alexa cannot make such a grave mistake. Think of it," she begged him. "Don't you want to marry a woman you *love*?"

Mr. Tolly's jaw clenched. He swallowed hard. Olivia

believed she understood him—he'd offered in haste and he regretted it. In a wretched moment, he'd seen a woman in distress and he'd believed, as Olivia had, that all would be lost for Alexa if someone didn't step in to prevent it.

"Mr. Tolly . . . you have been so good to me," Olivia whispered. "Alexa has ruined her life, but you cannot allow sympathy for her to ruin your life forevermore. My heart breaks for my sister, truly it does, but she and I cannot drag someone as good as you—"

Mr. Tolly suddenly reached across the table and covered her hand with his, squeezing gently. His touch startled Olivia right out of her thought. She stared down at his hand, twice as big as hers, at his fingers wrapped securely around hers. "You will make yourself ill," he said low. "And surely you know me well enough to know that I am not an incautious man. You must understand that I did not make such an offer lightly. I need a bit of time to think of another way that she and I might avoid it and yet save her reputation—and yours."

The feel of his hand on hers was powerful in a way that made Olivia's heart pound. There was so much in his touch—protection, assurance. *Do not let go my hand, never let go my hand.* "It's so unfair," Olivia murmured, her gaze fixed on his hand, on a small freckle on the back of his thumb. "Where is she? Is she all right?"

"She is at the dowager house." Mr. Tolly made no effort to remove his hand from hers, and Olivia imagined that he was infusing her with his strength. She could almost feel it flowing between them.

"She is understandably upset and confused," he continued, "but she will be quite all right. Lady Carey, look at me," he commanded softly.

Olivia didn't want to look away from his hand. She wondered when that freckle had appeared on his thumb, if he'd spent his youth in the sun. She wondered so many things about him—

Mr. Tolly squeezed her hand, and she reluctantly lifted her gaze to his.

"Do not fret," he said. "I will see that your sister is well cared for."

"I have no doubt that in your hands, she will be better cared for than she has ever been. But I fret for *you*, sir. What of your personal affections and desires? You are a young man, scarcely older than me. You will want your own love and children, and yet you will throw all that away?"

Mr. Tolly's gaze dropped to Olivia's mouth, and she instantly felt a draw from her toes, spiraling up her legs and into her spine, warming her cheeks. Her heart skipped; her fingers curled around his.

"If I may be so bold," he said, as if weighing each word, "my personal affections lie with a woman I can never marry for a number of reasons. If it comes to it and I marry Miss Hastings—and I am not convinced that it will—you must believe that the arrangement will suit me perfectly."

The sound of Edward striding down the hall reached them; Mr. Tolly's hand slid across the table and into his lap. He continued to hold her gaze as Edward entered the breakfast room. Just as Edward looked up from the papers he was holding, Olivia picked up her teacup and brought it to her lips, hiding behind it. It was empty; she daintily replaced it in the saucer and surreptitiously glanced at Mr. Tolly.

"Olivia, you may take your tea to your rooms," Edward said dismissively.

She stood. "Good day, Mr. Tolly. Edward." She could feel Mr. Tolly's gaze follow her as she walked around the table. Her heart was fluttering as she walked out of the room, her head filled with the image of those gray eyes, and a small shiver was sneaking its way down her spine at the intensity with which he had looked at her.

CHAPTER FIVE

Sunday evening, Harrison had a small contretemps with Miss Hastings, his would-be fiancée.

"You sound like a husband, Mr. Tolly, and the vows not even said," she petulantly complained.

As Harrison had never been a husband, he had no idea how one sounded. In his opinion he sounded as if he were the only reasonable person in the drawing room. Miss Hastings was determined to go to her sister and weep on her shoulder, but Harrison was just as determined that she not do so until Lord Carey had departed Everdon Court.

Carey's mood had been particularly foul that afternoon after Harrison explained that his younger brother, Lord Westhorpe, had made a series of decisions for the Carey estate in Surrey that had cost a significant sum. Lord Carey did not tolerate mistakes in anyone. He thought himself above making them, and expected others to be above them as well.

"David will ruin us," he said sharply. "After centuries of building this family's fortune—since Edward the Second sat the throne!—he will bring it down with his spendthrift ways and inattention to details!"

Harrison considered himself fortunate that, for whatever reason, the marquis listened to him. Carey heeded his advice, sought his counsel, and, for the most part, treated him as an equal in the management of the vast Carey holdings, which rivaled those of the richest men in the kingdom.

Harrison was an excellent and capable steward, trained by the best in England. But he was not so naïve as to believe that he was somehow immune from instant dismissal. He'd seen it happen too many times.

He liked to think he had prevented some of that at Everdon Court. He couldn't help but feel protective over the servants there—they were powerless people, displaced on the whims of powerful men like Carey, and he'd spent too much time in their shoes as a child. He'd watched his mother worry herself ill and struggle to keep the gentlemen who provided for her engaged in any way she might, for when they were finished with her, that was the end of their largesse. One of Harrison's most painful memories was the night his mother had learned that her benefactor had been seen in the company of a younger paramour. She'd collapsed in a heap, sobbing, and he'd felt a deep uselessness. He could not help his mother. He could not give her peace.

A fortnight later, they moved to meaner surroundings—him with his books, his mother with the jewels she used to pay for their living.

Now, Harrison was in a different position. He was powerful in his own right, because the Carey family trusted him.

Harrison firmly believed that he'd remained in good favor as a result of the relationship he'd enjoyed with Lord Carey's late father. The marquis's father had employed Harrison based on the recommendation of one of his mother's lovers. He had kindly overlooked Harrison's situation and had grown very fond of Harrison. He'd always treated him as an equal. His son had followed his lead and had come to rely on Harrison just as his father had.

Today, however, Harrison had detected a slight change in the marquis's tone, and it had to do with Alexa Hastings. As Harrison had gathered his things to leave, his lordship had stopped him with a question: "What do you intend to do with the whore?"

Harrison bristled at the term—Miss Hastings was an eighteen-year-old girl who'd made a singular, life-altering mistake, but he resented the judgment of her. "I intend to search for a situation that will suit everyone involved, and if I cannot find it, I intend to marry her," he'd said flatly.

A dark look had come over Lord Carey's face. "I am shocked. I have given you every respect, and this is how you repay me? By taking a whore as your wife while in my employ?"

"I beg your pardon if I have offended you," Harrison responded evenly. He knew how to appeal to Carey's ego. "But if someone does not marry the girl, the scandal could very well be ruinous."

Carey hadn't said anything to that, but had eyed him shrewdly.

"It is my duty here to look after the estate," Harrison had said, and had steadily returned his gaze, daring him to challenge that he'd been anything but steadfastly loyal in every way.

Carey had finally looked away. "I cannot understand your desire to meddle in the affairs of the Hastings family and ruin your own life in the course of it, but if that is your desire, so be it. I will insist you find a solution quickly, whilst I am away," he said, turning his attention to the papers before him. "And send her somewhere out of my sight. I cannot bear to look at her and she is unwelcome in my house. If you find that objectionable, keep in mind that I'd sooner banish her for good."

Harrison knew that Carey meant what he said. The marquis had banished his own cousin for racking up unmanageable gambling debts two years ago. He'd reduced his stipend and sent him off to Scotland with the promise that he'd remove the stipend altogether if he dared show his face in England again. "Very well," Harrison said, and took his leave before he said something he regretted.

He'd left Lord Carey humming a jaunty little tune.

He'd returned to the dowager house, wondering why he'd stayed in his post as long as he had. Was it the generous salary? No—money was not everything. Was it because of the Rues of the world, who needed someone like him to look after them? Perhaps. The work? He liked what he did.

Whatever the reason, Harrison stayed and endured the prejudices and bigotries of the marquis. Even if this Fish fellow were to be believed, he could not leave here.

Harrison didn't care to think of Ashwood. Of the possibility that there was a place for him to go, to belong, to be his own man. If he thought of it, he felt unsettled, a sensation he didn't care for in the least.

Yet he was feeling quite unsettled when he'd entered the house the Careys had graciously made his while he was in their employ. The dowager house was a manor house that was, in some ways, vastly superior to houses owned by other lords and ladies. It was far too large for one man.

Rue was on hand that afternoon to take his wet things. "Is it raining yet?" she asked, holding his dripping coat.

Harrison suppressed a small smile at the obvious. "It is. Where is Miss Hastings?" he asked as he started for his study.

"She's putting on her cloak and such. She's to the big house."

"Is she," he drawled. "Where is she now?"

"In the drawing room, my lord."

"Sir," he corrected, and proceeded to the drawing room.

He found Miss Hastings in her cloak, fitting her hands into gloves. "Good afternoon."

She glanced at him from the corner of her eye. "Mr. Tolly."

"May I inquire where you are going?"

She suddenly whirled about to face him. "You sound like a husband, Mr. Tolly, and the vows not even said. You cannot keep me from my sister!"

Harrison clasped his hands behind his back and lowered his head. "I have no intention of keeping you from your sister," he said, as if speaking to a child. "I hope that over the fortnight, while the marquis is away, you may spend every possible moment with her. But he has not yet departed and you must stay here until he does. It is not open to debate."

"Why?" she demanded. "He cannot do anything to me. He is not my father."

"I beg to differ," Harrison said. "There are few men in this land who are as powerful as your sister's husband. If he wants to see you publicly ruined, he can do so with a word. A single word, Miss Hastings. If he wants to banish you, he will do it, and no one will challenge him. *No* one."

She winced at that. "I just want Olivia, Mr. Tolly. I want to be with my sister. You cannot imagine how difficult this is for me."

"Your sister desires to be with you, as well," he assured her. "Nevertheless, you must trust me that it will be to your benefit to wait. His lordship is to London on the morrow, and when he is gone, you may come and go as you please."

"Thank the saints," she muttered, and glanced down at her gloves.

"So . . . if you will kindly remove your cloak and gloves," he said.

Miss Hastings did not remove them. She glanced up at him, chewing her bottom lip. "Mr. Tolly . . . I should not like you to think I am ungrateful for your intervention on my behalf, for I am not. But I do not wish to marry you."

Surely the foolish girl didn't believe that *he* did. "I understand completely," he said. "No need to say more—"

"On the contrary, I quite desperately need to say this," Miss Hastings said earnestly. "I realize that I am in no position to argue, but I really cannot, in good conscience, *marry* you, for I do not . . ." She glanced around the room as if searching for something, finally fixing on a small porcelain angel Rue had put on an end table. "I do not love you," she said softly.

She said it as if he'd made some declaration of his esteem for her, and Harrison couldn't help smiling. "Of course you do not love me. You scarcely know me."

"Yes, well . . . there is also the matter that you are a steward. I had hoped for a better situation."

Miss Hastings's gall was as fascinating as her brutal honesty. But that remark put a small hole in Harrison's bubble of goodwill. "I am indeed a steward," he said. "And you are carrying a child out of wedlock."

Miss Hastings blushed furiously. "How dare you speak of it?"

"How dare I not?" Harrison countered. "You surely must realize this is hardly an ideal situation for either of us. I sincerely hope that I might find a way to avoid a marriage, for both our sakes—"

"I can't wait to learn what way *that* might be," she muttered sarcastically.

"But if I cannot," he continued, ignoring her skepticism, "you must keep in mind that you are in rather desperate need of a husband, and it is my duty to keep scandal from the Carey name—"

"Why?"

The question astonished him. "*Why?*" he repeated.

"Yes, Mr. Tolly, why is it *your* duty to keep scandal from the Carey name? I cannot see that you would suffer from it."

Harrison shifted uneasily at the truth in that.

"It seems to me that *you* would wish to marry someone whom you esteem, someone you find compatible in temperament and station."

"Naturally that would be my preference, but I think perhaps it is too late for me. And, I daresay, too late for you."

"Why is it too late for you?"

For the second time today, Harrison was forced to say aloud a secret he'd carried for many years. "As it happens, Miss Hastings, the woman who holds that particular allure for me is regrettably unattainable. That is all that needs to be said of my situation. We are speaking of *your* situation."

"Who is she?" Miss Hasting asked curiously.

"That is neither here nor there."

"I say that it is. If we are to be married, I have a right to know."

He arched a dubious brow. "Are we to be married, then?"

She rolled her eyes. "Who is she?" she asked again.

He smiled as patiently as he could manage, given the uncomfortable direction of the conversation. "Let us call her Lady X."

Miss Hastings laughed. "Lady X? Who might that be? Olivia?" She laughed at her jest, and Harrison smiled, too. "Is it Olivia?" she asked, her eyes wide with surprise.

"That is an absurd suggestion."

"Oh, I know who it is!" she said suddenly, her smile brightening. "Lady Martha Higginbottom. Yes, it must be! Olivia said she calls quite often, and she never has much of anything at all to say."

Harrison chuckled. He'd played this guessing game at the Cock and Sparrow as his friends teased him about his mysterious Lady X. They had their theories, as well.

"You must see my point, do you not, Mr. Tolly? If you esteem Lady Martha, you must find a way to marry her. I should think that Lord Higginbottom would be quite pleased to marry her to a steward. She is the third daughter, after all."

He smiled wryly. "I do not intend to marry Lady Martha, Miss Hastings. Now then, I would suggest that as we are two reasonable people, we keep our attention to the problem at hand and determine how we shall find our way."

"Meaning?"

"Meaning . . ." God in his heaven, Harrison had no idea what he meant. He no more wanted to marry this girl than she wanted him to marry her. And as she'd astutely mentioned, he had no hope that he'd find a workable solution. But Miss Hastings was so young she didn't understand that the few choices she'd had as a female in general had been eliminated the moment she'd conceived the child she carried. "Meaning, we must plan carefully. For your sake, and for the sake of your sister. Are you quite certain that the father of your child will not stand up to his responsibility?"

Miss Hastings's cheeks turned crimson and she glanced down. "I shall be perfectly frank, Mr. Tolly. I do not care to speak to you of such personal matters. I should like to speak to Olivia."

"I am trying to help you, Miss Hastings. If you are frank and honest with me, the better we might see our way out of this quagmire."

thought, and in the next moment, Edward stumbled into her room, blinking at the light. "What are you about?" he demanded.

Olivia put the book aside and smoothed her lap. She could smell the whiskey on him from across the room. "I was reading."

"Reading!" He snorted as if he didn't believe that she was capable of reading. "I sincerely hope you are reading something that will improve your mind," he said, and began to untie his neckcloth, yanking at it. "Frankly, I find your education lacking, Olivia. You have no knowledge or opinions on matters of import."

Olivia wondered how this man, who couldn't stay out of the bottoms of his cups, could possibly think he knew what her opinions were on anything. He never inquired and was quick to cut her off when she did try to speak. "What matters?" she asked casually.

Edward sighed impatiently. "That is precisely my point. I should not have to enumerate them for you, should I? What are you reading?"

"A book."

"Clearly it is a book! What is the book?"

"*Castle Rackrent*," she said, and stood from her chair, walking to the hearth.

Edward paused from his fumbled attempts to disrobe and peered at her, swaying a bit. "That does not sound like a book with any redeeming value. What sort of book is it?"

And here they went, Olivia thought grimly. "A fictional tale," she said with a shrug.

Edward dropped his hands from his waistcoat, his face darkening. "Must I instruct you in everything? Is your judgment so poor? I do not approve of your reading *fiction*, Olivia. For God's sake, if you choose to read, do me the small courtesy of reading something of value. Not something that will weaken your mind any more than it suffers already."

Olivia imagined herself with her archery bow, an arrow pulled taut, and letting it go, watching it pierce Edward between the eyes. "Yes, dear," she demurred, and when he eyed her suspiciously, she smiled as innocently as she could.

But of course Edward was not satisfied. "Where did you obtain this fictional tale?" he asked snidely.

Olivia hesitated only slightly, but long enough for Edward's face to redden. "I asked you a question."

"Mr. Tolly lent it to me."

Something flickered in Edward's eyes. "Tolly," he said. He turned away from her and worked at his waistcoat. "That one seems to be entirely too involved in the affairs of women of late," he said, at last managing to discard the waistcoat. "I will admit that I was rather disappointed in his stepping forward for your whore of a sister. But then again, he himself is a bastard. Who better to raise a bastard than a bloody bastard?"

"Edward!" Olivia said, appalled by his remarks.

"How can you say such a thing? Mr. Tolly has always been steadfast in his service to you and this family."

He shrugged. "Does that make him any less a bastard? Is he not the child of a whore, just as your sister's child shall be?"

Impotent anger tightened like a vise around her chest. She knew better than to argue, but she could not hear Mr. Tolly or Alexa maligned and not speak. "Alexa is *not* a whore—"

"And now I find that he is passing books about to the feebleminded," Edward continued as if she hadn't spoken. "I shall have to address his lapse of judgment." He swayed as he pulled his shirt from his trousers.

"It was not his lapse of judgment," Olivia said quickly. "I asked him to bring me a work of fiction and he did as I asked."

Edward stilled. He lifted his head; his eyes had gone hard. "You *asked* him?"

Olivia's pulse ticked a little faster, but she looked him directly in the eye. "I did. The days can be rather tedious without an occupation." She cringed inwardly at the look that came over Edward, the frown of disapproval that deepened the creases between his brows.

"Well." He threw his shirt aside and stood with his narrow chest and arms exposed. "It seems I must explain to the *marchioness*," he said, his voice full of disgust, "that Mr. Tolly has responsibility for overseeing four estates and various business interests on behalf of this family."

"I am well aware of his responsibilities, Edward."

"Are you truly, Olivia?" he asked snidely. "For surely, if you were aware of his responsibilities, you would understand that it is beneath the man's time and effort to be sent on a chase for fictional tales to amuse *you*."

"For heaven's sake, it is only a book—"

"Do not presume to tell me what it is or isn't!" he snapped. "You are ignorant, Olivia. You bring to mind a cow standing before me now."

Olivia hated him. Reviled him. She hated his constant belittling, hated the way he smiled so cruelly, hated the air that he breathed, the space that he occupied. Her hope of a happy marriage had been so foolish, so naïve! For so long, she'd believed the best way to endure him was to agree with him. And in the beginning, there had been less trouble for her. But as time went on, the things she was forced to agree upon were more and more ludicrous or demeaning. Tonight she felt as if she couldn't abide it another moment.

There would be a price for it, but Olivia folded her arms and looked away.

"Fear not, my love," Edward said, as if they were playing a game. "I do not hold you entirely responsible for your many shortcomings. I think it is a defect of your birth . . . just as your inability to conceive a child is a gross defect." He chuckled. "An inability to conceive children or ideas," he said. "I married an imbecile."

Olivia started toward the dressing room. As she

moved to pass him, she said, "It is more likely that the defect is in *you*, husband."

Edward's response was lightning quick—he caught her, locking his fingers in a vise around her arm and yanking her toward him. "You think I am the defective one?" he breathed, and twirled her around, pushing her facedown onto the bed.

Olivia instantly pushed herself up and off the bed. "You will not force yourself on me again," she said breathlessly.

Edward's eyes turned black. He backhanded her across her mouth. The force of the blow sprawled Olivia onto the bed once more. It stunned her, but she managed to come up on her elbows and touch her fingers to her lips. He'd drawn blood.

Olivia's fury soared. She didn't care that copulation was his legal right. She didn't care that her mother had once told her that a wife's duty was to submit willingly to her husband. She would *not* allow him to lay a hand on her, not without defending herself as best she could. She jumped up off the bed and faced him fully, her fists curled at her sides. "You are a *beast*. Keep your hands from me."

Edward's laugh was loud and booming. Grinning like a madman, he lunged for her. Olivia tried to dart out of his reach, but he was too quick, too powerful. He threw her facedown onto the bed again and pinned her there with his body. "You stupid, stupid, bitch," he breathed hotly onto her neck, filling her nostrils with the stench of his drink. "Do you think I took you to wife for your scintillating conversation? Your comely looks? I took you as a wife for one thing only, and that was to give me a bloody heir. And I will keep trying for what you *owe* me until you bear me one!" He put his arm across her neck and pressed her face into the coverlet. "If you cannot or will not provide me with my heir, I will see to it that I never have to look at you again. Do you understand me?"

With that, he removed his arm from her neck, and as Olivia dragged air into her lungs, he took her by the shoulder and roughly flipped her onto her back. "So I ask you, Lady Carey, do you intend to open your legs to me as an obedient wife? Or shall you force me to take you?"

Olivia was shaking, her fury was so great. She rose up on her elbows, lifted her face so that it was just below his. Edward misunderstood her; his gaze dropped to her lips and he lowered his head as if to kiss her. But Olivia turned her head to avoid his mouth and said, "I will *never* willingly submit to you again."

Edward's mouth curved into a hideous smile. "Then you leave me no choice," he said, and shoved her onto her back.

Olivia fought him, but it was no use. In moments, he had her hands pinned above her head with one hand. He dragged her skirts up around her waist as Olivia kicked against him, then pried her thighs open with his knee as he freed his cock from his trousers and thrust into her like the beast he was, glaring down at her in dark triumph for having managed it.

When he had finished with her, Olivia rolled onto her side, clutching the gown he had wrenched off her shoulders to cover her breasts, then closed her eyes and recalled Mr. Tolly's broad hand on hers, squeezing her fingers reassuringly, infusing her with his calm.

CHAPTER SEVEN

E ven in the flurry of activity that surrounded the marquis's departure from Everdon Court, Harrison noticed a difference in his lordship's demeanor. As the coach was loaded and the horses harnessed, Carey seemed distracted and distant. One might even say distrustful.

And distrustful of him in particular.

They stood in the drive along with Brock. A coachman held open the door of the chaise with the black plumes and elaborate gold scrolls painted on the sides. "All is at the ready, my lord," he said.

"Thank you." The marquis moved as if to put himself inside the coach, but with one foot on the step, he paused and looked back, his gaze raking over Harrison. "You like to read, do you, Tolly?"

It was such an odd question that Harrison felt the hackles on his neck rise. "I do."

"Works of fiction?"

Harrison wasn't certain he'd actually heard the slight drip of derision in the marquis's voice. "From time to time."

"I believe fiction is a waste of an educated man's good time," Carey said as he smoothed the glove on his left hand. "Nevertheless, I suppose it is a personal choice." His gaze locked on Harrison. "However, if my *wife* chooses to read, I will have her read something more enlightening than fairy tales. She has enough foolish thoughts in her head without adding to them."

Harrison didn't know what to say to such a baffling, narrow-minded view.

But Carey was not finished. His polished boot dropped from the coach step and he turned around to face Harrison fully. "I should like to know on what occasion you presented my wife with books."

He said it as if Harrison had presented her with a key to his private rooms, along with an engraved invitation to adultery. "The occasion was a chance encounter, my lord," he said evenly. "As I do enjoy a fictional tale from time to time, I'd sent for books from London. On the afternoon they arrived, her ladyship happened by as I was perusing them."

"Just happened by, did she?" the marquis asked skeptically.

Harrison had rarely wanted to strike a man as he wanted to strike Carey in that moment. He had never been anything but unfailingly honest with the marquis. On more than one occasion, Carey had praised his frankness. "Yes. She happened by," Harrison repeated coolly.

And still Carey peered at him, as if he were looking for any sign that he was dissembling. He moved a step closer. "Tell me, Tolly—did you have the books delivered here for her?"

Of all the years he'd served this man, he'd never once, not once, done anything that wasn't entirely honorable. "Of course not," he said curtly. "They were for me, just as I said."

If Carey noted the hardness in Harrison's voice, he did not show it. In fact, his features seemed to relax. His gaze raked over Harrison once more, and then he turned away and climbed into the coach.

"Godspeed, my lord," Brock said.

The marquis did not respond. The coachman shut the door behind him, then jumped on the back runner and called out to the driver. Seething, Harrison stood with his hands clasped tightly at his back as the coach pulled away.

When the coach had disappeared from view, Harrison demanded of Brock, "Has something happened?"

"Nothing out of the ordinary of which I am aware, sir," Brock said as the coach disappeared from sight behind him. "But one cannot say what goes on behind closed doors, if you take my meaning."

Harrison's anger soared. "Is Lady Carey about?"

"I believe she was tending to her correspondence in the green sitting room."

Harrison strode to the main house ahead of Brock, his pulse racing with indignant anger. He headed for Lady Carey's sitting room and rapped insistently. "Come!" she called, and Harrison strode inside.

Lady Carey was seated at a table with a cup of tea at her elbow and a thick stack of vellum. The quill of her pen was bobbing quickly across the page. When she looked up and saw him there, her face lit with a sunny smile. He could see the sparkle in her blue eyes across the room. Her lovely face was free of the frown that often creased her brow. She was shining with happiness.

Harrison's own smile suddenly faltered.

"Good morning, Mr. Tolly!" she said brightly. "Isn't it a beautiful day? I never thought I'd be quite so happy to see the sun, but after all the rain we've had, I feel a bit like dancing. You look astonished. You mustn't fear—I promise I won't." She laughed. "Would you like some tea?"

"Madam, I . . . Are you all right?"

Her smile disappeared. "Of course!" She suddenly stood and walked to the windows, pushing back the open drapes even further. "I am determined to have a turn in the garden today and soak up the sun."

He moved toward her, but she deliberately kept her profile to him, leaning up over the deep window well and peering out. "The rain has made everything so green, has it not?"

Harrison was too intent on the mark on her face to respond.

"I should ask Brock to open the windows," she said, and turned away from him again, moving back to the desk. Her hand skimmed along the edge of it as she walked around it, keeping her head turned to one side. She glanced at him sidelong, then fidgeted nervously with her hair, gathered up in knot at her nape. "Mr. Tolly, you stare so intently that I feel a bit uneasy."

"I beg your pardon," he said instantly. "I do not mean to stare, but I was startled by—"

"A mishap," she interjected, and looked away. "It is nothing. I assure you it appears much worse than it is."

"A mishap," he repeated skeptically. His heart was racing as the truth sank in. He could not believe Carey would lift a hand to her because of a bloody *book*. "Madam . . . please look at me."

She sighed softly and reluctantly did as he asked. He could see plainly the bruise on her skin. "It is truly nothing, Mr. Tolly," she said quietly, and glanced at the footman who was standing at the door, ready to serve. "A mishap. Please believe me."

Harrison looked at the footman, too. "Richard, please leave us so that I might discuss some private matters concerning Everdon Court with her ladyship."

Richard nodded and walked out through the open doors.

When Harrison was certain he'd gone, he turned back to Lady Carey, his eyes on her mouth. His heart reacted with a little leap at the sight of it, then constricted. Lady Carey stood behind the desk with her head bowed like a chastised child. Harrison wanted to say something to comfort her, but he hardly knew what to say. "If I may be so bold—"

"How do you find Alexa today?" she asked, turning away from him again.

He swallowed down his frustration and tapped his fist against the edge of the desk. "She has calmed considerably." That wasn't precisely the truth. Over tea the previous evening, she had railed at him about the unfairness of life, and then had fallen into quiet contemplation. "However, I think she is not quite resigned to any plans regarding her future."

"Then she must be *much* improved," Lady Carey said with a wry chuckle. "My sister has never been resigned to any plans regarding her future." She folded her arms across her middle and stared up at a pastoral painting above the hearth. It was a green valley where cows grazed, and in one corner, a family with three young scampering children picnicked beneath a massive oak tree.

"In this instance, I suppose I can hardly blame her," Lady Carey continued thoughtfully. "I had my fate planned for me, and it never has resembled what I'd imagined or hoped."

Harrison knew how her future had been planned for her; he'd been part of it. "Life has a disconcerting way of behaving in precisely that way." He gazed at the happy family at their picnic and thought of the first night he'd seen Lady Carey. Harrison had been reared on the fringes of London's high society, and there was nothing he'd not seen: beautiful women, dangerous men, and the games they played with one another. But the night Olivia Hastings had come with her parents to dine at Everdon Court, he had been bowled over. To him, she was the embodiment of feminine beauty with her creamy blonde hair, a smattering of freckles across her nose, and eyes as blue as violets. She'd been a shy eighteen-year-old girl, her life spent on country estates in the protective circle of her mother and stepfather, her governess, and her tutors. Her smile was easy and warm, free of the artifice in the games of seduction played in London.

That young girl had been an innocent, laughing prettily at Lord Carey's awkward attempts to tease her. She'd sung like a bird when pressed to perform after supper, and had innocently trumped Lord Carey at whist with a happy laugh of triumph. Harrison had stood by, his gaze riveted on her, his envy of Edward Carey growing by leaps and bounds.

But when the Hastingses had said goodnight for the evening and put themselves in their ornamental coach and driven away, Lord Carey had shrugged and said, "She'll do, I suppose. As long as she can bear an heir, eh?" he'd said congenially, and had clapped Harrison on the shoulder as he'd strolled up the stairs to his rooms.

Harrison had been stunned that Carey could see the beautiful and charming Olivia Hastings and have such a very different reaction than he himself had had.

"I really should have been more resistant to all the planning for my future," Lady Carey said, her gaze still on the painting. With a wry smile, she gave Harrison a sidelong look. "Will you be surprised to know that I never questioned it? I was told from the time I was a child that I would marry a certain sort of man and live a certain sort of life, and that I would take care of Alexa, and I never questioned it."

"I think we are all told as children what we are to become."

"Were you?" she asked.

Harrison was told that doors would never open for him. That he'd be a bastard and illegitimate to society at large until the day he died. "I was told more what I could not be."

"Oh." She sounded surprised. "I think you could be anything you desired to be, Mr. Tolly. I did not have the imagination, or perhaps the freedom as a child, to imagine all the things I might be."

He found that interesting. "Do you now?"

She looked at him then. "Oh, yes," she said emphatically. "My imagination is now quite vivid."

He would have given anything to know what she imagined. The innocence was lost in her, but in its place was a worldliness he found captivating. "Perhaps then, you understood that your parents wanted what was best for you," he suggested.

She gave him a dubious look, then turned her attention to the painting again.

"My parents saw this match for what it was—an opportunity to advance their own standing as much as mine."

That was true. Harrison was well acquainted with Lord and Lady Hastings—he'd negotiated their daughter's dowry on behalf of his lordship. He'd overseen the posting of the banns and some of the more bureaucratic elements of a marquis's wedding. He'd had many occasions to meet Miss Hastings and her parents before her wedding and found her to be a delight in all things, always happy, always agreeable.

He'd found them to be opportunistic.

He looked at her now, with her head tilted back, her flaxen hair shimmering in the low light of the day, and thought of her on her wedding day. She'd looked so radiantly happy, so hopeful for the days ahead of her. And in Harrison's personal experience, he'd never seen Lady Carey do anything but work hard to please her intractable husband.

She'd entertained family and friends because Carey desired her to do so, and he criticized her choice of menu and entertainment. She made over the red salon, and he said her tastes derived from agrarian society. She tried hunting with him, and he said she sat her horse like a child.

Harrison had never heard Carey compliment his wife or say anything kind, yet he'd never seen her be anything but unflaggingly cheerful.

Until recently.

Recently, he'd noticed a hairline crack in her serene façade, and the crack seemed to spread along with the marquis's increasing fondness for drink.

Unfortunately, there was only one thing about this beautiful, agreeable young woman that could please the marquis, and that was conceiving an heir. Carey had said as much to Harrison—early in their marriage, he'd remarked that his wife had had "more than sufficient time" to find herself with child, as if it were a matter of selecting one at the local dry goods shop. As time went on and she had not conceived, the marquis complained that Lady Carey's mother surely knew she was incapable of conceiving, and had "saddled" him with a barren wife.

But after her ladyship had erroneously believed herself to be with child, something in the marquis changed. He openly insinuated that his wife was willfully not conceiving his heir.

Harrison had been exposed to all sorts of men in the course of his upbringing, but he'd never heard a man speak of his wife as disrespectfully as Lord Carey. The worst of it was that his lordship was so cunning in his criticism of her, making his remarks so matter-of-factly that a casual observer might believe that his statements about her were indeed true.

But in their six years of marriage—six years of scrutiny and belittlement—Harrison had never known Carey to hit her.

Yes, he'd tried it once. He'd been foxed out of his

mind and Harrison had stopped him. Carey had been contrite and apologetic the next day, and Harrison had believed it was a moment of madness brought about by inebriation.

"I never questioned the plans, and perhaps I should have," Lady Carey continued. "Now my sister questions the plans for her future, but unfortunately her actions have left her no options. Still . . . I have been thinking, Mr. Tolly," she said, and turned her attention to him. "I believe that while my husband is away, cooler heads might discuss what is to be done with Alexa. By that I mean your head and mine, for Alexa's thoughts are not particularly helpful." She gave him an apologetic smile.

"I understand. You mentioned a cousin in Wales—"

"No," she said, shaking her head.

No? Harrison had been nursing some very high hopes for the cousin. "I understand that his lordship did not—"

"The truth is that it has been many years since I have corresponded with her. I cannot say with any certainty that she is indeed in Wales . . . or that she has four children. That is the best of my recollection. I offered that idea with a bit of wishful thinking and a lot of panic, to be perfectly truthful."

"Ah," Harrison said. That certainly limited their options.

"I think *you* must find a situation that might be suitable," she said hopefully. "I would do it myself, if I could do so without causing talk or suspicion. I cannot bear to think what Edward might do if he thought I was cavorting about the country looking for a widow as a companion or a widower as a husband for my sister. He is one cousin removed from the king, you know."

Harrison heard the hint of sarcasm in her voice.

If only he knew of a situation for her sister, but it wasn't as if they were hanging from trees, ripe for plucking. Lady Carey was not the only one who had spoken out of hope and a bit of panic yesterday.

"We've a full fortnight before Edward returns. I thought perhaps you might . . . you might say you are traveling to the properties at Ridgeley, but use the time to make some delicate inquiries."

"I must be honest, madam. I am not very hopeful."

"Yes, but we must try, Mr. Tolly."

He shook his head. "It is a strange request to make of anyone."

"I have thought about that," she said, nodding. "I have saved all my pin money. That should help."

That was the amount Lord Carey allowed her for the things she might want. "How much?" Harrison asked.

"Seventy-two pounds."

If the situation weren't so dire, he might have laughed. "Good Lord, Lady Carey. That might keep her until the child is born—"

"I have jewels I can sell, as well," she quickly amended.

He felt an all-too-familiar twist in his gut at that. It

was precisely what his mother would have done—she sold jewels for lodging, to bribe Harrison's way into a proper boy's school. To pay for his apprenticeship. "Let me do what I can first," he said.

She smiled gratefully. "Thank you. I will do what I can, too. We'll begin today?"

Where exactly did one go to place an unwed woman carrying an unknown man's child?

"Discreetly, of course," she added.

"Of course."

"We will find something," she said, as if he were the one who needed reassurance. "It must be settled before Edward returns, as there are only two options he will entertain if I have not settled it. I can't have my sister banished from me; she is all the family I have."

"What is the other option the marquis will accept?" Harrison asked curiously, looking for any angle he might exploit.

She blinked up at him; the mark on her lip clear in the direct sunlight. "That I should find myself with child. If I could deliver him an heir, the entire kingdom would be mine for the asking." She smiled ruefully.

It moved Harrison, such bone-deep sadness glimmering in such beautiful eyes. How many times had he tossed in his bed, imagining those very eyes in some impossibly intimate circumstance? How many days had he walked about the sprawling Everdon Court, hoping for just a glimpse of them? To see the depth of her sorrow was as hopelessly frustrating as when he'd been a boy, unable to help his mother. He wanted to touch Lady Carey, to hold her and soothe her. To stroke her hair.

Lady Carey said, "I beg your pardon. I have made you uncomfortable with my woes."

"Not at all," he said, but it was true that he felt anxious, as if he had skated onto a newly frozen lake, uncertain of where the ice was thin. Yet he couldn't keep himself from skating farther and farther away from his shore. He'd held himself back for so long, had kept his true feelings so deeply buried under duty and honor. He wanted her to know happiness, to understand how a man could feel about a woman.

Harrison hardly realized what he was doing as he put his fingers under her chin, turning her face so that he could see the bruise. "The truth is, madam, that you deserve a kingdom and more," he murmured, and lightly passed his thumb over the bruise. "You do not deserve this."

Lady Carey's breath caught. Her eyes widened with surprise. But she did not move away from him. Bold desire swelled in Harrison. He gently touched the bruise again, wishing he could erase it.

Lady Carey's eyes shut. "You have always been so very kind to me, Mr. Tolly. What would I do without you?"

The words wrapped like a tendril around his heart. If only she knew, if only she understood how his heart called to her, had sought her from the moment he'd first laid eyes on her.

"I pray that neither of us must ever know the answer to that," he murmured. "We shall find a solution, madam. I give you my word."

She opened her eyes, and Harrison felt something. It was small, but fierce, like the flutter of a humming-bird's wings between them.

The sound of the door opening startled them both, and Harrison quickly dropped his hand.

"What is happening here?" Miss Hastings demanded.

CHAPTER EIGHT
꧁꧂

"A lexa, for heaven's sake," Olivia said. She was shaking. It had taken every bit of strength she had to move away from Mr. Tolly—she'd been one breath away from falling into his arms. *His arms!* What was she thinking? Was there anything that could possibly make her existence worse than it was? Was there anything more *dangerous*?

"What?" Alexa demanded.

"We are speaking of your predicament, naturally, for there is nothing quite as urgent to occupy our thoughts," Olivia said as she moved across the room.

Alexa looked curiously at her. Then at Mr. Tolly.

Olivia's heart had begun to beat the moment Mr. Tolly had touched her, and now it throbbed with a want that made her breathless. She put her hand to her chest in a futile attempt to calm it. "On my word, I do not know what I would do without Mr. Tolly's counsel." She dared not look at him, certain that her burning cheeks would give her away. Instead she continued on to the sideboard and examined the various decanters there.

She could feel Alexa's gaze on her as she picked up a crystal decanter. "Whiskey, Mr. Tolly?"

"No, thank you." His voice was as calm and confident as always.

"Whiskey?" Alexa said suspiciously. "I was not aware that you had a liking for whiskey, Livi."

"Yes, well . . . I do." Olivia poured a small amount and then drank it like water, coughing a little at the burn. Perhaps whiskey was not the best idea. "What has kept you?" she asked, and put the tot down. When she glanced up, she caught her reflection in the mirror above the sideboard. Gray shadows dusted her eyes and the bruise was dark against her skin.

"I did not feel well this morning, if you must know," Alexa said. "I am fatigued quite a lot."

"Here then, you must sit," Mr. Tolly offered, and moved a chair closer for her.

Alexa eased herself into it.

"I should like— Olivia!" Alexa said suddenly. She came out of her seat and grabbed Olivia by her arms, staring in horror at the bruise. "Dear God—what happened?"

Olivia turned her head away and moved out of Alexa's grasp. "A mishap."

"A mishap! *He* did this! I suspected him to be the sort! The man has a black heart."

"Alexa!" Olivia said, and looked at the open door. Mr. Tolly understood her and moved to close it. "Have a care what you say in this house," Olivia warned her sister. "You are speaking of my husband and, at present, your benefactor . . . and the walls have ears," she added low.

"I do not care if they do! You must leave him, Livi!" Alexa insisted. "You cannot allow such treatment!"

Sometimes it seemed as if Alexa were eight instead of eighteen. "Do you think I *allow* it?" Olivia said hotly.

"You allow it by staying here, with him," Alexa snapped. "You should leave this place."

"And exactly where do you suggest I go? To do what, pray tell?" Olivia demanded. "I cannot *leave* Edward. He is my husband and he has the legal right to do with me what he will. Even if he allowed me to leave him, where would I go? With *you*? To a convent in Ireland?"

Alexa flushed. "I only mean that you should not have to bear such treatment."

Olivia softened. "I know what you mean. But have a care, darling. And do not fret. He is not in the habit of hitting me, in spite of how it may appear." She felt the bile rise in the back of her throat with those words. Her mother had once told her that men who beat their wives were like wolves—once they'd had a taste of blood, they couldn't go back to eating rubbish. "Unfortunately, you and I are two lambs in this world, Alexa. We have no family, no money of our own, no laws to protect us. Until we can devise a better solution, we must do as he says."

"It's entirely unfair, how men may do as they please, and we must do their bidding," Alexa said bitterly. She looked distrustfully at Mr. Tolly as she resumed her seat. "Might we speak alone, Livi? I should like to speak to you in confidence."

"No," Olivia said. "We need Mr. Tolly's guidance. He is in our confidence, and we desperately need his help."

Alexa wilted in her seat. "He wouldn't let me come to you yesterday, you know. He is the steward here, and he is instructing *me*. I am the daughter of a viscount, Olivia. I should not be made to marry a steward."

Olivia gasped; one of Mr. Tolly's brows rose high. "Have you ever heard the saying that you should not bite the hand that feeds you?" he asked.

Olivia found her sister's arrogance breathtaking. "You might have thought of your requirements whilst you were in Spain."

"Lord!" Alexa said to the ceiling. "Must I constantly be reminded of it?"

"Alexa!" Olivia cried, horrified.

"Olivia, please!" Alexa complained. "Why can't we go somewhere and live? You would be happier, you know you would."

"Think of what you are saying, Alexa," Olivia said impatiently. "We have no money. How would we live?"

"I shall find an occupation," she said. "I could be a governess."

Olivia snorted at that.

"Why not? I am perfectly capable. At least I'm trying to think of a proper solution!"

"If I may?" Mr. Tolly asked calmly.

"I am not the least surprised you want to add your voice to the chorus," Alexa said dispiritedly.

"Oh dear God," Olivia groaned.

But Mr. Tolly was unruffled. He said calmly, "My mother bore a child out of wedlock—me."

Alexa gasped. Her gaze flew to Olivia, her expression full of shock.

Olivia was likewise shocked to hear him say it so plainly. "Mr. Tolly, it's not necessary—"

"I beg your pardon, Lady Carey, but if you will allow me, I think I can be of some help," he said, and clasped his hands behind his back and stared down at Alexa. "My mother was not so fortunate as to find work as a governess. She was a paramour."

Alexa gaped at him.

"She was forced to rely on her body for income. It was not her first choice, but unfortunately, her only realistic choice."

Startled by his honesty—or perhaps by the truth— Alexa suddenly stood and walked away from him.

But Mr. Tolly casually followed. "As for me," he continued, "I didn't know my father's identity until I reached my majority. I had only seen him from a distance. I can't even tell you where the name Tolly comes from. I was shunned by proper society and my playmates were the children of servants. My mother sold the jewels she received from her lovers to bribe the headmaster of a proper boy's school, who used her, took her jewelry, and still refused me. So she bargained with one of her benefactors to provide my tutoring."

"Mr. Tolly, you have said enough," Alexa said. The color had bled out of her face. Olivia wasn't certain it hadn't bled out of hers, too; her heart and imagination were racing.

"She sold her jewelry again to gain me an apprenticeship," he doggedly continued. "Had it not been for that, I shudder to guess what my occupation would be today. I had no sponsor, no protection, and now that my mother is gone, I am utterly alone in this world, for I have no legitimate relations. That is the reality of your situation, Miss Hastings. Your sister is determined that you not be forced to the same fate as my mother, and that your child not grow up in the shadows."

Olivia was stunned. She'd never heard Mr. Tolly speak of his childhood and she'd never imagined it to be so hard. He gave off no hint of it now . . . which made him seem all the more remarkable to her.

His remarks had some effect on Alexa, too. "I beg your pardon," she said dramatically. "I am sorry. I *am* sorry, Harry."

"Harry!" Olivia exclaimed.

"It's all right," Mr. Tolly said. "Alexa and I have endeavored to find some common ground."

"I do not mean to be unkind, Livi, and I do appreciate what he's just told me. But I do not wish to marry him. I've been quite honest in that."

It was the worst sort of frustration, being unable to do anything for Alexa when she needed Olivia most. Not to mention being unable to make her face the truth about her situation. She was so blessedly naïve for a woman about to be a mother! "I understand," Olivia said, trying not to sound angry. "It is not ideal for either of you. Mr. Tolly and I still hope to find an alternative."

Alexa snorted. "If there was an alternative, we would have thought of it already and taken it to your wretched husband."

Olivia could hardly dispute that.

"If only Mamma lived," Alexa added wistfully. "She'd know what to do. She always knew what to do, did she not?"

Olivia clucked her tongue. "Mamma believed the answer to all her troubles was to marry well."

At Alexa's startled look, Olivia shrugged. "When my father died, Mamma was arranging her marriage to Lord Hastings whilst in her widow's weeds. And when *your* father died, she scarcely bothered with a mourning period at all, but fled to Italy in search of a third husband and found a willing Signor Ruffalo." Her mother was not so different from Mr. Tolly's mother, Olivia realized, in that all she had to bargain with was herself, and she'd had two children who depended on her.

"But Mamma was in love with Signor Ruffalo," Alexa argued.

Olivia did not believe that for a moment. Her mother had been a true survivor. She'd maintained her position in society in the only way a widowed woman without inheritance could manage—she married well. Olivia had no idea what her mother truly felt for Signor Ruffalo, but she knew what her mother had needed. It was the same thing Mrs. Tolly had needed—security.

Olivia's mother and sister had been planning their visit to Spain when she passed away. A month before their planned departure, Olivia's mother complained to her husband of feeling fatigued and had retired early. The next morning, her maid could not rouse her; she'd died in her sleep. Just like that, Bettina Hastings Ruffalo—Olivia and Alexa's rock, their guide, their confidante—was suddenly and tragically gone from their lives.

Olivia would give anything to have her back, if only for a day.

Alexa, poor dear, had been inconsolable. She suddenly had no home. What little funds their mother had been able to leave to them were hardly sufficient to maintain Alexa. Signor Ruffalo had no desire to provide for her, and had returned to Italy shortly after the funeral.

The situation was precisely what Olivia's mother had always prepared her for—to take care of her sister. Naturally, Olivia had assured her sister she would always have a home with her . . . but privately, she was thankful she'd never had to put that to the test, given Edward's opinion of Alexa. And now Alexa's situation had forced her hand.

After their half-year of mourning was complete, Lady Tuttle, a friend of their mother, had offered to go to Spain with Alexa in her mother's stead. It seemed that Lady Tuttle had always had a desire to see the churches there. Alexa was restless and eager to go. "It is precisely the sort of diversion I need, and I daresay Mamma would have urged me to go," Alexa had reasoned with Olivia.

Olivia was relieved, as Edward had been growing increasingly impatient with her presence at Everdon Court. Moreover, Olivia had been happy for Alexa to have a suitable diversion. She'd thought Alexa too young to fret about her situation, and it was clear that there would be plenty of fretting to be done in the years to come. So she'd sent Alexa off with her blessing.

Now, back at Everdon Court, Alexa sighed. She moved absently across the room. Behind her, Olivia and Mr. Tolly exchanged a wary look. "If I *must* marry Mr. Tolly," she said, "I might be easily persuaded if he were to give me a town house in London."

Mr. Tolly chuckled.

Surprised, Alexa said, "I won't require servants. Only a cook. And a chambermaid. But no one else. I shall rear my child myself." She said it as if she were offering it as fair trade.

"Do you mean that Mr. Tolly should pay for this cook and this chambermaid and this house yet remain here at Everdon?" Olivia asked impatiently.

"Why not? Would you not prefer that arrangement, Mr. Tolly?" To Olivia, she said, "It's not as if he has any great desire to marry *me*, you know. He loves another, he told me plainly."

That news was so unexpected that Olivia was struck momentarily mute.

Mr. Tolly seemed likewise stricken.

"He does not care to speak of it, for she is a lady." Alexa toyed with the sash of the drapes. "Lady X."

"Lady X?" Olivia repeated weakly.

"He did not divulge her true identity to me, for he hardly knows me well enough to trust me with something so important. Which is precisely my point."

Olivia looked at Mr. Tolly, whose jaw was clenched. *Lady X . . .* could that be *her*? Olivia's pulse leapt so hard that her breath caught. *No, no, it's preposterous.* He was the Carey family's loyal steward, a model of decorum and decency. He would *never*—

"Miss Hastings, you have taken something I said in confidence and made much more of it than there is," Mr. Tolly said, his voice cool.

"Have I?" Alexa asked idly. "You seemed quite serious to me." She shifted her gaze to Olivia and gasped. "Oh dear, it is not *you*, Livi, if that is what you think. It is obviously Lady Martha Higginbottom."

"*What?*" Mr. Tolly said. "It is certainly not Lady Martha!"

"When I presented you with her name, you turned almost crimson!" Alexa said accusingly.

Olivia stood up, hoping that her wildly beating heart would still. Of course it was Lady Martha. She was young, unmarried, and her dowry surely suitable for a man in Mr. Tolly's position. But it was surprising. Astonishing, really. Lady Martha hardly seemed the sort of woman that would interest a man like Mr. Tolly. She was bookish and often tedious and always timid, particularly for a man as virile as he . . . But then again, what did Olivia really know of him or his affections?

"You are mistaken," Mr. Tolly said to Alexa, his voice stern.

"Well, whoever it is, you should not think to marry me if you love another," Alexa blithely continued. "You do not want him to compromise his true happiness, do you, Livi?"

"Of course not!" Olivia snapped. "But your carelessness has left us with very few alternatives. Now we must all redouble our efforts to find a suitable arrangement for you."

"What do you mean, a suitable arrangement?" Alexa asked suspiciously.

"Such as a widow in need of a companion?" Olivia said. She could hardly think of anything else at the moment—she could not get Mr. Tolly and his Lady X off her mind.

"A *widow*?" Alexa repeated disbelievingly. "Am I to sit about doing needlework and filling snuffboxes?"

"I should think that infinitely more enticing than a convent. Perhaps you are not aware that convents are cold, and the sisters pride themselves on austerity. There are no gowns, there is no society. There is work and devotion, nothing more. Or perhaps you prefer the life of the paramour after what Mr. Tolly has shared? Merciful heaven, have you heard anything we've said, Alexa? You have brought us an insurmountable problem, and expect everyone around you to solve it, yet you refuse to be pleased with any option, and you refuse to see the reality of your situation. There are no easy answers to this dilemma, and I have yet to hear you offer any sort of help at all! Don't you see what great sacrifice Mr. Tolly has made in offering to help you? Can't you be at least a *bit* grateful?"

The blood drained from Alexa's face. "It is not my wish—"

"Yes, you have made it crystal clear that it is not your wish. Do you think it is Mr. Tolly's wish? Or *mine*? Have you not considered that perhaps Mr. Tolly made the offer because he knows that the alternative for you was so much *worse*?"

Alexa pressed her lips together. "I beg your pardon. Of course I know what you mean, but please understand that this has all been quite difficult for me. And

I do not want to impose on Mr. Tolly, as he has professed his esteem for Lady X, and he's also inherited, and I do not wish to be a burden."

Inherited! What did that mean? Olivia's head was beginning to ache.

"Good God, Alexa, that is not your affair!" Mr. Tolly said.

Olivia was suddenly exhausted. "Please go, Alexa. Go and lie down or something," she said, waving her hand to the door.

Alexa blinked at her. "But I—"

"No. I cannot bear to hear any more from you today. You have imposed on our relationship and Mr. Tolly's generosity without a thought and have shown yourself to be utterly selfish."

Alexa gasped. Tears filled her eyes. "Livi, how could you?" she asked weakly, but Olivia waved her hand at the door again. She could not tolerate her impossible, imprudent sister another moment.

With a wide-eyed look of hurt, Alexa left without another word.

Olivia didn't move. She couldn't breathe. She couldn't bring herself to look at Mr. Tolly. But when she did at last, his gaze was intent on her.

"You didn't have to tell us about your . . . mother," she said uneasily.

He smiled at her discomfort. "I have nothing to hide, madam. And I think she needed to hear it. She will eventually accept the truth. At present, I suspect she is full of fear and uncertainty about the rest of her life."

He was right. "Thank you," Olivia said gratefully. "I know that must have been difficult."

He shrugged.

She swallowed and looked at her hand. "You have inherited. I was not aware." She glanced up.

He hesitated, then said, "I think the circumstances are questionable. And it has no bearing on this."

"It has every bearing on this." Her heart felt as if it were shrinking. "Will you be leaving us?" *Please say no, say no . . .*

"No," he said quickly. But then he looked down and amended, "That is to say, I don't know." He suddenly turned about. "There are many uncertainties, madam, but I think the most pressing issue is the problem of your sister. I shall go straightaway and make some inquiries, if I have your leave?"

Olivia could not think. It felt as if the earth were cracking beneath this house, preparing to swallow them up.

"Madam?"

"Yes," she said, and glanced to the window. Air. She needed air. "Thank you, Mr. Tolly. As always, thank you."

She heard him go out of the room, and she remained standing, her body stiff, her breath shallow.

What would she do without him? How would she bear it?

CHAPTER NINE

Alexa Hastings was a petulant, inconsiderate, disagreeable child. Harrison had alternated between wanting to shake some sense into her and sending her off to nap. How in heaven would he ever help the chit find a proper situation? And what exactly *was* a proper situation? Marriage? He prayed that acquaintances of the Carey family kindly forgot their arithmetic when the child was born, but he had no hope of that. It amazed him how dangerously inept some members of the Quality could be when balancing their own books, but how accurate they were in calculating the point of conception.

A governess? He snorted. Even she should have known that was impossible with a growing belly. No parent would care to explain to their children why their governess's belly grew without a husband about.

Companion? That was perhaps his only hope—to foist her on some lace-capped doddering old widow in need of someone to keep her company while she warmed her feet at the hearth. Harrison wracked his brain. He had to think of at least one widow because he could *not* marry Alexa Hastings.

But he knew he would, if no other solution could be found. He would because he had to protect that unborn child from the life that he had experienced.

As Harrison rode into Everdon, he methodically examined every conceivable angle, dismissing them all as either too public or too cruel. He couldn't bear to see Lady Carey distraught. But he couldn't bear to think of her with another bruise, and like her, he feared that if the situation with her sister was not quickly resolved, Lord Carey's ire would grow. Harrison no longer knew what the man was capable of doing. The drink seemed to have washed away his senses.

He arrived at the Cock and Sparrow to seek the counsel of Robert Broadbent, his closest friend. Robert was a blond-haired, brown-eyed bachelor squire who had a reputation for seducing widows and young ladies alike. He was the master of a small estate, an excellent hunter and gambler, full of personal ambition and a zest for living. Harrison had been hunting woods and public houses around Everdon Court with Robert for more than ten years.

The proprietor of the public house greeted Harrison when he strolled inside. Benny was as thin as a weed, and his wife was built like a barrel. "Mr. Tolly!" Sue said as she wiped up some spilled ale from a table. "We'd wondered where you'd gotten off to."

"Did you miss me, then?" he asked, and grabbed her chapped hand to kiss her knuckles.

"You know I did. I always miss you when you don't come round, love." Sue smiled coyly.

Harrison laughed and winked. He turned around and came face-to-face with Fran, a serving girl. "Did you miss me?" she asked as her gaze wandered the length of him.

"My days were incomplete without you," Harrison said, and stepped around her.

"Perhaps you missed me enough to pay a call, then, eh, Mr. Tolly?"

"Never." This from Robert. He was seated at his usual table in the common room, from where he held court most days for an hour or two, receiving his friends and dining on watery stew. "If Mr. Tolly pays a call to any woman, it is to Lady X," he said, grinning.

"Lady *X*," Fran said, looking half intrigued and half jealous.

Harrison laughed. "Do not give up hope, Franny. There is no Lady X."

"The hell there isn't." Robert held up two fingers to Fran. "A pair of ales, lass, and be quick."

"I've got them just here," Benny said, appearing at Robert's side. He placed two tankards of warm ale before Harrison, who slid one across to Robert.

"Where've you been, then?" Robert asked, and drank from the tankard. "What madness has the marquis frothing at the mouth this week?"

"He does not froth," Harrison said easily. "He's to London for a fortnight."

"A full fortnight? Without you?" Robert said, waggling his brows. "Your Lady X must be all atwitter. How long's it been since you've had time to steal away to the lady's boudoir?"

Robert would be shocked if he knew how long it had been since Harrison had been inside a boudoir. "A while," he said with a sigh. On occasion, when he was in London, Harrison called upon a house tucked away near Regent Street to relieve his lust. But he'd found it impossible to forge any romantic attachment with any woman, given his feelings for Lady Carey. He could think of no one else.

Robert grinned at him. "A while, is it? And here you sit with a pint. You're mad, lad. Go on with you then, go and see your ladylove. Tell me where she is and I'll see you there."

Harrison chuckled and drank his alc.

"Bloody tight-lipped rooster you are," Robert said, eyeing him shrewdly. "I'll discover her identity, you know," he said, and tapped his pint against Harrison's. "Why are you here when you've got a bit of freedom?"

"Because I've a bit of a problem for which I need your help."

"Me?" Robert asked. "The advice usually flows the other way between us, aye? What help?"

Harrison pushed aside his pint. He'd shared very

few things about his work with Robert through the years, as his discretion was one of the most important aspects of his occupation. This problem was doubly painful, as it was embarrassing for the Careys and brought to mind the difficulties Harrison had experienced in his own life. Difficulties he had managed to put behind him. But now, he recalled the first time he'd realized what it meant to be fatherless in this world, when three older boys had fallen on him as he returned from market, beating him as they labeled him a dirty bastard. Or when his mother's lover had given Harrison a tutor, but had told his mother in front of Harrison that he would not put him in school for fear of being associated with the by-blow.

Harrison swallowed down those old hurts and said, "May I speak openly?"

"Aye, you know that you can, Harry."

He glanced around to assure himself that no one was listening in. "It has to do with her ladyship's younger sister, Miss Hastings. You've met her, have you not?"

Robert nodded. "Wee thing, with hair the color of honey."

Harrison relayed to Robert what had happened, including today's debate. He trusted Robert, and told him everything . . . except that he'd so rashly stepped in and offered to marry the impudent girl. That omission was a matter of pride—he did not want Robert to know just how foolish he was.

When he'd finished, Robert drained his pint and put it aside. "This is a sad but common tale, lad. I suspect a convent in Ireland is no worse than what the lass might experience in society, given the marquis's determination to banish her."

"She deserves better than that," Harrison said curtly. "Give me a solution, Robert. Tell me what might save this bloody little fool and keep her close to her sister."

"Harry, lad," Robert said sympathetically as he leaned back in his chair and propped his boot against the wall. "You do not need me to tell you there is no better option for her, unless you magically produce someone who will marry her. Even then, I suspect Carey would disown her outright and save himself a deepening scandal. If she were to marry very quickly, she might spare them a bit of scandal, yet still . . ." He shook his head. "What gentleman would give his name to a bastard child? Not I."

Harrison knew better than anyone that gentlemen did not freely give their names to bastard children. "I had hoped you might know of a situation where we could at least send her for the term of her confinement."

Robert snorted. "You know very well that I do not, on principle, acquaint myself with the sort of decent folks who would take a lass in."

"Aye, but you do acquaint yourself with widows," Harrison pressed. "Perhaps you know of one in need of a companion?"

"I only keep company with young, comely widows, and not one of them would entertain it. Come to think of it, I haven't been with a young widow in an age. Bess Walls was the last I—"

"Old widows, then," Harrison said impatiently, before Robert began enumerating his conquests.

"No," Robert said.

It was as Harrison had guessed—there was nothing to be done for Miss Hastings. Or for himself, for that matter. He'd been confident that he'd find a solution when he'd intervened yesterday and had offered to marry Alexa; finding solutions to seemingly insurmountable problems was his gift. But his bag of tricks now felt woefully light. He had succumbed to the look of terror on Lady Carey's face that afternoon in the marquis's study and had opened his foolish mouth, and now he would have to live up to his word.

"For you, Harry, I shall do my best to uncover someone that will assist." He smiled. "Cheer up, lad."

"Thank you Robert," Harrison said. "Any help you might offer is greatly appreciated. And I needn't tell you that time is of the essence."

Harrison finished his pint and talked about other things before riding dejectedly back to Everdon Court and the dowager house. He wasn't giving up, not yet. He decided he should have a talk with Miss Hastings out of Lady Carey's earshot. A talk in which he would lay down the rules of their association and impress on her that he would not tolerate her bad behavior.

Rue was inside the small foyer, polishing a brass planter, when Harrison walked in. "Good afternoon, Mr. Tolly!" She continued to rub the planter.

"Good afternoon, Rue," he said, and discarded his gloves. "Where might I find Miss Hastings?" he asked as he unfastened his cloak.

Rue stopped rubbing. She squared her shoulders. "Miss Hastings has retired. She was in need of rest after all the chatter." She spoke as if reciting her letters.

Harrison tossed aside his cloak. "What chatter would that be?"

Rue blinked. She cast her gaze thoughtfully at the fresco on the ceiling for a moment as if trying to recall it. "Why, mine, I suppose," she said, as if she'd just arrived at the truth. She shrugged and went back to her polishing. "Aye, she went up to rest, and then Lady Carey said I was not to disturb her if she was resting—"

Harrison turned. "Did Lady Carey come to the dowager house?"

"Aye." Rue smiled proudly, as if she'd arranged it herself.

Lady Carey never came to the dowager house.

"Lady Carey was here . . . in search of her sister?" he suggested to Rue, hoping to speed her recollection along.

Rue nodded. "But Miss Hastings had gone up to rest, and her ladyship said I should not disturb her, and she said that she might have a word with you when you'd returned from your pint—"

"My *pint*?" Harrison said sharply. "For God's sake, Rue, what did you say to her that would cause her to believe I was off having a pint?"

Rue's fat bottom lip began to tremble and tears welled in her eyes.

It took a supreme act of self control for Harrison to remain calm. "Why in heaven would you tell Lady Carey such a thing? I didn't tell you where I was going. For all you know, I was on my knees in church praying for everyone here."

Rue gasped; her little eyes widened and looked like a pair of pennies. "Thank you, milord! I ain't never had no one to pray over me!"

Harrison sighed. "Rue—"

"I didn't know where you'd gone! And Mrs. Lampley said if you wasn't here, and you wasn't with her ladyship, then perhaps you'd gone to the village for a pint, for sometimes you are wanting a pint of ale!"

"For goodness sake, Rue," he said. "Hear me now— in the future, you are not to guess where I have gone. Say I am not within, and leave it at that. Do you understand?"

"Aye, my lord," she said timidly.

"*Sir*," he said, and strode to the door, catching up his cloak on the way.

"Thank you kindly for your prayers, Mr. Tolly!" Rue called after him.

"God in heaven," Harrison muttered as he went out.

CHAPTER TEN

At the main house Brock directed Harrison to the gardens and he spotted Lady Carey by the hedges. She wore a wide straw hat that had slipped off her head and hung down her back. Sunshine glinted in her hair. She was dressed in a white dotted swiss gown with pink and green ribbons, and a green spencer coat. She looked like spring.

She carried a basket of clippings on her arm. A ribbon had been threaded around the handle but had come undone and trailed behind her.

She was studying some newly planted rose bushes, and he admired the elegant curve of her chin and her long slender neck as he approached. For some reason, her profile reminded him of her wedding day. He'd never forget how she looked standing next to the marquis, dressed in a silk the color of morning clouds. A shy smile of pleasure had graced her lips, and she'd peeked up at the marquis, her eyes shining, her expression full of radiant happiness and hope.

Harrison had thought her the most beautiful of brides, and even then, he'd felt a small ache in his heart that he could not have her as his, that she was sealing her fate to Carey's forevermore.

Lady Carey heard his footfall on the gravel; she suddenly turned her head and her face lit as she spotted him striding down the garden path. "Mr. Tolly!" she said, as if he'd been gone a month instead of hours. "You've returned rather quickly from your pint, haven't you?" Her smile was impish.

He would not disappoint her—he was entirely abashed. "I beg your pardon, madam, but my maid was guessing at my whereabouts."

Lady Carey laughed, and the sound of it, so light and airy, startled him. It seemed out of place among the events of the last few days, and as he rarely heard her laugh, it rattled old memories in him—of those days and weeks after she was first married, when her laughter had filled the long corridors of Everdon Court.

"I hope you at least finished the pint before you hurried back to your post. Honestly, I will be disappointed if you do not tell me you've drunk an entire barrel of ale after the interview with my sister." She grinned at him.

Harrison smiled. That heartwarming grin was a welcome change after the unpleasantness with Alexa in the study. "Every last drop," he said. The sun glinted off the braid that hung below her hat. He imagined unbraiding that length of hair, of feeling the silken strands brush against his skin. He wondered how the marquis could look at this woman every day, at her crystalline blue eyes, at her plump ruby lips and feathery brows, and not fall to his knees in gratitude that she was his.

"I hope you will forgive Alexa, Mr. Tolly. She is not usually so . . ."

Arrogant? Thoughtless?

"Childish," she said, with a sheepish wince.

Childish. A good word for Miss Alexa Hastings.

"The poor thing is truly at sixes and sevens, for I've never known her to be so obstinate."

Harrison was not reassured.

She clearly saw that he was not. She sighed as she turned to a leggy rose to trim it. "I should not have come to the dowager house without first sending a messenger," she added. "Your girl was a bit unsettled by it, I think."

"My girl is perpetually unsettled," Harrison dryly assured her. "And you, madam, are most welcome at the dowager house at any time of your choosing."

"Thank you," she said with a pert little smile. "I promise I shall not make a habit of it."

Disappointing, but expected.

"I had come to see after Alexa and have a stern word with her, but she was resting." Lady Carey paused and absently brushed a small leaf from her sleeve. She sighed again and lifted her gaze to Harrison. "Will you walk with me, Mr. Tolly? It is such a glorious early spring day, and in spite of our troubles, I cannot help but rejoice in it after such a long and miserable winter."

"I'd be delighted," he said. "May I carry your basket?"

"Thank you," she said, and he reached for it, his fingers brushing hers as he took the basket from her.

They strolled through the garden, Lady Carey pointing out some of Mr. Gortman's new additions. They came to an old wooden gate that separated the manicured gardens from the park. Lady Carey unlatched the gate, stepped onto the bottom rung, and swung out with the gate before hopping down again.

Harrison's heart smiled at her playfulness.

"Shall I tell you a secret, Mr. Tolly?" she asked, using her hand to shade her eyes as she looked up at him. "I came to speak to you."

"Pardon?"

"Today, at the dowager house. I told Brock I'd gone for a walk and then I walked up the servant's path to the dowager house to speak to you."

Harrison was imprudently pleased by that admission. "Did you?"

"I did. I know I keep saying it, but you are so very good to us, sir. I am forever in your debt."

He couldn't help a slight smile. He was not the least bit good—he coveted another man's wife. That was the stuff of reprobates, of adulterers. "Surely you did not come to tell me that. And by the bye, I am not good. It is my du—"

"No," she said, throwing up a hand. "I implore you, do not say it. Do not dare tell me duty compels you to kindness." She smiled. "I know better than most that duty will only compel one so far."

He did not want to think about the meaning behind that statement.

Lady Carey cocked a brow. "Am I wrong? Does your kindness not stem from something else entirely?"

Harrison's heart lurched a little, and he felt the flush of warmth at his nape. He fully expected her to say out loud for God and all of England to hear that she knew he loved her, had loved her, had coveted her for more than six agonizing years. "I am afraid I do not understand your meaning."

"It is quite obvious," she said sympathetically. "Perhaps you are not aware that while others may not see your true nature, I know that you are tenderhearted and cannot bear to see suffering in anyone. There is no one who would have taken little Rue in, but you did. You would give up your own happy future to keep someone from suffering."

Harrison's gaze fell to the bruise on her lip. He was not tenderhearted; he was bloody besotted. He looked at her waiting for him to speak, to confirm that he was tenderhearted.

I love you. It was what he wanted to say, it was the pressure he could feel in his chest. He loved her so much that he wouldn't have known how to say it even if he'd had the courage. It seemed there ought to be words to describe such a feeling as his, and yet he could think of only three simple words. *I love you.*

When he did not say anything, Lady Carey bit her lip and looked away. "Oh dear," she said. "Mr. Gortman ought to come and tidy up a bit. Edward will be displeased to see so many leaves about."

"I will tell Mr. Gortman," Harrison said, relieved for the diversion.

They walked on, Lady Carey's fingers trailing along the hedges again, and Harrison feeling that old desperation to touch her. They came upon a maze, and strolled inside to the middle. "Will you sit with me a moment?" she asked.

Sit. Yes. Harrison needed a moment to collect himself and reinforce the wall he'd built up in bits and pieces around his heart.

They sat together on a bench that faced an elaborate fountain built around three horses rearing up on hind legs, their forelegs entwined in some strange horse dance. Below the horses, a flock of birds bathed in the shallow pool.

Lady Carey settled onto the bench, her graceful hands in her lap, revealing the tiny white scar across the back of her knuckle that he'd noticed countless times before. She looked skyward. "I adore the spring, with its promise of new beginnings. What is your favorite season, Mr. Tolly?"

His favorite season, of all things. "Spring," he said instantly. "I like new beginnings as well." He wished for a new beginning to this day. He wished for a new beginning to his life seven years ago, one that might have involved her. He even allowed himself a moment of imagining his arm around her now, her head on his shoulder, perhaps even a child or two trying to catch the birds bathing in the fountain.

Lady Carey began to fidget absently with the end of her braid. "I am being callous, I know. I am speaking of new beginnings when my sister faces an uncertain one and you have offered to sacrifice your future for her."

Harrison's happy little fantasy vaporized.

"You must be allowed to pursue your own path to happiness, Mr. Tolly, no matter what else. I am quite determined on that. And I am equally determined to find a solution for Alexa's predicament. I hope you will help me, as I have thought on it until I can think no more."

"As have I," he admitted. He wanted to reassure her somehow, but he could not.

"We have very few options, don't we?" she asked.

Harrison had always found her to appreciate a straightforward approach, and decided he had to be frank now. "Very few. I cannot think of anyone close by who might take her in during her confinement. But I could go to London and perhaps find something there."

"Heavens, no," Lady Carey said. "If my husband were to discover you there, I cannot imagine his ire.

And I think there is no one in London who may be trusted with such a delicate secret."

"Nor do I, in truth."

"I know it all seems impossible. But my mother once told me that we Hastings had a way of landing on our feet. She likened us to cats." Lady Carey smiled suddenly. "When I was a girl, she would use coal to draw a kitten's nose and whiskers on my face." She laughed at the memory. "She always cautioned us to never forget that we Hastings girls are lucky, and will always find another chance. Some may believe our luck has run out since her passing, but I am optimistic." She smiled hopefully.

"I am fully prepared to do as I said I would," Harrison said.

"Oh, Mr. Tolly!" she said impatiently. "I think you have missed my meaning completely! You are too accustomed to solving all our problems. Do you recall the supper Edward hosted in honor of Captain Granville's return from the war?"

"Of course."

Her smile widened; her eyes sparkled. "Do you recall the seating?"

Harrison smiled, too. "How could I possibly forget it?" Seating thirty-six illustrious guests was daunting for the most seasoned of social secretaries. Unfortunately, neither he nor Lady Carey was very well versed in that sort of thing. "We spent two days in the formal dining room rearranging name cards."

Lady Carey laughed with delight. "We moved Lord Rothbone a dozen times if we moved him once! We could not determine who would pay the price of sitting next to him."

"'I've a liking for haddock,'" Harrison said, mimicking the portly old Lord Rothbone, "'but not in sauce. Haddock in sauce reminds one of gristle in bile.'"

"'My husband does not care for *gristle*,'" Lady Carey said, mimicking the high-pitched voice of Lady Rothbone.

Harrison chuckled. "'Have you venison, then? I should like a bit of venison. But not overcooked. Overcooked venison brings to mind a crofter's shoe. Have you ever seen a crofter's shoe? Quite a lot of muck and mire, as it were.'"

Lady Carey laughed roundly, pressing her palms against her belly as if to contain the laughter. "I think Lord Braxton has never forgiven us for putting Rothbone with him."

"I can scarcely blame him," Harrison said. "I could not bring myself to look the poor gentleman in the eye after that supper."

She smiled fondly at him, then put her hand on his. The touch jolted Harrison; his hand fisted beneath hers. "I could not have done it without you, Mr. Tolly. I was lost when I came to Everdon Court, as green as summer grass and timid as a mouse. If you had not been here to lead me, I would have faltered badly."

He remembered the young and inexperienced marchioness, wanting badly to do it all just so. "You give me too much credit, madam. You've always known what to do. I have not led you; I merely assisted you."

"You are far too modest." She removed her hand from his. "When my mother died, it was you who helped me make the arrangements."

"That is the nature of my work for this family."

"Perhaps. But like now, you went beyond your duties. I sat in your office sobbing like a child, and you sat beside me, your linen handkerchief at the ready."

He had wanted nothing more than to wrap his arms around her that day and hold her in that moment of heart-wrenching grief. But he'd had to make do by clutching his handkerchief.

"And what of the blue silk you brought from London? I had only heard of it from my friend Bernie, and you bravely ventured onto Bond Street in my stead and found one to match the description. You had a square of it tucked away in your pocket, as if you feared someone might see you with it. Yet you cannot imagine how thrilled I was with the square. I sent for the silk straightaway, and now it is my favorite evening gown, and all because you were kind enough to seek it out and bring it to me."

Harrison was beginning to feel exposed. She'd worn that blue silk to attend a soiree at the Earl of Elmont's. That evening, he could scarcely look at her in the silk without feeling the blood rush in his veins, pooling in his groin, making him uncomfortably hard as he watched her leave on the arm of the bored marquis. He recalled how she'd cast a smile at him over her shoulder, and had fluttered her fingers at her gown as if to ask him if he approved. Oh yes, he'd approved.

"Madam, you give me far too much credit."

"I do not. I depend on you more than anyone." She smiled so fondly that he could once again feel the blood begin to rush in his veins. "Truthfully, this is another time I want so desperately to depend on you, Mr. Tolly. But unfortunately, your help is not to be borne. Not this time. I expressly refuse to allow you to marry Alexa."

Harrison arched a brow in surprise, and she lifted her chin as if she expected an argument. "Will you not?" he asked gently. "For if there is no relative that Miss Hastings may go to, no widow, no Good Samaritan to take her in, then for her sake, and for *your* sake, and particularly for the sake of that unborn child, she must marry and marry quickly."

"Yes, yes, I agree. But not to *you,* Mr. Tolly."

"I shall try not to take offense," he said easily. "Have you someone else in mind?"

"Not yet. But I have my jewels with which to barter, and I shall think of someone desperate for them. I am not completely without connections."

She was naïve. Harrison shifted a little closer. "Madam, forgive me, but I think you do not understand." He leaned in, speaking softly. "Any man you may consider for your sister likely would not accept her child. And even if you found a man who was kind enough to see his way to it, he would not accept the child as his own. As much as it pains me to do so, I must say this out loud: Alexa is ruined. Without some agreement, without some promise of continued enrichment—which I can advise you in confidence that his lordship will *not* provide—there is no one who will touch her."

Lady Carey suddenly turned about on the bench and faced him fully, her expression earnest. "How can you *bear* it?"

"Pardon?"

"I must know, Mr. Tolly. How can you offer yourself when your affections lie with another? When you have *inherited*! Do you not deserve to take your inheritance and make your own happy ending with your Lady X?"

Hearing her say those words startled him. "Lady Carey—"

She leaned in, her gaze locked on his. "Have you not witnessed enough unhappiness here to warn you against an arranged marriage? Do you wish such turmoil and despair for yourself?"

Her admission unnerved him; a nauseating mix of fury and sorrow filled his gut.

"This situation you would put yourself in is insupportable. You are a fine man, and you deserve a wife you esteem and children and the happiness that most people only aspire to. What you propose is madness! Do you fear my husband? Do you fear what he will do to you or to Alexa? Is that why you would turn your back on your Lady X, the woman you esteem above all others—"

"I cannot have her." He said it more sharply than he intended, but he had to stop her before she enumerated the many, many things he would never know with her. His fingers curled into a fist against his knee. "It is as simple as that."

She cocked her head to one side, seeming confused. "Why ever not?"

Did she truly not see why not? Did she not see how he looked at her now? Harrison swallowed and pushed down the urge to touch her, to say words that he could never say to her. "I think it is impossible that you can understand it so I beg of you to not even try."

But Lady Carey was undaunted. She touched his fist. "I think perhaps you are the one misjudging the situation, Mr. Tolly. Are you *certain* you cannot have her?"

"Entirely," he said firmly, and shifted just enough to move his hand from beneath her fingers.

Lady Carey drew a breath. "I beg your pardon. It is not my place to interfere, or to offer advice . . . yet I cannot help but tell you that I am certain Lady Martha would be quite *pleased*. And if she is not, I would be happy to intervene."

It took Harrison a moment to understand what she thought, and the realization shot him to his feet. "Lady Martha!" he exclaimed. "Good God, madam, please extend me the courtesy of assuming that I would be attracted to someone of greater . . ."—he could not think of the word that described the simpering, dull, Lady Martha—"*vigor* than Lady Martha! I have no regard for the woman!"

She reared back, her eyes widening with surprise. "But if not Lady Martha, then who?"

Harrison faced her, his hands on his hips, and stared down at her.

Something seemed to register in Lady Carey. Her lashes fluttered with a thoughtful frown, and her gaze dropped to her lap. "My goodness . . . does she . . . does Lady X know of your regard?"

"Apparently not," he said dryly.

Lady Carey bit her lower lip. "But if she knew, she might . . ."

"She might what?" he asked impatiently. "Leave her husband and live in reduced circumstances with her reputation destroyed? No, madam. To confess my affection and esteem to Lady X is to compromise her completely, and I would never dishonor her."

Lady Carey looked up then, her eyes full of under-standing.

And sadness.

Harrison regretted saying anything at all. He should have allowed her to continue believing his affection lay with Lady Martha—

Lady Carey stood, and surprisingly, she touched his cheek. Harrison was so flustered by that single, soft touch that he was rendered speechless.

"Poor man," she murmured. "I understand better than you know."

Harrison was suddenly tumbling off a precipice. He'd balanced on that rim for all these years, standing practically on the tips of his toes, never falling into the abyss, but standing close enough that he could smell the roses that scented her hair, feel the softness of her touch. And now he was falling, falling so hard and fast that he couldn't even say what happened next. He only knew that his arms were suddenly around her, and that his mouth was on hers, on lips that were as soft and succulent as he knew they would be, yet searing him like a hot coal.

He cupped her face, tasting her as he had longed to do all these years, his tongue against the seam of her lips, and then plunging inside her mouth, swirling about her tongue as he fell, tumbled, and disappeared into the desire he'd kept bottled inside him.

Lady Carey kissed him back, tumbling right along with him, her body rising up to his, pressed against his. She gripped him as if she feared she would fall, wrapping her arm around his neck when he encircled her waist with his arm to hold her there, to keep the feel of her shapely form against him as long as he could. His erection strained against his trousers, demanding he fulfill his body's need to be physically sated. Somewhere in the depths of his conscience, he was acutely aware of the danger in kissing her, but in that moment he didn't give a damn.

His hands roamed, sliding over the curve of her hip, up to her rib cage and to her breast, filling his hand. Only then did Lady Carey make a sound of alarm in his mouth. Only then did she recoil, jerking back and away from him.

"Oh my God," she said hoarsely, and pressed her palms to her cheeks. "What have I done?"

The look in her eyes was of sheer panic. "Breathe," he said to her.

"That should never have happened," she said frantically. "What if someone had seen us? It was a mistake, a dreadful mistake!"

"Please do not panic—"

"It is too late for that!" she said sharply, and grabbed up her basket. She moved to pass him, to flee, but Harrison caught her arm.

"Madam."

She looked up at him, and Harrison saw unbridled desire mixed with fear in her eyes. "Let go of me," she said, and yanked her arm free.

She rushed up the path, the basket's ribbon dragging behind her. What he had seen in her eyes was the worst sort of yearning. He knew, because it ran deep in his veins, cutting deep crevasses into him.

When she'd disappeared around the corner, Harrison groaned and ran both hands over his head.

"*Goddammit.*"

CHAPTER ELEVEN

In the dowager house salon, a glum Alexa examined the pianoforte. She thought it out of tune, but her skill was only passable, so she wasn't entirely certain.

Alexa's mother had possessed a pianoforte that she had claimed had come all the way from the Palace of Versailles. Alexa didn't know how her mother could have possibly acquired such a thing, but it was made of the finest wood and the keys were polished ivory. She felt confident that Mr. Tolly's pianoforte had *not* come from Versailles. She rather doubted it had come as far as even York.

She sighed heavily and played a few notes.

Carlos undoubtedly had a fine pianoforte. His family was wealthy. Not that she'd ever inquired, but it was apparent. Carlos Alfonso de la Fuente lived in a castle overlooking Madrid.

Alexa had met him quite by accident. Lady Tuttle had taken ill one day, fainting dead away as she and

Alexa had toured the gardens of the Plaza de Oriente. Carlos had come to the rescue out of thin air, speaking flawless English with a lovely accent, and had directed his servants to see Lady Tuttle to the hotel where she and Alexa were staying. When he understood they had no doctor, Carlos had sent his personal physician to see after Lady Tuttle. When the physician had declared Lady Tuttle must convalesce before resuming her travels, Carlos had offered a cottage that belonged to his family for Alexa and Lady Tuttle's use.

And so had begun their torrid affair. He was tall and darkly handsome, with dancing brown eyes and a smile as sparkling as the Mediterranean Sea. He called every day to see after Lady Tuttle's welfare, and within the week, he was escorting Alexa out into the streets of Madrid to show her about.

Alexa had never intended for anything to happen between them. Admittedly, she was taken by his physical beauty. And she'd been so grateful for his help and held in thrall by his buoyant company. But she was not prepared for how quickly she'd fallen in love with him! Her eyes teared just thinking about it. God help her, she had loved him.

He was charming and sophisticated. He'd taught her Spanish history and the Spanish language. He'd wanted to know everything about her, and he'd looked at her in a way that had made Alexa's heart pound and her palms dampen.

One month turned to two, and two to three. Carlos grew bolder, teasing her with kisses and playful touches. And Alexa grew softer, welcoming each touch, smiling with pleasure when he kissed her. Then had come the day of rain, when it was too awful to go out but too tedious to remain within the two-room cottage Alexa shared with Lady Tuttle.

Carlos had come, and while Lady Tuttle slept in one room, Carlos led Alexa to a place she'd never before been—into a man's arms, and his body into hers. It was physically magical, and emotionally enthralling. Alexa had felt as if she was his, and that he belonged to her. She'd never felt anything so deeply in her life.

Alexa continued to have intimate relations with him, assuming that they would marry. It wasn't entirely her imagination; Carlos had said things such as, "One day, we will be like that old couple," and point to an elderly couple strolling together. Or, "Our children will be fearless."

Alexa had believed it with all her heart.

He spoke eloquently of his life and his work. He described where he and his family lived in an ancient fortress in the hills, which they had turned into a home. While Lady Tuttle snored down the hall, Alexa would lie in the bed with him, imagining his family. She imagined a raucous gathering of siblings, some married with children, others not. She imagined their family meals, and she imagined, heaven help her, she imagined sitting among them, one of the family.

"I want to meet them," she'd said one day.

"*Si*, of course. When the time is right, *mi amor*," he would say, and Alexa trusted him.

Lady Tuttle began to mend. She wanted to go home to England, to be near her son, and Alexa began to think about how she would tell the old woman she didn't intend to return to England. She'd even penned a letter to Olivia with the news that she would remain in Spain with Carlos.

But she never sent that letter.

One day, Carlos did not come. Nor did he come the next day. By the end of that week, Lady Tuttle was determined to carry on with their tour, and Alexa was frantic—she knew by then that she was carrying his child.

She played another few notes on the pianoforte in the dowager house, then settled in with both hands to play a song she remembered from her childhood as her mind wandered through her memories of Madrid.

At first she'd been angry with herself for not knowing more about where Carlos lived. She'd wondered if he'd intentionally kept her in the dark, for she had only a few vague descriptions of where the house was. So it was astounding that she was able to discover where Carlos lived. It had taken a bit of ingenuity to find her way there—a discreet question to the florist who delivered his flowers to her, a smattering of Spanish words to help wend her way through Madrid's crowded and confusing streets. But Alexa had done it—she'd found him.

She could recall standing at the bottom of the hill and admiring the old castle. It looked just as Carlos had described it, with wisteria climbing the walls and a fountain at the bottom of the drive. Alexa had walked up the hill to the gate. She'd intended to send a note in to him, and she'd never imagined she would see him standing on the drive, almost as if he was waiting for her.

But he was not waiting for her.

It was interesting, Alexa thought numbly, the things she remembered about that sun-filled morning. Such as his horse, and the saddle with the tassels and a red scroll embroidered on the seat. That the bougainvillea along the stone wall at his back needed trimming.

Alexa remembered with painful, searing clarity, that as she lifted her hand to call to him, a woman came bounding onto the drive. That was when she noticed the other horse, and that the woman was dressed for riding, as was he. And she was beautiful, with inky black hair and dark red lips. The two of them had been laughing and speaking in their native tongue at a pace Alexa hadn't been able to understand.

She'd stood outside the gates, unnoticed, watching with a nauseating swell as Carlos had taken the woman's elbow and leaned in to kiss her cheek. The woman had pressed her hand on his back and rested her cheek against his shoulder, and Carlos put his arm around her shoulders and hugged her close.

A light of understanding had shone in Alexa's head at that moment. Without a word, without a whimper, she had turned and walked down the cobblestone hill. And she'd kept walking, heedless of the people or the animals or carts that crowded the street, seeing nothing but the image of Carlos kissing the beautiful woman. She'd kept walking until she'd reached the cottage where Lady Tuttle had commanded a small army to pack their things.

Even now, a month later, the memory was still too painful to bear.

Alexa played more of her song, but it sounded dreary. She was determined to put the past behind her; what else could she do? She'd done something wretched—she'd fallen in love with a Spaniard, and fallen so far, and so deep, that she had conceived his child. Happily conceived it, eagerly conceived it. And then she had discovered that he was married.

There was no other explanation. His sudden disappearance from her life, the kiss to the woman's cheek . . . Alexa guessed that his wife had been away while he seduced her. He'd left her one rainy afternoon with kisses and promises and a bright smile and he'd gone home, apparently, to his wife.

Alexa never saw Carlos again. She'd left him a note thanking him for the use of the cottage, and she'd come running home to Everdon Court and Olivia, the only place she could go.

She couldn't say what she thought would happen once she arrived at Everdon Court. She supposed she'd wanted to sweep it all under the rug and pretend it hadn't happened.

But Olivia had guessed the truth. That was the way

with her, and it had always been. She was so perfect in her conduct, so terribly clever. All of Alexa's life, Olivia had been held out as the ideal, what Alexa should strive to be. It didn't matter that Alexa did not care to be as prim and proper as Olivia. She was told she must be if she wanted a match when she grew older. Alexa had never been as concerned about appearances as her sister. She had believed Olivia was making a bad situation even worse with her insistence that they tell Edward, who was so cold and distant. She didn't want to end up like Olivia, married to a cold-hearted man.

But then Alexa had seen the bruise on Olivia's lip, and that had given her pause. The physical evidence had made her realize that she had to stand up and face the consequences of what she'd done, for if she didn't, Olivia would.

If only Alexa knew *how* to face the consequences without being banished to Ireland! She really had no options, but the more she resisted, the more Olivia would pay the price for her mistake with her beast of a husband.

Alexa knew she'd been awful to Olivia and Mr. Tolly, and truly, she'd not meant to be. But she'd been feeling so many confusing, conflicting emotions. She did not want to *marry*. She pined for Carlos still, as hurt as she was. She'd agonized over everything he'd said, wondering how she could imbue his words with so much promise, or how he could have lied to her as easily as he had. She cried herself to sleep more times than she could count and had given up all hope. She wanted only to return to the cottage where she and Carlos had spent so many blissful afternoons, and wake up tangled in his legs and arms, her head on his shoulder. Alexa had struggled mightily to let that dream go. But she did not want to live in a convent, and she would *not* give up her child.

Today, Olivia had managed to penetrate the fog that had surrounded Alexa since that day in Madrid and convinced her that her situation was dire. This afternoon, Alexa had methodically examined her options and found them distressingly absent. She thought of what Harry had said about his life. She thought of the child she was carrying. What if it was a boy, like Harry? Would he be shunned? Not allowed in school? Alexa didn't have jewels to sell, and the thought of doing what his mother had done to provide for her child made her shudder.

Olivia was right. She had to marry.

Mr. Tolly seemed to be as good a candidate as any. He was agreeable, he was handsome, and he had inherited something, so hopefully her child would not want. But the most appealing thing about him was that the alternatives were too grim. He simply would have to do.

Harrison returned to the dowager house without actually recalling the walk—his head was full of Lady Carey's kiss, his body still thrumming, his nerves skating on a guilty edge. He'd held back his desire for her for so many years that he was startled by how quickly he'd succumbed. As if he'd been blown off his precipice by a slight spring breeze. In a single moment, his life had forever changed and he would never be the same man he was only hours ago.

Worse, he knew he would do it again without a moment's hesitation.

Harrison walked into his foyer with the intention of retiring to his study and a bottle of whiskey, and was brought up short by the surprising sound of music. It was the old pianoforte from his mother's salon, though he'd never heard her play it.

Curious, he walked to what he optimistically called the music room.

Alexa was seated at the pianoforte, her golden head down, her play light, and a frown of concentration on her face. Harrison cleared his throat; she looked up and smiled thinly. "There you are."

"Here I am," he said as he moved into the room. "Please carry on. This house has not heard music during my tenure. It might shake loose a few old cobwebs or hidden treasure."

She smiled shyly and put her hands in her lap. "I am not very practiced at it. I was merely biding my time, waiting for you. May I have a word, Harry?"

Harrison suppressed a groan. He was hardly in the mood for her at present, as he had his own bad behavior to sort out. "Could it possibly wait? I have quite a lot of work—"

"It won't take but a moment," she said, rising from the pianoforte, holding her hands tightly at her waist. "Please, sir. I know I have been wretched, but on my word, I shall not be so again."

The contrite little promise surprised Harrison. She even *looked* contrite. Still, Harrison was wary. "Go on, then."

"I, ah . . ." She took a deep breath, then began again. "I have thought quite a lot about what you and my sister have said."

Harrison was no longer interested in aiding her—quite the opposite. He wished she'd flit away.

"And . . . I have come to the conclusion that you are quite right."

Now there was a heavenly miracle if ever he'd seen one. Did she truly expect him to believe that? He gave her a dubious look. "Have you, indeed? Pardon me, Alexa, but that does not sound like the young woman I have come to know."

"I am aware of that." She swallowed hard. "You were so kind to offer me marriage and a name for my baby, given my impossible predicament, and I . . . and I realized I have been foolish and ungrateful in return. But upon reflection . . ."

She paused and swallowed once more, and Harrison resisted the roll of his eyes, waiting for what he suspected she would say next. *I cannot marry you, et cetera, et cetera.*

"Upon reflection," she said again, her voice soft, "I

have come to the conclusion that we might indeed find our way, and perhaps even be . . . happy. Therefore, I should like to accept your offer of marriage."

He couldn't feel his heart beating; he couldn't feel anything, for everything had stopped moving. The air, his breath. Time. He stared at Alexa; she pressed her lips together, her chest rising and falling with each anxious breath. He had no idea what to say—his entire world had been turned on its head after kissing Lady Carey in the garden, and his heart was a twisted, tangled mess. And now *this*? He couldn't speak, couldn't move.

Miss Hastings paled. "I know what you must think. That I am petulant and uncooperative, and for that I apologize. But on my word, sir, I have never in my life faced such a dilemma. I apologize for my poor behavior."

Was he dreaming?

"Please say something," she pleaded.

"Is this a jest? Some sort of trickery?"

"What? No!"

Harrison folded his arms across his chest. "Then may I inquire what happened in the last three hours to bring about this stunning change of heart? How is it that I suddenly meet with your approval?"

"I never said that you didn't," she said weakly.

"You seemed crystal clear about that to me."

Alexa glanced down and traced her finger along the edge of the pianoforte. "I think that I was not ready to accept that I cannot . . . *be* . . . with the person I fell in love with. But I have accepted it. And I find you entirely agreeable, and frankly, sir, I fear what will become of Olivia if I do not put my situation to rights."

That, at least, was something they had in common.

"I hope we might find a more palatable solution for us both, but if not . . . I am humbled by your kindness," she said.

Harrison walked across the room and sat down heavily. He could only think of Lady Carey. Not this wisp of a girl.

"No doubt this would be easier for us both if we were more familiar with one another," she said nervously. "Perhaps we might speak of how to exist in each other's company until familiarity takes hold?"

Harrison was dumbfounded. He no more wanted to marry this girl than he wanted to walk into the jaws of hell. But he'd put the wheels in motion by opening his bloody mouth, and now, he couldn't even begin to think how he'd manage his way out of it. A weight of crushing disappointment and frustration settled onto his shoulders. Was there no way out of this nightmare?

CHAPTER TWELVE

After that stunning, disturbingly arousing kiss in the garden, Olivia had to escape the thoughts and feelings that had flooded her, so she went to the one place where no one would look for her. The one place no one, and especially Edward, would venture: the nursery.

She hurried up the back staircase and pushed open the painted green door with both hands, then quickly shut it and turned the lock. She stood there a moment, her forehead and hands pressed against the closed door, trying to catch her breath.

But it would not come; it had been snatched clean from her lungs.

Olivia turned and surveyed the room. With windows facing north and west and the walls painted a sunny yellow, it was a bright, happy room. Snowy white brocade draperies matched the coverlet on the child's bed. The dark cherry wood of the cradle gleamed in the sunlight streaming in. Edward had commissioned it during the two months Olivia had believed herself to be with child. It had been in the center of the room, the nurse's bed nearby. Now, the cradle was pushed to a corner.

Near the hearth, painted yellow flowers adorned the child-sized table and matching chairs. The stuffed bear Olivia's mother had given her was sitting on a shelf, waiting for the child that would never inhabit this room.

Olivia did not think of that today. She thought only that it was too bright and cheery for her state of mind. She began to pace the yellow and green carpet, nibbling anxiously on one thumbnail. She didn't know what to do, what to *think*. How had it happened? How had Harrison Tolly come to kiss her—or had she kissed *him*?

Olivia hardly knew what had happened. One moment she was talking, and the next she was kissing Mr. Tolly, sinking into him and her deep-seated fantasy. "What in heaven has come over you?" she chided herself. She'd put them both at extraordinary risk, yet she hadn't stopped because she had wanted that kiss more than she'd ever wanted anything in her life.

More than anything.

The weight of her longing pushed her down onto her knees, her hands braced on either side of them, dragging air into her lungs. Which was worse—the fear of discovery, or the pain of wanting more?

Olivia touched her fingers to her mouth, desperate to remember every moment, every sensation. The way he'd tasted—like cinnamon—and how he'd smelled like linen.

In all her life, she'd never been kissed so passionately, but it was also surprisingly tender. He desired her. Not just her body, but *her*.

Olivia closed her eyes, pressed the back of her hand against her mouth. She could see his face, his lips, his eyes brimming with wild desire. She could feel his mouth on hers, the tight hold of his arms around her, all his desire for her.

How unfair it is! To receive that sort of kiss with the power and strength of a man's desire, and feel the ache for more, all while knowing she could never have it, was heart-wrenchingly painful. Olivia slowly slid one arm across the carpet until she was lying on her side, her head resting on her outstretched arm. She closed her eyes and brazenly imagined Mr. Tolly's hard, warm body fluidly entering hers. She imagined his hands on her skin, stroking her, caressing her, slipping into her secret folds. She imagined his mouth and tongue on her skin, and the way he would look at her as he took her, his hair falling over his brow, his arms holding himself above her, his expression filled with desire and affection.

Pain swirled in Olivia's chest, and a tear of frustration slipped from her eye. She wanted him more than air. It was the worst torture knowing that he should be the last thing on this earth that she might have.

I am his Lady X.

How could she not have known it? With a groan, Olivia rolled onto her back, staring up at the mural painted on the ceiling, a quaint little scene of boats bobbing about a lake, rowed by bears wearing waistcoats and neckcloths. What was it Mr. Tolly had said? That he could never have his Lady X, he could never ask her to leave her husband and live in reduced circumstances with her reputation destroyed.

"*Oh, yes, yes, yes, you can,*" she moaned. She would not hesitate to leave Edward and everything else behind. She'd lived too many years in her miserable little birdcage to care for circumstance or reputation. She'd live in a hovel with Mr. Tolly and pluck chickens and bake bread and grow wheat.

But what about Alexa?

She couldn't beg Mr. Tolly to take her away; she had to consider Alexa and her child now. And as much as it pained her to admit it, Mr. Tolly was the only viable option she had for saving her little sister.

But it was more than that. Edward would never agree to set her free. He would never concede that he'd been cuckolded; he would never seek or allow a divorce. No, Edward would prefer to keep her and torment her. He was half mad, and he would never, *ever* allow his reputation to be sullied with slander. He would sooner destroy Harrison. And Alexa. And her.

Olivia closed her eyes, willing back the tears that threatened to fall.

She was trapped in a loveless marriage for the rest of her life, living in a gilded birdcage that grew smaller each day until she was pressed up against the bars, unable to breathe, unable to move. Slowly suffocating to death.

She pushed herself to her feet, tucked in the hair that had come undone, and dusted off her skirt.

It wasn't as if she hadn't realized the truth of her life before. But today she'd had a glimmer of hope for something different. The sooner she walled off that hope, the better.

Maybe—she took a deep breath and released it— maybe she could wall Edward in his study first. She imagined tying him to a chair, then calmly laying one brick on top of another as he shouted at her to stop, going as high as she must until she could no longer see him or hear him. What a happy difference there would be if she no longer could see him or hear him.

Olivia walked to the window and gazed down at the garden where she'd kissed Mr. Tolly. "Stiff upper lip, lass," she murmured. She had enough problems without creating new ones.

Nancy Carthorn, a buxom ginger-haired young woman with great aspirations, had been employed as a ladies' maid at Everdon Court for four years. She enjoyed her occupation, particularly as she spent her days in the marchioness's private rooms amid all the finery and the gowns and the glittering jewelry. Her post was far superior to any other in the house, with the exception of perhaps Mr. Brock.

It was certainly better than what poor Lucy Krankhouse faced every day in the kitchen, working alongside a tetchy Miss Foster. Lucy was firmly under Miss Foster's oppressive thumb—she'd been quite cross with Lucy when she thought her special ladle had gone missing—and to Nancy's way of thinking, the girl was being unfairly treated. The lovely thing about Nancy's post was that she could say she thought so to Lady Carey, and her ladyship would speak to Mr. Brock. She'd done it when Fred wouldn't leave Nancy be, and now Fred was in the stables shoveling manure and not chasing her up and down the servant's stairs.

That evening, Nancy mentioned Lucy's unhappiness as she dressed the marchioness's hair. But Lady Carey didn't seem to hear her. That puzzled Nancy. Generally, Lady Carey listened politely to what Nancy had to say, and often offered her personal opinion, which, naturally, Nancy would rush downstairs to deliver at first opportunity. But Lady Carey seemed distracted, and Nancy paused. "Beg your pardon, mu'um, are you unwell?"

"Hmmm?" her ladyship said, and glanced up.

"You seem a bit pale, is all," Nancy said.

Lady Carey looked at herself in the mirror, squinting a bit. "I suppose I am fatigued," she said with a bit of a shrug.

Fatigued, pale . . . Nancy's hand stilled on her ladyship's hair. Good Lord, was it possible her ladyship was with child? That would bring a bit of lightness into this gloomy old house! Everyone knew that an heir was the only thing that would make the marquis happy.

"Nancy? What is it?" her ladyship asked, peering at Nancy's reflection in the mirror.

Nancy instantly resumed putting up her hair. "Pardon." She slipped a pin into Lady Carey's hair to hold it. "I was thinking that you should have a care not to overtax yourself, mu'um. Must keep up your strength."

"Keep up my strength for what?"

Now she'd gone and said too much. Nancy turned away to fetch more pins. "No reason in particular," she said. "I'd not like to see you under the weather." She turned and smiled. "That's all."

Her ladyship said nothing, but sat quietly brooding as Nancy finished her hair. When she was done, Lady Carey stood and looked at herself in the mirror for a long time. She was wearing a gown that looked almost as if it were spun gold. It hugged her bodice tightly, and with his lordship away, Lady Carey had foregone the bit of taffeta that she generally wore as a modest collar. Tonight her décolletage was powdered and perfumed, and a pair of diamonds dangled from her earlobes. If she'd donned a coronet, she'd look like a princess. "Very pretty, mu'um," Nancy said admiringly.

"Thank you." Lady Carey gave Nancy a ghost of a smile before she went out, the train of her gown trailing behind her.

Nancy smiled to herself as she began to tidy up the room. The entire estate waited on tenterhooks for Lady Carey to provide an heir, and wouldn't it be nice to have a baby toddling about? She could scarcely wait to tell Miss Foster and Mrs. Perry what she suspected.

CHAPTER THIRTEEN

꩜

The red salon seemed empty without Edward's oppressive presence. He had a tendency to suck the air from the room. Olivia was required to meet him here each evening before supper; Edward liked her to embroider while he read his newspapers. It did not matter to him that Olivia had never taken to needlework, or that her creations generally required some repair by Mrs. Perry, or even that neither of them had any desire to be in the other's company. Edward believed it was what married couples should do.

Tonight, Olivia was alone with the footman Bruce, who stood silently beside the sideboard in case she required anything.

Olivia pressed her hands to her abdomen as she walked across the room. *Breathe, damn you*. She couldn't seem to find her bearings after what had happened this afternoon.

"Olivia!"

The sound of Alexa's voice calling to her from the hallway set Olivia's nerves on edge. She swallowed, took another deep breath, and turned around just as Alexa came hurrying in.

"There you are! Where have you been? I looked for you earlier and I could not find you."

Olivia's pulse fluttered with the realization that Alexa could have seen her with Mr. Tolly. Merciful heaven, all of Everdon Court could have seen them! So reckless, so *foolish*. "Ah . . . I had some correspondence." She saw the footman glance at her, then look away again. Did he know she lied?

"I must speak to you, Livi," Alexa said. "I have something I must say."

If Alexa's anxious demeanor was any indication, she had, yet again, something dreadful to impart, and Olivia wanted to scream. "Bruce, if you would, a bit of wine," Olivia said. "Alexa, please do not vex me this evening," she said quietly as Bruce turned to the sideboard. "I've had quite enough for one day."

"Vex you?" Alexa repeated, as if she were surprised by the notion that she could be vexing. "No, Livi, I do not mean to *vex* you." At Olivia's dubious look, she sighed. "All right, I suppose I can hardly blame you for that. I am aware that I have been wretched. I want to apologize for it."

An apology was the last thing Olivia expected from Alexa, who had never been very keen on them. Her sister was decidedly *un*apologetic. She must have been gaping in disbelief, for Alexa said a bit tetchily, "Must you seem so shocked?"

"I *am* shocked," Olivia said. "And I cannot help but wonder what has brought on this sudden change."

"As it happens, I have had some time to think." She paused as Bruce handed Olivia a glass of wine, then took Olivia by the elbow and led her across the room to a window seat. She glanced at Bruce again, and whispered, "I *am* sorry, Livi. I have no excuse for it, really, other than I've not been ready to accept that I . . ." She leaned in so that she could whisper in Olivia's ear. "That I cannot marry the father."

Olivia perked up at that—Alexa had been loath to mention him at all. "But are you certain, Alexa?" she whispered, seizing the moment. "I've been thinking . . . what if we sent for him? Perhaps if we offered—"

"*No*," Alexa said sternly and squeezed Olivia's hand. She glanced anxiously at the footman.

"Thank you, Bruce," Olivia said. "You may leave us."

With a nod of his head, he went out.

"All right, then," Olivia said. "I will ask you again, Alexa. Can't we send for this man? Should we not appeal to him on the grounds of his moral responsibility?"

"No!" Alexa exclaimed.

"For heaven's sake, why not?"

"I know that is what you want," Alexa said impatiently. "Do you not think that is what *I* want, as well? Of course I do! But my acquaintance with him is . . ."

She bit her lips and looked down. "It is surely not as you must imagine it."

"How I *imagine* it?" Olivia echoed crossly. "This man has put a child in you and therefore bears a responsibility, whether you or he want to admit it! I think it a much better solution than any other we've thought of thus far."

"I understand—"

"You do not understand!" Olivia said. "If you understood anything at all you would tell me more, tell me his name, so that I might at least *help* you—"

"No," Alexa said firmly, and stood.

"That is so very like you," Olivia said angrily.

"Meaning?"

"Meaning that your consideration for your own desires outweighs those of everyone else."

"I resent that!" Alexa said. "I have my reasons."

"*What* reasons?" Olivia exclaimed heavenward.

"And that is so very like *you*, Olivia. So superior and sure of yourself."

"In this I am very sure," Olivia said. "If he is a *decent* man, he will—"

"Will you please stop this, Olivia? I know without question that his situation will not allow him to help me."

Olivia sighed and looked out the window. It was what she'd suspected all along. "He is married, then."

Alexa made a sound of displeasure and whirled around, marching to the sideboard. "Do you want to hear what I have come to tell you, or not?"

"Of course I do," Olivia said wearily, and hoped to God it was something simple.

Alexa braced her hands on the sideboard. "I have come to the realization that you are right, and I do need your help."

"Thank God for that."

Alexa turned around. "And that you were quite right about Mr. Tolly," she continued. "He has done me an incredible kindness."

Something twisted deep inside Olivia. Surely Alexa did not mean—

"I am trying to say that Harry and I have agreed—"

Olivia suddenly couldn't breathe. She surged to her feet and looked around, uncertain where to go to avoid hearing what she instinctively knew Alexa would say. What had happened? What bolt of lightning had suddenly struck to change Alexa's heart?

"We have agreed that in the absence of any other option, my best course is to marry. He and I have discussed it—"

"What? When?"

"Today," Alexa said, taken slightly aback. "This afternoon. Why do you ask?"

"Just . . . go on," she said tightly, and braced her hands on the window casing.

"There's really not much left to say, is there? I realize you would have preferred to put me in some old widow's home, tucked away from society, but I prefer this. At least I might have some semblance of a life."

She would have a life? What of Mr. Tolly?

"Harry seems kind, and he is physically appealing—"

"Must you call him Harry?" Olivia interrupted. "Even I am not so familiar with him, and I've known him many years. I have seen him every day of my married life and I have never called him by his given name."

"If I am to be married, I cannot always address him as Mr. Tolly," Alexa said with a shrug. "And we agreed that we must put ourselves on familiar terms if there is any hope that we might grow to affection."

Oh, that dagger to her heart, knifed cleanly and all the way through. Olivia closed her eyes. "He said that?"

"They were not his exact words, but that was surely his sentiment."

So while Olivia had lain on the floor of the nursery fighting an overwhelming desire for him, mourning him, Harrison Tolly had been promising a future to her sister.

Her heart had just been rent wide open.

"Livi, please," Alexa said behind her. "I am endeavoring to do as you wish."

There was nothing Olivia could say. Alexa was doing exactly what Olivia had counseled her to do. But that was before this afternoon, when Olivia had known a moment of bliss so pure and deep. Yet it was only a moment—she'd gotten on the wrong boat floating down the river of her life several years ago. The boat she wanted was on the opposite shore, but the current was too strong, and there was no reaching it.

Gather yourself! Olivia swallowed. She pressed her hand against the cool windowpane and said, "It is indeed the best option we have. And I think you will be happy in spite of the circumstances. Mr. Tolly is . . . He is . . ." *He is everything.* He was her security, the one person she could look forward to seeing every day. He was laughter and light in her dark world. He was her happy dream.

"Well, at present, he is right here," Alexa said casually.

Olivia hadn't heard him come in, but when she turned, there he was, standing just inside the door, his hands clasped behind his back. He looked . . . virile. Desirable. And pained.

"My sister was on the verge of saying something complimentary about you," Alexa said and turned to the sideboard to resume her examination of the bottles there. "However, she seems to find herself a bit tongue-tied with my change of heart. I seem to have astounded everyone today."

"It was a rather astounding turn of events, to be sure." Mr. Tolly's gaze locked with Olivia's.

"Let it never be said that Alexa Hastings doesn't see her way around to what is best," Alexa said, and poured water. "Whiskey, or . . . port, perhaps, Harry? I suppose I ought to learn what you drink in the evenings."

"Whiskey," Olivia said softly.

Alexa looked at her with surprise. She smiled. "I assume you are referring to Harry's preference and not your own?"

"A whiskey will do nicely," Mr. Tolly said, and started for the sideboard. "Allow me."

Alexa moved away. "Have you recovered from your astonishment, Livi? Might we speak of the arrangements now?"

Arrangements. That sounded so . . . final. Olivia sank onto a chair.

"I was thinking perhaps a small affair, here at Everdon Court," Alexa said lightly.

"Impossible," Olivia muttered.

"Why?" Alexa asked.

"I should think that the marquis would not care for it," Mr. Tolly said evenly. "Perhaps you might think of something smaller."

"How small?"

"The two of us."

Alexa snorted. "Without even Olivia? Or a friend or two?"

"I think, given the nature of our . . . union," Mr. Tolly said, as if searching for the right word, "we should go to Scotland and take care of things quietly."

Dear God, he meant to do it straightaway. Olivia averted her gaze. She could not look at him now and think of him hurrying off to Scotland to marry Alexa.

Nor could Alexa, apparently. "Scotland!" she exclaimed. "I had thought we might go about this as normally as possible. Not elope!"

"We must remove ourselves from public." Mr. Tolly

sounded calm, but Olivia could hear a bit of tension in his voice.

Alexa didn't have an opportunity to complain, for Brock entered at that moment and informed them that supper was served.

"Thank heaven. I am famished. May we continue this as we dine?" Alexa asked, and walked out behind Brock, seemingly oblivious to Olivia's hesitation and to the tension in Mr. Tolly's jaw.

Mr. Tolly was not oblivious, however. His eyes moved over Olivia's face as if he had not seen her in an age. He looked as if he wanted to speak. Olivia could feel her defenses eroding already, her body warming.

He held out his arm to her as he'd done a thousand times before. Olivia hesitated; she was afraid to touch him, but just as afraid to let the opportunity for at least a small bit of contact pass. She laid her hand lightly on his arm. He instantly covered her hand with his, slipped his fingers beneath hers, and lightly stroked the inside of her wrist.

It was hardly anything at all, but it reverberated through her body. Somehow, she managed to walk to the dining room at his side. With her gaze straight ahead, Mr. Tolly caressed her wrist down that long hallway.

In the dining room, Alexa was already seated. Mr. Tolly handed Olivia into a chair. "The soup smells divine," Alexa said as Brock ladled soup into their bowls. He went out, carrying the tureen.

Alexa picked up her spoon and sampled the dish, then put her spoon down. "Olivia," she said, as she idly traced the scroll pattern on the silver, "you undoubtedly agree with Harry that it is best we go to Scotland, but won't everyone in Everdon speculate as to the need for such haste? I should think it would produce more scandal where we might avoid it."

"It wouldn't make the slightest bit of difference if we were married at Westminster Abbey, Alexa," Mr. Tolly said patiently. "The moment the vows are said there will be speculation, since there is only one reason to marry with such haste. Furthermore, it will not be long before anyone who sees you will understand the reason for it."

Alexa blushed and looked plaintively at Olivia. "All right, I understand, I do, but this is the only wedding I shall ever have. I should like at least a *small* affair."

"You may have your small affair upon our return," Mr. Tolly said firmly. "When you are very married and thus incapable of causing any more harm to the reputations of everyone around you."

Alexa looked again to Olivia like a child looking for a different answer from another parent. Olivia wanted to name a thousand reasons why Alexa and Mr. Tolly could not possibly marry. But now was not the time to mope. She could nurse her wounds later.

She put her spoon down. "Perhaps there is a way to cast this situation so it does not look entirely . . . disgraceful," she said carefully.

"I would welcome any suggestions," Mr. Tolly said dryly.

Olivia glanced at her soup bowl. "I think we simply say that the two of you had occasion to meet and it was love at first sight." She managed to say it without choking on the words. Mr. Tolly looked away. "And that as we had no idea how long the marquis would be away, you could not bear to wait. It is a . . . love story." Her heart was breaking. "We might invite a few ladies for tea and plant the seed," she added as an afterthought. Dear God, was she actually saying these words?

Alexa mulled it over, then smiled. "I think it is a splendid idea, Livi."

"There, then, Alexa, you have your explanation," Mr. Tolly said. "Now let us discuss when we will make the trip to Gretna Green."

Alexa and Mr. Tolly proceeded to speak of it as Olivia picked at her meal. She noticed that the familiarity between Mr. Tolly and Alexa was not limited to names; they'd struck up some sort of friendship at the dowager house, the sort of acquaintance where they might have an intimate discussion such as this without inhibition. Olivia tried to convince herself that their familiarity was good and necessary. The situation was difficult enough as it was; they needed a certain comfort with each other to weather it.

When Olivia had married Edward, she'd been timid, uncertain when to ask questions, when to speak her mind. As a result, she'd always felt anxious around him.

What a young little fool she had been.

What a hardened woman she was now.

Her private and deeply personal loss keened through her, swelling in every vein. Mr. Tolly had been her friend, her confidante, and she would never have that again. Because of their kiss, she would now always be cautious, careful not to reveal too much. Because of Alexa, Olivia could never reveal her true feelings to anyone. It was a devil of a place to be, frightened of being alone in Mr. Tolly's company, and frightened that she never would be again.

The worst torture of all would be to watch her sister grow and bear Mr. Tolly's children, while she wasted away at Everdon Court with a brute of a husband.

"Is the meal not to your liking, Livi?"

"Pardon?"

Alexa looked at Olivia's plate. "We've been nattering on about the arrangements, and there you are staring at your lamb. I will agree it is not the best roast Miss Foster has made."

"There is nothing wrong with the lamb. I simply do not have much of an appetite."

"Oh, Livi," Alexa said sympathetically. "I know how difficult this is for you, but I do mean to put it all to rights, straightaway." She patted Olivia's hand.

Olivia smiled thinly, looked at her plate, and imagined hurling it across the room. "Have you decided when you will depart, then?" she forced herself to ask.

"Not yet. I shall need at least a few days to gather

my wits about me and put together a trousseau," Alexa said.

A trousseau. Good Lord.

"I should think by week's end," Mr. Tolly said quietly.

"So soon?" Alexa asked, forcing a smile.

"Have you forgotten that you've agreed to abide by my decisions until we are certain that the scandal has been held to an absolute minimum?"

"I did not realize that extended to my wedding."

"It *begins* with your wedding," he reminded her.

Alexa opened her mouth to argue, but quickly closed it. She glanced at Olivia from the corner of her eye. "All right, then. To assure you I will be as dutiful a wife as any woman is meant to be, I will agree."

Mr. Tolly said nothing. He turned his attention back to his meal. Olivia couldn't help noticing that he'd not eaten much, either. Alexa, bless her, seemed entirely incognizant of the strain around that table. She was too occupied in her attempt to put as much dignity and pageantry to her wedding as possible given the unfortunate circumstances, and chattering to fill the silence around her.

Fortunately, Alexa's chatter left Olivia to her own thoughts. When the main course had been cleared and Brock returned to set puddings before them, Olivia looked up and her gaze met Mr. Tolly's. He was watching her. Olivia's heart sank deeper into her despair. He knew her well, this man. He knew her better than anyone.

And as if on cue, as if to reassure her that he did, Mr. Tolly smiled at Olivia. It was the same reassuring smile he'd given her nearly every day for the past six years. The same sort of smile that had made her love him.

CHAPTER FOURTEEN
〰৶ঔৎ〰

After supper, they retreated to the salon. For what? Harrison wondered. More talk of trousseaus and teas that had already set his teeth on edge? He stood near the hearth, counting down the minutes until he could escape this interminable evening.

He could see that Alexa was trying to wrap this wedding about her like a rope, something secure to hold on to, yet she still did not seem to fully grasp how perilous her situation was. She rattled on about it as if Harrison had gone down on one knee and asked her to join him in conjugal felicity. Even now, she was speaking earnestly to Lady Carey about a gown. She was so intent on what she might wear that she didn't seem to notice how distant Lady Carey was.

Harrison had clearly expressed his reservations to Alexa after her surprising turn. He'd been frank that marriage was not his desire, but necessary to save her from banishment, save her sister from the marquis's wrath, and then save the Carey family from damaging scandal. Alexa had assured him she understood, and that she was very grateful for his generosity and his help, and that she would endeavor to be as good a wife to him as he deserved.

What he deserved was to be kicked in the head for having kissed Lady Carey in the garden. He'd taken an unthinkable liberty with her, yet here he stood, still unable to take his eyes from her. That kiss had done nothing but make his absolute hunger for her grow. Harrison had warred with himself all day—he'd imagined himself inside her warm, tight sheath, her legs around his waist, her eyes glistening with the carnal pleasure she had been denied for so many years, and that he would be very happy to show her. Bloody hell, his body began to swell at just the idea of giving her that pleasure.

He turned his back and pretended to look at some books on the shelves, forcing down his desire.

Lady Carey stood at the window, peering out into darkness, as if she might leap into it at any moment. He couldn't blame her; her life was spinning wildly out of control. So was his. For a man who had made his own way in this world, who had been master of his destiny at a very early age, he was now a slave to a situation that was not of his making, but one into which he had rashly entered. He could all but hear the iron gate banging shut behind him and the key turning in the lock. He would have liked to join Lady Carey at the window and contemplate jumping, too.

Then suddenly—or perhaps not so suddenly, for Harrison had ceased to hear what was being said—Alexa stretched her arms high above her head and yawned. "Please excuse me, but I am quite fatigued."

"I shall see you to the dowager house," Harrison said instantly, anxious to be away from this distressful tableau.

"I think I am too tired to walk there. And really, I should return to the main house while the marquis is away, should I not? I hardly think Rue qualifies as a proper chaperone. May I, Olivia?" Alexa yawned again.

"Hmmm?" Lady Carey said, turning from the window.

"I prefer to sleep here."

"Yes, of course," Lady Carey said with a slight but dismissive flick of her wrist. "Whatever you like."

"Thank you," Alexa said, and stood up, crossing the room to kiss her sister's cheek. "Good night." She smiled at Harrison as she walked across the room, her hands pressed against her back as if it pained her.

He and Lady Carey watched her go from the room in silence, both of them rooted to the floor. Harrison's pulse ticked up as he heard Alexa's step on the stairs. He had a moment, if that, to explain what had happened after he'd left the garden. He turned around to Lady Carey.

Her blue eyes widened. She put her hand to her nape, a gesture she made when she felt unsettled. She looked at the open door and suddenly started toward it, walking briskly. "If you will excuse me, Mr. Tolly, but I must bid you a good night as well—"

Harrison was not going to allow that—he moved quickly, beating her to the door and closing it firmly. He turned about, his back to the door. "Are you trying to escape me?"

"Yes!" she exclaimed, and whirled around, retreating from him.

"Lady Carey—*Olivia*," he said earnestly.

She kept her back to him, but her shoulders lifted with a deep breath.

"Olivia," he said again, his voice softer.

"You mustn't call me that."

"At least allow me to explain—"

"There is nothing to explain," she said, and moved again, deliberately putting a chair between them. She put her hands to either side of her face, pressing her fingers into her temples.

"I think perhaps you fear that I kissed you in the garden as I did, and then turned about and pressed my suit with your sister," he said, advancing carefully. "No, Olivia. She caught me completely unawares, as I am sure she did you."

"Mr. Tolly!" she cried, throwing up her hand. "Do not speak of it!"

Harrison impulsively reached out and caught her hand. She tugged against his hold, but he would not release it. "*Harrison*, Olivia. My name is Harrison."

"Stand back!" she said sternly, and tried to pull

her hand free and turn away from him, but Harrison caught her face with his fingers and forced her to look at him. "Olivia, listen to me—"

"Do not say my name!" she cried, and gasped as if the words had taken the wind from her.

"How am I to help it?" he asked, his gaze skating over her face, as beautiful to him as any he'd ever seen. "I have kissed you, and I—"

She hit him square in the chest with her fist. "Do not *say* it!" she said, her breath coming in gulps. She hit him again. "Do you hear me? Do not say it, Harrison Tolly! I forbid you to say my name, for every time you say it, I *shatter*."

Harrison grabbed her up into his arms and held her tightly. She gripped his arms, her fingers curling into the fabric with the strength of a drowning woman. "Do not say it, never say it," she begged him. "I did not mean for it to happen, but now that it has, I cannot bear it. I cannot *bear* it," she said again, and hit his arm with her fist.

"Be still," he soothed her. "And for God's sake, breathe." He held her, his cheek pressed to her temple, until he could feel her breath calm and steady. She didn't let go her grip of his coat, but he felt her begin to soften, the tension easing from her body. At last she turned her head, laid her cheek against his shoulder, and sighed wearily.

They stood that way a long moment until she straightened, dabbed beneath her eyes with one knuckle, and drew a steadying breath. "Well," she said. "This is rather awkward."

"It is not."

She smiled and touched his cheek. "It is. You know it as well as I do. Mr.—" She hesitated. "Harrison," she said carefully, testing his name. "I have thought of little else other than what happened in the garden. I did not mean for it to happen. I never dreamed something like that *could* happen. But my defenses deserted me, and I felt . . . I felt . . ." She closed her eyes, her lips slightly apart with the exhalation of her breath.

Harrison braced himself. He expected her to say she'd felt guilty or compromised, while he had been lifted up by that kiss. He'd felt himself soar in that kiss, and he would not apologize for it. Not to her, not anyone.

"I felt alive," she said, and opened her eyes.

He blinked with surprise. His heart began to swell in his chest. "Olivia—"

"But I have no right to feel that way!" she exclaimed, and let go of him. "I am married and when I thought of what would happen if my husband—my *husband*, the man to whom I have sworn my fidelity, for better or worse. *You* know, you know better than anyone that it has been for worse. What would happen if he were to discover that kiss?" she exclaimed in anguish.

"It would not go well for either of us," he agreed. "I never meant it to happen, either, Olivia. And it will not happen again; I give you my word. I will keep my distance from you—"

"I do not want your distance!" she cried. "God help me, I know I must have it, but I do not *want* it."

Harrison was at a complete loss. He didn't want to keep his distance, either, but he had no choice. To be near her was to court disaster; he'd already discovered that the wall he'd built around his heart over the years was as weak as a house of cards. "Tell me what you want and I will do it, whatever it is," he said. "I will help you in any way that I can."

She made a sound of frustration. "If you could help me, you would have done so long ago. I am beyond help."

The truth in that statement sliced through him, made him feel like less than a man. He could not save the one person who meant more to him than any other. Harrison shoved his fingers through his hair and desperately sought his footing. The only thing he knew was that he wanted to touch her again, to take her in his arms and into his bed.

"Do you know what I truly want?" she asked, her voice soft and breathless.

"What? Tell me, and I will give it to you," he said earnestly.

"But I want what I can never have—I want *you*, Harrison."

He caught his breath. It was the last thing he'd thought he would ever hear from her. A week ago, he would have rejoiced at her declaration. He would have swept her away from Everdon Court, as far away as he could take her. But now . . . now everything was different. He took her hands in his, his gaze on her slender fingers.

"I have astonished you, haven't I?" she said. "You cannot imagine how I have come to depend on you. You have been my rock these years, Harrison. You are the one who has kept me breathing."

His heart constricted. What a sad pair they were. He lifted her hands and kissed her knuckles. "Those words fill my heart with equal joy and despair. They are words I never dared to dream of hearing from you."

"And today," she said, "today, I knew a few moments of bliss. There are no words to describe how devastated I am to know that I will never feel that again."

"If only I had known," he said. "You must know, you must have sensed that I have adored you these many years, from the moment you first appeared at Everdon Court wearing that sunny yellow gown and pearls."

Olivia looked up with surprise. "You remember what I wore?"

"I remember everything," he said. "I remember the day you went riding, and you returned with twigs in your hair and your hat missing, lost when you attempted to negotiate a low-hanging limb. You laughed and called it a fool's daring. I thought you were so vibrant."

"Oh, Harrison."

"I recall one summer day when you hosted a tea in

the gazebo, and Miss Shields told you a tale that had you laughing so soundly that your hands were pressed against your abdomen and tears filled your eyes."

"How can you recall that?" she asked, smiling with pleasure. "You were not there."

"I watched you from an open window in the study. I remember the occasion of your first anniversary, and the silver gown you wore. You looked every bit a princess, and in the middle of the dancing, you caught my eye and winked."

She smiled softly. "You seemed rather forlorn, standing to the side all alone."

"Not forlorn," he said, his gaze on hers. "Mesmerized. Always mesmerized."

Olivia blushed. "By me? I have always felt so uninteresting."

"You?" He shook his head. "Never. Do you recall a night, two or three years ago, when a heavy snow fell and we played Écarté? You soundly bested me and took three crowns from me."

"You were so cross about it," she said, and grinned up at him. "What else do you remember?"

Harrison's smile faded. "I remember the joy that shone out of you like sunlight when you believed yourself to be with child, and the despair that darkened your face afterward. And I could not . . ." He swallowed. "I was helpless to remove the pain of it."

That sober reminder caused Olivia to look away and pull her hand free. "You remember so much."

"I remember it all, Olivia. Every moment, because I have admired you most ardently from the moment I first saw you."

"Why did you never tell me?"

"*Tell* you?" He smiled and shook his head, brushed his knuckles against her cheek as he had longed to do a thousand times. "How could I? As you say, you are a married woman. You are above me in society, in matrimony, in every way a woman can be above a man. And I esteemed you far too much to put you in jeopardy with my feelings. Until today. Today it was quite beyond my power to resist you."

"Harrison . . . it was I who could not resist *you*," she murmured. Her eyes began to glisten with tears. "I wish . . . I wish I could steal a moment in time. I wish I could carve out a few days of happiness, all to myself, with you. Alas," she said, her gaze falling to his mouth, "that is not my lot in life. Or yours. It is imperative that what happened between us today never happen again."

But her gaze belied the words she spoke. Her gaze didn't leave his mouth, and it was heating his blood. He touched his fingers to hers, lacing them together.

"It is best for all concerned," she said, as if trying to convince herself. The tip of her tongue darted out to wet her lower lip, and Harrison's pulse began to throb. It was a supreme act of self-control to keep his hands from her.

"We must endeavor to put this behind us," she said. "We *must*. But Harrison, I cannot live without your friendship. If I don't have that at least, I shall perish here in this drafty old house and this dark marriage. Promise me. Promise me that we shall always be friends."

A small, hairline crack snaked its way across Harrison's heart. Without question, he would always be her friend. The idea that he would never have more with her was cruelly disappointing. It felt a bit as if he'd run the race, but had fallen just short of the finish line. It was an unsatisfying request of a desire that had now been opened up to the heavens. But Olivia's expression was so earnest, he said, "Not only will I be your friend, I shall always be close. And I will always hold you in my heart, Olivia." He lifted his hand to his chest, pressed it against his breast.

"Oh dear," she said, her smile tremulous. "How can such tender words sting so? My good and loyal friend."

She was trying to climb above her feelings and put their regard for one another in its proper place, but Harrison did not want them there. He wanted her as his own. And he wondered how he would ever put down that desperate, soul-devouring want.

For her sake, however, he would. He smiled. He leaned in. And he let his lips brush her temple. He inhaled her scent, his mouth on her hair, her hand in his. He could feel the draw of her breath and the warmth of her sigh on his neck. It whispered through him, spreading tiny little vines through him, attaching to his veins, his bones.

He was loath to leave her, loath to leave this moment behind—but he let go of her hand and made himself walk away from the only woman he would ever love.

As he reached the door, Olivia said, "Harrison?"

His heart winged with foolish hope; he turned around.

"I already miss you."

It took every ounce of his strength to walk out the door, to leave her standing there. *Olivia, sweet Olivia.* He walked, and he did not look back. Yet his heart was still divining, still seeking her, and he felt the acute pain of having lost her when he'd never even had her.

CHAPTER FIFTEEN

Olivia awoke the next morning with a start. In that state between dream and consciousness, she'd felt an invisible weight bearing down on her and had bolted up, looking around the room.

There was nothing out of the ordinary. Everything looked just as it had when she'd turned in last night.

Olivia pressed her hand to her chest. What had awakened her, she realized, was extraordinary sorrow and anger and frustration with everyone and everything about her.

She missed Harrison more than she believed was possible.

She buried her face in her hands. She'd lain awake for a long time last night with an aching head, her thoughts on how Alexa had come round to this marriage, and had somehow embraced it completely, wanting even a wedding. It was heart-wrenching. Completely, utterly heart-wrenching.

But Olivia couldn't fault her for it. Her own marriage had been arranged, and she'd embraced hers as well. It's what young women in their position did—they were trained to want the best match in fortune and social standing, not the best match of affections.

Olivia lifted her head and leaned back against the pillows. At eighteen years of age, she'd been astounded when the Marquis of Everdon had expressed an interest after one supper at Everdon Court. Edward had sent Harrison Tolly to negotiate her dowry. She remembered how he'd ridden up to their home, his cloak flying out behind him. He'd leapt off his mount and swept his hat off his head and had grinned at Olivia and Alexa, who stood behind Lord Hastings on the drive.

Her stepfather had brought him into their home, had offered him tea. Harrison had sat at the small tea table, the cup looking like a toy in his large hand. "If I may, Miss Hastings," he'd said to Olivia, "Lord Carey is a fortunate man." Olivia could remember her blush of pleasure and the smile he had given her. She'd thought him handsome and charming. She'd believed Harrison was an omen, a portent of what was to come at Everdon Court. She'd believed her life was on the verge of opening like a rosebud, the petals of it stretching out, reaching for all the world had to offer.

Dear God, how naïve.

But Olivia supposed that Alexa must be feeling some of that, the promise of something new, the hope of a bright future, particularly after the emotional turmoil she'd suffered through.

And Olivia had no doubt that Alexa would have a bright and happy future with Harrison.

Just like she'd thought she would have with Edward.

"Fool," she muttered under her breath and got out of bed. She walked to the windows and pulled back the drapes, looking out into the early morning light. She tried to recall the moment or the event or even the day that marked the beginning of her disillusionment. Was it when she'd discovered Edward's thirst for whiskey? Or when she'd realized how indifferent he was toward her, even blaming her for it? Was it when he'd casually informed her that she was tedious, or when he demanded to control her, wanting to know where she was and whom she saw? Was it his utter lack of desire for her? He'd never wanted anything but to rut on her like a pig and put his seed in her, then leave.

When Olivia told her mother, Lady Hastings had begged her to be more enticing in bed. But try as she might, Olivia could never seem to entice him to anything but anger.

Was it perhaps when she'd realized that he had a mistress? Oh, how devastatingly obtuse she'd felt! They'd only been married a little over two years when they were invited to the home of the rotund Major Barrow along with a dozen couples for a long weekend of shooting. From the beginning, Olivia had felt as if there was something everyone was hiding from her. There seemed to be no end to the averted looks, or to the whispering that stopped when she entered the room. The only person who didn't seem to whisper was Mrs. Bronson, who had come with her husband, Mr. Bronson.

Olivia rather liked Mrs. Bronson. She'd been lively in conversation, speaking of the latest fashions in London, who she had dined with, and who was expected to shine in the upcoming Season. And she'd seemed very intent on Olivia.

At last, Mrs. Barrow had taken mercy on Olivia and had pulled her aside. "My dear . . . do you not understand who Mrs. Bronson *is*?"

"Who is she?" Olivia had asked innocently.

"For heaven's sake! She is a particular *friend* of your husband's."

She'd said "friend" in such a tone that Olivia had suddenly understood. She'd been humiliated. There she'd been, chatting it up with Edward's mistress all weekend while everyone had watched.

In all these years, the one person who brought any warmth into her life was Harrison. He was always ready with a smile, a wink, a jest. He was on hand to play cards with her when there was nothing to do on long winter evenings. He was there to help her plan the social evenings she and Edward had hosted, to ensure that Everdon Court was ready when members of Edward's family arrived for extended stays.

Harrison had always been there to save her.

Olivia turned away from the windows with a cluck of her tongue, annoyed with herself. She marched across the room and picked up her brush and began to rake it through her hair, wincing when it caught a tangle.

It wasn't as if Harrison had died, for heaven's sake. He was marrying her sister and he would still be very much in her life. There was no point in moping about it. Olivia had suffered through too many years to be dragged to the bottom of her despair now.

She was suffering from useless desire, from pointless mourning. She would put on her best face and she would soldier on, just as she'd always done.

How best to defeat her doldrums? A small smiled curved her lips. She would invite Miss Bernadette Shields of Harkingspur Grange and Lady Martha to Everdon Court. No one could make her laugh like Bernie. And she always included Lady Martha in her teas, for the poor dear was so shy, she'd have no society at all were it not for Olivia's invitations from time to time.

But the true reason Olivia wanted to invite the ladies to Everdon Court was because Edward could not abide them. He could not abide the company of anyone whom he hadn't himself selected for Olivia, but neither could he deny her friendship with these two particular ladies, as their fathers were influential in the shire. If Edward wanted to give the appearance of being a benevolent little king in this corner of England, he would have to allow Olivia their company.

And they, unwittingly, would help her endure the loss of Harrison. She would have Brock send a messenger to them directly after breakfast.

Mrs. Lampley sent Rue from the dowager house to the main house for fresh linens. "You cannot use so much lye, Rue," she chastised the girl with a shake of her head. "It eats the linens whole if you put in too much."

"Aye, mu'um," Rue said.

Rue was rarely out of the dowager house, as she was too fearful of being accused of doing something wrong. She ambled up the path, taking her time, happy to be in the sunlight. When she reached the kitchens of Everdon Court, no one was about. There was a plate of muffins on a wooden table, amid some pottery bowls and a sack of flour. She helped herself to a muffin.

"Rue!"

The girl was so startled she dropped the muffin. Miss Foster swept in, her apron full of eggs. "What in blazes do you think to be doing? Do you see anything on that table that invites you to help yourself?"

Rue looked at the table.

"No, you do not," Miss Foster answered for her. "Pick it up."

Rue bent down and scooped up the muffin. She didn't know what to do with it and stuffed it in the pocket of her apron.

"Do not think to come into *my* kitchen and do as you please! That may be the way of Miss Lampley's kitchen, but it will not be tolerated here!" Still holding the corners of her apron, Miss Foster leaned across the table, pinning Rue with a look. "Those muffins happen to be for Lady Carey. She is partial to them." She leaned back and began to put her eggs in a bowl. "I expect her appetite will be increasing very soon, if you take my meaning."

"Hungry, is she?" Rue asked through a mouth full of muffin.

"Oh, she's hungry, all right," Miss Foster said, and chuckled. "Hungry enough for two."

"I am hungry like that when I forget to break my fast. By the afternoon, I think I might faint away."

Miss Foster sighed impatiently. "Not because she forgot to eat, you little simpleton. She is eating for *two*."

Rue blinked. That was precisely what she meant. Sometimes she felt as if she ate enough to feed two people.

Miss Foster clucked her tongue. "A *baby*," she whispered, and smiled broadly. "Have a care that you don't repeat that to anyone, do you hear? The marquis is away and it wouldn't do to have that sort of talk going round."

Rue frowned a little. She had heard Miss Lampley say that the marchioness was barren. Perhaps she'd meant something else entirely.

"Do you intend to stand about all day? What do you want?"

"Linens," Rue said.

"Linens! Do I look as if I have a key to the linen closet? Go and find Mrs. Perry and stay out of my kitchen."

It was a half hour before Rue returned to the dowager house, having taken her sweet time wending along the servant's path back to the dowager house. When she stepped into the foyer, she almost collided with Mrs. Lampley. "Oh! Beg your pardon," she said, dipping a curtsy.

"What are you curtsying to me for?" Mrs. Lampley said, and took the linens from Rue's hands. "Chamber pots need emptying. What is that?"

"What?" Rue asked.

Mrs. Lampley nodded her gray head at Rue's lap. Rue looked down; the rest of her muffin had been smashed and had stained her apron pocket. "I'm sorry!" she cried as Mrs. Lampley frowned at the stain. "How was I to know her ladyship needed a muffin to feed two people!"

"What? What are you prattling about?"

"Miss Foster said the muffins were for her ladyship, for she was eating for two, and I wasn't to have one."

Mrs. Lampley blinked. And then a smile slowly lit her face. "Well, well, well."

CHAPTER SIXTEEN

Alexa was too nauseated to eat when she awoke and decided instead that she needed some fresh air. She walked down to the dowager house to collect a few things, since she had no intention of staying there while Edward was away.

The day was beginning to turn gray and smelled of more rain, which didn't please her. The journey to Scotland would be difficult enough without bumping about in a coach on rutted roads. She put her hand to her abdomen, thinking of the child she carried.

Perhaps she might persuade Harrison to wait a few more days.

At the dowager house, she stood on the front steps and knocked the mud from her boots. As she did, a messenger rode into the small circular drive. Alexa paused and looked curiously at him. "G'day, miss. I've a letter for Mr. Tolly," he said.

"Wait here," she said, and walked inside.

Rue and Mrs. Lampley emerged from the drawing room when Alexa called. Mrs. Lampley bobbed her head and quickly went the other way, her arm full of linens. Rue, bless her, looked as she had every time Alexa had seen her—as if she didn't know what she was to do with herself. She stared wide-eyed at Alexa. "Oh!" she said. "It's you, miss."

If Alexa was to be mistress of this house, she intended to make a few changes, beginning with a butler or a footman—someone who knew how to properly handle people coming and going, and wasn't forever surprised by it. "There is a messenger outside with a letter for Mr. Tolly," Alexa said. "Will you fetch him?"

"A messenger!" Rue cried, apparently delighted by the news. "I'm to give the messengers coin when they come," she added, and hurried to a small alcove just off the entry. Not noticing the small footstool at her feet, she stretched up to the tips of her toes, her hand scarcely reaching a bowl on the top shelf. She managed to get two fingers in the bowl and then held the coin up triumphantly to Alexa on her way to the door.

"I have your coin, sir!" Rue called out proudly to the messenger, and went out.

Alexa rolled her eyes. She untied her bonnet and set it aside, and was removing her cloak when Rue bounded back, holding the letter aloft.

"Where is Mr. Tolly this morning?" Alexa asked.

"I think he's gone off already," Rue said, frowning

a little as she thought it over. "But I'm not to say he's gone for a pint."

"A pint! Rue, for heaven's sake!" Harry said, appearing on the stairs above them in his shirtsleeves and waistcoat. He started down. "I've not gone off, and neither have I gone for a pint." He smiled at Alexa as he reached the ground floor. "Good morning."

"Good morning, sir," Alexa said, and forced herself to smile sunnily.

Harry looked at Rue again, eyeing the letter. "What have you got there?"

"A letter! A messenger brung it," Rue said. "I give him the coin, just as you said."

"Just as I said, eh? Then we must mark this day on the calendar, Rue. That is splendid news," Harry said, and held his hand out for the letter.

A beaming Rue placed it in his hand.

"Would you like some tea?" Harry asked Alexa. "Seems rather damp out."

"Terribly damp," she said. "Yes, thank you."

"Am I to fetch the tea, then?" Rue asked.

"You are to fetch the tea," Harrison said, and gave Alexa a small shake of his head as Rue scampered off. "Come into the study."

Alexa followed him into the study and accepted his offer to sit in one of the chairs at the hearth. "Excuse me a moment, if you will," he said politely, and broke the seal on the letter.

Alexa watched him read it, a slight frown of concentration on his brow. His hair looked as if he'd combed it back with his fingers, and his trousers—buckskins— fit him very well, indeed. He was quite handsome, really; well built and strong, and not too thin.

Moreover, he had been polite and kind to her in spite of all the difficulties. Perhaps, Alexa mused, she had made the best decision after all. Perhaps she might really come to love him.

She glanced around at the room as he read. It was sparsely furnished, like the rest of the house, and there were so many books! They were stacked on his desk and on the table between the two chairs. There was a wall of bookcases, too, stuffed full of them. She couldn't imagine the desire to own as many books as this, or the expense of obtaining them. It seemed that one or two would be enough. An atlas. A Bible, of course. Perhaps an historical or scientific book. What more was necessary?

Harry sighed heavily and Alexa turned her head as he tossed the letter onto his desk. "Is something wrong?"

"No." He stared at the large window a moment, his jaw clenching and unclenching. Then he seemed to remember that she was there and smiled once again. "I hope you rested well," he said as he took the chair beside her.

"I did, thank you."

He absently drummed his fingers on one knee, clearly distracted. "I think it shall rain."

Lord! Is this what they would speak of in each other's company? The weather? How rested they were? "Is everything all right?" Alexa asked.

"What?" he asked. "Yes, everything is fine." His fingers stopped drumming. "And with you, as well?"

"Fine," she said, feeling exasperated now.

"And how does the day find Lady Carey?" he asked.

"I did not go down for breakfast. I was feeling a bit ill."

Harry's gaze flicked to her abdomen a moment. "Recovered now?"

"Quite."

"Very good," he said, and glanced at the fireplace once again.

"I think you are right. I think rain is coming," Alexa said, watching him closely. "And I was thinking that perhaps we might wait until the rain has passed before we undertake a long trip."

Harry nodded, but then glanced at Alexa. "Pardon?"

"It is a long way to Gretna Green," she said.

"Having second thoughts?" he asked quietly.

"Not at all," she quickly assured him. "But I find that I do not travel as well as I have in the past." She put her hand to her abdomen.

He nodded and stood up. "I should think the ability to travel will only become more difficult for you. But I will consider it. You must not fret, Alexa. All will be well."

She couldn't imagine why he thought so. The situation was a terrible mess. She watched him walk to the desk, pick up the letter again, glance at it, then toss it down again.

"Will all be well with your Lady X?" Alexa asked.

That brought his head around. "I beg your pardon?"

"Lady X," Alexa said again. "You seem rather distracted, and I thought perhaps that *you* are having second thoughts."

His face darkened, and Alexa flushed. She had overstepped her bounds. Again. And unintentionally. "Perhaps it would ease you to know that I have no expectations," she said, in a feeble attempt to smooth over her gaffe.

That seemed to amuse him somewhat, judging by his softly wry smile.

A loud crash of glass and metal startled them both. "Oh *lud*!" they heard Rue exclaim.

"What in blazes is it now?" he said. "I'll be back when I have assured myself that it was only a tea service and that the house is still standing." He walked determinedly out the door.

Alexa stayed in her seat a moment. Things seemed so strained between them. How on earth would she ever find her way with him? She sighed and leaned back. Her gaze fell to the open letter on his desk. Outside, in the hall, she could hear him admonishing Rue to be careful, that she might cut herself.

Alexa rose and strolled toward the desk. She glanced surreptitiously at the open letter. The handwriting looked to be that of a woman's. She cocked her head and glanced at the signature. *Lady Eberlin.*

It was her! This was his Lady X.

Someone else had joined the chorus of voices outside; she could hear Harry's calm, deep voice as two women argued over each other. With a furtive glance over her shoulder, Alexa leaned over the desk and scanned the letter.

And then she read it a second time.

When she walked to the window and blinked out at the gray day, she scarcely saw a thing. Her mind was whirling.

Good heavens. She was on the verge of marrying a man who was the legitimate heir to the Ashwood estate in Sussex, and, if Lady Eberlin could be believed, entitled to the title of earl.

Which meant she would be a countess. At the very least, an heiress.

Suddenly, she saw how she might endure her marriage to Harry. Suddenly, everything seemed possible.

CHAPTER SEVENTEEN

It seemed to Harrison that everything that could go wrong in the next few days did. Wool that had been sheared and cleaned for market had been lost in transit. A bridge over a small river was lost in flooding. Harrison received notice that Lord Westhorpe owed arrears of more than two thousand pounds. And on top of it all, he was the only one who could make all the discreet arrangements that were necessary for the trip to Gretna Green.

As a result, Harrison did not see Olivia. She kept to the main house, and he kept to his post. While he believed that was the only way he could carry on, it was agonizing.

Visions of her danced around in his thoughts, making concentration impossible. Every woman's voice, every feminine laugh, caused his heart to leap with the hope that it was her. He was disappointed over and over again. When he received the letter from Lady

Eberlin—formerly Lady Ashwood—urging him to take his rightful place as heir to Ashwood, Harrison had toyed with the fantasy of stealing Olivia away and retreating there.

It was a ridiculous thought, he knew—they could not hide away at Ashwood. He was in love with a married woman, and she was married to a very powerful man. And then there was Alexa. He could not leave the foolish girl to her own devices. And he could not leave her child to suffer the same sort of upbringing he'd suffered.

But as curious as he was about Ashwood, Harrison had no intention of taking Alexa there. He had no intention of leaving Everdon Court. He'd never sleep again if he abandoned Olivia here with the marquis.

He'd never sleep again if he could not see her, every day. He tried to imagine himself at Ashwood, existing without her. It was impossible to do, and after two days of these thoughts he felt quite unlike himself. He longed to see Olivia, but the only woman he saw was Alexa.

It appeared as if Alexa had rounded an emotional corner. As if she'd made her decision and was now settling into her future role as Harrison's wife. She spent several hours at the dowager house, was polite and solicitous to him, and more than once, she offered to help him in any way that she could.

There was another, more subtle change in her that Harrison couldn't help but notice, and it was one he did not care to face. Alexa's smile was different than it had been; it was softer, more alluring. One might even say seductive.

And there were the casual, discreet little touches.

The first time Alexa had touched him, Harrison had instantly stiffened. She had smiled, had let her hand slide off his arm, and when she'd taken her leave, unwelcome images of what was to come began to swirl in Harrison's mind. Alexa Hastings was a comely young woman, yet Harrison could feel nothing amorous for her.

Of course he'd considered that if he wed Alexa, he would need to treat her as a husband ought to treat a wife. In all respects. Including the marital bed. Harrison intended to honor the marital vows he would take . . . but he hoped for a bit of time. A few months. Perhaps a few years.

He had to somehow carve Olivia out of his heart first. Was that asking so much? Did he not deserve at least a few weeks for making this sacrifice? Given Alexa's attention to him, he guessed that she would think it was too much to ask, and it was making him unusually cross.

The reality of his colossal mistake would come crashing down on him on the morrow, when he planned to leave for Scotland if the weather held. It had rained all week, but the sun had made a weak appearance yesterday. Alexa was right in that the rain had made the roads difficult and slow to travel, but

Harrison was feeling anxious. He had only three days to address the problem of Alexa; any more than that would leave the estate management lacking in the marquis's absence.

And for Olivia's sake, he had to have this settled and be back at his post before the marquis returned, for his lordship would be furious if he found Harrison gone and Olivia's sister the cause of it.

Unfortunately, today had dawned with gray and heavy skies. But if the rain held off, Harrison planned that he and Alexa would leave at dawn.

That afternoon, when Harrison went up to the main house to record the rents, he noticed a carriage from Harkingspur Grange in the drive.

In the foyer, he stripped off his wet hat and cloak and handed them to the butler. "Thank you, Brock," he said. "I am expecting Mr. Fortaine. Best not to allow him in the front door, as he has been shearing sheep in the rain and has a peculiar smell about him. Nor can I vouch for the sanctity of his boots."

"Yes, Mr. Tolly."

"Who has come to call?" he asked curiously.

"Miss Shields and Lady Martha," Brock said.

Harrison walked down the corridor that led to the offices at the corner of the southern wing. The door to the salon was open; he could hear the ladies laughing as he neared. He saw them as he walked past, gathered around a card table. Alexa's back was to the door, seated across from Lady Martha. Olivia and Miss

Shields sat on either side of her. Olivia was sitting on the edge of her chair, her gaze fixed on Miss Shields, who apparently was in the middle of a tale.

"On my word," Harrison heard the jovial young woman say as he walked past, "the very moment Lady Rollingoke spotted Mr. Carver entering the room, she went after him like a fat little goose after bread crumbs."

Alexa laughed gaily.

"Mr. Tolly?"

Olivia's voice caught him off guard; Harrison jerked around. She was leaning out the door of the salon.

"Olivia!" he heard Miss Shields call. "I've not yet told you what Mr. Carver said to her inquiries."

"One moment, if you please, Bernie," Olivia said, and stepped out of the salon, walking quickly to where Harrison stood. Her eyes were full of longing; he could feel the draw in his own heart. "Alexa informs me you intend to leave on the morrow?" she whispered.

Was it his imagination, or did he hear a world of suffering in her voice?

"If the rain holds off," he admitted.

"Oh. When will you return?"

He clenched his jaw and took her in, head to toe. "In three days."

Olivia's lashes fluttered as if she'd been struck. But she lifted her head and smiled. "That shall give me just enough time to find a proper wedding gift for you."

"Olivia—"

"Mr. Tolly, I am quite at ease," she said. "Long ago, I learned the art of accepting things as they are."

"Then perhaps you might teach the skill to me, for I have not mastered it, try as I might."

"It's really quite simple. You mourn. And then you remind yourself to be grateful for what you have, and that it could be worse. Far worse."

"*Could* it be worse?" he asked low.

Pain glimmered in her eyes, but she kept smiling. "Yes, it could be worse. Come now, Mr. Tolly, you've always been so ready with a smile."

Mr. Tolly. She had retreated from him. "One cannot look at you and not smile, Lady Carey," he said, and he smiled, for her.

But there is so much left unsaid. I love you. I have always loved you. I will always love you.

"I should like to see you off, but . . ." She shrugged lightly. "So I shall wish you Godspeed." She turned away.

Harrison couldn't let her go like that. He impulsively caught her fingers with his. It was an infinitesimal amount of what he needed from her, but it was all he would risk.

Olivia didn't turn her head. But she wrapped her fingers around his and squeezed them tightly, then let go and walked on, her hips softly swaying, her head high.

Harrison stood alone in the corridor, the touch burning his fingers, spreading the ungodly heat of anger, frustration, and sheer longing through him.

"Am I right, Olivia?" he heard Alexa ask as she entered the room.

"About what, darling?" Olivia said, her voice clear and bright.

Harrison turned the other way and walked on to the office, his heart constricting tighter and tighter, until he wished it would disappear altogether.

Olivia had no idea what she'd intended when she'd dashed out in the hallway to Harrison—to simply look at him, she supposed. To see his eyes, to see his smile, which had been woefully lacking this afternoon. She had not intended to say what she had. Not until she'd seen the hunger in his eyes, the same hunger that was eating her from the inside out, and she had realized with excruciating clarity that she had to stop wanting him. For both their sakes.

It was impossible to stop wanting him, perhaps even more so now that Alexa had had such a miraculous change of heart. Her sister was suddenly chatting about the wedding and her marriage as if Harrison had courted her as any suitor would, then had offered for her hand. And the more Alexa came to accept her fate, the more Olivia felt stifled by hers. The bird in the little cage continued to grow, and she strained against the bars.

"Aren't you going to play your card, Olivia?" Bernie asked.

Startled out of her thoughts, Olivia glanced at the table. She played her card.

"Oh dear," Bernie said. "That won't do us a bit of good, will it?"

Olivia looked at the card and instantly realized her mistake.

"How extraordinary," Lady Martha said as she picked up the discarded cards. "Miss Hastings and I win again."

"Olivia, I have never known you to play so poorly," Bernie said, eyeing her shrewdly. "Have you something on your mind? You must tell us what it is, for the rain has washed away all our diversions."

Warmth filled Olivia's face. Was she so obvious?

"Don't be shy, Livi," Alexa said with a sweet smile. "I hardly care if the whole world knows it."

Olivia blinked.

Alexa's smile brightened. "Shall I tell them, then?"

Now Olivia's heart seized. She had said they would plant a seed. Surely Alexa did not intend to tell them—

"I am to be wed," she said happily, and turned her smile to Bernie and Lady Martha.

"Alexa!" Olivia cried.

Lady Martha looked stunned, but Bernie cried out with delight. "Miss Hastings!" She grabbed Alexa's hand, squeezing it. "How could you two possibly keep this from me? Who? Who has been so fortunate as to win your hand in marriage?"

"It is really the most amazing thing," Alexa said happily. "When I returned from Spain I had only one thing in mind, and that was to see my sister."

Oh dear God.

"But I met someone else here, and I must tell you that it was love at first sight. Well, second or third sight, really, as I had met him briefly before. But I had not had occasion to speak to him, and when I did, I was smitten."

"Do not say it is Mr. Broadbent," Lady Martha said, looking very ill at ease.

"No, no," Bernie asked excitedly. "It is Baron Peterman's son, is it not, Miss Hastings?"

"No," Alexa said, and grinned. "It is . . . Mr. Tolly."

Lady Martha gasped. "Mr. Tolly!" she repeated, sounding shocked.

Miss Shields squealed with delight. "Mr. Tolly! Oh, I cannot begin to say how that gladdens my heart! I have long admired him, in truth. Such a handsome, thoughtful man! And generous to a fault. Do you know that he has been paying the rent for Mr. Gaston for the last two years?"

"What?" Olivia asked. She'd never heard of this.

"It's quite true. I am certain he is far too modest to speak of it, but I heard of it from Mrs. White. Mr. Gaston badly damaged his arm thrashing wheat and now he is quite unable to do it. When he appealed to Mr. Tolly for a bit of time until he could find someone to take his croft, Mr. Tolly wouldn't hear of it. 'What will you do with your children, sir,'" Bernie said, acting as if she were Harrison. "'Go and be a good father to your children and work as best you can, and I shall see to it that your rent is paid.'"

"You don't mean it," Alexa said.

"I do! Everyone at the church knows it. He is universally adored, Miss Hastings. You have come into good fortune with this match."

Alexa suddenly laughed. "Greater than you know."

"And when are the nuptials to be held?" Bernie said. "When it is warmer, I should hope. A wedding breakfast is so dreary in the wet spring."

"Oh," Alexa said. She looked at Olivia, who merely shrugged. Let Alexa talk her way out of this. "Well," she said carefully, "Mr. Tolly and I thought we might just . . . just dash off and wed."

Bernie's mouth gaped. Lady Martha looked as if she would be ill.

Olivia sighed. It was difficult to imagine how Alexa could make this any worse, but she'd just done it. "What Alexa means," she said calmly, "is that we cannot be certain when my husband will return, and it doesn't seem proper that they reside in such close proximity—"

"Of course, of course," Bernie said. "I do see your point. This spring, sometime, then?"

"Miss Peugeot is marrying this spring," Lady Martha said, her point lost on Olivia.

"We've not decided as yet," Alexa said, and shifted a little in her seat.

Olivia very much wanted to kick her in both shins for saying anything. The girl never thought before she opened her silly mouth! "But naturally you shall both be among the first to hear of it," Olivia said. "Shall we play another round before I ring for tea?"

"Please," Alexa said, and picked up the cards to shuffle them.

"April is a lovely time of year," Bernie remarked. "When I marry, I should like a wedding in April. Your wedding was lovely, Olivia, but it was February, and the day was dreadfully cold and gray." She shivered.

"Yes, wasn't it," Olivia replied. "Cold as ice."

"Madam." Brock had entered the salon and bent his head to whisper, "Pardon, but his lordship has arrived."

That announcement stunned her—Olivia wasn't expecting Edward for at least another week. "Here? Now?" she whispered.

"Yes, mu'um. He and his brother and some other gentlemen have just ridden into the drive."

"What is it, Livi?" Alexa asked.

"Ah . . ." She forced a smile. "It would seem my husband has returned a little earlier than I thought."

"Because he cannot bear to be away from you," Bernie said blithely.

Olivia stood up. *So soon!* Alexa looked just as stunned; she stood, too. "I suppose we ought to . . . ?"

"We should," Olivia agreed.

"But this is splendid news, Miss Hastings!" Bernie crowed. "Now that he has come back, there is no need to rush! You may wait until the weather has warmed and treat your family to a lovely spring wedding."

Olivia's knees quaked a little at the thought of Bernie saying something like that to Edward. He would explode with rage. But at the moment, her most pressing issue was greeting him and his guests, for if she were not on hand to do so, she would pay for it later.

"Please excuse me," she said as lightly as she could and swept out of the room, unthinkingly rubbing her palms on her skirts.

CHAPTER EIGHTEEN
✤

Olivia stepped outside just in time to see Edward slide off his saddle and land on one knee beside his horse. He laughed as a footman rushed to help him up, then pushed the young man away before staggering up to his feet.

"Have a care you do not break your bloody leg," his younger brother, David, Lord Westhorpe, said. The two gentlemen in their company laughed. Olivia had met them before: Lords Fennick and Keddington.

A laughing Keddington took Edward's arm and draped it around his shoulders, then helped him to walk up the steps.

"There she is, my beautiful wife," Edward slurred as they had tromped past. "To look at her, one would believe I am a fortunate man."

"You *are* a fortunate man," Keddington said.

"Olivia, darling," David said, walking up the steps, his arms open. Olivia smiled at him; he wrapped his arms around her in a warm embrace and kissed her cheek. "Beautiful as ever, love. How it gladdens my heart to see you." He kissed her cheek again, then linked his arm through hers. "What news have you? I've heard your sister has come back from Spain," he said as he led her into the foyer. Edward and his friends had left mud across the clean tiled floors of the entry.

"She has, indeed," Olivia said.

"Tell me," David began, but a commotion in the corridor caught his attention. The gentlemen had apparently encountered the ladies. Olivia could hear them begging the ladies to stay and entertain the weary travelers.

As Olivia and David entered the corridor, she saw Alexa extracting Bernie's hand from Fennick's grip. "Please do allow Miss Shields and Lady Martha to take their leave," she said with a sweet smile. "Their families cannot spare them another moment." She fairly pushed Bernie along down the hallway, who was enjoying the attentions of the gentlemen, in spite of their drunken revelry.

The one person who did not seem to find her charming was Edward, who glowered like a sullen child, leaning up against the wall as he waited for his friends to return their attention to him.

"Miss Hastings, how good to see you again," David said, stepping away from Olivia to greet Alexa. Olivia took the opportunity to escort Bernie and Lady Martha to the foyer.

"You will have your hands full, will you not?" Bernie asked gaily as she accepted her cloak from a footman.

"I always do," Olivia said.

The footman opened the door and Olivia was dismayed to see the rain had begun again.

"You really must convince your sister to wait to marry until the weather improves," Bernie said. "It's a bad omen for it to rain on a wedding day."

Olivia's heart began to beat in her chest. "I will do my best. Thank you for coming!" she said cheerily, hoping to hasten her friends' exit before they said something to Edward.

When she had seen them into the carriage, she released a sigh of relief, and hurried back to the hallway. David and Alexa were standing there, Alexa with her back to the wall, David leaning in as if imparting a great secret.

"David!" Edward bellowed from within the salon. "Where are you?"

"Coming!" David said something to Alexa that caused her to laugh.

Edward suddenly appeared at the door of the salon, his gaze hardening as he saw what kept David.

"Miss Hastings, will you join us in the salon?" David asked as he started after Edward.

"Perhaps another time," Alexa said. "I've a beastly headache and must retire for now."

"A pity," David said, his smile charming. "I shall console myself with your lovely sister." He held out his hand to Olivia, who quickly gave him hers, lest Alexa change her mind.

Aware that Edward was glowering at them both, Olivia said softly, "Go to the dowager house and stay there. I will come later."

Alexa glanced at Edward, then walked quickly down the hallway.

Olivia did not look at her husband, but allowed David to drag her into the salon, where Lords Fennick and Keddington had managed to find the whiskey.

Edward followed them, accepting a glass of whiskey from Fennick. He looked at Olivia, his gaze hard. "Perhaps you might be more comfortable in your sitting room," he said.

"Her sitting room!" David laughed. "You will deprive me of the pleasure of her company? You know my high regard for your wife, Edward."

"You may reacquaint yourself with her over supper."

"Yes, of course," Olivia said. "Welcome home, my lord," she said, and left the room.

The day didn't improve as the rain turned into a deluge. Olivia could hear the men's boisterous laughter echoing through the house, Edward's voice louder than them all.

When Olivia joined the gentlemen for supper, her mood was grim. The evening was exactly as she might have imagined: her, alone, in the company of four gentlemen who had managed to while away an entire afternoon with billiards and whiskey. In the course of it, they'd drowned their table manners. They delighted in uproarious laughter over the most trivial matters.

Edward was the worst. When he entered the dining room, he'd cast his arms wide. "Ah, my darling wife." He'd put his arms around her and kissed her mouth hard, much to the delight of the others. When he lifted his head, it was a miracle that Olivia managed to keep from dragging her hand across her mouth to wipe the kiss from her lips.

"Did I tell you that David has missed you?" Edward asked loudly as he walked a bit unevenly to his seat. He waved away the footman who was there to pull out his chair. "He insisted on coming to Everdon Court just to see you."

"As I recall, *you* insisted that I come," David said as he helped Olivia into her seat. "You specifically threatened my stipend," he added, and fell into a chair next to Olivia. "He tortures me, Olivia. If it were not for you, I'd not abide him."

Olivia smiled.

David put his hand on his chin and smiled up at her. "How lovely you are, my dear. I've always thought you the handsomest of women. And with such a sunny disposition, as well. How fortunate that I may enjoy the favor of your smile and your conversation during my meal."

"You are always so very flattering, my lord," Olivia said. "One cannot help but wonder if you come by that talent naturally, or if you practice it in various dining rooms and salons in London."

"So fair, and yet so skeptical."

"I have known you several years," she said with a slight wink.

David laughed and brought her hand to his lips, kissing her knuckles. "I do adore you, Olivia."

"Where is your sister?" Edward demanded as he lifted his wineglass to be filled.

"Yes, where is that comely sister of yours?" David asked, looking around the room.

"She has taken to her bed with a headache," Olivia said, and Edward snorted.

"And Tolly?" David asked. "Where has our man Tolly gotten off to?"

"What are you waiting for?" Edward barked at one of the footmen, who stood patiently at his side, waiting for him to approve the wine. "Fill the glasses, man!"

The footman hurried to do so.

"I am in deep despair, Olivia," David said with big, doleful eyes. "My brother tells me I have entered dun territory and threatens my stipend. But I have every confidence Mr. Tolly will set it all to rights."

"You should learn to keep your coin in your pockets instead of spreading it among the light-skirts of London," Edward scoffed.

"Do you blame me?" David asked cheerfully. "I haven't the luxury of having a comely wife to occupy my bed."

Olivia flushed.

David chuckled and winked at her.

"Fennick, what of Basingham? What's this I hear of his debts?" Edward asked, and lifted his wineglass to his lips, drinking as if it were water.

Olivia glanced to the window as the men talked. She could hear the rain falling in great swaths, soaking Everdon Court and everything around it. She pictured the house floating down the valley toward the sea, pictured herself on the roof, jumping onto a rock just as the house was flushed out into the sea. And she imagined watching the whole thing sink, whiskey bottles popping up to the surface when the house had gone down.

After a meal that seemed to stretch on forever, port was at last served. It was a wonder to Olivia that Edward could manage to remain seated.

She was debating how and when to make her escape when David leaned over to her. "What are you thinking?"

Olivia looked at his dancing eyes. "I am thinking that you are all quite foxed," she whispered back.

He laughed and lifted his glass in a mock toast. "There is nothing to be done for it, I fear. When four men are confined to the house because of rain, they cannot help but fill their cups and think of life."

She laughed. "What a curious thing to think about when one is filling one's cup."

"Tell me something," he said, planting his arms

on the table. "Has your sister any suitors? Anyone in particular that she esteems? She is handsome, and my brother informs me I am in need of a wife. Come now, tell me. Has she set her sights on anyone in particular?"

Oh dear God, this the last thing Olivia could endure. "I cannot rightly say."

"You can," David said, touching her arm. "You are her sister. What do you think? Would she find a man in dire financial straits appealing?" He laughed at his jest.

"I don't know," Olivia said, laughing too. "But in truth, I think there is someone she esteems. She's been quite coy about it, really, but I rather think so."

David's eyes narrowed suspiciously. "I am an earl and I come from a distinguished family. Is her interest in someone with a better position than that?"

"I cannot say," Olivia said, "but I shall inquire."

"That is all I ask," he said. "You know me well, Olivia. We are good friends, you and I. You know that I would not enter into matrimony with someone who is not comely, or whom I cannot speak to. I can speak to you. You've always been very frank. I want someone like you to be my wife." He grinned, as if that should please her beyond measure. "You will help me, won't you?"

"If I can," Olivia said.

Apparently satisfied with that, David leaned back in his chair. "Cards, gentlemen," he said loudly. "Shall we have a round or two?"

"I thought you'd never ask," Fennick said.

Olivia's gaze happened to meet Edward's.

He was glaring at her, which was her cue to leave. She stood from her chair, nodding to the footman, who hurried to pull it back. "Gentlemen, if you will excuse me, I will leave you to your cheroots and your cards."

The men all stood with varying levels of success as Olivia quit the room, her gaze straight ahead.

In her suite, Olivia removed her jewelry and headpiece, debating if she would even mention David's interest to Alexa. She was working the stubborn clasp of her bracelet when the door opened and Edward stumbled in.

Olivia gasped with surprise; then braced herself, prepared for anything. Prepared for the worst.

Edward steadied himself on a chair; his gaze raked over her. He very clumsily began to tug at the knot of his neck cloth. "Lady Carey," he said, slurring her name slightly, "I cannot discern from your expression if you are pleased to see your husband or not."

"Nor can I tell from your expression if you are pleased to see me," she said warily.

"Me?" His hold on the chair slipped; he caught himself again. "I cannot imagine what you mean. I am always happy to see you, Olivia. And I am always hopeful that you will become the wife I deserve."

Olivia's blood instantly ran cold.

"You came quite close to it this evening, I must say," he added as he gave up the untying of his neck

cloth and concentrated on making his way to her bed.
"A more charming hostess I could not ask for." He fell
onto his back on her bed, hitching himself up on to the
pillows and crossing his feet at the ankles. He smiled
at her and patted the bed beside him. "Come here, my
love."

No, no, not this, not now.

"Why do you hesitate?" he asked coolly.

Olivia swallowed down a swell of revulsion and
walked across the room. She sat carefully on the bed
next to him.

Edward stroked her arm. His glassy-eyed look told
her that he was terribly inebriated. She just wanted it
over with. The sooner he'd attempted what he'd come
for and grew frustrated with his inability, the sooner
he would leave.

"I saw a different side of you tonight," he said
thickly. "Kind. Gracious. It made me wonder what I
must do to enjoy that lovely countenance at my table
every day. *Hmmm?*" he asked, and wrapped his fingers
around her forearm.

Perhaps if he did not strike her, or take her without
her consent, she might feel more inclined to smile at him.

"Have you no thoughts, precious?"

Precious? The word, spoken with his port-soaked
breath, made her nauseous. "Perhaps kindness is
reciprocated."

He squinted at her, and his head lolled to one side.
"Am I not kind?"

She looked away from him, unwilling to have this ridiculous conversation.

"So *that* is my failing as a husband," he said, and chuckled as he clumsily righted himself once more. "I have not been kind!" The mattress sagged as he moved closer to her, propping himself up on one elbow. "I vow to be kinder," he said, and pulled a hairpin from her coif. One thick tress tumbled down. "I shall be as kind as a man can be to a wife. The kindest man of all." He pulled another pin free, and more hair tumbled down.

Olivia braced herself for what was to come. She'd taught herself that if she would relax, the discomfort was not as great.

"I will . . . *lavish*," he said, searching for the word. "Yes, lavish my attention on you, wife. Is that what you want?" he asked, and with an arm around her shoulders, he dragged her down onto her back.

Olivia lay on her back, staring up at the ceiling. Edward touched his finger to the mark on her lip. It had almost disappeared in his absence. "*That* was not very kind, was it?"

"No."

"I should not have done it," he said, and stroked her cheek. "I am sorry, Olivia. Truly sorry for it. But neither should you provoke me."

She bristled at the notion that she had somehow provoked him. She was always careful *not* to provoke him. But Edward was smiling magnanimously, as if he'd just shown her the kindness he had spoken of, and Olivia could not let it pass. "Does that include my breathing?" she asked simply.

His nostrils flared. But his smile remained. "Dearest Olivia," he sighed, and kissed her cheek. He smelled as if he'd bathed in port and sweat. "My foolish little wife," he said, and kissed her lips. His mouth was nauseatingly sticky and warm.

"I will be kind and gentle with you, my love . . . unless you find my brother more to your liking? Say the word, and I shall invite him into your bed."

Every fiber in Olivia tensed. "What nonsense is this?"

"Would you like David to put his cock inside you?"

Olivia cried out and instantly tried to roll away from him, but Edward moved surprisingly fast for being as drunk as he was, pinning her half with his body and half with one arm. "Do you think David would be kinder than *me*?"

"Stop this, Edward!" she cried, and shoved against him.

"Do you know, can you guess, how humiliating it was for me to watch you smile at *him*? And speak to *him* as if you share a secret?"

She shoved him again, and Edward fell onto his side. "He is your brother! Therefore, he is a brother to me," she said angrily. "How dare you suggest anything so vile!"

"Do not lie to me, Olivia," he said, and grabbed her around the waist, flipping her on to her belly. "I cannot bear to look at you," he muttered, and started to paw for the hem of her gown.

Something burst in Olivia; she reared up and hit him hard in the ear with her elbow. Edward cried out in pain and let go of her to grab his ear. She twisted about and shoved him as hard as she could.

Too close to the edge of the bed, Edward toppled off, hitting his head on the nightstand.

Olivia cried out and leapt to her feet. She leaned over him, afraid to touch him. Had she *killed* him? She knelt down, lifted her hand to touch his neck—

Edward suddenly moaned and put his hand to his head. "Bloody hell," he muttered, and rolled onto his side.

Olivia clambered to her feet and fled her suite. In the hallway, she looked wildly about. She dared not run toward the main staircase—she had no idea where his guests were. She ran for the servant stairs.

There were no candles lit, so using her hands, Olivia felt her way down to the ground floor, her steps soundless on the carpet runner.

On the ground floor she paused to catch her breath, pressing her hand to her heart to contain its wild beating. She strained to hear any sound that would indicate Edward was coming after her, but could hear nothing.

It was dark in the hallway; she slowly started walking. She would walk the full length of the house to the library and sit on the couch there until she could think what to do next. She could hear the gentlemen laughing and chatting in the small salon, the clink of glasses, the smell of tobacco . . . and what sounded like snoring.

Olivia slowed her step and quickly pulled down the last of her hair from the chignon she'd worn earlier; she then wrapped one long tress around the rest to make a tail, which she draped over her shoulder. She took several deep breaths to slow her heart. When she was as calm as she could be, given the circumstances, she continued down the hall, intending to dart past the small salon without being noticed. But as she moved, she heard Harrison's voice.

That stopped her mid-stride.

"For the love of God," she heard David say. "The game is impossible with three. Tolly, go and fetch the marquis so that we might have a fourth and finish the game."

"I hardly think he'll be any help," Keddington said laughingly. "He could scarcely hold his hand as it was."

Olivia stepped forward and peeked into the salon. David, Keddington, and Harrison were seated at the gaming table. Lord Fennick was sprawled on the settee, one arm dangling off, and he was snoring.

Olivia suddenly had an idea. She'd take Edward's place. If he awoke, she would say she'd been here. She'd make him think the whole thing was a drunken dream. She stepped into the room.

Harrison glanced up, and his eyes sparked when he saw her. One brow rose in silent question. There was no place she felt safer than near him, and Olivia moved forward, clearing her throat.

David and Keddington twisted about; Keddington clumsily gained his feet and looked sheepishly at Fennick.

"Good evening, sirs." She shifted her gaze to Fennick.

David had managed his feet by this time and laughed. "You must not mind him."

Olivia nodded. "What are you playing?"

"Commerce," David said. "A tedious game with only three players. Will you be a love and go and fetch that foxed brother of mine?"

Olivia smiled and clasped her hands behind her back as she eyed the coins stacked at their elbows. "I hardly think I could rouse him if I tried."

"If I may, my lord," Harrison said without looking up from his cards, "Lady Carey is quite an expert player."

"Well now," David said, eyeing Olivia. "Have you any stakes, Lady Carey?"

She held up her arm, from which the diamond bracelet with the stubborn clasp still dangled. "I do."

Keddington looked surprised; Harrison laughed.

"You won't mind partnering with your steward, will you?" David asked.

Olivia smiled at Harrison. "I cannot think of anyone I would rather partner with," she said.

David grinned and casually kicked a chair back for her.

This wretched evening was beginning to turn around.

As luck would have it, Olivia and Harrison won the first round because of a mistake Lord Keddington made.

"Good God, man," David complained. "We are playing against a lady and her steward. If we cannot win against them, what good are we?"

"My lord, a person's gender or occupation does not determine their skill at cards," Olivia said, and trumped the card he'd played to open the next set.

"Your point is well taken, madam," Keddington said, and trumped her card.

"I suppose I should count myself as fortunate that I am able to stand upright at all," said Harrison, and to Olivia's delight, took the set. "Well played, Lady Carey."

"The credit is all yours, Mr. Tolly," she said with a gracious incline of her head, and raked the pot to her side.

They played a few more rounds, Olivia and Harrison winning more of them. When it was Harrison's turn to deal the cards, Olivia excused herself and went to the sideboard for water. As she poured some into a glass, Lord Keddington said, "If I may be so bold, madam . . . but has your sister settled on a suitor?"

The question startled her. "Ah . . ." She turned around. Harrison was dealing the cards, but she could see him fighting a smile.

"A very interesting question, my lord," Olivia said as she walked back to the card table.

"Save your breath, Keddington," said David. "I've already inquired."

Harrison suddenly looked as if he'd choked, and Olivia had a devil of a time keeping herself from laughing. It was all so impossible! It was a tale fit for a stage! "While she has not said anything to me," Olivia said, "I rather think she has."

David and Keddington both looked quizzically at her. "Who?" David demanded. "I know you well, Olivia, and I know you are keeping a secret. You claim not to know who it is, but I think you do. Who the devil is it?"

Olivia smiled at Harrison. "Surely you do not ask me to break my sister's confidence, my lord," she said sweetly. "Perhaps I do more know than I can say. The only thing I can tell you is that the gentleman is quite handsome and very kind."

"I don't give a damn if he is an angel. What is his fortune?" David demanded.

"Oh, that, I cannot say," Olivia demurred, and smiled devilishly at David's snort of impatience. "It would be untoward of me to inquire."

"I think I know who you mean," Harrison said suddenly, surprising Olivia. "Bit of a foolish chap, is he not?"

"Perhaps a wee bit," Olivia agreed. "But he means well."

"A sycophant, is he?" Keddington said irritably as he threw down his card.

Harrison laughed outright. "While her ladyship's sentiment is pleasing, I have long suspected the gentleman's trouble is his mouth. Seems to flap about without benefit of thought."

"Sometimes one can think entirely too much before speaking," Olivia countered. "I rather enjoy his lack of judgment."

Harrison smiled so fondly at her that she shivered. "I suspect he enjoys making you smile with his nonsense."

"What in blazes are the two of you talking about?" David said, and threw down a card that Harrison instantly trumped.

"You are wrong about him, Mr. Tolly," Olivia said. "He is not foolish. He's a fine gentleman. A good man."

"Bloody good for him then," David said, and trumped Olivia's card, taking the round.

Olivia looked across the table at Harrison and smiled.

They played until the early hours of the morning, long enough for Fennick to rouse himself. When he did, Olivia excused herself, and with one last furtive smile for Harrison, she returned to her rooms.

Edward was exactly where she'd left him: on the floor, snoring loudly.

Olivia carefully touched him with the toe of her slipper. He didn't move. She left him there and went into the adjoining dressing room to wash and dress for bed, then stepped over him and climbed into her bed.

She slept soundly that night, her dreams filled with Harrison.

A sliver of light was creeping in through the drapes when Olivia was awakened by the presence of someone by her bed. She sat up with a start.

"I'm sorry, Olivia," Edward said thickly.

She scrambled across the bed and landed on her feet. His hair was mussed, his clothing wrinkled. He'd undone his neckcloth and waistcoat, and had pulled the tails of his shirt from his pants. "I beg your pardon," he said.

What was happening? Edward never apologized for the slightest thing. The only time he'd apologized was after he'd hit her—

It suddenly dawned on her—he didn't recall what had happened. "Do you honestly think an apology is enough?" she asked, testing him.

He grimaced and looked down. "As I said, I do beg your pardon. You will have to be content with that, for there is nothing more I can do." He walked out of her room, his coat in his hand, the sleeve dragging on the floor behind him.

Olivia blinked, then sank onto the edge of the bed in disbelief. The fool assumed he'd done something worse than he had. And she was more than happy to allow him to think it.

Nancy arrived just after sunrise to change Lady Carey's basin water and to stoke the fire. As she reached the top of the stairs she saw his lordship stagger by, clutching his coat in one hand and looking as if he'd been rolled about on the lawn. He didn't speak to her as he passed.

She hurried on to her ladyship's room.

"Good morning, Nancy," Lady Carey said when Nancy poked her head inside. She was sitting in the chaise by the fire, which had been stoked. His lordship must have done that.

"Is it still raining?" her ladyship asked.

"It is." Lady Carey was never one to smile in the mornings, but this one was a nice big and bright smile. "How do you fare, my lady?"

Lady Carey laughed. "Very well," she said, as if she was surprised by it. "Very well, indeed." Still smiling, she turned her attention to the fire.

Later, when Nancy made her way to the kitchens with the used linens, Mrs. Perry and Miss Foster were seated at the kitchen table, sipping tea.

"There you are," Mrs. Perry said. "I had the girl wait to begin the laundering until she had her ladyship's linens. Whatever took you so long?"

Nancy blithely dropped the linens onto a pile of soiled napkins. "Lady Carey was not alone this morning."

"Oh?" Miss Foster said, sitting up and turning her attention to Nancy.

"His lordship come stumbling out of her room half dressed, he did, and looked as if he'd had a time of it."

"Oh my," Mrs. Perry said, and blushed as she laughed.

"Lady Carey had a smile as wide as the Thames and she was up sitting before a stoked fire as if she made a habit to rise like that every morning. Was quite cheerful—not like her at all, really."

"That very thing happened to me when I was carrying my third," Mrs. Perry said sagely. "Couldn't sleep a wink! I was up with the dawn every morning."

"Think she's told his lordship?" Miss Foster whispered loudly.

"I think she has," Nancy said. "It's not like him to stay in her bed the whole night. I gather it was a special occasion, if you take my meaning."

The three women giggled girlishly, and began to debate when Baby Carey would make his or her debut.

CHAPTER NINETEEN

Harrison sat on the edge of his bed and absently watched a pool of water forming at the base of the window where the rain was leaking in.

He had always prided himself on the ability to confront difficult situations headlong and forge a path through. It was a skill he had learned in London, in the absence of anyone to guide him, and he had navigated his way through many difficult situations. But he was having a devil of a time seeing his way through this one.

What a bloody mess he'd created. He was conflicted, terribly conflicted, and the burning desire he felt for Olivia did not help him think clearly. Sitting across from her at the card table had been unbearable. He was sick unto death of remaining reserved and disinterested when she was about. He had wanted only to smile, to engage her, to have her all to himself. He'd watched her tease her brother-in-law, and had imagined himself with her every evening, her lovely smile to warm him, her laughter to soothe him.

When he tried to imagine spending every evening with Alexa, he could not.

It was maddening that he couldn't slake his thirst for Olivia. Every time he saw her eyes twinkling at him, he felt more crazed. His desire had been building for years, drinking from tiny snatches of hope until it was a living, breathing thing inside him. It had a life of its own, and he was powerless to stop it. He couldn't force it down; he couldn't beat it into submission. He was trapped by its strength and moored to the wretched situation of wanting what he could not have.

How could he continue this charade with Alexa? Was he destined to make her life miserable with his inability to care for her as a husband ought? It was madness, utter madness, and he could not see his way clear.

He supposed the only thing to come of this wretched weather was that it put off any hope of making it to Gretna Green quickly, which gave him a bit of time. But for what? More flailing about? He felt as if he were waiting for his execution.

Harrison washed and dressed, then went downstairs. Mrs. Lampley was lighting the fireplaces. He tried to read, but his thoughts kept swirling wildly about his predicament, and with images of Olivia lying naked beneath him.

Shortly after breakfast, a footman from the main

house appeared. "His lordship asks that you come, as his guests mean to take their leave and Lord Westhorpe requires a word."

Harrison was grateful for the diversion.

He met Westhorpe in the marquis's study, and as the congenial young lord idly tapped a pen against a teacup, Harrison reviewed the Cornwall estate finances with him.

After a few minutes of at least attempting to listen, Lord Westhorpe impatiently tossed the pen aside. "Enough of that, Tolly," he said. "I trust you to do what must be done to straighten out the finances."

That was precisely Westhorpe's problem—he had no patience for running a vast estate and preferred leaving it to someone else. His affairs suffered from his lack of attention.

"I will do what I can, my lord," Harrison said. It was impossible to manage the interests from this far away, which Harrison had explained to Lord Carey and Lord Westhorpe more than once. "However, I must remind you that it is imperative that you give the mining your attentions. Most mines are seeing vast profits, but our mine has cost more to operate than it has earned."

"I vow to play close attention," Westhorpe said with a disarming smile. "Now then, what of my stipend? You will speak to my brother, will you not, Tolly? He has threatened to reduce it, and I cannot possibly live on less."

Harrison gave him a skeptical look.

Westhorpe shrugged sheepishly. "I know you believe that I live beyond my means, but maintaining one's position in London society is an expensive proposition."

"I am certain that it is," Harrison said. "The invoices that have arrived from Madame Broussard's Millinery have been impressive."

Westhorpe grinned. "You understand my point. That is all I ask of you, Mr. Tolly. I need my stipend. Very well, then, I shall be off. I expect I will see you again in a fortnight or so." He winked at Tolly as he passed. "I should like to acquaint myself with Miss Hastings once more without Keddington about."

Harrison must have looked surprised, for Westhorpe chuckled. "I must be about the business of heirs one day, eh? And between the two of us, my sister-in-law seems incapable of giving my brother an heir. So a child born to me would be the heir presumptive." He grinned, as if it were perfectly acceptable to view matrimony solely for the purpose of inheriting. "You will keep that between us, I trust," he added lightly.

"Naturally." Harrison could only guess what Westhorpe would say upon hearing the news that Harrison had married her. His quagmire was getting deeper and deeper every moment, sucking at his ankles, pulling him down.

Lord Carey was on hand to see the gentlemen off, looking a little bleary-eyed, and leaning against the door as the men mounted their horses in the downpour. Rain blew in through the open door, wetting the marble entry. When they had started out, Carey turned and said, "A word, Mr. Tolly," as he passed.

Harrison followed him to the study and stood waiting as the marquis poured himself some whiskey. He held up the decanter to Harrison, who shook his head. It was half past ten in the morning.

"Tell me, what have I missed whilst I've been away?" his lordship asked, and sipped.

"Very little," Harrison said. "I spoke with Mr. Fortaine about his rents, and he assures me they will be paid in full by the end of the month."

"I am not inquiring about the bloody rent," the marquis said, and tossed down the whiskey. "I am inquiring about the slut who inhabits my house. Why is she still here?"

Harrison's entire body coiled. He sincerely hoped he could get through this interview without launching himself at Carey. "Arrangements have been made, but the rains have made travel difficult."

Carey's face darkened. "Let me tell you something, Tolly—Keddington inquired after her. Can you imagine the discomfort that caused me? What am I to say? That the whore carries a bastard child, but is free for the taking?" He made a sound of disgust. "If her condition is discovered, I will be made the laughingstock of all of England."

It galled Harrison that the young woman's life meant nothing more to Carey than how he would appear in society. The marquis suddenly seemed more despicable than ever.

"I intend to take her to Scotland as soon as the rains have eased," he said.

Carey glowered at him, and reached for the whiskey decanter again. "I think you've become entirely too bold, Tolly. Lest you forget, you are the steward here. You do not inform me what you will or will not do. Nor do you determine when."

Harrison stood calmly, his gaze unwavering, silently daring Carey to say more.

But Carey did precisely what Harrison would have guessed—he looked down and poured another whiskey. "Send her away. I don't care where you send her, but send her from Everdon Court."

Harrison gave him a curt nod and started for the door.

"One other thing," Carey snapped. Harrison forced himself to look around.

His lordship's gaze was piercing as he asked, "How did you find my wife while I was away?"

Every nerve in Harrison's body fired at the question. He'd found her sad, mistreated, and incomprehensibly brave in the face of it all. "I beg your pardon?"

"Was she congenial?" he asked with a shrug. "Did she engage? Or did she mope about the house missing her husband?"

What in hell was this? "I would not know, my lord. I hardly saw her."

"Indeed?" Carey said, smirking a little. "It is interesting you should say that, for when I asked Brock if you had occasion to speak to her, he told me that you had met with her in the garden one afternoon."

It was all Harrison could do to keep from launching himself at Carey and putting his fist in the middle of his face. "I did indeed meet her to discuss the situation with her sister."

"Then you saw her," Carey said with a smirk.

"On that occasion, yes," Tolly said. "Is there anything else about which you are curious?"

Carey frowned darkly. "Mind yourself, Tolly. You may go." He turned away, to the sideboard.

Harrison strode from the room, walking straight to his office and shutting the door. He stood with his hands on his hips, his anger ratcheting up with each breath, until he whirled about and punched the wall with his fist as hard as he could, breaking through the plaster.

"*Ouch,*" he muttered, wincing painfully, and stretched out his fingers, shaking his hand.

There had to be an escape, a solution. If he could think of how to remove Olivia from this house without ending up on the end of a noose, he could save them all. He just had to think how to do that.

CHAPTER TWENTY

The next afternoon, a restless Alexa heard Rue exclaim, "Goodness! Milady!" She stepped out of the parlor into the foyer to see Olivia hand a wet umbrella to Rue, who promptly stuffed it in the umbrella stand without shaking it off on the stoop.

"Good afternoon, Livi," Alexa said. "I didn't expect to see you here."

"I find the company here more appealing than at the main house," Olivia said. She smiled at Rue and handed over her cloak.

"Thank you, mu'um," Rue said, and curtsied.

"Hang it on the coatrack, Rue," Alexa said. As Rue moved to hang the cloak, Alexa asked, "Does your husband approve of your calling at the dowager house to walk among the fallen and the banished?"

Olivia smiled ruefully. "If I feared everything my husband would not approve of, I would never leave my bed." She linked her arm with Alexa's. "And I should be overjoyed to be banished to the dowager house, were I you."

"Come and have a look before you declare it," Alexa said, and pulled Olivia into the parlor. "You will find the furnishings rather dreary. I trust Harry will be amenable to a few small changes."

"Dreary!" Olivia exclaimed, looking around. "I find it charming. I hope you will not burden him with such things as furnishing."

"I do not intend to burden him," Alexa said impatiently. And besides, she intended to preside over Ashwood—not this old place. "But I think you are right—I shall be quite happy with Harry."

Olivia looked around the room. "I can scarcely imagine how anyone could be unhappy with him. Nevertheless, darling, why on earth did you announce to Bernie and Lady Martha that you intended to marry him?"

"I thought we'd agreed to it."

"We agreed to lay the seeds of it. Not to announce it."

"What difference does it make?" Alexa asked with a shrug.

"It makes all the difference," Olivia said patiently. "Surely you understand that if either of them speaks of it now—particularly since Bernie is convinced that with Edward returned, you should wait for warmer weather to wed—that everyone will wonder why you hurried up to Scotland."

Alexa sighed heavily. "I didn't think it would cause any harm. And now that I've said it, I scarcely think it matters, really. Will it not be evident to all in a matter of weeks? If you ask me, Harry and I ought to leave here altogether straightaway."

"Please do not say that," Olivia said. "It pains me to hear you say it."

"Very well, I won't say it. But I think it," Alexa said petulantly, and sat down. She wanted out of this house—it was beginning to feel like a prison. "To think it's been scarcely a fortnight since we came to this plan," Alexa said, shaking her head. "I wanted nothing to do with it, but now . . . now I see the wisdom in it." She smiled sheepishly at Olivia. "I am, for the first time in many weeks, quite looking forward to my life." Harry was not Carlos, but she had accepted the inevitable. She would never be with Carlos, and therefore there was no point in dreaming of it. "Who knows?" she added with a smile. "Perhaps we shall add another child to our little brood."

Olivia turned away from Alexa to examine the china bowl on the mantel. "Perhaps you will," she said, sounding distant.

Her sister feared losing her, Alexa realized. "I owe you a debt of gratitude, Livi," she said. "I mean that very sincerely. You have always been there to help me."

"Ah, well," Olivia said, and picked up the bowl. "You would do the same for me."

"Do you really think I would?" Alexa asked curiously. "I would hope that I would. But the shoe is never on the other foot, is it? I am the one who always needs you. I scarcely know what I'd do without you."

Olivia looked curiously at her.

"I know very well how I am," Alexa said to Olivia's obvious surprise. "I rely on you for everything. I always have and I suppose I always shall. But this time, you saved me, Livi." She put her hand on her belly and imagined having to bribe a headmaster to allow her child into a school. "I am sorry I didn't understand it sooner, but I see it now. You knew what I needed when I couldn't or wouldn't see it, and you saved me in spite of myself."

Olivia blushed. "You make too much of it, darling. I only meant to help——"

"But you always help," Alexa insisted. She stood up. "Thank you. For everything. For always indulging me, and for guiding me when Mamma died, and for saving me when I couldn't even see that I needed saving. I owe you my life, and the life of my child." She put her arms around Olivia and hugged her.

"Oh, Alexa," Olivia said, and squeezed her tightly, then let go. She smiled thinly. "Please, don't make so much of it."

The sound of the front door opening reached them, followed by a man's stride across the foyer. Harry appeared in the doorway, still wearing his cloak. He seemed surprised to see them there, and looked from Alexa to Olivia.

"Good afternoon," Alexa said.

"Good afternoon," Harry responded; his gaze was on Olivia.

"I, ah . . . I hope you don't mind that I've come," Olivia said, clasping her hands tightly before her.

The marquis had done that to her, Alexa thought. He'd made her afraid of her own shadow.

"Of course not. You are always most welcome. Always. Is everything—"

"Everything is fine, Mr. Tolly," Olivia said quickly, and smiled. "I wanted to see how Alexa was faring and to walk. I feel as if I have been caged by the weather, and I thought it would be nice to go out, even if in the rain." She put her hand to her nape. "I should go back."

"You needn't run off," Alexa said.

"Edward will wonder where I've got off to."

"Shall I walk with you?" Harry asked.

"No, no," she said, smiling at him. "You should stay and . . . and speak with Alexa. I am certain there is much you have to discuss."

"Indeed there is," Alexa said, and sat on the settee. "Quite a lot, Harry."

"At least let me see you out," Harry said.

He was a good steward, solicitous of the marchioness. Alexa hoped he was that solicitous of his wife.

"Thank you," Olivia said softly, and walked through the door. He followed her out without looking at Alexa.

Alexa sat on the settee and ran her hands along the velvet upholstery, her fingers sliding over a rough patch that was beginning to wear. She could hear Harry and her sister whispering in the foyer, then heard the door open and close.

Harry appeared a few moments later without his cloak. From the corner of her eye, Alexa saw Olivia dart by the window beneath her umbrella.

"How are you today?" Alexa asked cheerfully.

Harry looked at her strangely. "Fine, thank you. And you?"

"Very well, thank you." She smiled.

"Splendid," he said absently. "Rue!" he called. "Rue, what has become of the brandy?"

"The brandy, my lord?" she asked, popping into the parlor.

"Sir," he corrected her. "Yes, the brandy. An amber liquid in a crystal decanter. Quite necessary on a cold, wet day such as this."

"Did you not drink it, my lord?"

"I am not a lord," Harry said patiently. "And I did not drink an entire bottle of brandy. Please go and inquire of Mrs. Lampley."

"Yes, I will my . . . sir," Rue said.

"May I speak frankly?" Alexa asked when Rue had left.

"Of course," he said, and began to sort through the few bottles at the sideboard. "Feel free to speak whatever is on your mind."

"What is on my mind is Everdon Court. The marquis cannot bear the sight of me, and I can scarcely abide him. I should like to leave."

"I think it best if you remain at the dowager house for a time," he said.

"I had in mind something a little more drastic than that."

Harry held up a decanter and frowned at it thoughtfully.

"Are you listening?" she asked, and stood up. "Harry, let's leave here. Let's go somewhere the marquis is not. I cannot bear to be confined to the dowager house and not allowed to see my sister because it displeases her husband."

Harry spared her a glance then. "And go where, Alexa?" he asked, sounding a bit impatient with her.

"I thought perhaps we might . . . we might go to Ashwood," she said.

Harry stilled. He turned his head and stared hard at her, as if he could not believe he'd heard her correctly. His eyes narrowed slightly. "What do you know of Ashwood?"

His voice was dangerously low, and Alexa's heart began to flutter with uncertainty. "The man who came to see you said it. He said you had inherited."

"I don't recall that he said so to you," he said suspiciously.

"I overheard it," she lied.

His expression darkened.

"What?" she asked. "What have I said?"

Harry suddenly closed the distance between them and stared down at her in a manner that made her feel as if she were a child, incapable of understanding something. "You must not mention it again."

"But why?" she asked. The letter had been very clear that Ashwood belonged to him. Why would he not admit it?

"Because I have asked you not to. It is none of your concern, Alexa. We shall make our home here, as planned."

"*You* planned this. Not me. The marquis cannot bear the sight of me."

"Then you must resign yourself to the idea that for a time, at least, it will be a quiet existence. You will have enough to occupy you when the child is born."

Alexa gaped at him. "But it's not fair!"

"Not *fair*?" he snapped. "Shall I tell you what is not fair? That I am giving up my life for you. That your sister must languish in the prison of Everdon Court every day for the rest of her life. That *you*, in your astonishing lapse of judgment, have brought this on all our heads! *That* is not fair!"

Alexa was so taken aback that tears welled up and started to fall. She lowered her head, mortified but unable to stop it.

"Please do not weep, for heaven's sake." Harry sighed, and put his arms around her. "Come, come, Alexa. There will come a time that we shall both look back at this and find it amusing."

"I will never find it amusing!" she cried.

"You are right," he said, sighing again. "That was a wretched old chestnut. I think neither will I ever find it amusing, but these things do have a way of settling into comfort with time. I don't think you will despair for long."

Alexa sniffed and rested her head against his shoulder. She liked the smell of his spicy cologne. He was hard, and strong, and she felt moved by his comfort. She lifted her head and gazed at his face. "How can you be so certain?"

"I have faith."

Faith had long deserted her, and Alexa suddenly wanted some of his. She couldn't seem to help herself; she went up on her toes and boldly kissed him. She didn't know what she thought might happen, but she did not expect Harry to rear back as if he'd been stung. "What in blazes are you doing?" he demanded.

Heat flooded her cheeks. "I . . . We are about to be married. I thought . . ."

He moved away from her, putting the room between them.

Mortified, tears began to flow again. Alexa felt humiliated and confused, and when Rue walked in with the bottle of brandy, wide-eyed and mouth agape, Alexa thought she might die from the embarrassment at being so soundly rejected.

"Rue," Harry said, taking the bottle from her and putting it down on the sideboard. "I am going to the village to have a pint."

"Am I to say it?" she asked anxiously.

"I don't give a damn." He strode out.

CHAPTER TWENTY-ONE

✤

At tea Edward was still contrite, and politely greeted Olivia when she entered. He didn't comment when she ignored the needlework laid out beside her chair, nor did he complain when she stood up to look out the window as he read his newspaper.

But when she mentioned the rain seemed to be waning, he said, "That should make your walks to the dowager house more pleasant." He looked at her over the rim of his wineglass and drank deeply, then signaled the footman to pour more.

Olivia glanced at the decanter—it was almost empty, which meant he'd consumed most of it in the last hour or so. Which meant that anything might happen. She waited for his condemnation, and his decree that she was not allowed to walk to the dowager house. She waited for him to make a cruel remark.

When the footman had filled his glass, Edward instructed him to leave.

"I worry about your health, my love," Edward said, his eyes fixed on her. "Walking in the rain could make you ill."

"I wasn't too terribly wet." She warily resumed her seat, her eyes on the clock on the mantel, silently counting down the minutes and hours she must remain in his company.

Miss Foster arrived with the tea a few minutes later, bustling in through the oak doors and banging one against the writing desk. "Oh! Beg your pardon, my lord, my lady," she said cheerfully. "Brock asked me to bring tea around, as Mr. Dembly has come with a delivery. I fear I grow clumsy in my old age."

"Thank you, Miss Foster," Olivia said, and rose from her seat to help her. Edward frowned at Olivia but did not instruct her to sit.

But Miss Foster did. "Sit, madam, please! Allow me to serve you. I made a fig cake, especially for you. I know how well you like them."

Olivia didn't care for Miss Foster's fig cake at all, and couldn't imagine where Miss Foster had gotten that idea. "How kind. Thank you."

"Shall I pour?" Miss Foster asked.

"Yes," Edward said without looking up from his paper.

Miss Foster wasn't as deft with the service as Brock; there was such a clattering of china and pewter that Edward sighed loudly and lowered his newspaper to pinch the bridge of his nose between his thumb and finger.

Miss Foster did not seem to notice him at all. She put tea on the small table next to Edward's chair, then handed a cup to Olivia.

"Thank you, Miss Foster."

"It is my pleasure," she said enthusiastically. With a bright smile, she removed the cover from the fig cake with a flourish. She served up a thick slab of it and put it on the table next to Edward.

He ignored it.

Miss Foster lifted the knife to cut another slab, and Olivia said quickly, "No thank you, Miss Foster. I am not feeling well this evening. I will wait, if you don't mind."

Miss Foster looked crestfallen.

"I am certain it is delicious, but I am a bit under the weather," she said, and gestured to her stomach to indicate her distress.

Miss Foster suddenly brightened and winked at Olivia. "I understand completely. My sister was the same way when she was with child; she could scarcely eat a thing for a time."

For a moment, the words didn't make sense to Olivia. "Pardon?" she said. But then she realized what Miss Foster was implying at the very same moment that Edward did.

He looked at Olivia, then at Miss Foster. "What do you mean by that?" he demanded.

Miss Foster blinked. "Forgive me, my lord. I'm just an old woman, prattling on." She put the lid on the cake platter.

"That is not what I asked," Edward said, casting aside his newspaper. "What precisely did you mean by that?"

"I beg your pardon, madam!" Miss Foster said. "I spoke out of turn!"

"I asked you a question, woman!" Edward snapped. "Explain yourself!"

Miss Foster looked as horrified as Olivia felt. "There has been some misunderstanding," Olivia said, but Edward waved her quiet, his eyes locked on Miss Foster. He rose up out of his seat, squaring off in front of the poor thing.

"I meant only to say that when my sister was with child, she could not eat. And I thought . . . I thought perhaps that her ladyship—"

"Oh no!" Olivia cried. "No, Miss Foster, you are mistaken! I am not with child. Wherever would you get such an idea?"

The poor woman looked as if she might collapse. She looked frantically from Edward's cold gaze to Olivia. "Everyone knows it, madam. I've heard it said—"

"That will be all," Edward snapped, and pointed to the door. "Leave us."

Miss Foster scurried out of the salon, still holding the knife she'd used to cut the fig cake.

Edward's jaw was clenched, his gaze hard, and Olivia knew she'd already lost. "I am not with child," she said. "I cannot begin to guess why she would think so."

"Would you lie to me?" he asked, his voice dangerously soft.

"No, of course not. It is the one thing you want from me, Edward. If I were carrying your child, I would be dancing on the rooftop."

That did not appease him, judging by his dark look.

"You may have Dr. Egan come and examine me if you don't believe me."

"I believe you when you say you are not carrying my child, Olivia. So now I wonder, if not *my* child, then whose?"

"How dare you, Edward!" she cried. "I am not carrying *anyone's* child! I am faithful to you."

"Then explain to me why the staff of this house would believe that you are," he said, and suddenly lunged for her. Olivia cried out and tried to dart out of his way, but he easily caught her and shoved her up against the wall, pinning her in place. "You'd best not be lying to me," he said. "For if I discover you have cuckolded me and attempt to parade some bastard about as *my* child, I will kill you first."

She gasped. "Unhand me!"

Edward brought his hand to her face, his fingers splayed against her cheek, pushing her head back. "*Do not lie to me.*"

"I do *not* lie to you." Olivia brought the heel of her shoe down hard on his foot. Edward hissed with the pain and let go. Olivia quickly moved away from him, putting the settee between them.

"It's Tolly, is it not?" Edward seethed. "He is your lover."

"You are mad," Olivia said heatedly. "First you accuse me of your brother, and now Mr. Tolly? I will tell you again: I have always been loyal to you, even when I found it exceedingly difficult to be!"

His eyes widened and he shook as he pointed his finger at her. "You will pay for this, Olivia. Dear God, you will pay."

Despite the shiver of fear that coursed down her spine, Olivia lifted her chin. "You cannot possibly punish me more than you have in these last several years."

Edward picked up his wineglass and hurled it across the room. It smashed into the wall and fell in pieces; wine ran down the papered wall. "*Liar,*" he roared, and pivoted about, striding out the door. "Liar!" he shouted in the hall.

Olivia grabbed the back of the settee and sank down as fear, anger, and loathing choked the air from her.

At the dowager house, Rue was gathering up Mr. Tolly's boots to be shined when she heard a banging on the door.

She dropped the boots and ran to the top of the stairs just as the door was flung open and the marquis almost flew into the foyer. "*Tolly!*"

Rue gasped and the marquis looked up. "Come down here!" he snapped.

She did not want to go down, and took one hesitant step.

"*Now!*"

Rue ran down the stairs.

"Where is he?" the marquis asked when she'd made it to the ground floor. "Where is Tolly?"

His demeanor frightened her. His eyes were wide and almost shiny. Once, Rue's brother had trapped a rabid fox, and there had been a shiny look to his eyes, too. The marquis had eyes like that fox.

"*Where is he?*" the marquis bellowed.

Rue was trembling. She saw Mrs. Lampley in the corridor, saw her push her son behind her.

"By God, I asked you a question, wench!"

"I'm not to say!" she cried.

The marquis's eyes grew brighter, and he grabbed her arm and jerked her forward. "*Why?*" he breathed. "Why are you not to say?"

Rue thought she might faint with fright. "Because he doesn't like me to say when he's gone for a pint!" she shrieked and closed her eyes, certain the marquis would hit her.

He pushed her away, and Rue crumpled to the ground. When she opened her eyes the marquis had already gone, leaving the door wide open.

She slowly pushed herself up as the sound of a horse riding away reached her. Mrs. Lampley was suddenly at her side, her arms under Rue's. "Stand up, now, love," she said.

"Did you see him?" Rue asked. "He had the look of the devil about him, he did. And he smelled of drink!"

"You're not to say what he smelled of," Mrs. Lampley softly chided her. "Shut the door before the rain washes us away, then clean up the mud."

CHAPTER TWENTY-TWO

Robert looked annoyed when Harrison entered the common room of the public house. He frowned darkly as Harrison took a seat at his table.

"Is your neckcloth wound too tightly? Or perhaps your boots pinch?" Harrison asked as he removed his hat and cloak. "You seem a wee bit unhappy."

"As you would be, were you me," Robert groused. "One thinks he is well acquainted with a man and then discovers he hardly knows him at all." He held up two fingers to the serving girl to indicate they needed two ales, then glared at Harrison.

Harrison laughed. "All right then, let's have it, old friend. What has you behaving so petulantly?"

"When were you going to tell me, Harry? Are we not friends? Do you not trust me?"

"Of course I trust you! What is it that you think I haven't told you?"

Robert grunted at that and sat back, looking away from Harrison, folding his arms across his chest.

"Come on then, I cannot guess what has you wrought," Harrison said. "When was I to tell you *what*, precisely?"

"That you were planning to marry Miss Hastings, that's what," Robert snapped. "The very same Miss Hastings whom, a mere fortnight ago, you had hoped to put off on some widow!"

"Ah," Harrison said, sobering.

"*Ah*," Robert snapped.

Fran put the ales on the table without looking at Harrison and sashayed away. No smile, no inquiry after his health, no brushing against him as she was wont to do. Harrison groaned and hung his head for a moment. This month had to be the worst of his life. "I guess everyone within a radius of Everdon has heard it, then?"

"I'd wager a few," Robert drawled. "And still, you've not answered my question. When did you think to tell *me*? When the first child was born?" He snorted and drank from his ale.

So did Harrison. "I didn't mean to keep it from you, Rob. But I hadn't determined how exactly to make the announcement."

Robert's eyes rounded. "So it is true! Ach, I always believed you to be against marriage, in principle. I thought we were of like minds—better to bed them than to wed them."

"I do not believe we are of like minds in that regard," Harrison said with a wry smile. "But neither have I been eager to join the ranks of the married. However . . ." He glanced around them. "Some things have changed."

"Have you fallen in love, then? Have you lost your esteem for your Lady X, and found it for a woman who is scarcely more than a girl? And before you answer that," he said leaning forward and pointing at him, "I must warn you that I will not believe you if you say you have. Miss Hastings is comely and she might be quite agreeable, but I would wager all that I have that she is not as enticing as your Lady X."

"I can't deny it," Harrison said. "She is not. Nevertheless, Miss Hastings finds herself in a bit of a bind, and I, in my infinite wisdom, agreed to help."

"Why?" Robert demanded.

"Why not?" Harrison countered. "It's not as if I might ever have Lady X."

"I do not see why that is so," Robert said stubbornly.

"Isn't it obvious?" Harrison asked impatiently. "She is married. And not to me." He drained the rest of his ale.

"Aye, I've had my suspicions," Robert said. "Yet you've managed well enough until now. You've seemed perfectly happy until now! And now, out of the blue, you decide to marry someone you hardly know?" He shook his head. "It hardly sounds like you."

"It is not my first choice," Harrison said flatly. "But I have put myself into a corner. By the bye, how in blazes did you hear of it?"

With a roll of his eyes, he said, "Bernadette Shields rather enjoys the sound of her own voice."

Harrison groaned and signaled for more ale. "I haven't the slightest idea how Miss Shields learned of it, but I would wager Miss Hastings is equally fond of the sound of her voice."

"By all that is holy, Harry," Robert said with great exasperation. "If you are not inclined to marry this girl, do not shackle yourself. It will only lead to resentment and unhappiness. Are you prepared to live the rest of your life in that manner?"

God no, he was not prepared—not at all. He didn't want to speak of it; he did not want to *think* of it. He wanted an hour or two of freedom from it. "No, I am not, but I gave my word. Bloody hell, it is even worse than that—I *offered*, Robert. In a moment of pity for the girl, I offered, and now it is impossible to extract myself from my word."

Robert gaped at him. After a moment, he shook his head and looked sadly at his friend. "When?"

"In a matter of days," Harrison muttered. "As soon as the rain lets up." He shifted in his seat, chafing at the invisible binds cutting into him. "Come then, give me some news. Let me drink an ale and not think of my troubles for a few minutes."

"I do not think I can best your news, but I shall try," Robert said with a sigh, and settled back. "Andrew Penstock has been accused of poaching," he began, and was in the midst of telling the story of Mr. Penstock's unfortunate encounter with a constable when the door of the public house opened with a loud bang, startling everyone. The entire room of men twisted about to see who had come.

Lord Carey walked into the public house a bit unsteadily, but his gaze calmly surveyed the crowded room as he pulled the fingers of his glove from his hand one by one.

The sight of him confused Harrison. He couldn't recall ever hearing of the marquis stopping at the public house. When the marquis's gaze landed on Harrison, and he began to noisily push through the tables to him, Harrison believed it must be something to do with the estate.

"He looks as if he's been swimming in a keg of ale," Robert muttered.

"I imagine he has," Harrison said low, and stood up. "My lord?" he said as Carey clumsily pushed one last table out of his way with such force that it toppled over. Harrison heard Robert rise behind him.

Carey looked at Harrison with venom. He grabbed the back of a chair to brace himself against it and said, "Did you honestly believe that you could strut around Everdon Court like a bloody peacock, and I wouldn't learn of your betrayal? Did you think *you*, a bastard, could cuckold *me* and not suffer the consequences?"

The room was suddenly so silent that one could hear a coin fall. *Good God!* Harrison's pulse began to pound with raw anger. He gestured to the table. "My lord, perhaps you might be more comfortable if you were to sit—"

"I do not want to bloody well sit!" Carey snapped, swaying a little against his chair. "I know you have lain with her, Tolly! I know you have put a child in my wife!"

"God in heaven," Robert muttered.

"You are *quite* mistaken, my lord," Harrison said sternly. "Please sit before you embarrass yourself further."

"Traitor," Carey said acidly. "After all I have done for you—"

"I will not stand here and allow you to besmirch your wife's good name or mine with your slander. You are mistaken."

Something sparked in Carey's glassy eyes. He lunged forward and poked his finger in Harrison's chest, pushing him. "I will see you hanged, Tolly. I will bloody well see you hanged for taking my wife to your bed!"

Harrison slapped the marquis's hand down and grabbed his arm, holding it in a vise grip. "That is enough," he said low. "You are making a grand fool of yourself. Sit down *now*, before you do irreparable harm."

He was aware that Robert had moved to stand beside him, aware that everyone in the room was watching with mouths agape.

Carey didn't seem to understand. He looked as if

he would swing at Harrison at any moment, and Harrison prepared himself for it. But Carey was a coward through and through. He jerked his arm free of Harrison's grasp and stumbled backward, colliding with a table. "You do not know what you have done," he said. "You do not yet understand how you will pay for this." He jerked around, colliding once more with the table, and with cry of rage, he sent it sliding across the room before he pitched out into the night.

No one moved; no one as much as breathed. When a few moments had passed and it appeared that the marquis would not return, people slowly began to take their seats. A din of whispering voices began to rise, and then looks were cast in Harrison's direction.

Harrison jumped when Robert put his hand on his shoulder. "Sit down. The longer you stand there, the longer they stare," he said, and pushed Harrison down into the seat, and his tankard of ale into his hand.

Harrison curled his fingers around the handle; rage tightened across his chest. "I should take my leave," he said. "I cannot imagine what he has done to Lady Carey, if this is what he shows me in public."

"Wait," Robert counseled him. "Find your bearings. You won't be of any use if you are as angry as he."

Robert was right, but Harrison couldn't stop imagining the many ways Carey might have harmed Olivia. His blood pumped that much harder.

"Well then," Robert said as he lifted his tankard. "I suppose the secret of Lady X has been revealed."

"Christ in heaven," Harrison muttered, then lifted his tankard. "Ale!" he called to Fran. "Bring me ale!"

He had to take Olivia away from here.

Ashwood. It was all he had, the only place he might escape to. He thought of Alexa, of Olivia, of the loyal staff of Everdon Court. Robert was speaking earnestly about something, but Harrison's thoughts were whirling, the blood rushing like a river in his ears. Everything had just spun out of control and he didn't know how to get it back.

The door to the Cock and Sparrow flew open again, and Harrison instantly came to his feet, whirling toward the door.

It was not Carey; it was a young man who shouted, "Help! Someone come, there's been an accident!"

"What is it?" Harrison demanded as several men rushed out to see what had happened.

Another man stumbled in, his eyes filled with horror. He looked around the room, finally finding Harrison. "You must come, Mr. Tolly! It is the marquis! He rode too fast, and the horse slipped in the mud—broke her leg."

The loud report of a gunshot sent a shock through Harrison. "Where is the marquis?" he asked quickly. "Is he harmed?"

The man gulped. "I think he's dead, sir. Broke his neck."

CHAPTER TWENTY-THREE

Y ou have violated my trust," Olivia said angrily to
Nancy.

Her tone caught Nancy off guard; the young woman
paled and gaped at Olivia. "I . . . I don't know what you
mean, mu'um."

"Don't you?" Olivia asked. "Who else in this house
would be so presumptuous as to think they know
something as intimate as a pregnancy?"

Nancy looked as if she might be ill.

"I am *not* with child, Nancy," Olivia said, her
hands curling into fists to keep from shouting. "But
your unseemly speculation has caused a horrible rift
between me and my husband."

"I beg your pardon, Lady Carey," Nancy muttered
tearfully with a curtsy.

"It is too late for that." She pointed to the door. "Go.
Leave me."

Nancy's chin began to tremble as she fled. Olivia

could hear her sobs as she ran down the hallway. She had never raised her voice to any servant, but the old accommodating Olivia—the one who feared angering her husband—was gone. She didn't know what would happen next, but she would meet it head on.

She began to pace, her mind racing through all the possibilities. She'd never seen Edward so angry. She grabbed the iron fireplace poker and hid it behind the chair where she could reach it. She was prepared to use it—Edward would never force himself on her or lift a hand to her again, not if she could help it.

The sound of voices downstairs reached her. Her heart was racing so badly that she feared it might leap out of her chest. It sounded like several men had come with him. Olivia strained to hear. The voices were growing louder, and it sounded as if someone cried out. That was followed by footsteps moving swiftly down the corridor toward her room.

Olivia reached for the poker, her hand closing around the handle. Her breath was coming so hard and fast now that she was afraid her heart would stop. The hard rap on her door shot white-hot fear down her spine.

Another hard rap, and she lifted the poker.

"Lady Carey!" Brock called through the door.

Olivia dropped the poker.

"Lady Carey!"

She hurried to the door and yanked it open. Brock's face was ashen. "Brock! What is it? What is wrong?"

She had never seen him like this; the poor man could scarcely speak. She put her hand on his arm. "Brock! Brock, it's all right. Tell me what has happened."

He swallowed and put a hand to his neckcloth. "You must come, madam. There has been a horrible accident."

Harrison. Edward had killed him! Her knees began to weaken, and her stomach dipped. She grabbed the door frame to keep herself from collapsing. "Edward—"

Brock nodded, and her heart constricted painfully. "His lordship was thrown from his horse," he said, his voice cracking. "The horse slipped in the mud and they both went down."

Not Harrison. Her head spinning, Olivia released the breath she was holding. "Dear God, Brock, is he badly hurt?"

Brock shuddered. "Madam, he is . . . *dead.*"

Olivia stared at the butler. It wasn't possible. Someone else had been killed—not Edward. When Brock didn't speak, she blurted, "My husband is dead?" unable to even grasp those words.

"Lady Carey."

Harrison! He was suddenly there, her haven, very much alive, his expression grim. His cloak was wet and the hem muddied. His wet, dark hair was mussed. Olivia wanted to fling herself into the safety of his arms.

"It's true?" she asked, her voice scarcely a whisper.

He nodded.

"Where?" she said, her voice breaking. "Where is he?"

"He has been taken to the morning room," Brock said hoarsely.

"I must see him."

"I would not recommend it," Harrison said, his voice steady and strong. "His neck was broken in his fall."

Olivia looked directly into Harrison's eyes. "I *must* see him," she insisted. She had to see with her own eyes that he was really dead.

Harrison exchanged a look with Brock, then held out his arm. "I will take you."

There were men in the foyer, all speaking in low tones. They stopped talking when Olivia and Harrison began their descent down the stairs, looking up at her with expressions that seemed almost suspicious. Only one of them spoke as she moved through. "My sympathies, madam," he said.

Harrison swept her past them, down the long hallway to the morning room.

Two men were inside and she could see Edward's boots sticking out from the end of the table where they had laid him. His boots were still wet. He hadn't been dead long enough for his boots to have dried.

Olivia let go of Harrison's arm and walked forward, her eyes fixed on those boots until she reached his side. His clothing was thoroughly soaked; his dark golden hair was stuck to his forehead. Blood trickled from a gash across his cheek and the mud had made his neck-cloth brown. His waistcoat was torn, and Olivia irrationally wondered why.

She made herself look at his face. His skin was gray, his lips blue, and his head lolled to one side at a peculiar angle. He was dead, truly dead.

Edward was dead.

Olivia covered her mouth with her hand and stared in horror at his corpse. The gentlemen around her shifted and avoided looking at her.

He was gone. He could not hurt her again. Yet Olivia would never have wished death on Edward. He was young; he'd had his entire life ahead of him. Still, she felt such an overwhelming rush of relief that she sank down on her knees beside him. In death, he looked so relaxed. There was no frown between his eyes, no gripped fist. He looked like the young man she'd met seven years ago. He looked like the man she'd believed she could make happy.

She stepped back, away from his body, and somehow managed to turn around.

Harrison stood a few feet away, his hands clasped tightly at his back, his gaze fixed on her. "We must send for the family," she said softly. "And the vicar."

"Of course."

"And the undertaker."

"You mustn't worry, madam. I shall mind all that needs to be done."

"Thank you." Olivia made herself look at Edward

once more. *Dead*. Thank you for bringing him home," she said. "If you will excuse me . . ." She suddenly needed to be alone. She put her head down and walked out of the room, away from her dead husband and the oppression she had suffered, had believed she would always suffer. She walked down the hallway away from the foyer, almost unseeing.

Her thoughts were racing along with her heart; she still had not caught her breath. Olivia walked to the service stairs and ran up one flight of stairs, and then another, and made her way to the nursery.

The room was cold and so dark that she could just make out the furnishings. She walked into the room, then sank onto the end of the little bed and began to gulp air into her lungs.

How was it possible? What miracle was this, that she had been freed from her prison? He was dead! A surprising swell of sorrow rose in her, but was quickly overcome by the stronger swell of relief. The tension began to seep out of her body as the reality began to sink in. She was free of him. She was *free*.

Olivia remained in the dark, cold nursery, staring at the pattern of rain on the windows, feeling something she had not felt in so long that at first she didn't recognize it.

It was hope. The tension was gone, and in its place, she was filling up with hope.

But there was something else there, too; something nibbling at the edges of her relief—guilt. She had said things she knew would anger him. She had caused him to rush from Everdon Court in a state of inebriation. Was she not, in part, responsible for his death? Had she not fantasized about it time and again?

The relief, the guilt, the confusion, was overwhelming.

The house was quiet when Olivia finally quit the nursery and walked down the steps. How long had she been in the nursery? She moved silently to the ground floor, and as she turned the corner into the main corridor, she saw the light of a single candle.

Harrison was sitting outside the morning room beneath a wall sconce. His elbows were on his knees, his head in his hands.

As Olivia walked down the carpeted hallway, he didn't lift his head.

"Harrison?"

He jerked upright at the sound of her voice. When he saw her, he hastily stood.

"Are you all right?" she asked.

"I am fine," he said. "A bit stunned."

"As am I." She looked at the door of the morning room.

"The undertaker has come," he said. "He and his wife are within and Brock is with them now. Messengers have been sent to London to give the news to his family."

He'd taken care of everything, just as she'd known he would.

"Olivia—"

"I can scarcely believe it, Harrison," she blurted, before he could speak, before he could say things that she could not answer. "It feels as if I am moving in a dream."

"I understand."

"I am free of him." Tears suddenly clouded her vision. "I dreamed of freedom, but I never wanted to be free of him like this."

Harrison nodded. He looked as if he wanted to speak, but he pressed his lips together and touched her face. "There are many things to consider. But at present, there are many arrangements to be made."

"Yes."

"You should get some rest while you can."

"I cannot possibly rest!"

"Try," he urged her. "Scores of people will begin to arrive in the morning, and the marchioness must be on hand to meet them and direct the funeral proceedings."

He was right. Olivia nodded and caressed his hand, then walked past the closed door of the morning room, half expecting Edward to come lurching out, demanding to know where she was going and why she didn't maintain a vigil by his side.

But the door did not open. He was truly dead.

CHAPTER TWENTY-FOUR

※⚮⚮⚭⚭

The sound of sniffling woke Alexa the next morning. She pushed herself up onto her elbows. Rue was standing at the wardrobe, her cap on backward, folding Alexa's things and putting them away.

With a groan of exasperation, Alexa rolled onto her side. "Please try not to weep so early in the morning, Rue," she said, and closed her eyes.

"I beg your pardon, miss," Rue sniffed loudly. "It's all my fault, it is. I'm not to say he's gone for a pint, but I did, and that's the reason he's dead this morning."

Alexa opened her eyes. "*What* did you say?" She sat up. "What are you saying? What has happened to Mr. Tolly?"

Rue gasped, her eyes widening. "Did something happen to Mr. Tolly?"

"For God's sake, you just said he was dead!"

"Not Mr. Tolly, miss! Oh no!" Rue cried. "I could not bear it if something were to happen to Mr. Tolly!"

Alexa climbed out of bed. "Then who are you sobbing over?" she asked.

"His lordship. It's him who's dead."

Alexa gasped. "By all that is holy, girl, tell me what
you mean! Why do you say that?"

"It's true!" Rue cried. "He fell off his horse and
broke his neck. He's gone and died, miss!"

The news was so stunning that Alexa couldn't make
sense of it. Edward, *dead*? "Help me dress," she said.

It was as if the marquis's death had wiped all the rain
from the early morning sky. It was the deep blue of a
robin's egg, and sunlight glinted off the moisture that
clung to the trees.

As Alexa rushed up to the main house she saw
coaches in the drive, and among them, the undertaker's
black carriage. She still could not believe it had happened, that the marquis was gone. She'd heard it all
from Mrs. Lampley, who was eager to share the rumors
that were flying about Everdon. The marquis had ridden
into the village in the rain, Mrs. Lampley said, and had
gone into the public house, and before God and everyone, had accused Harry of making a cuckold of him.

"What do you mean?" Alexa had demanded. "He
accused Mr. Tolly of an illicit affair with my sister?"

"Even worse," Mrs. Lampley said. "He accused Mr.
Tolly of putting a child in her!"

Alexa had been too stunned to speak, and Mrs.
Lampley had taken that as invitation to continue. She

said the marquis had left the public house in a rage and ridden away too fast for the night and the muddy roads, and he and the horse had both gone down.

Both beasts were dead now.

Alexa did not give the marquis's accusations any credence. Olivia would never forsake her marriage vows; propriety would always come before desire. Olivia was more concerned with appearances than her own happiness.

At the main house, a somber footman directed Alexa to the salon. She could see Olivia within, facing a pair of gentlemen who were wearing black armbands. Olivia was dressed modestly in black, her hair knotted at her nape and wrapped in black crape. She saw Alexa hovering at the door, and asked the gentlemen to excuse her for a moment. She steered Alexa into an anteroom and shut the door.

"He's gone, Alexa," Olivia whispered. "Can you believe it? He's dead!"

Olivia looked wan, as if she'd not slept at all. But there was something entirely different about her. It took a moment for Alexa to realize that her sister's face seemed younger. It was free of tension. "I am astonished," Alexa said. "It seems impossible."

"I couldn't believe it until I saw him. And still, it seems almost too . . ." Olivia shook her head. "The family has been sent for. The funeral shall be held on Friday. He will lie in state until then."

Alexa didn't care about the arrangements. She

waited for Olivia to say more, to at least acknowledge the events surrounding her husband's death. But Olivia just gazed distantly at the small window. It seemed as if she were miles from this small room.

"Are you not concerned about how it happened?" Alexa asked carefully.

That drew Olivia's attention. She gave Alexa a quizzical look. "He was thrown from his horse and broke his neck."

"Oh dear God," Alexa said as realization dawned. "You are not aware of how what happened, are you?"

"What do you mean?" Olivia demanded. "Speak plainly. He drank too much and he was thrown from his horse."

"No, Livi." Alexa reached for Olivia's hands. "You don't know what everyone else knows. You don't know what happened last night."

"What in heaven are you going on about, Alexa?" Olivia demanded. "I told you what happened last night. Stop speaking in riddles and say what you mean."

"I mean that the marquis went to the village last night, to the Cock and Sparrow, where Harry was with his friends, and before everyone, he accused Harry of making a cuckold of him and putting a child in you."

Olivia gasped as if she'd been struck. "In the public house!" she repeated disbelievingly. "No, there is some mistake," she said, shaking her head. "I've not heard any such thing."

"It is true. Edward was foxed, and he made a very

public accusation. Harry stood up to him and told him he would not stand by and listen to him slander you, and Edward left. That's when the accident happened."

Olivia stared at Alexa, her eyes clouding with confusion. "I have not heard this," she said again, a frown creasing her brow. "Why did Harrison not tell me when they brought Edward home?"

"Perhaps he didn't want to distress you any further," Alexa guessed.

Olivia pressed her fingers to her forehead as if her head ached. "I must speak to him," she said softly. "I must hear from him what happened."

"Shall I fetch him?" Alexa asked, wanting to be helpful.

Olivia shook her head. "He has gone to Everdon to arrange for crape and funeral tokens."

Someone rapped on the door. "Lady Carey, the Earl of Manbrooke has arrived," a male voice called.

"I must go," Olivia said. She took Alexa's hand and squeezed it. "Find something black to wear. We must pay attention to appearances."

Alexa snorted at that. "Why? Edward cannot dictate to you any more, Livi."

"Because we are now living at the mercy of the Carey family, Alexa. *That's* why. Please just do as I ask," she said, and went out to accept her condolences.

The morning moved into day, and that into the next, and slowly, it all began to make sense to Olivia: the looks from the men last night when they'd brought Edward's body home, the curious looks from the staff. Olivia wanted badly to speak to Harrison about it, but there wasn't a moment that she was alone. The business of burying a marquis was a complicated task.

When Olivia did see Harrison, it was always in the company of others. He worked tirelessly to make sure the arrangements befit a man of Edward's stature. Funeral tokens were arranged, mutes hired for the procession to the church, speakers to attest to Edward's esteemed life.

Edward's family arrived one after the other, all of them grief stricken. His sister, Lady Belinda Mathieson, embraced Olivia more than once to sob on her shoulder, and urged Olivia to do the same. "You must be in a state of shock," she said tearfully to Olivia. "It is unhealthy to hold it in; you must release your emotions, Olivia."

"I am past the point of shock," Olivia tried to assure her, but Belinda would not have it.

"You *must* be in shock, dearest. You've not shed a single tear."

Olivia allowed Belinda to embrace her again. "You are right, Belinda," she said sullenly. "I am shocked that he is gone." And as Belinda stood there, her arms tightly around Olivia, Olivia wondered if the Careys had heard what had happened the night he had fallen from his horse.

David seemed the most stunned of them all. "I can

scarcely grasp it," he told Olivia the night of his arrival. "I never dreamed I would take over for Edward. I feel so ill equipped. How shall I ever live up to the standard he has set?"

"You will," Olivia assured him. "Mr. Tolly will guide you."

"Yes. Thank God for Tolly," David said. He looked at Olivia and smiled weakly. "Thank God for you. You are so dear to us all, Olivia. We're all deeply concerned for you. My sister, my aunts and uncles and cousins. You must not worry about your future. We've all agreed that you have a place with us and a stipend for as long as you need. We are aware there is no one to see after you."

To see after her. She had no money of her own, no one to turn to, save Alexa. Everything had happened so quickly that she hadn't thought about what would happen when Edward was buried and the family returned to their lives. She wished she could speak to Harrison, to seek his counsel and his comfort.

Olivia hoped that Alexa had misunderstood what had happened the night Edward had died. If anyone would know, it was Harrison. If only she could speak to him.

The opportunity did not present itself until the morning of the funeral. Olivia couldn't sleep, so she rose before dawn and dressed herself in her funeral garb of black bombazine and black ribbons. When the procession began, she would add a black hat and veil.

When she had dressed, Olivia moved through a silent house, down to the receiving room where Edward lay in state. She could hear the faint sounds of pots in the kitchens as Miss Foster prepared for the day. Olivia had no appetite.

She slowly opened the door to the receiving room—she had yet to get over the shock of seeing her husband deceased—and was surprised to find Harrison there. He was standing at the windows looking out, his clothing somber and marked by the black crape tied around his arm. He turned as she entered, and a smile softened his weary features.

Olivia quickly shut the door behind her. The two of them stared across the room at each other. "What are you doing here?" she asked.

"Waiting for the undertaker. He will arrive shortly to prepare for the move." His gaze roamed her face, drinking her in. Neither of them made a move toward the other, unwilling to do so with Edward's corpse in the room. "How are you?" he asked, his voice a little hoarse.

"As well as might be expected. I've been desperate to speak to you. Alexa has told me what others are saying happened the night Edward died. But I must know from you, Harrison—is it true?"

Harrison's smile faded; he glanced down at his hand.

"Oh dear," Olivia murmured. She sagged against the closed door. "Everyone heard his accusation?"

"Everyone," he confirmed.

She looked at Edward then, and a small shiver of foreboding coursed her spine. She knew that no matter how untrue the accusation, it mattered.

Harrison knew it, too; his gray gaze seemed a little older. "Rumors spread like a cancer, particularly about someone as notable as the marquis. You must prepare yourself for the questions his family will inevitably ask."

"They've not asked me," she said. "They must not have heard it."

He smiled sympathetically. "Perhaps not yet. But they will. And when they do, think carefully what you will say. Your standing with them has been reduced with the marquis's death, as you know."

"Yes," she said. "But David is very fond of me."

Harrison looked skeptical. "He is the marquis now, Olivia. That has a way of changing one's perspective."

She knew he was right, that she could take nothing for granted. Olivia suddenly felt very tired. She pushed away from the door and walked across the room to him. It seemed like miles. He watched her approach, his body tense, his hands at his sides. It was wrong, so wrong, but Olivia needed his comfort one last time. She leaned forward and put her cheek against his shoulder. Harrison lifted his arm and put it around her back. He turned his head, his mouth on the crown of her head. "Have a care," he whispered. "You are a widow without an heir. When one adds scandal to that, it's as if you are standing on the end of a thin tree limb. It is not a question of if it will break, but when. And then the question is how far the fall."

She closed her eyes. "On my word, I don't know what to do."

He tucked his finger under her chin and made her look up at him. He smiled softly, reassuringly. "Be who you are, love. Be the vibrant and beautiful woman you have always been. After the funeral, we will determine the course of our future."

Olivia's heart skipped a beat or two.

She heard the sound of a carriage coming down the drive. Harrison dipped his head and kissed her cheek, his lips warm on her cool skin. "Be brave," he whispered. He stepped around her, walking out of the room to greet the undertaker.

When he had gone, Olivia glanced at Edward's waxen face. That cold shiver ran down her spine again, and she pressed a hand against her abdomen, pushing down a swell of nausea.

CHAPTER TWENTY-FIVE

At the funeral, Harrison sat directly behind the family, his gaze locked on Olivia's back. She was seated between Westhorpe and Lord and Lady Mathieson.

The funeral was everything Carey would have wanted; Harrison had made doubly sure there was a lot of pomp and flowery words attesting to the fine man Carey had fancied himself to be.

After the burial, the Carey family received mourners who had come from all over England to pay their last respects. Olivia was regal in her role as the widow. She spoke to each person, the mournful wife, grateful for the respect paid her husband, concerned for their grief, and dignified in the face of the whispers that seemed to float about the room.

Harrison could feel the scrutiny. More than one suspicious eye was cast in his direction, more than one black fan raised so that gossip might be exchanged.

He stood off to one side, available if the family needed him, but removed from the activity so as not to prompt more talk.

As people began to trickle away, Harrison watched Westhorpe draw Olivia aside. He gripped her elbow and bent his head to hers, speaking earnestly. Olivia looked up at him, nodding, her face serene. When Westhorpe let go of her arm, Olivia turned around and looked at Harrison across the room. He knew instantly by the look in her eyes that the time had come, that the Carey family had heard the rumors of what had happened the night the marquis had died and would confront them.

A footman appeared at Harrison's side. "Mr. Tolly, if you please, Lord Carey should like a word in the study."

The new Lord Carey. "Thank you, Bruce," he said. He hadn't exactly worked out what he would say, but he was quite clear in his head about one thing—he would not accept any responsibility for what had happened to the marquis. The bloody bastard had done it to himself. Harrison only hoped Olivia would remember that, too.

In the study with Olivia, Westhorpe seemed a bit uncertain about how to proceed. Harrison had always been fond of him. He'd been raised as a second son with no responsibility to speak of. His thirst for pleasure had been encouraged by his father, who found it easier to shower money on him than to sort out a useful occupation for him.

Westhorpe nervously cleared his throat. He stroked his chin thoughtfully. He walked to the window and looked out before he turned around and smiled at Olivia, albeit rather thinly. "Olivia, you know how fond I am of you, do you not?"

"As I am fond of you, David. We've always had such a grand time in one another's company, haven't we?"

"Yes, well." He drew a breath. "Unfortunately . . . my fondness for you cannot help me overlook the very disturbing things my family and I have heard in these last few days. Particularly about my brother's last few hours." He glanced at Harrison.

"I regret that you've heard anything at all," Olivia said. "But Edward was mistaken. Terribly mistaken."

Harrison leaned back against the wall and folded his arms over his chest. "The problem with tittle-tattle is that it is rarely based in truth."

"This is not tittle-tattle, Tolly. This is the account of several people who were in the public house when my brother confronted you." Westhorpe looked at Olivia. "As much as it pains me to say it, I was told that my brother had gone into the village to confront Tolly and accuse the two of you of making him a cuckold. And that there was mention of an unborn child."

"Oh, David," Olivia said sadly, as if she were disappointed in him for even suggesting it to her. "I regret that your family has heard such wretched things. But they are not true. I did not cuckold him. I am not with child."

"But why should he think it? Why should he ride into the village in the rain, at night, to confront him?" he asked, gesturing to Harrison.

"Because he was a drunkard who mistrusted everyone around him," Harrison said flatly.

Westhorpe gaped at him in shock.

Harrison pushed away from the wall, his gaze steady on Westhorpe. "Have I ever been less than truthful with you, my lord? Have you not suspected your brother's fondness for drink was beyond abnormal? You know very well that I, of all people, would never sully your brother's name to you or anyone else, but the circumstances are exceptional. Lord Carey was given to drink and distrust, particularly where his wife was concerned. He listened to the misguided utterings of a housemaid, and that is the truth."

Westhorpe seemed confused. He ran his hand over his head. "I know very well how servants talk," he admitted. "But I also knew my brother rather well, and I do not know him as the man you describe, Tolly. Yes, he liked his drink, but not more than anyone else. And he was a rational man—not one to listen to gossip or rush to judgment. Didn't you think so, Olivia?"

Olivia hesitated, and for a moment, Harrison thought she would deny it. But she slowly shook her head. "He was rarely rational where I was concerned. He was cruel to me."

Westhorpe looked completely astonished. He stared at Olivia as if he'd never seen her before. "How do you expect me to believe this is true?" he demanded. "He never once mentioned any distrust of you, Olivia. But even I have noticed a friendship between you and Mr. Tolly—"

"David, Mr. Tolly intends to marry my sister."

"Lady Carey—" Harrison started.

"Mr. Tolly has been my steadfast friend in this house and in this marriage for many years. Edward could not abide me, David. He even struck me. And the night he died, he was foxed and he was irrational. Yet contrary to the gossip you have heard, I have been loyal to him, as has Mr. Tolly. As I said, Mr. Tolly has an understanding with Alexa."

Westhorpe looked utterly shocked. He looked from Harrison to Olivia. "Miss Hastings," he repeated, and looked to Harrison for confirmation. "You are to marry Miss Hastings."

Harrison nodded.

"Why on earth would she agree to it?" Westhorpe asked. "She has many options to marry a titled man with a legitimate name and improve her situation," he said, as if marrying Harrison would drag her down to the depths of society.

"*She* is the one with child," Olivia said softly.

"Good God," Harrison muttered. "Lady Carey, there is no need to divulge any more."

"He must know the truth," she said simply. "He has lost his brother and he must know the truth."

Westhorpe did not seem particularly appreciative

of the truth. He glared at Harrison. "So this is how you repay my brother's generosity?" he asked angrily. "By corrupting his wife's sister?"

"I have sought only to save her reputation," Harrison said, and would have said more had Olivia not stepped in front of him.

"You misunderstand, David," she said softly. "The child my sister carries is not Mr. Tolly's. Mr. Tolly has generously offered to help her."

Westhorpe blanched. "What in blazes has been going on here?" he exclaimed. He turned away from them. "I am not prepared for this. It's unfortunate news, all of it," he said. "To think of what went on behind my brother's back, and that your sister is *ruined*." He turned back to them. "And now we have a scandal that shrouds my brother's death. All of England will talk of it, if they aren't already. Rumors are rampant. And it seems as if they will only grow worse, given this news!"

"What can be done for it?" Olivia asked. "We sought to avoid scandal—all of us. Unfortunately, Edward's mistrust and suspicions, mixed with whiskey, brought his end."

"Is that what brought his end?" Westhorpe scoffed. "It would seem to me that between you and your sister, Edward was driven mad."

"That is not true," Olivia said, her voice shaking with indignation. "How dare you say such a thing—"

"I do not know what I should do," Westhorpe said,

cutting her off. "But I do know that this will not be tolerated within the family. We cannot allow anything to give rise to more talk, and as long as the two of you remain here, particularly if Tolly marries Miss Hastings and she has a child—Do you see, Olivia? The scandal gets deeper, and at a time when I must assume control of the family titles and holdings. Everyone will look to see what I do. I don't see how it may be avoided."

"How *what* may be avoided?" Olivia asked.

"I think what his lordship suggests is that Alexa and I must go," Harrison said.

"Yes, at the very least," Westhorpe agreed. He shook his head. "The last guests are leaving. I should be there. I will speak with my uncle about this and determine what is to be done. Come now, Olivia. Our guests will expect you to bid them farewell."

Olivia looked helplessly to Harrison, then allowed Westhorpe to lead her out.

When they had gone, Harrison's hands fisted at his sides. He had a bad feeling about this. A very bad feeling indeed.

CHAPTER TWENTY-SIX

The Careys met after supper in Edward's study. All of them but Olivia, that was. At half past eleven, they retired for the night. Olivia knew this, for she'd remained in the salon, waiting.

Not one of them spoke to her as they passed the open door, save David. He stepped into the salon and stood at the threshold, his hands on his waist. "Well then," he said. "We've come to a decision."

"Have you?" she asked, rising to her feet.

"I think it is no surprise that we will ask Tolly and your sister to leave at once. I should like to have kept him on to help me, but that is impossible, given the situation he has placed himself in with your sister."

As if Harrison had caused this. As if Harrison was somehow responsible for Edward's demise, or Alexa's situation. Olivia knew from David's demeanor that she would fare no better. "And as for me?" she asked calmly.

"As for you," he said, sighing, "we should like you to remain at Everdon Court and mourn Edward as he deserves to be mourned, in a manner befitting a marchioness. After the mourning period, we will . . . we will see to it that you have what you need."

It seemed as if she would be banished, after all. "That sounds rather ominous."

David sighed again. "My uncle is not as forgiving as am I, Olivia," he said softly. "It is his suggestion that we make it clear: If you do not cooperate with us and do as we ask, we will see to it that you are left penniless and cut from our society. Naturally, that would extend to your sister as well. My uncle has no wish to lay eyes on you again, but I persuaded him that you ought to at least have your period of mourning."

Olivia blinked. "You would throw me out?"

David glanced away uncomfortably. "As my uncle points out, you bring us nothing. The benefit of this marriage has all been to you, in fortune, in standing, and in connections. Therefore, we will use that benefit to ensure you do not cause us any more painful scandals."

"I am astounded," Olivia said softly. "How can you speak to me as if I am a criminal? Not a fortnight ago, I was your dearest friend, remember?"

David's gaze sliced across her. "You should really get some rest, Olivia," he said, and turned and walked out of the room.

Olivia did not move. She stood looking at the open door, at the corridor beyond, wanting her chance to

speak. She wanted to tell them all the truth about
Edward. She wanted to apologize for imagining all the
ways she might rid herself of him, and then somehow
managing to do it. She wanted to tell them she was
sorry for their loss but glad to be free.

How ironic, Olivia thought, that the guilt was
almost as unbearable as her marriage had been.

At half past midnight, Olivia found herself wandering about the darkened house, a single candle to
light her way. It was odd, she thought, how still a house
could seem when a soul had left it. She'd always been
able to sense Edward's presence in this house, even
when he wasn't nearby. But she couldn't feel him any
longer. The place where he'd been was just . . . still.

She moved silently down the corridors, pausing
once to look out the window, where a full moon spilled
milky light over the gardens where she and Harrison
had shared a kiss. Olivia closed her eyes, recalling every
moment of it, feeling the memory warm her.

She would lose him, she knew.

Olivia knew the Careys well, understood their desire
to be perceived as above reproach. Even a hint of scandal—particularly one so intimately tied to Edward's
death—would not be tolerated. She suspected Harrison knew it, as well. He would be given the opportunity to leave on his own terms, and in exchange they
would offer him letters of recommendation to find a
new post.

But what would become of her? She had no money

of her own, save her dowry. How long would that keep her? She didn't think it was enough for a house, much less the upkeep. And then there was Alexa, whose secret Olivia had tried so very hard to keep. Now the entire countryside and half of London would speculate about them in ways Olivia couldn't begin to imagine. The Hastings girls were supposed to land on their feet, but in the end they'd toppled off the mountaintop in a most spectacular fashion.

Olivia turned the corner of the hallway, walking slowly. Ahead of her was a hint of light, and as she drew closer, she saw the light was coming from beneath Mr. Tolly's office door. Olivia quickened her pace. She laid her hand on the smooth wood door, pressed her cheek against it, warring with herself. She should walk on, leave well enough alone. They had caused enough trouble as it was. But the temptation to see him, to hold him, was unbearable.

Before she fully realized what she was doing, she'd put her hand on the knob and turned it.

When she opened the door and peeked around it, Harrison was standing behind his desk in his shirt-sleeves. He'd discarded his neckcloth, had unbuttoned his waistcoat, and his gaze was fixed on the door. When he saw it was she, he came around the desk.

Olivia slipped inside and shut the door, then put her candle aside.

He looked concerned, as if he thought something was wrong. "Olivia?"

There was no conscious thought, nothing but emotion racing through her. Olivia ran to him. She threw her arms around his neck, buried her face in his collar.

Harrison's arms wrapped around her like two iron bands. He breathed a long breath and kissed her temple. "Are you all right?"

Olivia shook her head. "I will never be all right," she said, her emotions bubbling to the surface, her will to remain above her desires swiftly eroding. "I want to know a moment of happiness, Harrison," she said. "Just one."

"Ah, sweetheart," he said, and roughly smoothed her hair back. He looked down at her with concern and despair and love, all of it. She could feel the connection to him, could feel the pull of his heart to hers. Everything she had ever wanted was standing right there in front of her, and yet the gulf between them seemed even wider than it had before Edward had died.

Olivia lifted her head, rose up on her toes, and kissed Harrison with everything that she was feeling.

But he instantly put her down on her feet and held up one finger between them. "Do not touch me, Olivia. My power to resist you has been severely compromised, and I cannot promise that I will not take full advantage of any encouragement you show me."

"A moment is all I ask. To know, for once in my life, what it is to be loved."

Harrison's gray eyes flashed darkly as he crushed her to him, his mouth on hers, kissing her hard, holding her as if he were afraid she would fly away if he let go.

Olivia knew very well what she was doing. She was giving credence to the gossip, she was betraying her sister—but in that fog of deep arousal and desire, she also knew it was the only time in her life she would ever know what it was to be wholly desired, and to desire someone completely in return. She would not shy away from it—not this time.

She was free.

Harrison whirled her around and pushed her up against the door, locking it. His mouth, so warm and wet on hers, was as tormenting as it was pleasurable. It jolted her, rattled every bone and nerve. Her body curved into his and she felt as if she blended into him, as if she fit his arms and his body as though they were meant to be together like this. She clung to his hard frame, felt his muscles moving beneath her hands.

She'd never felt anything so strongly as the need for him, on her, in her, around her. As his tongue swirled around hers, and his hands caressed her sides, her torso, then her breast, Olivia forgot about Alexa, about Edward, about everything that had happened. She saw, she felt, only Harrison. She was emboldened by his obvious desire and admission of affection. He'd finally unleashed his desire, and it was clashing with hers in one luscious storm of pleasure.

He eagerly explored her mouth while his hands moved on her body, sliding down one curve, up another while she sought his hair with her fingers, then his neck and chest.

Harrison suddenly lifted her off her feet, twirling her around and setting her on the chair. He dipped down to the hollow of her throat. "At last, I feel your heartbeat," he said. Her racing, galloping heart. Olivia dropped her head back with a moan as Harrison sought the skin of her bosom with his mouth. White-hot shivers of anticipation shimmered down her spine, sparking in her groin, making her damp. When Harrison pressed the hard ridge of his erection against her leg, she inhaled a ragged, ravenous breath.

He cupped her face, pressed his forehead to hers. "You cannot imagine the power you possess over me. With a look, a sigh, a smile, you reduce me to nothing but hunger."

"It is the same power you possess over me," she said, and pushed back a lock of dark hair from his brow. Harrison kissed her tenderly, and slid his hands to her shoulders, then her rib cage, sliding them down, to her hips. He dipped one hand beneath the hem of her gown and slid it up her leg.

Olivia moaned and pressed against him, encircling his neck with her arms, teasing him with the tip of her tongue. He moved his hand higher, touching the soft flesh of her inner thigh.

She gasped at the galvanizing sensation. A small voice told her to close her legs, to stop before she'd gone too far and given up everything she'd ever believed. But another voice, a stronger voice, urged her to seize this moment, for it would never come again. She opened her legs a little wider.

Harrison groaned. He stroked her thigh as he kissed her face and neck. When his fingers brushed the apex of her legs, the exquisite sensation ran through Olivia like a river.

She reached for his trousers, her fingers finding the buttons and undoing them. His member sprang free of his clothes and into her hand. She closed her eyes as he stroked her, willingly riding the wave of pleasure that was building, stroking him, feeling him swell and harden. His fingers swirled around the core of her pleasure, sliding deep inside her, moving faster. He anchored her with one arm around her, his eyes on her face, watching her succumb to his touch and to pleasure she had never known.

"*Harrison*," she said, her voice rough.

He moved between her legs. "Let go and allow yourself this." He began to stroke her again, and when Olivia teetered on the edge of a climax, he pushed into her, filling her up.

Olivia gasped loudly at the sensation of Harrison's body in hers. She fell back against the chair, clinging to his arms, moving with him, against him, rising up to meet each thrust. He moved in her as he caressed her, riding her into an explosive climax that shattered around her. It felt as if pieces of her were raining down around them. In the next moment, Harrison groaned and yanked free of her, spilling his seed on her thigh. Olivia clung to the arms of the chair as she fought for her breath. Harrison touched his forehead to hers as he sought his. "Never," he said breathlessly. "Never have I been more fulfilled. Never have I desired a woman as I have desired you for more than six years. Only you. Always you."

She cupped his face in her hands and kissed him on the mouth, lingering there, exalting in the sensation of having joined with him so completely.

Harrison kissed her cheek, her forehead, and then tenderly kissed her mouth before gathering her in his arms and holding her to him.

Olivia had never felt so connected to another. Her heart was beating against his chest, trying to leap into his. She could feel unshed tears in her eyes, could feel her blood flowing hot and heavy through every vein. The heavens were shimmering above them, blanketing them.

Several moments passed before Harrison put his palm to her cheek and kissed her, softly, languidly. And then he leaned back.

"No," Olivia said, reaching for him, but Harrison gained his feet. He straightened and fastened his clothes. He smiled down at her as he ran his fingers through his hair, then reached down and stroked the crown of her head.

She pressed her cheek into his palm and closed her eyes, desperate to memorize every moment, every sensation. But reality began to seep back in like smoke, curling in around her tender thoughts for Harrison, sneaking in between them.

He came down on one knee beside her and cupped her face. "Let us leave here, Olivia," he said softly. "Let us leave Everdon Court behind, once and for all."

Olivia took his hand and pressed it between hers, and kissed the tip of each finger, one by one.

"What do you say?"

"Where would we go?"

"Ashwood," he said instantly. "I've inherited Ashwood. We'll go there—"

"Scandal would follow us," she said.

"I don't give a damn about scandal," he said earnestly, and cupped her face with both hands, forcing her to look at him. "You are the only thing that concerns me, Olivia. You are the only thing that has concerned me all these years. Do you know how much I love you? I *love* you, and God knows I have longed to tell you so, to kiss you, to make love to you. And now, in the misfortune that has befallen this family, a miracle has happened—I no longer have to love you from afar. I can love you every day, provide for you and care for you in every way."

She could feel a torrent of tears building in her head and chest. She swallowed them down and took his hands in hers. "I cannot come with you," she murmured.

Harrison made a sound of impatience, but Olivia squeezed his hand. "What of Alexa? I cannot leave her behind for the sake of my own happiness."

"She will understand—"

"She won't. She honestly believes she will make a good life with you, that you will give her child a name." She looked into his eyes. "You of all people know how important that is. She knows her situation is desperate and she has fixed all her hopes in you. Should I tell her that now that my husband is dead, I want you, and she is to fend for herself?"

"She may reside with us at Ashwood—"

"The three of us?" Olivia said. "Harrison—Alexa is hopeful for a future that *we* gave her. That we convinced her she should seize. And now she can sleep knowing that her child will not suffer the same fate that *you* suffered. How can I take that from her? She is my sister—"

"I don't care," he said roughly.

"Perhaps not now. But in the years to come, when you see Alexa and her child, will you not feel at least a bit of remorse? I think you will. I think you will feel as if you pursued your own happiness at the expense of an innocent child."

"But I love *you*," he insisted.

"And I love you," she said sadly. "Unfortunately, fate sometimes intervenes in our happiness."

He pulled his hands from hers and stood up. "If you are determined, you will think of many reasons why you cannot come with me. But have you thought of why you should? Have you thought of *your* happiness? You are free now, Olivia. You are *free*."

Olivia looked down at her black bombazine and shook her head. "I am not free. I've simply moved to another cage. I am held captive by my esteem for you, and the fact that I am all that my sister has in this world. Alexa is not free—she is held captive by a bastard child. And the child . . . the child is not the least bit free, is it? The child faces a lifetime of censure."

Harrison groaned with exasperation and whirled around, locking his fingers behind his head for a moment. The heaviness of his disappointment filled the room and pressed against her. "Is this truly what you want?" he asked bitterly.

"Of course not. I want to be with *you*. But I recognize that there are others who are hurt by my wants. Edward is dead because of them. You and Alexa teeter on the edge of ruin because of them."

"You're not making any sense—"

"Because you do not want to see it," she said, coming to her feet. "I am responsible for all of this, Harrison. Edward is dead because of me. You are to be cast out because of me, as is Alexa."

"That is absurd!"

"Is it, truly? Think of it—had I not kissed you, had I not fallen in love with you, would Edward have ever believed that an affair between us was even possible?"

He stared at her in shock. "You do not truly believe that." He gathered her to him, holding her tight. "It is not your fault, Olivia. The marquis was foxed and he was mad and he was reckless. It's as simple as that."

"But I gave him reason to ride—"

"Hush," Harrison said, and pressed her head against his shoulder. "*Hush.*"

It was impossible to explain the guilt she felt—guilt that Edward had believed she'd been unfaithful, which she truly had been, in her heart. Guilt that she didn't feel more sorrow for his passing. Great swaths of guilt as heavy as Harrison's disappointment in her, as heavy as the bombazine she wore.

She gazed up at him, wincing at the pain and hurt in his eyes. "I love you, Harrison. More than words could ever convey. But I cannot go with you." She stepped out of his embrace and walked to the door. She hesitated there, hoping he would call her back. But when he did not speak, she glanced back. "I have always loved you, too," she said. "And I always will."

"That is scant comfort," he said coolly.

"For me either," she agreed. There seemed nothing more to say. She picked up her candle and went out, her heart cracking and falling to pieces.

CHAPTER TWENTY-SEVEN

Rue announced to Alexa that Mr. Tolly wanted to see her in his study before breakfast. He was dressed in gray tails and black trousers, a pristine white neckcloth tied perfectly, and a dark gray waistcoat. Had it not been for the armband of mourning and the dark circles under his eyes, he would have looked as if it were any other day. It was obvious that the marquis's death had taken a toll on him.

"Thank you for coming," he said coolly, as if she were a servant. "I thought you should know that we will depart for Ashwood at week's end."

Alexa gasped with surprise. She was elated, surprised, and suddenly very hopeful that her life would consist of something more than the drab walls of the dowager house. "This is most welcome news! I thought you were determined to stay on."

"Things have changed with Lord Carey's death."

"And we shall reside there," she said, to make doubly sure she understood him.

"Yes."

A wide grin spread across her face. "Thank you, Harry," she said. *And thank you, Olivia.* "I know you do not wish to leave Everdon Court, but I think it is for the best. You shall be an earl!"

"I would advise you not to count your chickens before they hatch, Alexa. I do not know what we will find there, much less if the possibility of a title is even viable. Let us be content that at least we have a place to go for the sake of your child."

"Yes, of course," she said. He was a cautious man, but she had every confidence that they would be titled before the end of the year.

"That is all for now," he said, and picked up his pen.

Alexa leaned over to see what he was writing and noticed the letter was addressed to Mr. Fish. "Does Olivia know?"

"No," he said, and began to write.

"I shall tell her this morning, shall I?"

When Harry did not answer, Alexa walked around the desk and looked out the window. Another sun-filled spring day. Flowers would be blooming before long. She hoped she had gardens at Ashwood. Countesses ought to have gardens.

She was still smiling when she turned about and put her hands on Harry's shoulders. His body tensed instantly and she quickly withdrew her hands. "I beg your pardon."

"If you please, Alexa, I have quite a lot to do before we take our leave."

Alexa was mortified. Her mother had always assured her that in an arranged marriage, affection would come, but it might take a little longer than when one was free to choose. She certainly hoped that was true.

Most of the Careys had taken their leave by mid-morning, leaving only David behind. Belinda said an awkward good-bye to Olivia, then hurried off to the coach where her husband waited for her.

No one else spoke to her.

When the family had gone, David asked for Olivia in the study.

She made her way there, the bombazine dragging on the carpet behind her.

She didn't want to speak to David. She wanted to walk down to the lake and sit on a rock and remember the happy times she'd spent in Harrison's company.

David was pacing when she entered the study. He cleared his throat. "My uncle and I thought perhaps you might be more comfortable at the dowager house." He glanced at her uneasily, as if he expected a hysterical display.

At least it wasn't a convent in Ireland. "And Mr. Tolly?" she asked.

"He has been asked to leave."

She sighed and sank onto the edge of a chair. "After fifteen years of service to this family, he is cast out on the basis of rumor."

"You cannot be surprised," he said. "It is obvious to all concerned that something happened here, although none of us can agree as to exactly what. Nevertheless, the decisions have been made and we think a quiet existence at the dowager house is perhaps the proper way for you to mourn your loss."

As if she could not be trusted to be mourn properly.

"I beg your pardon, am I interrupting?"

Harrison's voice filled Olivia with hope. She quickly came to her feet as he strolled in. He looked so virile, so handsome. So competent. But he did not look himself.

And he did not look at her.

There was no ready smile for her, no warmth, and Olivia's heart sank. She should have expected it.

"Do come in, Tolly," David said. "We were just speaking of you."

"Were you, indeed? I came by only to inform you that Miss Hastings and I will depart by week's end. I will leave instructions on various accounts for my successor."

"As to that, is there anyone you might suggest?" David asked.

A cold smile spread across Harrison's face. "No one at all."

David frowned. "Have you any idea where you might go?"

"I intend to accept my inheritance and take my rightful place at Ashwood."

David snorted. When Harrison didn't smile, he eyed him skeptically. "What do you mean? Would you have me believe you have inherited the Ashwood estate in West Sussex?"

"I would," Harrison said calmly.

"But how?" David pressed. "How might a bastard inherit an estate such as that?"

"When the bastard's father has left no legitimate heirs and the original decree specifically grants the inheritance to any blood heir."

David laughed with surprise. "Bloody hell, I think you mean it."

"I do, indeed." Harrison looked at Olivia then, his gaze piercing hers.

Her breath was growing short. She felt a little dizzy, as if she might faint. "Must you leave so soon? There are so many details to be sorted out—"

"Lord Carey will have a new steward to sort through them."

"He's right, Olivia," David said. "And in the meantime, you might begin to acquaint yourself with the dowager house." He looked at Harrison. "We have asked Lady Carey to take up residence there. I assume there is some staff?"

"She deserves better treatment than that," Harrison said coldly.

David threw up his hands. "If my uncle had his way, she would have been turned out. It was the best I could do, given the circumstances."

"The best you could do?" Harrison scoffed. "The best you could do would be to believe her and admit that your brother was growing madder by the drink."

"I think it best if you go, Tolly," David said quietly. "Edward is not here to defend himself, and I will not tolerate the slander of his good name."

"Yet you will allow the slander of Lady Carey," Harrison said sharply.

David's face darkened. "She is no longer your concern."

Harrison glanced at Olivia. She had hurt him so deeply, she could see it rimming his eyes. He clenched his jaw. "No," he said quietly. "I do not suppose that she is." He gave her a curt nod. "If you will excuse me," he said, and walked out of the room.

Nothing Olivia had endured the last six years was more hurtful than watching Harrison walk determinedly away from her. There she sat, in her little tiny cage. She couldn't move. Her wings had been clipped.

CHAPTER TWENTY-EIGHT

"Can you believe it? I am to be a *countess*," Alexa said to Olivia. No one had ever expected that of her; Olivia had always been the one to be the lady. After all that had happened, Alexa couldn't believe that it was she who would find herself in this position.

"Yes, it would seem all has taken a turn for the better for you," Olivia said as she stared at the lace of her black shawl. She'd scarcely even looked at Alexa these last two days, which vexed her sister. Alexa thought that her excitement at the prospect of a life outside of the dowager house walls would have been much greater had Olivia not seemed quite so despondent.

Of course, Alexa wasn't so unfeeling that she didn't understand her sister's distress—she'd lost her standing in society, and her sister, and her friend in Mr. Tolly. And she was being made to move into the dowager house. But Alexa thought it would suit Olivia in the long run. Olivia would very much like the small study with the books and atlases and whatnot.

"Harry has left many of his books behind for you," Alexa offered, hoping that would cheer her sister. "He said that you were not afforded the luxury of reading before, and now you might avail yourself of many of his novels. Not all of them, however," she said. "We've stacks and stacks of books that must be brought along."

"That was thoughtful of him," Olivia said absently, and leaned back on the chaise longue to stare out the window.

"Really, Livi. I thought you would be at least a wee bit cheered that you are finally free of Edward."

"Alexa!"

"Am I wrong?" Alexa asked with a shrug. "Are you not at all relieved?"

Olivia snorted at that. "Freedom to one is just a cage to another."

Alexa rolled her eyes. She picked up two hats and held one, then the other up against her gown. "Which do you prefer?" she asked.

"The blue one."

Alexa sat it on her head, studying it. In the mirror's reflection, she could see Olivia's profile. Her head was bent, and she picked at the fabric of the chaise. Alexa had never seen her in such low spirits. Olivia was always so . . . *steady.* "Are you sad that I'm leaving? For it's not as if we won't see each other. You will come and visit me at Ashwood."

"I think you do not fully understand my position here, darling," Olivia said. "I haven't any money."

"Livi!" Alexa said laughingly. "You can very well afford it. You are still Lady Carey."

"Not for long," Olivia said with a shrug. "David will be about the business of marrying and producing an heir very soon. I consider myself fortunate to at least have a roof over my head."

"Now you are being silly," Alexa scoffed. "You will always be most welcome at Ashwood." She stood back to admire her traveling gown and spencer. "Harry will send for you," she said, and closed the small portmanteau with her things. "And before you say no to that, I must tell you that you are being rather difficult." Alexa looked at her sister and smiled. "I know you do not care for us to go, Livi. I wish you were to come with us. But we both must make the best of it, mustn't we?"

Olivia smiled wryly. "How ironic that you are content with the arrangements, and I am the one left to fend for myself. I suppose that means we've come full circle."

Alexa couldn't think of what to say to that. Wasn't that what Olivia wanted? "I suppose we have," she said with a shrug.

Olivia's gaze shifted to the window again. "When will you wed?"

Alexa would like to know the answer to that herself. "Harry claims he must see Ashwood and understand the finances before he will name the day. Soon, however. I told him that I thought it was terribly interesting that a mere fortnight ago, it was imperative that I marry straightaway. Now that the marquis has passed, it seems as if it can wait."

"Miss Hastings!" Rue called from the hallway.

Alexa rolled her eyes. "She never knocks," she whispered.

True enough, Rue opened the door and popped her head inside.

"Mr. Tolly says it is time."

The girl was beaming. She was wearing a new cloak. Why Harry thought it necessary to bring Rue along to Ashwood, Alexa could not say, but he'd made it clear that there would be no argument about it.

"Here," Alexa said, and handed Rue her portmanteau.

"Shall I put it on the coach?"

"I can think of no other way it might arrive at Ashwood," Alexa said.

Rue dipped a cheerful curtsy and went off with the portmanteau.

Alexa turned around and faced her sister. "I suppose this is farewell for now, Livi. But only for now."

Olivia nodded. She stood up from the chaise longue and held out her arms.

Alexa walked into them, and held her sister tight. She breathed in her sister's familiar scent and closed her eyes. "You will come, won't you, Livi? You know I am hopeless without you."

"And I am hopeless without you," Olivia said. She kissed Alexa's cheek and linked their arms. "I know you will be exceedingly well cared for," she said as they began to walk. "Promise me you will do as Mr. Tolly asks. Promise me that you will not be a bother to him. He has given up quite a lot for you, Alexa. He deserves your respect."

"Of course!" Alexa said. "You really must believe me when I say that after careful thought, I am happy with this arrangement. I think Harry and I shall get on well with each other. I think we shall be quite happy." Particularly when he was earl and she was countess, she thought warmly. "Now you must promise me that you will come when the baby is born, Livi."

Olivia smiled. "I will look forward to the happy news you have delivered a healthy child," she said.

Harry was waiting in the foyer for them in his cloak, which made his shoulders look broader than normal. He was holding his hat in his hands and stood with his legs braced apart. Alexa smiled at him as she and Olivia descended the stairs.

Harry did not smile in return. He was looking at Olivia, and Alexa noticed his hard swallow. Was it really so difficult for him? Was he so attached to this position and this family?

In the foyer, Alexa hugged her sister tightly once more. "Good-bye, Livi," she said and turned to the console to fetch her gloves.

"So this is farewell," Olivia said.

"For a time," Alexa said, and glanced over her shoulder to smile at her poor sister. But Olivia had made that comment to Harry. And she looked, Alexa thought, rather hopeless. That was odd. In all the years Olivia had been tormented by Edward, Alexa could not recall ever seeing her look like this. She'd seen Olivia despairing, fatigued, and sad . . . but not hopeless.

Alexa meant to say something pithy to lighten the moment, but she happened to glance at Harry, and to her surprise, her *great* surprise, she saw the same look on his face. And there was something more to Harry's expression: desire. Hopeless desire.

Alexa knew that look. A shiver of memory reminded her that she had seen that expression on Carlos's face more than once, that look of anguish mixed with desire. Seeing it on Harry's face was so startling that she wasn't certain what to do. Not that it mattered— neither he nor Olivia seemed to know she was still standing there.

"I'll . . . wait outside," she said, and fled the foyer. But as she went through the door, Alexa glanced back. They just stood there, staring at each other across the foyer.

Alexa's head was suddenly spinning, her mind racing back through all the moments she'd seen Harry and Olivia together. How could she have been so blind? How could she have missed what was so clearly before her? Why hadn't Olivia *told* her about her true feelings?

Alexa climbed into the carriage with Rue.

"It looks like a good day for traveling, aye, miss?" Rue chirped. "I've not been away from Everdon. Have you?"

"Yes," Alexa said absently.

"I wish Lady Carey could come, as well," Rue said, looking up out the window at the dowager house. "But I suppose the heir should be here with the Careys."

Alexa looked at Rue. "The heir? There is no heir!"

"But that's what his lordship said the night—"

"That was a malicious rumor, Rue! It wasn't true in the least, and you will not repeat it!"

"Oh. No, I won't. I won't say to anyone that the mistress's baby is not the heir."

Alexa would have taken Rue to task, but she saw a movement outside of the carriage window. It was Harry, striding out of the dowager house. He threw himself up on his horse, gave the signal to the driver, and the coach lurched forward so quickly that Alexa was tossed back against the squabs. She quickly righted herself, looked out the window, and saw Olivia holding on to the open door, watching them pull away, and it looked as if Olivia's knees would buckle.

Dear God. Harry and Livi were in love.

CHAPTER TWENTY-NINE

A shwood was not sufficiently far enough from Everdon Court and Olivia to suit Harrison. That was the most disappointing thing about the estate he'd inherited. Not that there weren't a great number of things with which to be disappointed—the peeling paint, the cracks around the foundations, the worn furnishings, to name a few—but if Harrison could have picked up this once grand mansion and set it down in Scotland, he would have done it.

As he could not, he had relied on whiskey to numb his anger in the week he'd been there.

What angered Harrison was that he had never run from anything in his life before now. He'd always run *toward* things, looking for that place of acceptance, and he'd believed that he'd found it in his employment with the Marquis of Carey. He'd known true acceptance in his friendships with Robert, with Mr. Dembly . . . and with Olivia. As a result, Harrison had made a dire mistake: he had believed. When the marquis had died, Harrison had believed that even a man like him could have the things that every man wanted: a woman to love and cherish, children to adore and who would carry on his name. A hearth, a home, laughter, memories.

To have that belief so thoroughly and suddenly dashed had sent him into an internal rage that was directed at the world at large. He'd long been accustomed to the censure he'd suffered among polite society for the circumstances of his birth and his mother's tawdry occupation, though he'd never really understood it. He was not his parents. He was his own man.

Lord Carey's father had been a man of true integrity who was willing to look at a man for what he was, not who bore him. Had it not been for the senior Lord Carey, Harrison would never have enjoyed the life he'd led these last fifteen years. He would never have met Olivia.

He thought often of his last moments with her in the foyer. So many thoughts had rifled through his head in the last few days, so many things he wished he had said to her. But he'd said nothing. Nothing! He'd been stung when Olivia, with tears shimmering in her eyes, had said, "Please just go, Harrison. Do not look back, for I will not dishonor this family or betray my sister. Not for you, not for me."

In that moment, Harrison could hardly look at her at all. He wondered if perhaps he had imagined the bond between them. Perhaps she had reached out to him in her grief, and not out of love as he had wanted to believe. Perhaps his love for her had colored his thinking.

Harrison knew only that he loved her yet, that he'd loved her for so long that he didn't know how to feel any other way. Except, perhaps, rejected. He'd learned how to feel that rather keenly of late.

Harrison also felt deprived of a full vetting of his feelings. He needed time, he needed a bottle, perhaps even a woman—something to take the hurt away. He needed something to keep him from missing her. But as he stood on the drive of Ashwood, staring at the façade, waiting for Mr. Fish to arrive, he recognized that Alexa was unwittingly serving as a constant reminder of all that he'd lost.

How could he marry her? How could he commit his life, his affection, his loyalty to a woman he did not love? How could he *not* marry her? They'd gone down a long road, and to cry off now would invite an even worse fate for Alexa and her child. Would he condemn the child she carried to the same fate he'd suffered? Had that not been Olivia's point in making him leave?

Yet his misgivings were becoming more and more obvious with each day. Alexa clearly sensed his reluctance. She had not pressed him, but she was growing impatient. Perhaps she was feeling reluctant, too. She had busied herself with taking full stock of the mansion, making lists of things they would need.

Harrison had assured her that once he reviewed the estate's ledgers with Mr. Fish, they would go about the business of giving her a child a name. That's how he had to think of it—he was giving her child a name. He could not think of it any other way, or that, God help him, he would have to make Alexa his wife in every sense of the word.

He heard the sound of an approaching coach and turned to see a barouche barreling down the road to the house, black plumes bouncing wildly. It rolled into the drive and before the coachman could remove himself from his perch on the back running board, the coach door swung open and out popped an attractive woman with black hair and pale green eyes.

"You are Mr. Tolly!" she called out to him, and came striding forward, her hand extended.

"I am," he said, and took her hand, bowing over it. "And you are ...?"

"I am Lady Eberlin," she said cheerfully. "Formerly Lady Ashwood, until we discovered that you exist." She smiled broadly. Behind her, a gentleman with wavy golden hair emerged from the coach. "May I present my husband, Lord Eberlin," she said, sweeping her hand in his direction and taking a slight step back.

As Harrison shook the man's hand, he saw Mr. Fish hop down from the coach, a thick ledger stuffed under one arm.

"Welcome to Hadley Green and Ashwood," Lord Eberlin said.

"Thank you," Harrison said. "Mr. Fish. How do you do?"

"Mr. Tolly!" Mr. Fish adjusted the heavy ledger he held under his arm. "I am very well, sir, very well! I am exceedingly glad that you have come after all."

"It was my letter, was it not?" Lady Eberlin said brightly. "My husband thinks I should not have written it, but then I heard you had come, and as I said to him, it must owe to my letter."

She smiled so hopefully that Harrison was hard-pressed to deny it. "You did indeed pen a very persuasive letter, madam," he said, and noticed Eberlin's wry smile.

"You must have so many questions," she said.

"A few," he agreed, and gestured to the house. "Will you come inside?"

As they walked inside, Alexa was coming down the staircase. Harrison noted with slight chagrin that if one looked closely, one could see the swell of her belly. She seemed surprised that they had guests, and Harrison tried to recall if he had mentioned it to her. "Allow me to introduce Miss Alexa Hastings. Miss Hastings, Lord and Lady Eberlin and Mr. Fish."

"A pleasure," Alexa said, curtsying. She looked at Harrison, clearly waiting for him to say more.

"Linford, will you bring tea?" Harrison said to the butler, and to the group, "Shall we?"

He did not miss Alexa's narrowed eyes as they walked to the salon.

They talked about the weather for a few minutes. Linford brought a tea service so quickly that Harrison wondered if he hadn't started brewing it after luncheon. Alexa served, but Harrison noticed she was unusually reserved, hardly speaking at all.

"How do you find the house, Miss Hastings?" Lady Eberlin asked.

"Lovely," she said. She sipped daintily from her teacup.

Lady Eberlin was eager to tell Harrison about the estate and the house. She was particularly proud of the unique staircase.

"It is a work of art," Harrison agreed. "Who was the artist?"

"My husband's father carved it," she said, beaming.

Eberlin did not look up from his cup of tea, and Harrison had the sense there were other secrets floating about the room.

"I tell you the history because it may not be apparent that Ashwood is a worthy estate," Lady Eberlin said. "I know that you were reluctant to accept it as yours."

Alexa looked at Harrison.

"I never thought the estate was unworthy, Lady Eberlin. I was dubious that I had inherited something so grand. And I preferred my work at Everdon Court. To accept my responsibilities here was to give up an occupation that I quite liked."

"But surely the title of earl and all the privilege afforded that title is more alluring than a stewardship?" Lady Eberlin asked laughingly.

"Yes, isn't it?" Alexa asked, looking at him directly, waiting to hear his answer.

Harrison ignored her and put down his teacup. "Perhaps you are unaware, Lady Eberlin, that I never knew my father. Only in passing, and even then, I was not aware that he was the man who had sired me until I was a young man. When Mr. Fish brought me the news that I had inherited his estate, I was not particularly intrigued by it. That is probably hard to understand unless one has been in my shoes."

"Actually," Lady Eberlin said as she put down her teacup and folded her hands in her lap, "I understand completely. He was my stepfather and I think he scarcely knew my name. I was quite surprised to have been named the heir, and quite reluctant to accept it. In fact, I fled to Italy and sent my cousin to oversee it—"

"Darling, perhaps we should leave that tale for another day," Eberlin said quietly.

"Right," she agreed. "The point is, Mr. Tolly, I can assure you from personal experience that you may come to appreciate this old place."

"May I ask why you gave it up? I never would have known about it, had you not sent Mr. Fish to me."

Her eyes widened with surprise. "Because it is not mine. It is *yours*." She smiled. "I would have handed it over sooner, but I did not know of your existence until we learned of Mrs. Priscilla Braintree, and if she hadn't been in possession of the portrait, we might never have discovered you. We are happy that we can put your rightful inheritance into your hands, and perhaps inquire after the jewels."

"Pardon?" Alexa asked.

"Lily, darling, I think you have rushed ahead of yourself," Lord Eberlin said, putting his hand on her knee. To Harrison, he said, "We sought the whereabouts of some priceless ruby jewelry that went missing from her aunt's things more than fifteen years ago. We searched the old earl's records, which led us to Mrs. Braintree. She had a portrait of your mother, Mr. Tolly, and in the portrait, your mother was wearing the ruby necklace from the collection. Mrs. Braintree didn't know what had happened to the jewels, but she did know of you. With a little digging, we were able to uncover your identity and your whereabouts."

"If I may be indelicate," Lady Eberlin said, "may I inquire if you know what happened to the jewels?" She leaned forward as if his answer was of the utmost importance.

Harrison frowned a little. His mother had quite a lot of jewelry. "Rubies, you say?" he asked, thinking.

"Yes, rubies," Lady Eberlin said eagerly. "A necklace, a coronet, and some earrings."

"Ah yes," he said. "I remember them well. She kept them in a box."

Lady Eberlin shared a look with her husband before pressing Harrison. "Do you know what became of them?"

He shrugged. "Wrapped around some grand dame's throat, I suspect."

Lady Eberlin looked crestfallen. Eberlin frowned down at his teacup.

"Have I said something wrong?" Harrison asked.

"Not at all," Eberlin said. "We rather hoped they might be found, to clear up an old mystery or two."

"I wish I could help you," he said. "The ruby jewelry was a gift to my mother. She occasionally had to sell large pieces to pay for our lodging and my schooling. I do recall the necklace quite well—she was fond of it and wore it often. But she sold it to a jeweler to pay for my apprenticeship."

"Oh dear," Lady Eberlin said, clearly disappointed. "Is it possible you might know where she came by the jewels?"

"It's rather obvious, my love," Eberlin said, and took her hand in his.

"From my father," Harrison said flatly. "Very plainly put, madam, he took them from your aunt to please his lover, and for that, I am very sorry. But I cannot be surprised. After all, he had a son whom he never acknowledged."

Harrison had not thought of the slights his father had given him in many years. But he was reminded of how painful it was to know that the earl had seen him, his son, so many times and looked right through him. It was as if Harrison had not even existed to that man. All those years he'd spent praying for a father, watching the men parading through his mother's life, wondering if any of them could be the one. When Harrison was very young, he imagined that one of them was his father and didn't know of him, and if only he could determine which one, he could tell them, *I am your son.* And in his innocence, he'd imagined the gentleman would fall to his knees in gratitude, would sweep him up and hold him tight, vowing to never let him go.

Harrison looked at Alexa. She was sitting very still, her gaze on a portrait above the hearth. She was surely thinking what he was thinking—that her child would be just like him. Harrison couldn't live with himself if he left her child to suffer that. He was doing the right thing. As privately painful as it was, he was doing the right thing for an unborn child.

"I did not mean to dredge up unpleasant memories," Lady Eberlin said. "I have been eager to solve the mystery of what happened to the jewels."

"And now you have your answer, my love," Eberlin said, and put aside his teacup. "Shall we leave them to the business of their estate? I am certain Mr. Fish has quite a lot of news to impart."

"I do indeed," Mr. Fish said, patting the ledger on his lap.

"Thank you for coming," Harrison said, and saw the Eberlins out. They paused in the foyer to look at the staircase.

"It's an astounding piece of work," Harrison said as he admired the meandering vine carved into the railing. "Your father is a master woodcarver, I take it?"

"He was. He is deceased," Eberlin said. A muscle in his jaw jumped. "He was hanged for the crime of stealing the ruby jewelry."

"I beg your pardon?" Harrison asked, startled.

Eberlin swallowed and looked at Harrison. "He was Lady Ashwood's lover. The old earl allowed him to be accused and to hang for the crime, so that he might give the jewels to your mother."

Harrison was shocked. "I . . . I don't know what to say."

Eberlin smiled. "There is nothing to say, Mr. Tolly. I have long since come to terms with it. I hope you will, too. By the bye, we've a box of things that we collected from Mrs. Braintree you might find of interest. I'll have it sent round on the morrow. Good day."

"Good day, sir," Lady Eberlin added, and allowed her husband to lead her out of the house.

"One cannot say Ashwood has not seen her share of tragedies," Mr. Fish said. "But I should like to think happier days have come. Shall we have a look at the books?"

They repaired to the study, where Mr. Fish gave Harrison a detailed discourse in the business of Ashwood. Mr. Fish was a thorough man and acquitted himself as well as Harrison would ever hope to do himself. It was clear the estate was suffering from poor fiscal management, but Harrison was seasoned at righting listing ships—Lord Westhorpe had given him ample opportunity over the years.

"I think we might reverse Ashwood's fortunes with a few strategic moves," he said as Mr. Fish prepared to take his leave.

"I agree, my lord," Mr. Fish said.

"I am not a lord, sir," Harrison corrected him.

Mr. Fish smiled. "Not at the moment, perhaps, but I think it inevitable. Lady Eberlin is determined that you shall have all that is rightfully yours."

"Yes," Harrison said. "About that. I would like to marry Miss Hastings as soon as is possible. It would be preferable if the posting of banns might somehow be avoided or expedited." He gave Fish a sidelong look. "Is that something you might arrange?"

Mr. Fish blinked, then nodded. "I think I might."

"You have probably guessed that time is of the essence. How soon might we stand before a clergyman?"

Mr. Fish's cheeks took on a slightly rosy hue. "I should think Friday. Shall I speak to the vicar on your behalf?"

"With all due discretion, please."

"Of course," Mr. Fish said.

Harrison could feel the heat in his neck, and clasped his hands at his back. "Thank you, Mr. Fish. Is there anything more?"

"No. I shall return on the morrow with the details you need."

Mr. Fish left—all but sprinting, really—and Harrison felt the heat in his neck climb to his cheeks. The die had been cast now. There was no turning back.

CHAPTER THIRTY
⊱♥⊰

Alexa dressed in one of the few gowns that didn't strain across her belly and would contain her swelling breasts. She would have to speak to Harry about suitable clothing for her spreading waistline.

She wondered when precisely she should do that as she donned her earrings. Since they'd arrived at Ashwood, she hadn't seen much of him. Should she mention it before their typically silent supper? Or after, during the silent respite in the salon before they retired?

Alexa studied her belly in the mirror, turning one way, then the other.

Ashwood wasn't what she had envisioned at all, really. It wasn't the house—the house and the grounds were worn, but she supposed that might be expected, given that no one had tended it for so long. The estate could all be made spectacular again with some funding and ideas.

What was wrong about Ashwood was Harry. Her would-be earl.

Alexa had believed they would marry, and she would be a countess, and she would spend her days readying her nursery and inviting ladies to luncheon. She hadn't really thought much beyond that. She'd avoided thinking beyond that. For when she thought of herself with a baby, she inevitably thought of Carlos, and the ache in her heart would flare and . . . well, she would rather not think of it.

But Alexa did like to think of how she might dress the nursery, and how she and Harry might walk about the grounds and have a look at things, and they would talk, and they would become the sort of friends she supposed men and women must be if they were married.

Yet they'd been here a little more than a week, and instead of growing closer as she had hoped, Harrison seemed to grow more distant. Moreover, he was cross. He was no longer the smiling, self-possessed man she'd first encountered at Everdon Court. When Alexa had made the mistake of remarking on it one night, he had curtly informed her that Ashwood required his attention at present, and he apologized if that did not meet with her expectations.

Alexa had retired that evening feeling childish and patronized.

Moreover, she did not believe him. It wasn't the business of Ashwood that had occupied his thoughts;

it was Olivia. Alexa had glimpsed the truth on the day she and Harry had departed Everdon Court, and Harry and Olivia could not seem to tear their eyes from one another. But Alexa had reasoned that all away. She and Harry had embarked on a new path now, and as they were a day's ride from Everdon Court, the affection between Harry and Olivia would fade.

She could no longer pretend that was so. The truth could not have been more glaring to Alexa this afternoon, when Lord and Lady Eberlin had called. Harry had introduced her only as Miss Hastings. He'd left their association to the imagination of the Eberlins, and Alexa had felt humiliated.

Harry couldn't even say it, and because he couldn't, the Eberlins undoubtedly thought she was his sister, or his housekeeper, or his mistress—any one of which would make a sudden marriage rather difficult to explain.

Alexa guessed she had at most a month before her situation was noticeable to everyone. Not to mention that the approaching date of the child's birth would become harder and harder to explain away in any believable way. She had agreed to tie her future to Harry, and now she was dangling at the end of very uncertain rope.

It was Olivia that kept Harry from noticing Alexa. In hindsight, she could see it all so clearly: the way they smiled at each other, as if they shared a secret. Or the times Alexa had come across the two of them, and their heads were together, whispering. She had foolishly believed they were whispering about *her*.

She recalled the day Olivia's decorum had slipped a little and she had referred to Harry by his given name, a sure indication that there was a certain intimacy there—Olivia would never step out of the bounds of propriety and call the steward by his given name. And of course, the day Alexa, Rue, and Harry had taken leave of Everdon Court. Standing in the foyer of the dowager house, Alexa had felt as if she were swimming through all the tension between Harry and her sister.

How could she have been so bloody blind?

It was so out of character for Olivia! She'd always been the quiet, studious one, the daughter their mother had once lamented was so good in character and disposition that she feared Olivia was missing any spice in her life. Yet it was Olivia, simple Olivia, who held Harry's heart in her hand. Alexa couldn't even gain his attention, much less wedge herself inside his heart.

She had to *do* something. She could not remain here at Ashwood, growing bigger and bigger and languishing on the edge of scandal, unloved, forgotten, and alone. She put her hand on the soft swell of her belly as she gazed into the mirror. It was time to be even bolder than she normally was. She would speak to Harry now.

The doors of the salon were open when Alexa arrived. Harry was already there, standing with one hand on the mantel, his head down as if he were deep in thought. One would think he wasn't even aware that a footman stood to one side, waiting to be of use.

When the footman saw Alexa, he said, "Good evening, miss. Shall I pour wine?"

Harry jerked around as if she'd snuck up on him.

Alexa smiled at the footman. "No, thank you, Louis."

"Alexa," Harry said. "How are you?"

"Well, thank you. And you?"

He nodded. He picked up his wineglass and drank, draining the remainder in one long swallow. He moved to meet her in the middle of the room, planted a peck on her cheek, and then gestured to the settee.

Alexa sat. He flipped out his tails and sat beside her and smiled. Not the easy smile she'd come to know. This smile did not crinkle the corners of his eyes. This smile seemed forced.

"How was your day?" he asked.

"Tedious," she admitted. "And yours?"

"Busy," he said. He fixed his gaze on the carpet. "There is much to be done."

Alexa had had enough. "Harry, may I ask you a question?"

"Of course." He was still looking at the carpet, hardly present at all.

"When shall we wed?" she asked bluntly.

Harry came off the settee so quickly it was as if he'd been burned. "Thank you, Louis, I think we might be alone now," he said.

The footman nodded and went out of the salon, closing the door behind him.

Harry turned around to face Alexa. "You might be a bit more circumspect in your remarks."

"Why should I? All of Ashwood shall know I am carrying a child soon enough. They will wonder why I am here with you, as much as I do."

"Not again," Harry groaned. "I thought I had explained it quite clearly. There are things I must attend to before we wed."

"What things?" she asked skeptically.

"As I have explained, there are many issues surrounding the inheritance and the legalities of marriage that must be settled."

"Why must they be settled before we stand before a clergyman?" she asked.

He sighed as if she were taxing him. "So that I might settle on you all the rights and privileges you deserve as my wife. Honestly, Alexa, if I am to be your husband, you must learn to trust me."

"Therein lies the problem, Harry," she said crossly, and folded her arms across her belly. "I do *not* trust you. I think it time we stop pretending."

"Pretending *what*, pray tell?"

"Pretending that you are not desperately in love with my sister, that's what."

"Good God," he muttered. He stalked to the sideboard and helped himself to more wine.

"Do you deny it?"

"Will you slander your sister with such careless talk?" he shot back, avoiding the question. "When I think of all that she has done for you—"

"I do not slander her!" Alexa said angrily, and came to her feet. "I am saying what we both know is true. A month ago, marrying me off and saving my reputation was of the utmost importance. Today, however, it can wait. Yet I am getting bigger, and you have become cross, and I think you have no intention of marrying me at all."

"You are imagining things," he said curtly. "You need an occupation."

"And yet you have not denied it!" she exclaimed. "I saw the way you looked at her when we left Everdon Court. I have seen the smiles between the two of you. I can *see* your regard for her, Harry."

"*Stop!*" he said sharply. "Regard for someone does not equate to love."

Alexa groaned. "Why will you not admit it?"

"Why will you not bloody well keep yourself out of my affairs?" he shot back.

Alexa gasped.

"You do not know me, Alexa. Do not presume that because I have extended my protection that you know *anything* about me." He turned away again, downed the wine, and slapped the glass onto the sideboard.

"I did not ask you to marry me, Harry," she said softly.

He shook his head and sighed heavenward. "No,

you did not," he said, his voice calmer. "I offered for you, and you accepted, and on Friday, we shall stand before a clergyman and join in matrimony."

"Pardon?" Alexa said as his words sank into her consciousness. "Friday?"

"Yes. Friday. As I said, certain things had to be taken care of first."

Alexa gasped with surprise and delight. She ran to him and put her arms around his waist, her head against his back. "Thank you, Harry! I was beginning to believe you would not honor your word!"

He sighed. He ran his hands over the top of his head and moved so that she had to drop her arms. He turned around to face her, his gray eyes studying her face. "Have you not realized it yet, lass? You are carry-ing a child who does not have a name."

"Yes but I—"

He took her chin between his fingers. "I will reveal a little secret to you, Alexa. I would give up all of this," he said, gesturing to the room about them, "to have known a father. I would give up everything I have ever had for the privilege of knowing what it is like to be held by a father. My life would have been far easier if I had had a legitimate name. That is what we must do for your child. The time has passed for any concerns over our own selfish wants, for there will soon be a helpless being who must take precedent."

Alexa eyed him closely, looking for something she wasn't seeing, a sense that they were together in this.

It felt very odd to her, as if his conviction was firmly in place, but his heart was nowhere to be found. "Do I have your word?" she asked.

He swallowed as if he were forcing down a bitter elixir. "I asked Mr. Fish to arrange it all today. He assured me that Friday we could be wed."

Alexa blinked. She put her hand on her abdomen and nodded. "Thank you." It was what she wanted, but it almost felt as if the floor slanted in this spot; she was having trouble finding the center of her balance.

"Shall we dine?" he asked, offering his arm.

Alexa had very little appetite, but allowed him to lead her to the dining room.

As was Harry's habit, very little was said as they consumed the first course of onion soup. Alexa scarcely tasted it at all. She couldn't seem to shake the unsteadiness of her feelings. She had what she wanted; why, then, did she suddenly feel so restless?

"I think," she said carefully, "that we should pay Olivia a call once we are wed."

Harry's head came up quickly.

"I am sure after all she's been through, she might like the company," Alexa said.

An emotion scudded across Harry's features. He picked up his fork and knife and cut his meat.

"Or perhaps we might invite her here—"

"No," he said abruptly, before Alexa could suggest her sister attend their nuptials. He put down his utensils and leaned back, his gaze on Alexa.

"It seems as if we owe her that, at least," Alexa said.

"No," he said again, his gaze unwavering.

Alexa looked away. The restlessness in her only grew. "Then I shall write her and tell her we will call at Everdon Court after the nuptials."

Harry didn't disagree. In fact, he didn't speak at all.

The disquieting feeling did not leave Alexa, and when she and Harry sat in the salon after supper— he with his book—she stared at the painting of a man on a white horse above the hearth. She couldn't find any physical comfort. It was as if she were sitting on a lumpy cushion and couldn't find the smooth place.

"Are you uncomfortable?" Harry asked.

Alexa hadn't realized he was watching her. She shook her head and smiled wryly. "I have suffered a lifelong curse of restlessness," she said sheepishly. "Livi would tell you that I always appear to be sitting on hot coals."

He smiled at that and returned to his book.

"Once, when I was a girl, my mother sent the two of us to call on our grandmother," Alexa continued. "I never cared for that old woman. She was quite ill and hard of hearing, scarcely even knew who we were, and she was cruel."

Harry closed his book.

"She was spiteful," Alexa said, surprised she had his attention. "Mamma said she suffered from senility, but I think she was very aware." She frowned slightly at the memory of the spiteful old woman who would strike them with a walking stick when she thought one of them misbehaved. "Nevertheless, my mother commanded we go and pay our respects. It was Olivia's responsibility to make certain I behaved and did not upset Grandmamma."

Harry smiled.

"We sat in my grandmother's parlor and she held a cane across her lap, and if she thought we did something we ought not to do, she would strike us with it. But that afternoon, she had taken quite a lot of laudanum for one pain or another, and she kept nodding off as she was speaking. I happened to see a little iron bird that sat on her table," Alexa said, sketching it with her hands. "It was the oddest little decorative bird. It was on a hinge and I supposed it would lean over and peck the table, then swing back up. I picked it up. Olivia told me to put it down, straightaway, but I was stubborn and I would not—I was restless."

"As you are now?" Harry asked.

She smiled. "Precisely as I am now."

"What happened?"

"I was holding the bird and Grandmamma began to rouse. Olivia grabbed it, and her finger got caught in the hinge. It sliced her, just there," she said, gesturing to the knuckle of her little finger. "Grandmamma opened her eyes and saw Olivia holding the bird and whacked her with the cane and said she was not to touch things that did not belong to her." Alexa smiled sheepishly. "It was all my fault."

One of Harry's brows drifted up. "I've seen the scar."

He had noticed the tiny scar on her knuckle? "She didn't cry out or utter a word of protest. She said only, 'I beg your pardon, Grandmamma.' And when we left, I told her I was dreadfully sorry, but she said I should not think of it, but that she would be pleased if next time, I would leave Grandmamma's things alone."

Harry chuckled. "It would seem she has been caring for you a long time, eh?"

"Yes." Alexa gazed into the fire a moment, thinking back. "Frankly, she is the only one who has cared quite so much for me."

"I've always enjoyed her humor," Harry said. "She has quite a keen sense of humor."

"Olivia!" Alexa said, surprised by that. "How do you mean?"

"Once, at a supper at Everdon Court, Lady Fenster attended. She can be opinionated and determined to share her opinions on any number of subjects. She was not enamored with the leek soup that was served and said that if the leeks had stayed in the ground past their prime, their taste was more of dirt than of leek. Implying, of course, that the leeks used in the soup were past their prime and tasted of dirt. Lady Carey was rather cheerful about it and apologized for the soup, and sent it back to the kitchen and requested another soup for Lady Fenster. Mind you, that probably took some doing."

"I can imagine it did," Alexa agreed.

"Weeks later, several of the same people were invited back for a garden party and they played croquet. Lady Fenster fancies herself rather good at croquet. Her favorite color is blue, so Lady Carey gave her the blue mallet and ball. But with every strike of her mallet, Lady Fenster sent her ball veering off to the side."

"Why?" Alexa asked.

"That is what Lady Fenster wanted to know. She complained loudly over it. Before everyone, Lady Carey picked up the blue ball and examined it. 'Oh, see here,' she said, to Lady Fenster. 'The ball is misshapen.' Lady Fenster demanded to know how that had happened. Lady Carey said, 'I imagine it was left on the ground past its prime.'" He chuckled. "Naturally Lady Fenster did not recall her remark, but others did. It was later revealed to me by the groundskeeper that Lady Carey had employed him to shave a bit off the ball and repaint it."

Alexa laughed. "Olivia did that?"

"She did indeed," he said, and smiled fondly.

Alexa had never seen that side of her sister. To her, Olivia was the person who was always there when she needed a hand, or a shoulder. She was the older sister, there for Alexa to run to when times were bad, and quickly forgotten when times were good and there were other, more diverting people about.

She'd never thought of Olivia as funny. Or mischievous.

Those thoughts plagued Alexa the rest of the evening.

When she retired for the night, she shooed Rue away and sat in a chair, staring into the fire until it was nothing but coals.

When their mother had died unexpectedly, Alexa had been full of grief and righteous indignation. She'd believed her life unfair. She'd lost her father and her mother. She'd been left with no money, and a stepfather who was on his way home to Italy practically before her mother's body had gone cold. She'd had no one but Olivia.

Olivia was the one who had urged her to take the trip to Spain. "You should go while you are young." She'd given Alexa the money she'd gained from selling one of her mother's pearl brooches, and Alexa had gone off to Spain with the idea that she was entitled to do as she pleased, for she had suffered.

Alexa never once thought of Olivia's suffering.

And in Spain, Alexa had done something she ought not to have done, obviously, and when her heart was broken, she had known without a doubt that Olivia would fix it for her. Olivia had done precisely that. She'd given Alexa the man she loved. Olivia had done it because she was married and she could not have Harry—but then Edward had died, and everything had changed . . . and yet, Olivia had made sure that Alexa was cared for.

It was time, Alexa thought, that she solved her

own troubles. It was time that she owned what she had done, as well as the consequences. She stood up and walked to the small writing desk in her room, sat down, withdrew a sheet of vellum, and dipped the pen in the inkwell.

Then she wrote a letter to Carlos.

CHAPTER THIRTY-ONE

On Friday morning, Mr. Fish arrived with the parish vicar, Mr. Meachamp, to perform the wedding ceremony. Mr. Fish would serve as a witness and Harrison had arranged for Rue to serve as well. When he'd explained to the simple girl that she would witness to his marriage to Miss Hastings, Rue had seemed confused.

"What is it, Rue?"

"My lord, do you not love Lady Carey, then?" she'd asked, clearly distressed.

"Sir," he corrected. "Wherever did you get the idea that I loved Lady Carey?" he'd asked, hoping that his feelings were not so obvious that even Rue could discern them.

"But that is why his lordship fell off his horse! Everyone knows it."

The girl truly had more hair than wit. Harrison had put his arm around her shoulders. "His lordship fell off his horse because he was foxed. And what have I told you about rumor and gossip? Are you to listen to it?"

Rue frowned. "No, milord."

"Sir. Did you recall what I told you before we left Everdon, that what you might have heard about the night the marquis died was all gossip and rumor?"

"No," Rue said, sniffing back a tear.

Harrison cocked his head to one side. "Will you try to remember it now?"

"Yes."

"Now listen carefully, Rue. I am about to tell you something that is not to leave this house. Do you quite understand?"

She'd nodded.

"Miss Hastings is with child. I am going to marry her so that the child will have a name."

"Miss Hastings!" Rue had cried. "You had your way with her, *too*?"

"For the love of God," Harrison had said, and pointed to the couch. "Sit, you foolish girl. And for God's sake, for once, will you listen?"

He had no idea if Rue had listened or not, but she was in the salon this morning, her gown pressed and a small mishap patched. She was also holding a handful of wildflowers that, she announced, she'd picked yesterday. But she'd neglected to put them in water, judging by their appearance.

"We are ready to begin, sir," the vicar said.

Harrison nodded. A strange shiver ran down his

spine. *This is not a prison sentence,* he told himself. *With time, I might come to care for Alexa.* The distance he felt toward her now wasn't Alexa's fault. It was that his heart was firmly entrenched in Olivia's.

He hoped that, at the very least, he would be a good father to Alexa's child.

"Linford, fetch Miss Hastings if you please," he said.

Who is to say we'll not have more children? Harrison liked the thought of that. He'd always wanted a large brood. Perhaps Aunt Olivia would come and visit.

That was absurd. Of course Olivia would visit, and he would feel the pain and misery of being so close and yet unable to touch her. To hear her laugh and know that it was not for him. No matter how he tried to paint a rosy little portrait, it always faded in the light of Olivia's beautiful face, her dancing blue eyes, a strand of white blonde hair teasing her cheek. *She* was the woman he loved. *She* was the woman he wanted. How in the bloody hell had he come to this moment?

There was no turning back now. So Harrison clasped his hands tightly behind his back and sought the strength to do what he had to do.

Alexa was staring at her reflection in the mirror when Linford came for her. She was wearing a sunny yellow ball gown she'd had made in Madrid that Rue had helped her alter, one she had planned to wear during the Season in London this year. It was pretty, and it made her look a lot more cheerful than she was.

But she was not a blissful bride.

Alexa followed Linford down to the salon, ready to say her vows. But when she stepped across the threshold, and saw Harry standing with those he'd assembled to witness their marriage, she felt something hitch in her heart.

"Alexa? If you please," Harrison said, gesturing to his side, as if he wanted it over and done so he might begin the work of burying it beneath the mountain of regret that he'd so clearly piled onto his shoulders.

She approached him slowly, feeling entirely at odds with herself.

Harrison frowned. "Are you all right?"

All right? How could she be all right? She absently put her hand on her abdomen and gave him a shaky little smile. "I am well, thank you. Perhaps better than I have been in some time."

His brows rose with surprise. "I am glad to hear it. If you will stand here, we might begin."

Alexa did as he asked, and curtsied to the vicar. "My lord reverend," she said, and leaned around Harrison. "Mr. Fish, thank you for coming. And you, Rue— thank you."

"I brung you flowers, miss," Rue said, thrusting a sad little bouquet at her.

Surprised and touched, Alexa took the bouquet. "Thank you." She noticed that her hand was shaking, so she gripped the bouquet tighter and lifted a smile to the vicar.

"Miss Hastings? Mr. Tolly? Shall I proceed?" the vicar asked.

"Yes," Harry said briskly. He was a man resigned to his fate.

The vicar moved Rue and Mr. Fish in a bit closer, to stand on either side of Alexa and Harry. "Dearly beloved," he began, his voice taking on a grave tone, "we are gathered together here in the sight of God . . ."

Alexa watched the vicar's throat bob as he spoke. This felt almost a dream. She glanced at Harry, and it struck her—what felt wrong was that Olivia should be standing here, not her. She was standing in Olivia's place.

"First, it was ordained for the procreation of children . . ." the vicar continued, and looked directly at Alexa. Of course if one was to have a child, one must be married. Of course she had to marry Harry for the sake of her child. Wasn't that what the vicar meant?

"Secondly, it was ordained for a remedy against sin and to avoid fornication . . ." he said, his voice rising a little.

Ah yes, the perils of fornication. Alexa knew them better than most, and had felt the depth of that anguish. Not because she'd done it, but because she still couldn't think of the moments she'd spent in Carlos's arms without feeling the ache of missing him. She glanced at Harry again from the corner of her eye and wondered if he felt anguish. How could he not? He loved Olivia, just as Alexa loved Carlos. *How deep is your ache, Harry?*

It should be Olivia standing here. Not her. But Olivia wasn't carrying a child. Alexa was.

". . . into which holy estate these two persons present come now to be joined. Therefore if any man can show any just cause why they may not lawfully be joined together, let him now speak, or else hereafter forever hold his peace." The vicar looked at Mr. Fish, who kept his gaze on the ground. He then eyed Rue, who furiously shook her head and stepped back.

The vicar then looked at Harrison. "Mr. Tolly, wilt thou have this woman as thy wedded wife, to live together after God's ordinance in the holy estate of matrimony? Wilt thou love her, comfort her, honor and keep her, in sickness and in health and forsaking all others, keep thee only unto her for as long as ye both shall live?"

Alexa felt all emotion draining out of her.

"I will," Harry said, his voice surprisingly clear and strong. He even managed a bit of a smile for Alexa.

Poor man. She felt numb.

"Miss Hastings," the vicar continued, "wilt thou have this man as thy wedded husband, to live together after God's ordinance in the holy estate of matrimony? Wilt thou obey him, and serve him, love, honor and keep him, in sickness and in health and forsaking all others, keep thee only unto him for as long as ye both shall live?"

Alexa hesitated. She looked at Harry, at his gray eyes. There was no emotion there, not even a flicker. *It should be Olivia standing here. Not her.* "I . . . say no."

No one spoke for a moment. "Pardon?" Harry asked, as if he'd misunderstood her.

But Alexa was suddenly very clear. "I cannot," she said, shaking her head.

"Alexa," Harry said softly. "What are you about?"

"I realize this comes at a very inopportune time, Harry, but I . . . I do not love you," she said apologetically. "I love someone else."

His face darkened. "For God's sake, Alexa," he whispered hotly, "I think we have established that—"

"And so do you," she whispered. "This is not the answer—there must be another way. For *both* of us."

"But Miss Hastings, you carry his child!" Rue whispered loudly.

Alexa glanced heavenward, then looked sheepishly at the stunned vicar. "Not his," she said. "Mr. Tolly was kind enough to pretend it, but I must be honest. The child is not his."

"Good God," Mr. Fish said, shocked.

"But you do carry a child. A fatherless child," Harry reminded her.

"Yes," Alexa said thoughtfully. "The child will bear my shame, there is no doubt. But will my baby also bear my compromise for the sake of appearances?" She was asking herself, really, although she knew the answer. And the answer was no. Her child might be a bastard, and never know its father, and be shunned in society. But Alexa would not destroy another person's happiness just to give the appearance that her child was not a bastard.

It all seemed so clear to her now.

The vicar and Rue both gaped at her. And Harry . . .

Harry sighed to the ceiling. "If you will excuse us a moment," he said, and gripped Alexa's elbow tightly, turning her about and marching her out of the salon to speak to her privately.

But Alexa had made up her mind and would not be swayed.

CHAPTER THIRTY-TWO
꙳ஐ꙳

In the first days after Alexa and Harrison had left Everdon Court, Olivia found herself watching the clock on the mantel quite a lot.

She had nothing to occupy her at the dowager house, nothing to do with the many hours in the day but think of Harrison.

She thought of Alexa, too, and wondered how she was getting on, but in truth, Olivia had begun to understand that she was very angry with Alexa.

Alexa had taken so much from her. Even as a girl, Alexa had been the one to gain the attention and favors from their mother and stepfather. She was bubbly and pretty, and had been the one to go off and experience the world, while Olivia was made to marry so that she might look after her sister when the time came.

And now Alexa had Harrison. She had Olivia's love.

Harrison had left a void in her life that was so deep, Olivia feared it would never be filled. His absence made everything around her feel so dull. Time was still, and minutes turned to years. The air was stale, and she felt short of breath. The silence, God, the silence—there was nothing, no sound, only the constant ticking of the clock. Olivia yearned for Harrison, ached to see the smile in his gray eyes.

Every day she awoke and braced herself for the emptiness to burrow into her. She tried to divert her thoughts, but nothing seemed to work. Needlework was pointless. She'd called on Bernie, but Bernie had seemed anxious. At first, Olivia didn't know why her friend was behaving so strangely, but it had finally dawned on her—the rumors.

Bernie's anxious cheerfulness was unusually grating. Olivia didn't want cheerfulness. If she'd had her way, the whole world would have joined her in dragging somberly about with heavy hearts and downcast eyes.

She found no society at Everdon Court, either. The Careys had departed shortly after the funeral, and when David returned a few days later, he was in the company of many friends. Or so Olivia heard from Mrs. Lampley.

"Mrs. Perry is at sixes and sevens with them about," she'd reported, shaking her head. "They gamble all night, sleep half the day, and won't come round for supper when it's served. And last night they had *guests,* if you take my meaning," she'd added, waggling her brows at Olivia.

Olivia could scarcely suppress a little smile. Edward would have been furious.

Olivia was not invited to the main house.

Her dark humor deepened day by day. Olivia could find nothing to laugh about, nothing to amuse her. Nothing could ease her pain.

One morning, as she wandered about the dowager house searching for an occupation, Olivia opened the door to the study. Mrs. Lampley had told her it was where Harrison had spent most of his time, reading or working.

"He loved his books, he did," she'd said.

Olivia had avoided this room. In addition to the bedchamber where he'd slept, this was where she would feel his presence most. But when she walked in, she wasn't overwhelmed with his presence. He was missing from this room, just as he was missing everywhere else.

She looked around her; the shelves were mostly bare now. He'd taken his collection of books, and there was nothing on the desk; it had been dusted clean. There was really nothing at all to say that Harrison had occupied this room for years.

Except for a small stack of books on a side table near the window. Olivia walked over and picked up the one on top, her fingers tracing the spine. She opened the book. *Camilla; or, A Picture of Youth*.

She turned the page and was surprised to find a note tucked inside.

To O: This book is written by Fanny Burney. In all the years I lived in London, I did not see the world she describes. Her novel opened my eyes to a very different town than the one I knew. H.T.

Olivia blinked with surprise and slowly sank onto the chair.

She put that book aside and opened the next. *Faust.* Inside was another note.

While I found this tale to be highly implausible, I found it wildly entertaining. As I pen this note to you now, it feels as if I have made my own deal with the devil. You must read the book to understand what I mean.

Olivia closed the book in her lap. The realization that Harrison had left her a parting gift in these books and these notes sent pain shooting through her. She gathered the books to her breast and bent over, sobbing. The feelings she'd spent so many years pushing down so that she could tolerate her life, finally flooded their shores, spilling onto these books that Harrison had touched and left for her. She sobbed until she could cry no more, and when the last tear was wrung from her, Olivia pushed herself upright then wiped her eyes with her sleeve.

"*Enough*," she said softly.

It was done. He was gone. He wouldn't be back, and

she couldn't carry on like this, mourning and pining away without hope. Would she be a woman to waste away in her widow weeds? Or would she pick herself up and carry on? She had a life worth living, and it was high time she started.

It was with a new outlook that Olivia emerged Monday morning. The day was gloriously bright, the spring colors magnificent. She donned her best boots and a bright red scarf, picked up the novel *Camilla*, tucked it under her arm, and went marching into the kitchen.

"Good morning, milady!" Mrs. Lampley sang. "You've come up with the sun, it would seem."

"Yes, indeed. I should like a luncheon basket, if you please, Mrs. Lampley. I mean to take a very long walk."

"Now there is a lovely idea," Mrs. Lampley said. "Not a cloud in the sky this morning."

Olivia smiled and picked up a muffin. She took a bite of it. "Delicious." For the first time in days, she actually noticed the taste of something.

"You'll not believe it when I tell you I've had a letter from Rue!" Mrs. Lampley said as she lined a basket with a linen cloth.

"Rue!" Olivia repeated skeptically. "I suppose my sister helped her write it."

"I hardly think so," Mrs. Lampley said. "The letter is written very poorly and the handwriting atrocious!" She laughed as she cut cheese from the wheel and put it in the basket. "She said that Mr. Linford, the butler at Ashwood, helped her to spell some of the words."

Olivia smiled. "She is well, I hope."

"Oh, very. And quite excited that she was asked to witness the marriage between Mr. Tolly and Miss Hastings. She's rather proud of that."

Olivia couldn't seem to draw a breath. She looked at Mrs. Lampley, who wore a cheery smile as she sliced through a loaf of bread.

"My sister and Mr. Tolly wed?" Olivia heard herself ask.

Mrs. Lampley's knife stopped. "I beg your pardon, mu'um. I assumed you knew. I'd heard it from Mrs. Perry."

Mrs. Perry! How would Mrs. Perry know, and not Olivia? "They married," she repeated.

"Aye." Mrs. Lampley withdrew Rue's letter from her apron pocket and handed it to Olivia.

Olivia read the letter twice, as there were numerous misspellings and strange marks. But it was clear that Alexa and Harrison had set a date to wed—three days ago—and Rue was to be a witness.

They had been man and wife for three days.

Olivia sank onto Mrs. Lampley's work stool, staring at Rue's crudely written letter.

"Are you unwell, mu'um?" Mrs. Lampley asked.

"I am disappointed that I wasn't there for the nuptials," she lied.

"Oh, of course. Perhaps they sent word and it was lost."

"Perhaps," Olivia muttered. The kitchen, with its

low ceiling and stone walls, was beginning to feel very close. "Well then," she said, handing the letter back to Mrs. Lampley. "I think I shall take that walk in the sun." She took the basket Mrs. Lampley had put together and forced a smile. "Good day, Mrs. Lampley."

"Good day, Lady Carey."

Olivia walked outside and stood in the garden with hens pecking around her boots looking for grain. It was just as well that she'd not known; she'd been on the verge of collapsing under her grief as it was. She couldn't imagine how ill with despair she might have been had she known the day, the hour, the moment he had pledged his eternal fidelity to Alexa.

It was done. It was over. He had married her sister, and of all the cruelties Olivia had ever been made to suffer, that had to be the cruelest blow. And worse, she'd delivered the blow to herself. She had insisted on it; she had sent him away, so she had only herself to thank for it.

Olivia was weary of it all.

She walked along the path down to the gate, hopped onto the bottom rung, and pushed it open, swinging out. She hopped down and shut the gate, and as she turned about, she saw two riders coming down from the main house. Olivia paused, adjusting her bonnet.

David and a gentleman pulled up alongside her.

"Lady Carey," David said, removing his hat. "How does the day find you?"

"Very well," Olivia said, remembering to curtsy to

him, now that he was the marquis. "I had heard you'd come down from London."

"May I introduce Mr. Eason?"

"Madam," Mr. Eason said, bowing over his horse's neck.

"Good day, sir," Olivia said.

"Mr. Eason is the new steward," David said, and put his hat on his head again.

"Ah." She smiled.

David looked at his hand. "I had intended to invite you for to tea, Olivia, but as long as we are here, I should tell you that we—that is, my uncle and I—thought that perhaps you might be more comfortable at the Greystone House on the Ridgeley estate."

Olivia's heart sank. She looked at Mr. Eason, who seemed very uncomfortable. "Ridgeley," she said.

David nodded.

"In Cornwall?" she asked coolly.

"Yes," David said. "Naturally, we will send you with a maid. And a cook. There is a couple who lives at the Greystone House to tend to things."

"But it is in Cornwall, David," she said. "My life is here."

"Yes, well . . ." He shifted in his saddle. "We need the dowager house for Mr. Eason. He is now the steward and he should be closest to me."

Mr. Eason looked as if he would like to crawl under a rock. Olivia stepped up to David's horse and put her hand on the steed's neck. "I thought we were friends."

"We are!" he said hastily. "Of course we are. We do regret the inconvenience, Olivia, but what are we to do?"

Yes, what was the family of a cruel and damaged man to do but cast aside his wife? "I suppose you are to exile me to Cornwall. My husband has been gone scarcely more than a fortnight and I've already been forced out of my surroundings."

"And whose fault is that?" David asked. He looked uneasily at Mr. Eason, but found no help there.

"I'll just ride up the path and have a look about, shall I?" Mr. Eason said, and spurred his horse on.

"Mr. Eason is prepared to bring his family to Everdon Court by the month's end," David said.

Olivia's gaze narrowed. "I have a week?"

David shrugged. "If there was any other way . . ." he said.

"There are many other ways, David. But you would like me out of sight and I am powerless to stop you. So be it. You have delivered your verdict, so if you will excuse me . . ." She started to walk down the path.

"Olivia," David said pleadingly.

Olivia twirled around, and continued walking backward. "Edward was a drunk, David! He was cruel and he was mad and forced his will on me! You know—you *know* what I endured! But I did not cuckold him!" She turned around and marched down the path.

She despised David. She despised all of the Careys. She despised that women had no voice and could be shoved about. She would be happy to leave Everdon

Court, but she would *not* go to Cornwall. David and his family could send her to Hades for all she cared—she would not waste away on some windswept cliff.

London, perhaps. Or perhaps *she* would go to Spain and take a Spanish lover! France! What was a little war when one's family turned against one?

Olivia was so angry, she'd marched all the way to the river before she realized it. She dropped her basket and her book, then collapsed onto her knees, glaring at the water rushing past.

When her breath had returned to normal, Olivia removed her cloak and spread it on the riverbanks. She looked in the basket, but she had no appetite, so she picked up the book and opened it, rereading the note Harrison had left her. She turned to the first page and began to read.

How long she read, Olivia didn't know. At first she'd found her mind wandering, and was forced to reread passages. But the story that began to unfold before her was about a seventeen-year-old girl who was naïve and too trusting.

Ah, she knew that girl well.

When she tired of reading, she rolled onto her back and watched the clouds scudding across the afternoon sky. Maybe she could carve a life for herself. Maybe she could put Harrison and everything that had happened at Everdon Court behind her and forge her own path. Maybe she could spend many afternoons watching the clouds float by. There were worse lives.

Resolved, Olivia gathered her things and started back to the house. She picked up a stick and wacked at the top of some leggy weeds, then let the stick drop. When she neared the gate, she inadvertently dropped her book. She picked it up, dusted it off, and wiped a bit of mud from the book's corner. Her hair had come loose, and she pushed a strand off her face, then looked up to the gate.

She dropped the basket and book again at the sight of Harrison standing there, his cloak billowing out on the afternoon breeze.

Something must have happened for him to be standing up on the hill as he was, staring down at her. *Alexa.* Had she lost the baby?

He started down the path, his stride long, and Olivia just stood there, paralyzed with uncertainty, her foolish heart beating like a little bird.

Harrison's expression was stern, his determination evident in the strength of his stride. He stopped before her, his gaze sweeping over her, from the top of her hair to the tips of her muddied boots.

Olivia couldn't find her tongue.

Something changed in Harrison's eyes; she saw a spark of light as he casually reached up and pushed her bonnet off her head, and with his thumb, wiped her cheek. He held it up to her. Mud.

"Where is Alexa?" Olivia asked breathlessly.

"At Ashwood. Hiding, I should think."

"Hiding? You left your wife hiding at Ashwood?"

"My wife?" He grinned. "No, Olivia. Not my wife."

"But we had a letter—"

"And I rather imagine you will have another shortly. We did not marry. That foolish girl refused me at the altar."

Olivia gasped. She should have been indignant, but the only sound she could make was mad laughter. *They were not married!* The wave of joy washing over her was strong enough to carry her off, and she would have gladly gone along with it.

They were not married!

"The baby," she said.

Harrison traced his hand across her cheek, his fingers sliding under her jaw. "Alexa is happy that her child will have an aunt and uncle who love him. I think it is time that you stopped minding your sister. She is a grown woman, and she is ready to make her own decisions and face her own consequences. She knows what she is about, and she is at peace with it. Now you must be, as well."

"Yes," she said, nodding.

He smiled. "Olivia, neither of us needs to pretend any longer. It's over. There is nothing left but us. I want you to come to Ashwood with me. Your sister and her child will always have a place there."

Ashwood. It sounded like heaven to her. "The Careys will ruin your career."

He shrugged. "I have inherited an entire estate, and with a few changes it will be quite profitable."

"Our reputations will not allow us into society."

"We'll have each other."

"Yes," she said, and threw herself at him, wrapping her arms around his neck. "Yes, we will have each other! I love you, Harrison. You cannot know how I have despaired these last few days. I should never have sent you away. I should never—"

"Hush," he whispered. "There are so many things both of us should never have done, but they are all behind us now. I love you, Olivia. I have loved you from the moment I first saw you, and I will always love you. I will never again allow you away from my side. We have new lives ahead of us. Come and gather your things. We are leaving Everdon Court."

CHAPTER THIRTY-THREE

Mrs. Lampley looked stricken when Harrison and Olivia walked in together through the back entrance.

"Mr. Tolly!" she cried. "You've come back!"

"Only for a night, Mrs. Lampley."

"But Mr. Eason is here. Oh dear, where are my manners? Felicitations on your nuptials, sir."

"Thank you, but that is not necessary. Who is Mr. Eason?" Harrison asked.

Olivia laughed. "The new steward."

"He's here, walking about, having a look at the place," Mrs. Lampley whispered, seeming distressed. "Says he has a wife and four children. *Four!*"

Harrison grinned. "I have full confidence that you will meet the challenge, Mrs. Lampley," he said. "I think I'll go and have a good look at the chap."

"But . . ." Mrs. Lampley turned to Olivia. "But where is Mrs. Tolly?"

"Oh, there is no Mrs. Tolly," Olivia said brightly. "However, I intend to remedy that straightaway. And by the bye, Mrs. Lampley, I shall be leaving Everdon Court."

"Leaving! Where will you go?"

Olivia grinned. "With Mr. Tolly to Ashwood. To become Mrs. Tolly. Alexa has decided she'd rather not."

She was still laughing as she ran up the stairs to her rooms, wondering if any widow had ever dared to wed as soon as she intended to.

Mr. Eason was in the study, bent over, pulling open the drawers of the desk.

"You'll find nothing there," Harrison said as he strolled in.

Mr. Eason jerked upright. "I beg your pardon."

"Harrison Tolly," Harrison said, and extended his hand, smiling at the man's look of shock.

"I don't understand," Mr. Eason said as he took Harrison's hand.

"I have returned for something I mistakenly left behind. And a few books." He walked to the little table where he had stacked the books for Olivia and picked them up. "I wish you the best of luck with Lord Carey, Mr. Eason. He hasn't the capacity for figures that his late brother did. And he enjoys spending freely. The late marquis was rather good at reining him in, but I cannot guess who might rein him in now." He smiled. "If you do not find someone who can reason with him, the Carey family fortune likely will be depleted within a year." It was hardly true, but Harrison couldn't help himself. "Good luck to you, sir," he said, and walked out, leaving a gaping Mr. Eason behind.

He took the stairs two at a time and went directly to the suite where Olivia had settled. She was inside, busily gathering her things; she hadn't even removed her cloak.

Harrison walked inside and put the books on her vanity. Olivia beamed at him. He'd not seen her look so happy in years. "Will you not remove your cloak?" he asked.

"No. I want to be ready to leave without a moment's hesitation."

He chuckled, and pushed the door shut. "You have my word that we will be gone by the morrow's first light. But I think there is something that requires our immediate attention," he said, turning the key in the lock.

Her smile brightened even more. "Immediate! It must be very important."

"Very," he said.

"Well then." She unfastened her cloak and let it drop.

Harrison smiled and reached for her. He'd ridden like a wild man from Ashwood, frantic to see her, to hold her. He would be forever grateful to Alexa for ending the madness that he had begun that day in the marquis's study, and for urging him to go and fetch

Olivia before it was too late. "They'll not keep her at Everdon Court," Alexa had argued the night of their failed wedding ceremony. "Lord Westhorpe will want his freedom and no reminder of Edward."

For a young woman who was very naïve about some things, Alexa was very wise about others.

"You are so beautiful," Harrison said to Olivia now. He kissed her lips. "And I shall make you mine, Olivia. Only mine."

"Is that a promise?" She wrapped her arms around his waist. "I have been waiting an awfully long time for it."

That wish detonated something deep inside Harrison. He needed to feel her body beneath his. He needed to end the wait, to know that their lives were about to change in a way they had both dreamed of for so many years. He drew her into him, holding her tightly as he kissed her.

Olivia smiled alluringly as she pulled the pins from her hair and let it fall down her back.

Harrison raked his hand through the silken hair he had admired from afar, lifting it to his face and breathing it in. Her grip tightened around his waist as she kissed him, her tongue seeking his. He moved her back, bumping up against the bed, his mouth on her neck now, his fingers on her bosom, curling into her cleavage, the scent of her perfume filling his senses.

His hands sought every curve, his mouth, every patch of skin. Olivia closed her eyes and dropped her head back, her sigh of longing making Harrison's blood rush and swell. He yanked off his neckcloth; Olivia's fingers flew down the buttons of his waistcoat and pushed it aside. Her hands ran across his chest, down to his waist, and pulled the shirt from his trousers.

He shrugged out of the waistcoat and hastily pulled the shirt over his head.

Olivia ran her fingertips down his chest, then leaned in and kissed where his heart was pounding in his chest. Her fingers fluttered over his nipples, and the slight indentation between the muscles that ran from his sternum and disappeared into the top of his trousers.

Harrison clenched his jaw, restraining himself as she explored him. But when she brushed the palm of her hand against the erection that strained against his buckskins, he said roughly, "I cannot bear to be near you any longer without possessing you." He felt almost feverish with the desire blazing in him. "I cannot *bear* it," he said again, then sank onto the bed with her.

Olivia giggled at his ardor, her hands everywhere, boldly exploring, caressing, and stroking. When her tongue flicked across his nipple, he groaned and found the buttons on her gown, then pushed it down her body. He released her breasts, caressed them, took them each in his mouth in turn, sucking the hardened peaks onto his tongue.

Olivia's hand surrounded his erection and moved

on him, sparking a fire in him that quickly roared out of control. She pushed him onto his back and began to trail kisses down his chest, to his abdomen, and below. When her lips surrounded his member, Harrison was lost.

She traced her tongue along the length of him, and Harrison gasped as he tried to keep from writhing and bucking beneath her. But it was no use; his self-control was hanging by a thread. She was pushing him beyond the limits of yearning. As madly pleasurable as it was, he needed to be inside her. He groped blindly for her, lifting her up to him and encircling her tightly in his arms. Her lips softly met his as he rolled her onto her back.

He moved over her, pushing her skirts up above her hips, then he slipped his hand between her legs. She was hot and slick, and her deep moan against his mouth came close to undoing him completely. His fingers slipped inside her heat; his thumb stroked her mindlessly until she made a little cry and shifted against him.

He moved between her thighs, nudging them farther apart with his knee. "I am at the end of my endurance, Olivia. I need you. I have needed you all my life." He slid into her and began to move. Olivia kissed him, lifting up to him, lifting her legs to his waist, drawing him in until he was moving deep inside her, his heart growing larger with each stroke, claiming her as his own in the most primal way a man could claim a woman. She moaned with pleasure, her body tightening around his, and then cried out as she shuddered and contracted around him.

Her climax drew Harrison's, and with a strangled sob of ecstasy, he released into her.

As he gasped for breath, he felt awed by what had happened between them. He was moved beyond comprehension. How could he have contemplated being without her for even a moment?

He tenderly gathered Olivia into his arms and rolled to his side. She nuzzled her face in his neck. They were covered with a sheen of perspiration, and they lay there until the heat had ebbed from their skin.

Still, Harrison did not let her go. He'd never felt so alive, had never felt anything so deeply. He knew that this was where he was meant to be, that *this* was where he was accepted. This was the rest of his life.

"Olivia," he murmured.

"Hmmm?" She sounded like a purring kitten, with a smile of satisfaction on her face to match.

"Let's go home," he murmured against her temple.

"I'm already there," she said.

CHAPTER THIRTY-FOUR

Rue was cleaning Alexa's room. She was forever cleaning Alexa's room, for her ability to tidy up was marred by her inattention to things that needed to be tidied. At present she was fussing with the sash on the drapes, and had stepped in front of the window, blocking the light.

Seated on a chaise, Alexa sighed irritably. "Rue, must you?"

"Yes, miss. You told me I must," Rue said.

"I told you that you must tidy up the room, not the sash. And must you stand before the window? I should like to feel the sun on my face."

"Oh, but you can't feel the sun when you are in the house. The sun is outside."

"Is it?" Alexa drawled, and stood up. "Then perhaps I shall go out to where the sun is, as you insist on blocking it."

"No, miss, it's not me," Rue said. "It's the house that blocks it."

Alexa groaned and picked up her shawl—her spencer would no longer fit across her breasts—and wrapped it tightly around her. "You should keep to sewing, Rue," she said, and paused to look at the infant gowns Rue had made that she'd lain out on her bed to admire. They were surprisingly beautiful. Alexa had discovered Rue's extraordinary talent as a seamstress when she'd altered the yellow gown. "Your skill is far superior to your housekeeping abilities."

Rue smiled proudly.

Alexa made her way downstairs, her hand on the banister, her fingers feeling the curving vines and leaves carved into the railing.

Louis, the footman with the kind smile, opened the front door for her. "Good afternoon, Miss Hastings."

"Good afternoon, Louis." She wondered if he or Linford or Mrs. Thorpe, the housekeeper, had noticed her increasing girth. How could they not? She felt as if she were bursting through everything she owned. But if they were offended, none showed it. They'd all been very kind to her, even after the disaster of the wedding.

Alexa stepped out onto the steps leading down to the drive. She heard riders approaching and glanced at the road coming into the drive. She wasn't surprised to see Harry and Olivia riding toward the house, but she was surprised at how well her sister could ride.

It was something else about her remarkable sister she hadn't noticed.

They rode into the circular drive and reined up. Olivia practically threw herself from her horse and strode across the gravel drive to Alexa. She wasn't wearing mourning clothes; she was dressed in a riding habit. She jogged up the steps. She didn't speak. She stared at Alexa, and before Alexa knew what was happening, Olivia threw her arms around her, hugging her tightly. "Thank you, darling," she said. "Thank you from the bottom of my heart."

Alexa felt a swell of relief and joy. "I *knew* I was right," she cried. "You *do* love him!"

Olivia laughed and stood back. Her eyes were shining, her smile bright. She hadn't looked this happy for years, not since long before she married Edward. "Yes. I love him with all my heart, and I have loved him for a very long time. I thought I'd lost him, but you made my happiness possible."

Alexa smiled. She felt proud of herself, in truth. She'd actually done someone a kindness. "I was forced to take matters into my own hands," she boasted. "You can be so blessedly stubborn, you know."

"I suppose I can," Olivia said, smiling fondly, and beamed at Harry as he walked up the steps to them. He smiled down at Olivia in a way that made Alexa's heart twist a little. That was love. That was what she'd believed she'd had with Carlos.

But Alexa pushed down that sadness—it was Olivia's turn at sheer happiness. "Come on, then, come and see your new home," Alexa said, taking Olivia's hand in hers. "A lot of work must be done, beginning with the salon. It's dreadful. Oh, and you will never believe what I have discovered—Rue is an excellent seamstress!"

"Little Rue?" Olivia asked, and cast a smile over her shoulder at Harry, who smiled at her with the same adoring look.

"Oh, for heaven's sake, the two of you will become tedious very quickly, with all that smiling," Alexa said, and tugged at Olivia's hand. "Mrs. Thorpe is the housekeeper here, and I can tell you, she will not approve of your arriving to marry Harry after I refused. She is very strict in her opinions, and even though you do not expressly ask for them, she manages to give them anyway. She's very skilled, that one. And you must speak plainly and precisely to Linford. He is the butler, and he is hard of hearing. Oh! This is Louis. He is our footman," she said, as Louis bowed and opened the door wide. "Louis, this is my sister, who will soon be the new mistress of Ashwood."

"How do you do?" Olivia said, but Alexa was pulling her along.

"Rue! Come down at once!" she called, and Olivia hurried to keep up with her sister as they entered to have a look at the place they would all call home.

CHAPTER THIRTY-FIVE

M r. Meachamp, the vicar, was called away from Hadley Green to attend to a dying parishioner in nearby Boxhill. The parishioner apparently lingered, for the vicar was away long enough for word to spread through Hadley Green that the new Earl of Ashwood would marry the pretty young woman he'd mysteriously arrived with.

In the meantime, Lily, Lady Eberlin, hosted a tea for some of Hadley Green's more illustrious denizens to introduce her aunt and uncle Hannigan, and her twin cousins, Molly and Mabe Hannigan. They joined her sister-in-law Charity and her daughter Catherine. The gathering of ladies had ample time to speculate as to why the new earl would travel with an unmarried young woman and only a maid for a chaperone.

Lady Horncastle was particularly disturbed by the inappropriateness of their arrangement. "He should have brought a proper escort for her," she'd said. "A sister, a cousin. Anyone would do, really, but you cannot convince me that the girl is so alone in the world that there is no one to look after her virtue."

"Perhaps she did not care to have her virtue looked after, aye?" Molly Hannigan asked innocently, and Charity chuckled.

"What a ridiculous thing to say, young lady," Lady Horncastle complained.

"He intends to set it to rights, does he not?" Lily said. "And really, madam, Hadley Green has seen worse scandal than that."

"Haven't we?" Miss Daria Babcock laughed. "It's all so diverting."

"Diverting, perhaps. But if that is the sort of person we attract at Hadley Green, it does not speak well for your future prospects, does it?" Mrs. Morton asked, and beside her, Mrs. Ogle nodded her complete agreement.

"I shouldn't mind a bit of scandal," Miss Babcock said with a shrug. "It would make life interesting."

"Perhaps more than you know," Charity said with a sigh.

The twins looked at each other and laughed, as if they shared some secret. The ladies of Hadley Green had no idea that Molly and Mabe Hannigan were renowned in Ireland for diabolical games.

All the talk prompted Lily to suggest to her husband that they pay a call to the new residents of Ashwood.

"Why?" he asked as they lay in bed late that night, their limbs tangled with each other.

"Because they are new here and they are to be married. They could use some acquaintances."

Tobin put his hand on his wife's breast. "I think you are looking for a diversion."

She smiled lovingly at him. "I have all the diversion I need in my husband, sir."

He kissed her forehead and rolled over on his side. "I refuse to call and annoy our new neighbors."

But Lily kissed his shoulder, her hand floating over his broad back. "I think I shall pay a call."

"Lily—"

"I shan't stay long. Just long enough to welcome them properly. The first time we met them, I was so interested in the jewels that I hardly thought of them at all. I've been rude. I should set it all to rights, do you not agree?"

Tobin sighed, and she giggled as she kissed the back of his neck. She knew she had him wrapped firmly about her little finger.

At Ashwood the following afternoon, the old butler Linford was trying his best to explain to the new master that Mrs. Thorpe, the housekeeper, felt a bit compromised by the arrival of the widow.

"Then perhaps she'd be more comfortable keeping house elsewhere," Harrison casually suggested.

The old man paled. "But Thorpe's been at Ashwood for thirty years, my lord."

"I am not a lord. I am Mr. Tolly," Harrison said

patiently. "Why is it, Linford, that I cannot seem to impress on anyone that I am not an earl?"

"Sir," Linford corrected himself.

Harrison sighed. "All right, here is what you say to Thorpe to soothe her ruffled feathers. Tell her that sometimes, events occur that are well beyond our control. And as soon as Meachamp returns from Boxhill, we shall set it all to rights. Will that do?"

"I hope for all our sake that it does, sir."

Louis appeared at the door. "Callers, sir."

"There, you see?" Harrison said, gesturing to the footman. "Louis understands perfectly that I am not an earl." He strode out of the study and into the foyer, and came face to face with Lady Eberlin. Behind her were two young dark-haired beauties.

"Mr. Tolly, how do you do?" Lady Eberlin said brightly. "I hope we are not imposing?"

Harrison bowed and said, "Welcome to Ashwood."

"May I introduce my cousins, Miss Molly Hannigan, and Miss Mabe Hannigan."

Harrison greeted them both and wondered how anyone could tell them apart.

Lady Eberlin beamed at him. "I would not have come without an invitation, but I have news!"

"And that is?"

"That Lord Eberlin and I intend to host a ball."

"Extraordinary," Harrison drawled. He heard someone on the stairs and glanced up. Olivia and Alexa were descending.

"There she is!" Lady Eberlin said, her face brightening with her smile. "Your beautiful fiancée. Why didn't you tell us that you and Miss Hastings were to marry? We would have feted you as you deserve, you know."

Alexa laughed. "There's been some mistake. Mr. Tolly and I have no intention of wedding."

"Oh." Lady Eberlin appeared confused.

"May I introduce my sister, Lady Carey?" Alexa said, gliding down the stairs.

"I will do the honors, if you please," Harrison said, stepping forward. He held out his hand to Olivia as she reached the bottom step.

"This," he said, "is Lady Carey."

"I am pleased to make your acquaintance," Lady Eberlin said. "And I am terribly sorry for your loss. We had heard the news."

Olivia blinked. "Oh," she said. "Yes, thank you. A tragic accident."

"Tragic," Lady Eberlin agreed, and looked at Harrison. "But . . . the entire village of Hadley Green is speaking of your nuptials, Mr. Tolly."

"Are they?" He looked at Olivia; they both laughed.

"Mr. Tolly intends to marry my sister, Lady Carey," Alexa said, as if it were perfectly natural.

"Alexa." Olivia sighed. "The news might need a bit more introduction than that."

Lady Eberlin looked shocked. She stared at Harrison, who nodded, confirming it. "It is a fact, ladies, that I intend to marry this woman. Not that one."

One of the twins gasped. Olivia gave a soft snort of laughter and quickly put her hand to her mouth to hide her smile.

"But . . . but we only just received the news about Lord Carey," Lady Eberlin said, as if trying to work it all out in her head.

"Yes, it would seem that we've all been involved in a rather large scandal," Harrison went on, enjoying himself now. "I feel confident the details of it will reach you soon enough."

Olivia could scarcely contain her giggles.

Even Alexa was smiling. "A lot of nonsense," she agreed. "But you mustn't believe it if you hear that I am carrying Mr. Tolly's child. It's not his at all."

Olivia's attempt to contain her laughter failed. She looked at Lady Eberlin, her smile almost effervescent. "I would have a care, madam, of associating too closely with us. We have broken every rule of polite society. But before you turn your backs completely, please know that we are determined to set it all to rights. We never meant any harm." She turned a brilliant smile to Harrison.

That smile warmed him to the core every time he saw it, and Harrison smiled back. "We will set it all to rights just as soon as the vicar arrives."

"We're really not awful people," Alexa added as she moved to stand next to Olivia. "But we've been beset by extraordinary circumstances that cannot be easily explained."

Lady Eberlin sighed and looked at her cousins.

The one on the right smiled. "Tell them," she said to Lady Eberlin.

"I could not. I *should* not."

The other twin said, "It seems if there is anyone in Hadley Green with whom you might be completely honest, it is them. Go on. Tell them."

"Tell us what?" Harrison asked.

Lady Eberlin smiled sheepishly. "What my cousins would like you to know is that we, too, have suffered through a bit of scandal because of extraordinary circumstances. To begin, another cousin pretended to be me—for *months*. And then she was discovered and forced to flee England altogether. I had to remain here and make my bargain with the devil."

Olivia and Harrison looked at each other, and said in unison, "Faust!"

Olivia reached out her hand to Lady Eberlin. "I think that settles it, Lady Eberlin. We shall be fast friends. Come and let us share a spot of tea and a wild tale or two."

On the day that Harrison Tolly took Lady X as his wife, the bride wore blue. The scandal of Lady Carey and the steward had begun to seep into the highest reaches of society, and it was on the tip of everyone's tongue.

But no one seemed to care about that scandal at the wedding of the newly elevated Lord Ashwood. There was scarcely anyone in attendance, save the bride, her sister, and the residents of Tiber Park, where Lord and

Lady Eberlin resided. That family was not particularly put-off by scandal.

As spring turned to summer, Alexa grew as round as a ball.

One afternoon, the family took tea in the gazebo near the lake. The Eberlins had come, and Lord Ashwood had retained the services of a fiddler to entertain them. They were in the midst of having their luncheon when one of the Hannigan twins glanced up and said, "Who is that?"

All heads swiveled about. Standing at the top of the hill was a gentleman in buckskins and a green coat. Ahead of him, Louis was striding down the grassy slope to announce him.

Alexa suddenly cried out and dropped her fork to her plate with a clatter. She stood, pushing the chair back so quickly that it toppled over behind her.

"Alexa!" Harrison said. "What is wrong?"

But Alexa was running toward the man as fast her pregnant body would allow her.

Harrison stood up, but Olivia caught his arm. "Let her go, darling."

"But who is it?" Harrison demanded.

Olivia smiled. "My guess is that Alexa's fondest wish just came true."

Outside the gazebo, Carlos saw Alexa the moment she leapt off the gazebo steps and he ran down the hill, grabbing her up in his arms. "Foolish, *foolish* girl!" he said sharply. "Why did you leave me?"

"Why!" she cried and threw her arms around his neck. "Why didn't you *come*? Because you were married, you wretched beast!"

"Married?" He exploded with a string of Spanish, kissed her hard, then set her down and ran his hand over her belly. "I am not married, *amor.*"

"Do not lie to me," Alexa said tearfully. "Because I love you, Carlos. I love you quite deeply, and I saw you kissing a woman behind your gates!"

"A woman!" he scoffed. "Who is this woman?"

Alexa told him about walking up to his house and seeing him kiss the beauty behind the gates.

"*This* is what caused you to run from me?" he exclaimed. "That was not my wife, Alexa. This was my *cousin.* I kiss her good-bye! I kiss her hello! I *kiss* her— she is my cousin!"

"Then why did you not come to see me? Why did you leave me for an entire week to wonder?"

A frown darkened his face. "I wanted to send a messenger to you, *mi amor,* but everything happened so quickly."

"What?" she asked skeptically.

He took her hands in his. "My mother, she suddenly took ill, and was gone within a day. My family, they came from all of Spain to mourn her." He frowned at her. "But *you* left me!"

"Of course I left you!" Alexa said. "You had left *me*! I don't know if I believe you."

Carlos let loose another string of Spanish. "Then

I will carry you back to Spain and you will meet my cousin and she will tell you. I love you, *mi amor.* Don't you know you are my heart? I searched all of Spain for you and could not find you. You carry my child. If I did not love you, if I were married, when I received your letter, would I come as fast as I could to find you?"

A small ray of hope began to shine in Alexa. "No," she said, and smiled. "So will you help me?"

"*Help* you? I did not come this far to help you! I came to marry you!" he bellowed.

"Oh, Carlos—"

"No, no argument. You argue too easily." He grabbed her up and kissed her.

When he lifted his head, Alexa took Carlos's hand and laid it on her belly. "You are my heart, too."

"Of course I am," he said. "How could you forget it, even for a moment?" he demanded, and wrapped her once more in a tight embrace.

It was agreed by all that Alexa and Carlos should marry straightaway, and return to Spain before Alexa was too far along to travel. In the space of a few days, they were ready to leave, along with Rue.

"I've never been on a boat, sir," Rue said to Harrison.

"My lord. You refer to him as my lord when addressing an earl," Alexa corrected her.

"But we're not to call him my lord," Rue said.

"It's all right," Harrison said, and gave Rue a squeeze of the shoulders. "Mind you don't lose your mistress,

Rue. I shudder to think what would become of you if you did."

Rue laughed. "I can't lose a person, milord. She's too big to lose."

Alexa winked at him over Rue's head. "I'll keep a close eye on her."

Alexa and Carlos said their good-byes, then loaded into the Ashwood carriage. Harrison and Olivia stood on the drive and waved as they watched them pull away.

Surprisingly, it was Harrison who felt the most dejected after her departure. "I confess to a soft spot for her. After all, she is the reason you are my wife."

"And she was the reason I very nearly was *not* your wife," Olivia pointed out. "But she is wildly happy, Harrison. I would rather her be happy and gone from us, than forever sad and with us."

"Yes, I suppose," Harrison said, and put his arms around Olivia's shoulders. "I have another confession, Lady X. I was looking forward to the birth of her child."

"Were you?"

"I was. I fancied myself a fine father figure."

"Well then." Olivia slipped her arm around his waist. "I suppose I shall have to give you one of your own." She peeked up at him and grinned.

Harrison's heart began to beat wildly. "Olivia, do you mean—?"

"Come next spring, you will be a father."

Later, Lady Eberlin would swear she heard Harrison's shout of joy all the way to Tiber Park.

Fantasy.
Temptation.
Adventure.

Visit PocketAfterDark.com,
an all-new website just for Urban
Fantasy and Romance Readers!

- Exclusive access to the hottest
urban fantasy and romance titles!

- Read and share reviews on
the latest books!

- Live chats with your favorite
romance authors!

- Vote in online polls!

 www.PocketAfterDark.com

26119